GABE

IN THE COMPANY OF SNIPERS

Book 8

IRISH WINTERS

COPYRIGHT

GABE - In the Company of Snipers, 8

Cover design and author photo by Kelli Ann Morgan,
http://www.inspirecreativeservices.com

Interior book design by Bob Houston, eBook Formatting

Editor: Lauren McKellar, McStellar editing,
http://mcstellarediting.blogspot.com

Editor: Katie Johnson, katiestefan333@gmail.com

ISBN Paperback: 978-1-942895-13-8
ISBN eBook: 978-1-942895-14-5
Library of Congress Control Number: 2015945955

Irish Winter's author website is http://www.irishwinters.com
or irishwinters.blogspot.com

In the Company of Snipers

You can find Irish Winters on Facebook: https://www.facebook.com/author.irishwinters

On Twitter: https://twitter.com/irishwinters1

For news on upcoming releases, sign up for Irish Winters' Newsletter at IrishWinters.com.

For more information about all my books, visit IrishWinters.com.

IN THE COMPANY OF SNIPERS

This series revolves around ex-Marine scout sniper, Alex Stewart, and his covert surveillance company, The TEAM, home-based out of Alexandria, Virginia. An obsessive patriot and workaholic, he created the company to give ex-military snipers like him a chance at returning to civilian life with a decent job.

This is not a serial with each book ending at a cliffhanger. I wouldn't do that to you. *In the Company of Snipers* is a collection of passionate love stories involving women and men who are tough enough to take on the world alone. Each is a stand-alone read, where in the course of an active TEAM operation, one agent comes face to face with his or her demons. The men and women I write about are all patriots and warriors, dealing with what they've lived through or the mistakes they've made

Spoiler alert: Every novel contains adult scenes including sexual situations (some explicit), language, and violence. I don't write sweet romance, so be forewarned.

At the end of each story, it's my hope that you, along with my heroes, will come to realize...

Love changes everything.

Chapter One

Pop! Pop! Bang!

Backfire? Gunfire? Could've been, either.

Junior Agent Gabe Cartwright jerked his gaze to the exit gate of the underground garage. He'd just parked his Land Rover in its assigned stall. With his revoked driver's license, he shouldn't have been driving, but he was. Barely had his feet on the ground.

His boss, Alex Stewart, lingered at the gate in a black SUV. Always in a hurry, the speed demon should've stomped on the accelerator and roared off into traffic by now.

Damn. Was that gunfire?

Gabe couldn't get to his boss fast enough, then couldn't believe his eyes. Alex sat slumped forward in his seatbelt, his forehead tilted down and his mouth open in shock. Three crimson bull's-eyes blossomed dead center of his white dress shirt.

"No! No! No!" Gabe jerked the door handle. Locked. His palms hit the window. "Boss!"

Alex didn't move. The damned engine still idled.

This can't be happening. Not here in America. Not to Alex.

Gabe grabbed his cell phone and stabbed 911, his heart roaring in his ears. He barked address and details to the dispatch operator, then his teammates two stories up. "Shooting. Parking garage. Alex. Get down here now!"

Where the hell had those shots come from? The busy traffic on the street looked normal. The office building across the way, too. No glint of a scope. No shadowy figure skulking away. It was just another sunny day in Alexandria, Virginia. *Like hell.*

No time to waste. Gabe braced the sole of his boot to the windshield and pushed it inward far enough to loosen the window seal, then jerked the entire sheet of safety glass out.

"I'm... shot?" Alex gasped.

Yes, damn it. Only Alex would be surprised at that. And still talking. *Had to be in shock.*

Leaning over the dashboard, Gabe shoved the shifter into park and unlocked the doors.

"Gabe?"

"Yeah, I heard you, Boss. Help's coming. You're gonna be okay."

Please. Don't let him die. Not Alex! Not my boss!

He didn't need CPR. He was still conscious, still huffing shallow breath. A sheen of sweat glistened on his upper lip. There just wasn't enough blood. He had to be hemorrhaging internally. *To death.*

"Kelsey," Alex whispered, his eyes glazed and his voice fading. "Tell... Kelsey..."

"No, Boss. You get to tell her yourself. Promise."

Lies. All lies.

Alex didn't curse. Not even once. He closed his eyes with a soft sigh, barely breathing.

Just that fast Gabe was inside the vehicle with him, releasing his seatbelt, easing him out of the SUV and onto the concrete. He locked his hands together and commenced first-aid, applying hard pressure to stop the bleeding.

Alex would not die. *Not today.*

The men and women of The TEAM tumbled out from the stairwell. Gabe heard the rumble of boots on concrete, but offered not one second of precious time to acknowledge them. All ex-military, they knew what the hell to do.

"Is he still breathing?" Harley asked, shoulder to shoulder with Gabe on the cold garage floor.

"Yeah. Three shots. Professional hit. Came out of nowhere." Gabe kept the pressure up. *Not Alex. I'm not losing another friend. Not again.*

Mark knelt at his other side with a fistful of sterile packing. He covered Gabe's hands with it, and together they applied enough pressure to make a grown man cry.

Alex never even groaned.

What kind of man survives three mortal wounds? Superman, maybe. Ironman. Alex was close to invincible, but the harsh reality of ballistics sucked.

Sirens shrieked. Maybe two. The paramedics barked orders for everyone to step back. They took over first-aid and had Alex off the ground and on the gurney in no time.

Gabe sucked in a lungful of stale concrete air. Damn. Could this be Alex's lucky day? Could he bully Death as he'd bullied everyone and everything else?

God, I hope so.

The medics loaded the ambulance, the clock ticking. Gabe stepped forward, going with his boss every step of the way.

"No riders." The driver secured the tailgate, his palm in Gabe's face.

"But I—"

"Follow in your own vehicle. We need to move."

They didn't waste time. Sirens blared away as quickly as they'd come.

Every team member scrambled to his or her vehicle. Gabe found himself pulled into Junior Agent Zack Lennox's family van. "Come on. He'll need Kelsey."

"You're not going after the boss?

"No, Gabe. We're not. We're going to take him his reason to live."

Good thinking. Gabe climbed into the van, wiping the blood off his fingers, needing the sticky stuff to stick somewhere else. Anywhere else.

"Did anyone call her?"

Zack only growled. Obviously not. This kind of news had to be delivered in person. With tender care. He aimed the van toward the elementary school where Kelsey taught.

Gabe pushed a fist to his sternum as if that could stop the drum roll in his chest, the creeping suffocation of an imminent panic attack. Triggers. It was all about managing his response to the triggers that initiated that claustrophobic sensation of the world closing in.

Not now. Keep it together. Breathe in. Breathe out.

By the time Zack roared into the school's loading zone and hit the school ground running, Gabe had it under control. He followed. Maybe Zack knew how to break this kind of news?

Yeah, right. Words always failed. How do you begin to tell a woman her husband had been mortally shot? How do you to tell her he may already be dead? That it could be too late?

Gabe flat out didn't want to know. K.I.A. notifications sucked.

The morning kindergarten class must've barely begun. Kelsey looked up, smiling from the two-foot high table where she sat surrounded by her teaching assistant and maybe a dozen adoring five-year-olds. "Zack? Gabe? Why are you—? What's wrong?"

"Alex needs you," Zack replied calmly, his hand outstretched to take hers, his fingers urging her forward. "Come on, Kels. We've got to go. Now."

The light left her eyes. She already knew. With barely any words of instruction to her assistant, she left the quiet morning behind and hurried with Zack and Gabe out the door and into the van.

"How is he?" she asked, her chin up, Zack's van already ten miles over the speed limit to get her to the hospital in time.

"Not sure," he replied evenly, squeezing her hand on the console between them.

"He's been shot before, you know," she offered quietly. *Hopefully.*

"Yes. He has," Zack agreed.

Sitting behind her in the van, Gabe kept his mouth shut. Kelsey needed to believe her fierce warrior husband could survive this time because he'd survived others. Too bad life didn't work that way. A man only had a certain number of chances before the bullet with his name caught up with him. The odds always decreased. Any dumb jarhead knew that.

Gabe glanced at his watch, needing to run instead of sitting on his ass. The trip took too damned long!

Finally at the emergency room, he joined his somber teammates with poor Kelsey sandwiched between him and Zack. As if that could stall the inevitable. As if anyone could protect her tender heart from what lay around the tiled corners.

She'd clutched Gabe's hand when he'd helped her out of the car. She hadn't let go. He couldn't bear to.

Junior Agent Izza Maher wiped her face when she looked up and saw them. Ember Dennison turned away. Their husbands, Connor and Rory, stood tall and silent.

Newbies, Taylor Armstrong and Maverick Carson were ashen. The office IT genius, Mother, bowed her head, her shoulders trembling.

Harley was nowhere to be seen.

Damn. We're too late.

That everyone was there should've been Kelsey's first clue as to how bad things were. Instead, like the lady of grace she was, she offered small talk to her too quiet friends. "Mark. Connor. My goodness. You're all here. Hi, Rory. Taylor. Any word yet?"

She made it sound as if this was simply another pickle Alex had gotten himself into. As if this too was all in a day's work for a covert operator. But Gabe caught the tightened grip of her fingers. She needed a lifeline. Someone to hold onto. He let it be him.

"The doctor's waiting," Mark said, his voice tight. "Come with me."

Kelsey nodded.

Gabe steeled his heart as they followed Mark beyond the waiting room, his whole being screaming, *'Hit rewind. Replay. STOP!'*

The corridors seemed to narrow with every step. Mark pressed the metal push pad to activate the wide emergency room doors. Once beyond, doctors and nurses in light blue scrubs hurried through the corridors as if Death didn't stalk right along with them.

At last, another door. Not just a curtained-off examination room, though. More like one of those family counseling rooms with solid walls. In case of crying. Cursing. Screaming.

A doctor had barely exited. "Mrs. Stewart?" he asked gently.

Kelsey's hand lifted out of Gabe's to her lips. "Yes?"

"I'm so sorry." The doctor reopened the door, ushering her into the room where Harley stood somber and still over a sheet-draped body. Bloody packing splattered the floor. The stifling drift of alcohol and antiseptics filled the air.

"No," she whispered. "Please, no."

Gabe didn't need to hear the words. He could read, and Harley's bleak, teary face was an open book with an ungodly ending.

Hell had come to The TEAM.

Alex Stewart was dead.

It took a while to figure it out.

The first clue? Gabe Cartwright, leaning over him, both clenched hands pressed to his chest, crushing the hell out of him, as if his life depended on it. The kid had crystal-green eyes, a fierce shade he hadn't noticed before. Full of life. Just as full of rage. Disbelief maybe?

The second clue? Softhearted Harley crying big, sloppy tears. The guy never should've been a soldier. Never should've been a sniper. Too much heart. Just wasn't mean enough.

But the third? Mark turned away with a too somber face and a tight lip, his jaw clenched, the way a warrior shuts down when he's seen too much. Gone too far. Can't bear any more.

Plus, he had stopped cursing. Even the unseen gentlemen who'd fired the killing shots had received no more than a mild rebuke, which was rare coming from a man with a formidable vocabulary of curses. The passion that had stoked his life only minutes before dissipated in the bright blurred light of— wherever he was. "Oh," became his strongest oath, somehow sufficient, maybe even a little bit over the top. Just—oh.

The fog in his head made everything surreal—the siren, the lights. The dark. The cold.

Air filled him with weightlessness until he was no longer bound to Earth by anger, bone, or muscle—a rare sensation for a man who'd once carried the weight of a few too many kills. Regret for never having been a better man. For all the wrongs he'd not been able to set right.

For Sara.

For Abby.

And now—Kelsey.

A brilliant light enveloped him from every side, blinding him to the strict methodology and logic that had ruled his life. Things like means, motive, and opportunity paled to mist and vapor.

Think.

But he couldn't. The light shone so purely he could barely focus. Numbing darkness followed. Then came the cold. Time drifted in this new place. This new dimension of—where am I?

He struggled to remember anything, but nothing came to him.

That was... then.

This was... now.

A man can't decipher nothingness.

But. Oh. Wait. This was weird. He floated over a casket while a collage of shadows marched by. The guy in the casket looked like—me? It couldn't be, could it? He slapped his heavy right palm to his chest for verification. That was what real men did. They proved they could keep on keeping on. But his hand hit nothing. No flesh. No bone.

The casket morphed into shadows, then people come to say—goodbye? To who?

Me?

How odd to see them, but not be able to shake a friendly hand, or tell an old Marine's lie. Friends. Governors. Congressmen. Faithful Marines. Soldiers. Airmen. Sailors. Sad and somber, they came and went.

He shifted through the dimension of here and now, pulled toward a somber group lingering beyond the coffin. He should've known right then and there. Something was dreadfully amiss, but nothing mattered because he'd caught a glimpse of her—the woman who'd saved his soul and breathed new life into his heart.

Kelsey. My Kelsey.

Her eyes searched for him. The hungering love of dewy brown riveted his heart to hers across time and space. She truly looked for him. More than once, he thought for sure she'd seen him.

He reached for her. God, he tried, but his fingers clutched nothing. They passed through her like shadows. She looked away, a tissue to her nose, a depth of sadness in her eyes. The kind of sorrow he used to be able to shield her from.

He would've cried if he could've cried. She'd always had that effect on him. She'd made him feel when others could not. She'd helped him remember the man he truly was. She made him want to live again. Even now.

Another man pulled her into a gentle hug of condolence. He whispered into her ear, like a knight of old swearing undying fealty to the queen of his fallen king. "I'm here for you, ma'am. Any time. Any day. You let me know what you need, I'll make it happen."

No. No. No! That's my job!

Who was he? Who did those startling green eyes belong to? Zack? Maybe Gabe? Maybe not.

Everything blurred, pulling him from the lovely, sad scene. He hurried to commit the exquisite details of Kelsey's face to memory. This might be his last chance to see her in this—this wherever he was.

Time ran out.

Her smile faded.

He couldn't breathe, the loss of his beloved more than a man could endure. His hand clutched the ragged hole where his heart used to be. Air no longer mattered. He had no reason to breathe. No more reason to live.

Realization dawned slowly. He'd just witnessed a funeral.

His funeral.

His widow.

Her tears.

He, Alexander Bradley Stewart, toughest dog in the fight, was nothing but a shadow. A memory.

A ghost.

Chapter Two

This might be the best job ever. All Shelby Sullivan had to do was stay with a young widow named Mrs. Kelsey Stewart while she recovered from her husband's untimely and tragic death. She lived in Alexandria, one of Shelby's favorite neighborhoods in all of North Virginia, and the deceased husband had owned some kind of a surveillance company. Two bodyguards would be staying at the residence as a precautionary measure since the husband had died under mysterious circumstances. Almost sounded exciting.

Shelby maneuvered her extremely economical and eco-friendly car through one last stop sign, then turned north. Morning traffic was light for a change, but her enthusiasm dropped when she pulled to the curb. The small house at her left didn't declare a prominent business owner had once lived there. Maybe a taxi driver. Or a milkman.

This can't be right. What have I gotten myself into?

But it was. The street address on the corner of the red brick home agreed with the GPS. She called Libby Houston to verify. Maybe she'd written it down wrong.

"Yes, Kelsey lives there. I know the house isn't what you might expect, but once you get to know Kelsey, you'll understand."

"If you say so." Shelby let her gaze scroll over what had to be a two-, at most a three-bedroom home. No garage. No extra parking pad for guests, either.

"Go on. Be brave, Shelby. I promise. It's an older neighborhood, but it's safe. The minute you meet Kelsey, you'll fall in love with her. Besides, she needs you."

"It's not what I was expecting, that's all. I'll be okay." *I hope.*

Shelby hung up, tapping her fingertips on the steering wheel while she reconsidered turning back before she actually walked across the street and met her new client. The house looked too small to accommodate a live-in care provider and two bodyguards.

Besides. What woman in her right mind wanted to live in this neighborhood? And her deceased husband had been an important businessman? *Beats me.* Sure couldn't prove it by this place. Couldn't they have moved somewhere—*anywhere*—better? Bigger? Newer?

Honestly, the lots of these old-fashioned, rinky-dink houses were no bigger than postage stamps. The homes crowded together, their hedges and bushes overlapping their neighbors like one untidy raggedy quilt with frayed edges. The lawns weren't much larger.

Old trees shadowed the sidewalks. All those leaves would be a mess to rake come autumn. Some of the concrete sidewalks were buckled and cracked.

The people north of the Stewarts had left their garbage cans on the curb, one now tipped on its side and empty, but filthy with streaks of moist grunge. A striped yellow cat prowled at its mouth, ready to crawl inside.

Ewww. The things people brought into their homes. Why anyone needed pets, Shelby didn't understand. Cats were dirty. Like dogs. Just the thought of the germs those *pets* carried made her shudder.

At least she didn't have any weeds in her front flowerbeds, though. The neighbors across the street sure did. Weeds galore. *Gosh. Some people. Don't they understand the concept of curb appeal? How hard could it be to pick a few weeds and paint their shutters?*

Details. Of all people, Shelby understood the extreme importance of the smallest details. *Sheesh. Why doesn't everybody? It's not rocket science.*

She girded up her loins and focused on the noble profession she loved instead of the neighborhood. She might not be as self-sacrificing as Florence Nightingale, but nursing had always been her calling and her aptitude. She liked helping people, especially women. Men were different. Smellier. Grumpier. Ruder. Someone else could take care of them.

Securing her rollup sun visor above the dashboard so the summer sun wouldn't fade her vehicle's interior, Shelby double-checked the rearview one last time. Lettuce in one's teeth did not make a good first impression.

The perky blonde smiling back at her certainly looked confident and competent. She ran a quick hand through her bangs, fluffing the sun-bleached strands to blend into her shoulder-length hair. *There now. Ready to go.*

Stabbing her index finger into the bridge of her brown-rimmed glasses, she gathered her purse and her courage and ventured forth. At least the bodyguards hadn't arrived yet. She'd been told to expect two men whose names she couldn't remember, just that they were agents and ready to assist Mrs. Stewart. The need to be settled in before they showed up hurried Shelby's step. She could stake her claim and those two guys could stay out of her way.

I can do this.

Glancing over her shoulder, she remote-locked her brand new red and white car. Dang, she hated leaving her baby on the street. It still had that new car smell. She'd only made two payments. But, oh well. That was the way it was. She had good insurance.

What could possibly go wrong?

Neither dared sit in the man's chair. Not Mark. Not Harley. That would've been sacrilege, as if Alex might storm through his door and catch them in the act of impersonating him. Damn, he'd be pissed. If he were alive.

Mark took his usual place at the small conference table instead, Harley at his right. Neither was willing to believe. Neither wanted to assume the mantle of leadership. Not yet.

Senior Agent David Tao certainly didn't. Since the shooting, he'd all but barricaded himself in The TEAM gym at ground level. The man was a study in opposites. He dressed professionally every single day, despite the fact that he ran the onsite gym. He changed clothes a lot. So what? It didn't matter. He still wasn't front and center where Mark needed him to be.

Drumming his fingertips on the table, Mark prepared to step up to the plate. The problem was, no one could hide from the gloom that filled The TEAM's once busy five-story building from basement to roof. The paralysis of shock and grief hung everywhere. The halls. The restrooms.

Reading Alex's will revealed the depth of his trust, another shock. He hadn't left his multi-million dollar covert surveillance business, The TEAM, to his wife, Kelsey, or to his old friends, Murphy Finnegan and Roy Hudson, though they were infinitely qualified. No. For some inexplicable reason, Alex had left it to his three trusted Senior Agents: David Tao, Mark Houston and Harley Mortimer. They were beyond rich. Disgustingly, sorrowfully rich.

The trust of his fierce mentor overwhelmed Mark as much as the man's death had. It didn't seem real yet that Alex, a guy bigger than life, could be gone so quickly.

Mark remembered the day at the hospital. Kelsey had fallen apart the moment the sad emergency room doctor had lifted the drape from Alex's face. She'd flung herself on his dead body, clinging to the man who'd changed her life, whose life she'd changed. And she'd cried, the shrillest keening Mark had ever heard. No words. No sobs. Just gut-wrenching grief thrown heavenward to a God who seemed deaf and blind.

Harley had outright bawled along with her. Zack and Gabe, too. The world of The TEAM had ended that day.

Since then, Mark's heart thumped out of control every waking minute. He couldn't sleep. He paced the floors of his home where he lived with Libby and his daughters, hoping he didn't wake them with his restless wanderings in the dark of night. His sudden transition from employee to top dog gnawed at him. Day in. Day out.

Alex had left a large pair of shoes to fill and Mark hadn't the faintest clue where to begin, so he started with something simple. The grieving widow. Kelsey.

He couldn't bear what she was going through, so he'd hired someone to stay with her. Certified Nursing Assistant Shelby Sullivan came highly recommended by Mark's wife, Libby, so he jumped at the suggestion, not that Kelsey was physically sick.

Just heartsick. Just living through the worst hurt of all.

If only he could hire someone to help The TEAM. The strain on them was paramount to losing a father. Days later, the shock hadn't decreased. If anything, it had only grown worse.

Harley had unraveled. Usually the coolest agent on staff, his post-traumatic stress resurfaced with a vengeance. His sunny disposition soured into pessimism and wild stories of a dead man walking. Where that wild notion came from Mark could only guess. It had to stem from the denial phase of grief. Harley and Alex always had a bond, Alex the anchor to a man adrift. Harley seemed to be floundering more than ever.

Mark studied him now. His sandy-haired friend stood staring at the window, his shoulders taut and tight with the chip he seemed to be carrying. More than once, he'd hinted at the idea of searching for Alex, as if he didn't already know the man rested six feet under, alongside his daughter and first wife.

"Remember when he tossed his chair out this window?" Harley asked, his palms flat to the plate glass Alex had shattered in a moment of frustration years earlier. That was another tough year, the year Harley and Kelsey had gone missing at the same time.

"I do," answered Mark quietly.

"Well, I don't! I was lost on the streets of D.C. with some crazy woman who knifed me. Remember that?"

"I'm the one who found you," Mark replied, searching the depths of his soul for more patience. It took next to nothing to set Harley off.

He slapped the window, his jaw clenched tight. "He didn't give up on me! Not even when he should have!"

"Alex didn't give up on any of us." Mark maintained his steady voice. Now wasn't the time to push his friend, not while he stood at a window large enough to jump through. "He's always been there for us. All of us. Any time. Any day."

"I didn't know he went to church every Sunday with Kelsey," Harley mumbled, lost in another memory, his forehead to the glass. "You'd think he would've told me something like that, wouldn't you? You'd think he would've asked me to go with them once in a while. I'd have gone. All he had to do was ask. Never knew he went to church. Wish he would've told me."

Poor Harley. He sounded more like a lost boy instead of the highly qualified ex-Army K-9 handler he was. Hell, poor everyone.

Mark swallowed hard. "It was a nice service, wasn't it?"

"It was." Harley scrubbed a hand over his head, his hair mussed and crazy from long days and too little sleep. "He helped me run an electrical line out to my barn last spring, but he could make me so damned mad."

"He was a good guy."

"Don't you think I know that? What the hell happened? Why him?"

Mark had no answers. He was as rattled as Harley, but business had to go on. Like life. "The FBI will be here in an hour."

Red-eyed and gaunt, Harley turned to glare at Mark. "Like we can trust them. They haven't been straight with us from day one. They're lying through their teeth now. I know they are. I can feel it."

"You might be right, but let's hear them out. We need to know who fired those kill shots. If they can help us, fine. If not, we'll run our own investigation the minute they clear the crime scene. Mother's already sifting through satellite images with Steven."

Harley's brows lifted at that news, so Mark continued. "You know how she is. She might be a busybody, but she digs in without being asked. She starts working angles some of us might not think about."

"What else is going on? Tell me everything."

"Well, I'm not the boss, but I think we ought to do what we're trained to do, don't you? Let's prepare ourselves to hunt the bastards who killed Alex down. We'll find them. They'll pay."

Harley blew out a deep sigh. Just getting him to calm enough to talk calmly was a major accomplishment. The sooner everyone resumed a regular schedule, the quicker everything would normalize, whatever that meant. "It shouldn't take long if his murder's related to the list of belligerents Charlie Oakes gave Alex. There was what? Ten of them?"

Charlie Oakes. A disgruntled ex-employee who'd stooped to treason and espionage. When Alex had caught him, Charlie had revealed an alliance of ex-military snipers who held a grudge because Alex hadn't hired them.

Alex hadn't taken the threat seriously.

He should have.

Mark did.

A soft light lit behind Harley's hazel eyes again. "Ten. Yeah. Have you found the list?"

"Not yet. Ember's looking for it. Hopefully she'll have something to tell us by the time the FBI leaves. I'm planning on holding a quick staff meeting before they get here. Anything you want me to tell The TEAM?"

"You gave Ember and Mother assignments?" The bewilderment in Harley's eyes told Mark how unstable his friend was. Hadn't he just explained what the two IT techies were doing?

"I didn't have to assign them. They're professionals. They pitch in. Remember?"

"Oh, yeah. They do." Harley nodded, his gaze drifting to the wall. "I remember now."

And that was the problem. Everyone remembered. No one could forget.

Harley took a seat just as the phone on Alex's desk rang. Mark tilted his chair backward to reach the receiver. "Alex Stewart's desk. Senior Agent Houston speaking."

His automatic response caught the caller by surprise. She gasped, and Mark regretted his thoughtless answer. "Kelsey? Is that you?"

Talking with Kelsey brought instant tears to Mark's eyes. He didn't care that he wept openly. Harley'd seen worse.

Mark just wanted to be tough enough to hold Kelsey and The TEAM together.

"Yes. You sounded so, umm... I thought... For a second there..."

Mark caught the drift. She was stuck in the same time warp as Harley. She thought Alex might actually answer this time.

"I'm sorry. How are you doing, honey?"

"I'm good. I'm okay."

Like hell you are. "What can I do for you?"

"I, umm, just called to ask if... You'll think I'm crazy, but..."

He waited while Kelsey composed herself enough to talk. He totally understood. She'd lost her best friend. Everything had to be hard for her right now.

"I... I want to exhume him, Mark. Can you help me? Do you know how to go about doing that?"

"Alex?" *God, why?*

"Yes, only I don't know if it's legal, or... or..."

"Has something happened I don't know about?" Mark asked gently. He was positive Kelsey didn't know what she wanted, and he didn't know if she was capable of making important decisions at the moment. Exhumation of her husband's remains was definitely one of those big decisions that might be better made in a year or two.

Silence was the answer he expected, but not the answer he got.

"I don't think it's him. It can't be. He can't be dead. I know you probably think I'm losing my mind, and to tell you the truth, I think I'm going crazy too, but..."

He could almost hear her tears falling through the phone line.

"I... I had a dream."

He wiped his face and listened. The rest of the world could wait. Harley, too. "What did you dream?"

"He... he came to me last night. I'm sure of it. It was so real, and he kept telling me he loved me, and it would all be over soon. That he'd never stop loving me. He wrapped his arms around me, and he snuggled into my neck like he does when he comes home late at night. When he used to come home... when he..." With a soft whimper, she broke down.

Mark squeezed his eyes tight against his own wellspring of tears. God, he could bawl at the drop of a hat these days, but exhume the body? He'd do it himself if the slightest possibility existed that someone else lay in that coffin. But everyone knew the truth. Kelsey just needed time to come to grips with what had happened.

Harley watched with piercing eyes, his brows furrowed and his hackles up again. "What's going on? Is she upset? Should I go over there? Tell her I can be there in twenty."

"No need." Mark covered the receiver with his hand. "She thinks she wants to exhume Alex's body. That's all."

"Good idea. I don't think he's in that grave, either." Harley clapped both hands to his knees. "Let's do it."

Mark shook his head. "Are you still there, Kelsey? Did your doctor give you anything to help you rest?"

"Uh-huh," she mumbled. "Do you think I'm losing my mind, Mark?"

"No, but it's possible the medicine you're taking has side effects. I'll ask Libby to check with your doctor for you. Maybe that's all this dream was about." Mark treaded carefully. Dream or side effect, Kelsey seemed as fragile as Harley.

She didn't respond, and he wouldn't crush her with any more logic. Despite the cold, hard facts, she needed to believe a little bit longer. Kelsey wasn't ready to let go.

He stalled. Maybe false hope wasn't such a bad idea. "To tell you the truth, I don't exactly know how to request something like that. How about I find out for you. It might take a little time, but I'll make it happen if that's what you want to do. Will that work for you?"

An uncomfortable silence stretched. At last she mumbled,"Yes. Okay. Thank you."

Mark bit his lip at her timid response. Of course, she wasn't okay. None of them were. The TEAM had devolved into a pack of lepers, losing bits and pieces of themselves every time they tried to help each other through this nightmare.

"Did Shelby arrive yet? Is she there with you?"

"Yes. She was here at the crack of dawn. I like her, Mark. Tell Libby thanks."

"It was the least we could do. I'm going to send Gabe and Zack over in a bit to check on you, too. We'll all stay close. If you need anything, and I mean anything, you call me or Harley, okay? We're here to help." Mark eyed Harley as he made this assignment to Gabe and Zack. There was a day Harley would have been the most logical man for the job, but no more. He needed emotional support as much as poor Kelsey to get through this kind of loss.

"Yes. Okay. Good. I will." Every word out of her mouth sounded so damned lost.

"Hang in there, Kelsey. Libby and I will stop by this evening for a quick visit. We'll bring the girls."

"Thanks, Mark. Goodbye." She hung up.

He turned to face an agitated Harley, whose fingers were tapping at his kneecaps. He looked ready to jump out of his skin, breathing hard again and his eyes blinking rapidly. "If she wants us to dig him up, then I say we start now. Let's go."

"Yeah. Find out how we go about doing that, would you?" Mark couldn't keep the sarcasm out of his voice this time.

"What? You don't think it's a good idea?"

"I'll do whatever she wants. You know that, but I'm hoping this is just a phase. I won't lead her on with some crazy ghost story. Damn it, man, we know who's in that grave. You saw him at the viewing. Hell, he hasn't been buried a week yet. We don't need to push her face in it all over again."

"But what if he wasn't in that coffin in the first place? What if that wasn't him?"

"Who else was it then? The guy sure looked like Alex to me. Think about it, Harley."

"You think about it! I'm tired of thinking about it!" Harley bellowed. "God, Mark. That's all I do. I can't sleep. I can't eat. Every time I close my eyes, he's lying there. Pasty white. Blood everywhere. Kelsey's crying and all I want to do is puke. Shit! Judy thinks I'm losing my ever-loving mind. She keeps nagging at me. Wants me to go to her Lamaze classes, but I can't. I get near a hospital and all I see is— him."

"You've been talking with Kelsey, haven't you?"

Harley didn't answer other than to push away from the table and stalk out the door without a backward glance. He was too close to Alex's widow, and just as emotional. They'd always had a brother/sister bond, but Mark needed him to help Kelsey out of her depression, not add to it.

This loss hurt deeper than others had. For some unfathomable reason, Harley was rejecting Alex's death as much as Kelsey was. While that was probably a normal reaction for people in the depths of grief, it spelled trouble. No matter. Harley needed to stay away from her and take care of his pregnant wife.

Mark waited for Harley to make it back to his workstation before he called his desk phone.

"What the hell do you want now?" Harley's snarl surprised Mark.

"How's Judy?"

"I've got a damned pager. She'll buzz me if she needs me."

"The babies are coming today?"

Harley's tone softened. "Yes. Maybe. Hell, I don't know. Her doctor says they could be here at any time, but she's had false labor before. God, I don't know if I'm coming or going anymore. What am I going to do with twins?"

"She opted out of a C-section?"

"You know how she is. The babies aren't in distress. Her pregnancy's gone smooth. She feels good and she's a nurse. She ought to know. I think she's bat-shit crazy to go the natural route, but I'm just a stark raving lunatic who wants to go grave digging."

Mark ignored the heavy sarcasm. Yes, he knew how Judy was. Everyone did. Harley's redheaded wife ruled the roost at the Mortimer home, a damned good thing for a guy from up-state New York with lingering PTSD. She brought order to Harley's chaotic life and would soon bring them the two healthy sons they never thought they'd have.

"You're no crazier than the rest of us right now, bro. Tell me if there's anything you need, okay?"

"You bet. Umm—"

"Don't worry about it, Mortimer. We're all wound pretty tight right now. Focus on Judy and those little guys. You're going to be a good father. Just wait. The second you see them, your life will change in a big way."

"Shit." Harley's voice cracked. "It already has."

Chapter Three

"Do you think I'm delusional?" Mrs. Stewart asked again.

She'd asked it twice, and Shelby had replied with the standard upbeat answers, but a question asked more than once meant something else was going on.

Kelsey had been a pretty lady before her husband's death, judging by the wedding portrait on the mantle. Long chocolate brown hair. Trim. Tan. Her dark eyes full of stars and the sappiest smile on her face. Mr. Stewart and she made a handsome couple. They seemed to have had eyes only for each other.

Shelby stopped reorganizing the hallway linen closet. She'd only meant to change the linen on Mrs. Stewart's bed anyway, but everyone knew pillowcases should be in pairs. The white with the white. The red with the red.

One thing led to another. Before she knew it, she'd stacked all the sheets, towels and pillowcases on the kitchen table so she could wipe the closet shelves down with a good disinfectant. Fresh and clean. Neat and tidy. The way every linen closet should be.

It could wait.

She closed the door and left her cleaning compulsion behind to join Kelsey at the kitchen table. "I guess everyone's a little crazy, Mrs. Stewart. Is there something you want to talk about?"

"I wish you'd call me Kelsey."

"I'm sorry. I keep forgetting, don't I? It's a habit. I try to maintain a formal line between my clients and me, but for you, Kelsey it is."

"Thanks. It's just that... I must be seeing things. My head tells me one thing, but my heart seems to have a mind of its own."

Shelby waited. She didn't have personal experience dealing with death and loss. Her parents were both alive. Her grandparents, too. The closest she'd come to losing anyone was a patient, a small boy who'd nearly died at the hospital. Only that wasn't so much grief as outright terror.

Her throat tightened remembering the awful thing she'd done. He'd been in her care. The walls closed in. Bile crept up the back of her throat as the day came back with a vengeance. Some memories never went away.

Thank God he'd lived, but that was why she'd fled the pressure and confusion of the hospital for the sanity of homecare. In a one-to-one private setting, she could maintain strict control over the minutia of healthcare for another. The sleep schedules. The diet. Prescriptions.

That day, the world became black and white. Controllable. It had to be. What had happened then would never happen again. Not with Shelby Sullivan absolutely in charge.

"I know better, but last night I could've sworn..." Kelsey's voice dropped, bringing Shelby back to her current client. Kelsey lifted one hand to her cheek. Her gaze drifted from the cup of tea in her hands to the open bedroom door at the opposite end of the hall. "I thought he slid into bed with me. I thought he told me he loved me. I'm sure I felt his breath on my cheek. His kiss. It seemed so real."

Shelby gulped. It sounded real to her, too. "I think it just takes a long time. I can't imagine what you're going through. This has to be incredibly hard."

Kelsey breathed out a ragged sigh.

"Maybe these, umm, *feelings* are just your mind's way of coping. You know, of easing you back into reality." Shelby bit her lip, hoping she was helping, not hurting.

"Maybe." Kelsey pulled her gaze out of the hall and forced a weak smile. "Listen. Don't worry about me. Would you join me in a nice cup of herbal tea?"

"What if I make breakfast instead? What would you like to eat?"

But Kelsey's gaze had drifted down the hall again.

Shelby squeezed her hand to divert her. "I'm here for you, Kelsey. If there's anything I can do, please let me know."

"I will," Kelsey promised, shifting her attention to the kitchen. "Honest."

Only Shelby knew better. She couldn't fix this problem with food, but she could prepare a solid menu and make sure her patient ate better. Toast and tea were not good enough. A good healthy breakfast ought to do the trick.

"Would you like an omelet?"

"Sorry. I haven't been to the store since—"

"Don't say another word and don't you worry," Shelby said, lifting out of the chair, glad to be useful and determined to get Kelsey back on her feet. "How about a spinach omelet with bacon on the side? Sourdough toast? Orange juice?"

"Oh, no." Kelsey resisted. "That's too much trouble. Besides, it's too early to go to the store and you just got here. I can make do with a piece of toast."

"It's no trouble at all. Trust me," Shelby promised, her car keys already in her hand and her mind made up. Kelsey needed a healthy menu plan to get her back on track. Maybe a bottle of vitamins, too. B-12. And chocolate.

Libby was right. Kelsey was a genteel woman who needed help while she learned to cope with her husband's death. *I might just get her a nice bright bouquet of flowers, too. Anything to make her smile.*

The funeral sucked. Three days later, the office still felt like a tomb, and Gabe wished he were somewhere else—like the other side of the world. The farther from the walking dead that used to be the best covert team on the East Coast, the better.

He sat at his desk staring into space and thinking.

The effect of the alpha male's death was instant. Everyone walked on eggshells. No one pointed a finger. Everyone seemed to understand. He hadn't killed his boss. It wasn't his fault. *Yeah, right. Some first responder I was.*

He used to think Alex had unusually elegant taste for a stiff-necked Marine. The black marble surfaces combined with polished aluminum created an attractive, yet functional work environment. Not anymore. The whole damned place looked cold. Like a morgue. Gabe had demons enough from his two tours to Afghanistan. He didn't need them at work, too.

He now had three supervisors instead of one. The day after *it* happened, Senior Agent Mark Houston stepped out smartly and took over most of Alex's workload. Someone had to. Senior Agent David Tao seemed to have filled the role as trusted but invisible advisor. He haunted the fitness center. A man had to track him down if he needed answers.

Harley was another problem altogether. He'd distanced himself in the ways of a man on the verge of a nervous breakdown. Nothing pleased him so everyone stayed clear.

None of this would've happened if Alex had stayed in his office that morning. But no, in his usual hardheaded way, he'd gone to the FBI meeting alone, not like that spelled a death sentence in and of itself. He'd just wanted the Bureau onboard with a perceived threat he'd received. When Alex made up his mind, people tended to get out of his way. He'd meant what he'd said, every damned time.

The whole mess stemmed back to that rat bastard, Charlie Oakes. He and his buddies wanted revenge because Alex had never looked twice at them, never would've hired them even if he had. Alex honestly believed in the concept of a few good men. He made schmoozing through a job interview impossible with that single telling question.

When's the best time to take a kill shot?

Gabe had looked at Alex long and hard the morning of his job interview. What the hell? Any USMC rifleman worth his salt knew that answer. *Like NEVER.*

Enough said.

Alex nodded just once, what Gabe now understood was his stamp of approval. And just like that, prior USMC

Sergeant Gabriel Cartwright became property of The TEAM and proud of it. He was done with the killing that went along with active warfare. Working for Alex promised less of it. Gabe had shot one too many as it was.

"Meeting in ten. You ready?" Junior Agent Taylor Armstrong leaned back in his chair and brushed his hair out of his eyes. He rarely spoke. He didn't have to. He'd proved his loyalty when it counted most—in battle. Their friendship ran quiet, but deep.

"Sure. Why not?" Gabe grabbed another gulp of coffee and stowed his emotion.

I've got nothing else to do.

It was time for a staff meeting as a supervisor instead of an employee. A first.

Mark gathered his thoughts and left Alex's office, determined to get on with the business of living.

Junior Agent Taylor Armstrong, ex-USMC scout sniper— as if there was such a thing—sat at his desk with his head down, no doubt working on his debriefing reports from his latest op. He was the strong and silent type, one-half American Indian, the other half crazy in love with his new wife, Gracie.

His buddy, Maverick Carson, yet another ex-Marine, jumped to attention the moment he spotted Mark. He might've made the same mistake Mark did when he was the new kid in the office, and called Alex *sir*. Alex had a thing about being inappropriately addressed as an officer. But that day was gone.

Mark nodded at Maverick, but kept going. Mental note to self: *He's wound too tight. Let him know he's in good company, that working with guys and gals who know the down side of war is good medicine, maybe the best for a vet come home from the sandbox.*

Their buddy, Gabe, seemed lost in thought, one leg stretched in front of him and staring at nothing. He'd grown quieter with every passing day since the funeral. Being first on the scene with Alex had left its mark. He blamed himself. What returned war hero wouldn't? Survivor's guilt always sucked.

Bottom line, Gabe needed to get his head back in the game, and Mark intended to remedy that in short order. No one blamed him. Every last agent on The TEAM knew exactly what happened. They wanted the shooter, plain and simple. And dead.

Newly hired Lisa Channing stood smartly at attention in her cammie cargo pants and TEAM polo. Somehow, she made that man's uniform look good, something Landon Truman obviously noticed. Odd. Of all the new hires, he seemed the most unaffected by the loss of his boss, probably because he kept flirting as if that were all he had to do. *Next time I see him hanging around her desk, we're going to have a talk. That bullshit stops.*

No big surprise. David wasn't at his workstation. No doubt he was in the first floor gym he'd persuaded Alex to build years ago. Same as Zack. He took his anger and grief to the fitness center and pounded it out on the weight bench. He'd spent a lot of time there lately.

The married couples surprised him. Usually discreet and professional about their relationship, today Rory Dennison stood at the window, his arm around his wife Ember's waist. They faced the bright light of another sunny day in Alexandria, but her shoulders heaved. He tipped his head into hers. Mark let them have their moment.

Izza sat stiff in the middle of her husband's desk with one boot on his armrest, a tissue at her nose. Connor's hand rested on her thigh. Tight-lipped and teary-eyed, this was the first time Mark had seen Connor's kickboxing wife cry. She sniffed and turned away.

Izza had a rule about crying—at least about being seen doing it.

Poor Junior Agent Steven Cross sat plugged in at Mother's workstation, as if she owned him. The man had the patience of a saint. Mother bossed him as if he wasn't the highly trained professional he was.

Mother. The quintessential Girl Friday. A genius computer geek. The go-to gal for everything technical. Mark's favorite covert hacker. Even she looked a little red-eyed and teary.

She'd shown up her first day of work under her given name, Sasha Kennedy. Once she got comfortable, she began doing what she did best—minding everyone else's business. Next thing anyone knew, Alex had nicknamed her Mother. Only he didn't mean it in a nice way. Damned if she didn't take it as a term of endearment, though.

Mark halted at her workstation and cleared his throat. "Hey, guys. Listen up."

Harley came to stand at his left while the others gathered around, the life kicked out of them but still on the job and ready to work.

"Yes, Boss," Rory replied like the good troop he was.

That word.

Mark faltered, the mantle of responsibility a weight he didn't want, not this way.

David and Zack joined the group with the same resolute expressions on their faces as everyone else. Mark had to give it to Alex. As hard as the guy could be on his team, he'd still earned the dedication of every one of them.

"We have two missions. First and foremost, we'll stay close to Kelsey. She needs to know she's still part of this team. Two, we hunt down the bastards who killed Alex. Until we know different, we're officially going after every last one of Charlie Oakes's buddies."

"The gang of ten?" Ember asked from where she stood with Rory.

"Yes. Did you find the list yet?"

"No. It's not on his computer. I still need to check his desk. He might've written it down somewhere. You know how he is, umm, was." She turned her face into her husband's shoulder at her misspeak.

"It's okay, Ember. We're all hurting. We're in the same boat." Mark took a deep breath. "We've all lost men before. It goes with the profession we've chosen, but Alex wasn't just another guy. It'll be tough for a while, but we can do this. We can carry on. We're the best team out there, remember?"

The TEAM. *My team. Damn.*

Reality suffocated the resolve he'd started with. "I'll tell you everything I know right now. Alex's will directed Harley,

David, and me to take over the business. None of you will lose your jobs. You guys should already know that. If you have any questions, come see one of us."

He sucked in a slow breath, relieved that the corners of Gabe's mouth twitched with the smallest smile. Good. The guy needed a measure of reassurance after what he'd lived through. "The minute the Bureau clears the crime scene across the street, I want a team on the roof to verify what happened. Check ballistics. Traffic cams. Everything. We'll find the SOBs who gunned Alex down. I can promise you that. Mother, call the county or city offices and find out how to exhume a body."

Everyone's brows lifted at that quick shift in direction. A couple agents gasped. *Well, hunker down guys. We're in this for the long haul.*

"I know how it sounds, but Kelsey's struggling. She thinks she wants to exhume Alex's body. I'm hoping she changes her mind before we bring in a backhoe, but until then we'll proceed with finding out how to do what she's asked."

Mark drew in a deep breath. "Taylor and Izza, the second Ember finds that list, I want you to track down every last name on it. Find out where those ten bastards live, what they ate for breakfast, and who their proctologists are. Everything." The more he talked, the more the weight of responsibility lifted from his shoulders. Delegation definitely spread the load.

"You got it," Izza muttered.

Taylor nodded one curt affirmative.

"Zack. Gabe. Pack up. You're going to stay with Kelsey for a while, maybe as long as a month."

Gabe's brows furrowed. Standing watch over a grieving widow was an unusual assignment for two ex-snipers and top-notch undercover operators, but he needed this assignment more than anyone else. "Sure. I can do that. Be glad to," he said.

"It'll be our pleasure. You think whoever killed Alex will go after her, too?" Zack asked.

"It's possible. I've asked Alexandria PD to keep an eye on her, but I'd feel better if we were posted at the house. I think she'd like having you guys with her, too. At least until she catches her balance."

"Do we know who killed him yet?" Gabe asked.

Several other agents glanced at the poor guy. He must not have been listening to the earlier assignment, a minor infraction for a man carrying a shitload of guilt.

His innocent question sparked Harley's temper. "Don't be stupid, Cartwright. It was one of those jerks he didn't hire. Who else?"

"Right now, we're assuming that's who killed him," Mark intervened. "Until the FBI lets us into the crime scene across the street, we can't be absolutely sure."

"Well, I'm sure." Harley glared at Gabe. "Hell. I'm not an idiot."

Regret washed over Gabe's face. Okay, so maybe Harley blamed Gabe for Alex's death, another problem Mark hadn't seen coming, but enough was enough. The TEAM was running on empty, Gabe maybe most of all.

Mark intervened again. "Gabe, listen. I need someone to stand with Kelsey. She needs her friends around her. Will you do that for me? For her?"

He nodded, swallowing hard. "Sure. Like Zack said. My pleasure."

Harley gave an impatient growl, but Mark kept going. "I know it sounds like overkill, but yes. On the long shot that someone might go after Kelsey, I want you guys to set up a perimeter around her house. Alex had a top-of-the-line security system installed. Use it. Push external coverage to a three-house radius for now. Maybe it's my paranoia, but let's stay close to her until we're sure what's going on. Sound good?"

"Yes, Boss."

Gabe's automatic response startled Mark again. They had to understand. "I'm not the boss here, guys. That was Alex. I'm just... me."

Blinking hard, Gabe opened his mouth to speak. Fortunately, Zack interrupted the awkward moment. "Maybe we'll do some painting while we're there. She'd like that."

"Good idea. Just take care of her, okay?"

Mark faced The TEAM. His team. Grief stared back. Despite bossing Steven earlier, Mother dabbed tissues against both eyes. Rory had Ember in a loving stranglehold while Izza and Connor both blinked fast and hard to keep their tears at bay. Softhearted Connor lost the contest.

Taylor looked every bit the fierce warrior he could be when needed. Harley's hand came to rest firmly on Mark's shoulder, his angst in control for the moment. Gabe looked ready to get the hell out of there, his fingers fluttering anxiously at his side and his feet tapping.

Still, Mark hesitated. Talking with his friends had never been so hard. The unsettling rumor that Alex wasn't dead had surfaced and Harley had fed it. It had to end.

"I know this isn't what you want to hear, but it needs to be said. I was there and I know what I saw. I watched Alex die. I couldn't get my hands on him, and I didn't administer CPR or first-aid like Gabe did, but he's gone." Mark took a deep breath, needing everyone onboard and moving forward. He measured his next words carefully. "Now that I've said that, you need to understand that I will stand by Kelsey with this exhumation order. I'll go to the ends of the earth to help her through this next month or two. Or three. Or twelve. If exhuming Alex is what she wants, by hell that's what we'll do."

"We're going to visit with her tonight," Rory offered. "Tyler wants to see his Grandma Kelsey."

"He drew a big sunshine for her," Ember said, a catch in her voice. "He pasted accordion arms on it. Said she needs a sunshine hug."

"We're going too," Mark said. "Maybe we'll see you there."

Izza's chin stuck out, masking grief with her usual mean-girl attitude. "Me and Connor are taking dinner in tomorrow night." She glared even as she wiped her eyes. "Yeah, guys. I can cook. Never said I couldn't."

"Nancy and I will wait a couple days to visit then," David said.

Mark clenched his jaw before emotion got the best of him. These people weren't just team members. They were family. And that family was closing ranks around their heartbroken friend in her time of need.

He gave them the best he had left to offer. "No matter what happened or what happens from now on, I'm here to tell you three things. Alex believed in you. Kelsey believes in you. And I believe in you."

Harley groaned and turned away. Mark kept going. It was a puny pep talk at best, but it was all he had to give. "Let's make Alex proud one last time. Gabe and Zack, keep Kelsey safe. Harley, go home. Help Judy bring some happiness into the world."

"Yeah, we need some good news for a change," Ember said. "Hurry up. Get those baby boys here so I can kiss them and hug—"

Harley clutched his forehead with one hand, covering his eyes. His shoulders heaved. "We're naming one of my boys... Alex."

Ember went straight to him. She wrapped her arms around her friend while he fell apart. "I'm sorry. God, Harley. I'm just so damned sorry."

Even stoic David wiped his eyes at the tender news. A baby named after their hard-as-nails boss? A shot straight to the heart.

Mark blinked the moisture out of his eyes, cleared his throat and said the only thing he could. "Dismissed."

Chapter Four

Get me the hell outta here.

Gabe followed Zack away from the depressing doldrums that followed Death. Thank God and Greyhound they'd gotten tasked to assist Kelsey. The assignment might not be out of the country, but anything was better than being stuck at TEAM headquarters.

Besides, she'd set him straight at the viewing with a hug and a handful of tissues. Kelsey held no malice in her heart that he'd been there when the shots were fired, that he hadn't been able to perform a miracle and save his boss. Gabe had outright asked for forgiveness, but received heartfelt gratitude instead.

"He always liked you," she'd said. "You remind him of himself when he was younger."

That teary exchange forged a link like no other. He headed for his locker one level up on the third floor, damned sure nothing would happen to Kelsey.

A special ops man always kept his duffel packed, and his gear bag ready to travel at a moment's notice. Gabe's duffel held a five-day supply of clothes and personal items. He also carried an extra bag for his spare bionic foot. He'd left more than empty shells and bad memories back in the Mideast.

His gear bag was something else. He'd packed it with the usual medical trauma pack, lock-pick kit, fingerprint lift cards, heavy-duty flashlight, spare lithium batteries, one hundred feet of nylon cord, his twelve-inch USMC knife, a baseball cap, ear protection and safety glasses. A guy always had to be prepared, even at the boss's house.

His boss's old house. Ex-boss. Oh, hell. Kelsey's house.

They stopped at the armory before they hit the elevator. It was nothing less than a vault, pure and simple. It housed an assortment of sniper rifles, sawed-off shotguns, grenade launchers, semi-automatic handguns, rifles, extra magazines, ammo—you name it. All small arms were stored in individual agent's lockers within the vault. That had been Alex's rule. No one carried on the job.

Gabe removed his SIG 290 from his locker and slung its holster over his shoulder. He secured five magazines into their plastic carrying case, and stuck a spare thigh-holster and a pocket pistol in his gear bag for added measure. It never hurt to be over-prepared, even if just standing watch over a sad lady friend.

Lastly, he included his laser scope, range finder, and a specialized digital camera for the lower rack on his pistol. "You think we'll need night vision?"

Alex had recently procured the latest NVG helmets, newly designed and downright futuristic looking. If Zack gave the word, two of them would be added to the growing stack of gear on its way out the door with them.

"Hope not. Here." Zack tossed a bag of dried dog treats. "Stow these instead."

Gabe lifted the plastic bag to view the contents. "Didn't know extra-large dog snacks were standard issue."

"They are now."

"We keep them in the armory?"

Zack grunted. "Why not? I've got a bag in my bottom desk drawer, too. A guy's got to be prepared for anything and everything."

It made sense. Zack always was one to take extra precaution. Gabe stowed the bag for the dogs Alex had left behind. Whisper and Smoke—the best tracking dogs in the state.

"You got the cameras and laptop? Tattle Tales?" he asked.

Tattle Tales were Mother's invention, a pesky minute version of a video and audio transmitter, small enough to escape most detection.

Zack pointed to another set of nylon gear bags. "Already packed. Let's stop for grub on the way. Don't want to eat her out of house and home. You ready?"

"Hell, yeah."

It took little time getting to Kelsey's. She and Alex lived less than a mile from his business. *Used to live. At least, Kelsey still lived there. Oh, hell.*

Gabe growled at the obvious hole in his head. His brain didn't seem able to move on any more than he could. *Takes time.*

His inner sniper's sixth sense pinged the moment the Stewarts' home came into view. No cars in the carport. "Thought the nurse was supposed to be here?"

"She was. Something's not right." Zack parked in the empty driveway.

"I'll check out back."

Gabe scrambled out of the SUV and headed into the backyard through the carport. Whisper and Smoke sat in their kennel, watching with bright black eyes while Zack unlatched the gate and proceeded toward the back door.

Nothing in the carport or back yard looked out of place. No foul play. He didn't like that Kelsey was gone, but okay. Maybe she felt good enough to go shopping or something. No problem.

Zack opened the patio door, a key fob in his right hand. "Come on in. Let's get settled."

"You had a key?"

"Sure. Alex gave me one years ago. Never needed it until now."

They no more than hit the front porch again when a red economy car zipped up to the opposite curb and parallel parked. A blond woman in powder-blue scrubs stepped out of the car with a bag of groceries in her arms.

"Looks like the nurse is back," Gabe said. "Without Kelsey. I've got a bad feeling."

"You two must be the bodyguards Libby told me to expect. Where's Mrs. Stewart?" she asked on her way up the walk.

"Don't you know?" Gabe countered. An icy finger of dread snaked across the back of his neck. "Isn't she with you?"

"No. I ran to the store for a few groceries. She was here when I left. Here." She pushed the bag of groceries into his arms. "Looks like you guys know your way around. Go put this in the kitchen. Don't drop the eggs. They need to go in the refrigerator. Top shelf."

Gabe bristled. If Zack hadn't been right behind him and already on his cell phone, he would've handed the bag back to the obnoxious woman and told her to do it herself. Instead, he did what she'd ordered. Women and their shopping. She'd bought a lot more than eggs.

"Hey, Mark. We might have a problem," Zack said. "Need you to track Kelsey's GPS. No. She's not here." He returned the phone to his hip holster. "You must be Miss Shelby."

"Nurse Sullivan to you," she answered peevishly. "And you are?"

"Agent Zack Lennox, ma'am." Zack extended a handshake.

"Gabe Cartwright at your service," Gabe offered the same, but she'd crossed her arms over her chest instead of accepting their offers.

"I don't see why she needs two of you. This neighborhood's a little rundown, but it's not like she lives in Anacostia."

"We come in pairs, ma'am." Zack unclipped the vibrating phone from his holster and raised it to his ear. "She's where?" He listened another second, hung up and turned to Gabe. "We've got to go. Now."

"Where?" Nurse Sullivan asked, but Zack didn't answer on his way out of the house. "Wait. She's my patient. I'm going with you."

"Then get in." Already in the SUV, he slammed the vehicle door and started the engine. "It might be nothing, but she's parked off the Mount Vernon Highway by the Potomac. Mark's sending coordinates."

Gabe buckled his seatbelt while Nurse Sullivan got into the backseat and did the same.

"What's she doing all the way out there?" she asked.

"You tell me." Zack put his foot to the floor and screeched out of the driveway. "How'd she seem this morning?"

"How do you think she seemed? She's grieving. This is hard on her."

"How long were you gone?" Gabe asked. Sullivan wasn't bad looking. Bossy as hell, but not too hard on the eyes. Blondes always did attract him, damned if he knew why. Had to be that California girl mystique the Beach Boys always sang about. Whatever it was, this woman had it.

"Not long. Maybe an hour and a half is all. I needed eggs for breakfast."

Gabe rolled the twinge of aggravation out of his neck. There was a helluva lot more than eggs in that grocery bag. Right out of California nights or not, Nurse Sullivan had a nasty air of superiority that tested his patience, and he didn't have much. Ninety minutes could be a damned long time for a woman at risk.

As usual, Zack stuck his foot in it and the vehicle flew. There was no sign of Kelsey's small blue sedan at the coordinates Mark sent—not that it mattered. You couldn't miss the flashing red and blue emergency lights or the bright yellow police tape. By the time Zack rolled the vehicle to a stop, Gabe had his feet on the ground.

Zack headed for the sheriff's car, Miss Sullivan on his six. Two local sheriff cars, one fire engine, a tow truck, and an ambulance stood with engines running and lights flashing. A long section of the road had been cordoned off with police tape while an officer routed traffic around the scene of what, Gabe couldn't tell. No cars. No accident.

He ran to the rear gate of the ambulance where two medics leaned against the back bumper, their arms crossed, watching the tow truck winch a car out of the river. Kelsey's car.

"Where is she?"

One medic lifted off the bumper. "Don't ask us. All we know is we've got one car in the river, but no driver. If you know anything, you need to be talking with the sheriff."

Gabe pivoted, his heart in his throat. He teetered back on his good foot, the life knocked out of him all over again. *God. This can't be happening.*

"Kelsey Stewart," he said hoarsely. "That's her car. She's my... friend."

"Listen, man." The medic cupped Gabe's elbow. "You'd better take a seat with us before you fall down."

"No. I'm good." Gabe brushed the kind suggestion aside, not willing to admit he wasn't as sure-footed as he'd like to be, but could things get any worse?

He headed toward the tow truck, its rear wheels still in the river, while Zack talked with one of the deputies.

Nurse Sullivan ditched Zack and tagged along with Gabe. "The deputy said if she's not here at the scene then she's in the river. He doesn't think we'll find her alive."

"Not Kelsey," Gabe ground out.

Sullivan seemed to be one of those types who needed to yak when they got nervous. "But he said it's the only thing that makes sense, especially since she was a grieving widow. Said he sees this all the time. An emotional woman loses control of her car on a turn, and—"

Gabe spun on his good heel, not going to entertain that idiotic conclusion for one second. "Not Kelsey, damn it. You don't know her like I do. And there's no turn on this stretch of highway. Why don't you look at the evidence before you jump to conclusions?" *And why don't you leave me the hell alone?*

"What evidence? All I see is mud and first responders."

He glanced over his shoulder, needing to put more distance between him and this annoying woman. She had one of those cute little perky noses that barely turned up at the end. For a scant second, remorse flickered across her face. And why Gabe noticed, he didn't know, but she seemed— lost. Maybe baffled. Out of her depth.

He gave her the benefit of the doubt and explained a few things to set her straight. "Look at the debris field," he muttered, pointing to the tire tracks leading down from the concrete highway all the way to the river. Another deputy stood in the center of the road with a camera and scribbling on his notepad, hopefully documenting the accident instead of just accepting his boss's version.

The more Gabe looked, the more things didn't add up to the sheriff's hasty conclusion of a driver losing control. He pointed to the muddy trail between the road and the river. "See there? Do you see any plastic trim or shattered glass?"

Sullivan followed the direction of his index finger. "I see some red plastic pieces on the highway, but—"

"Probably brake lights. That's all. But if a car rolled like the deputy said, there'd be a trail of litter and car parts all the way to the river. Side mirrors. Trim. Maybe hubcaps. Other stuff, too. And another thing." He scrambled back to the roadway where the alleged rollover began, dragging the nurse along to make sure she knew better. He pointed at the overabundance of black rubber on the road, most of it fresh and dark, arcing across the four-lane highway. "She had to be travelling west to east. What do you see?"

Sullivan shielded her eyes against the weak morning sun with her right hand. "Umm, nothing."

"Give me a break. Skid marks. You see skid marks. Look at 'em. See how they tend toward the river? Looks to me like someone hit their brakes and jerked their wheel hard to the right. And that one." He indicated a clear set of rubber to the east of the first arc. "Someone else braked hard to the left. And those."

He pivoted, needing Sullivan to understand the dynamics of what most likely happened on this stretch of road before she shot her big mouth off again. "Those wider patches are called yaw marks. All that rubber you're looking at is what gets left on concrete when tires are forced sideways. Normal skid marks are narrow except for the point where they turn. You see anything that looks like a car rolled now?" he asked, his Irish up and his blood pressure with it.

He would know. His ex-Air Force father, now a police officer in Texas, had once testified against a mob killing along the Trinity River. At that time in his teenage life, Gabe only cared about hotrods and racing his sixty-three Chevy Nova.

Watching his father's detailed testimony of automobile forensics in the courtroom, a testimony that resulted in the conviction of a powerful gangster, had turned Gabe's head around. He still loved a good race, which explained his revoked driver's license at the moment, but he also understood the dynamics behind laying a patch of rubber.

Funny how that particular insight precipitated Gabe's joining the Corps. Like father, like son? He only hoped.

Officer Nathaniel Cartwright was an honorable servant of the law and a father to be proud of. Gabe sure was.

This was no rollover. Whoever had committed this crime had left a map any good law enforcement officer should've been able to read. That this particular sheriff wanted to chalk it up to a bullshit reason like a grieving widow losing control of her vehicle shot a righteous dose of anger up Gabe's spine.

"Now that you mention it, no, it doesn't look like a car rolled. You really know your stuff, but the sheriff said—"

And enough was enough. Gabe bristled. "The sheriff should keep his big mouth shut until his deputies finish running the crime scene. This was no accident, damn it."

His heart pitched. The tow truck driver had just winched the butt end of Kelsey's car high enough that the driver's side door flopped open.

"So what do you think happened then?" Sullivan asked. "How many cars were involved? I mean, in your opinion?"

He raked an impatient hand over his head, wanting to be anywhere else but explaining collision dynamics to this particular woman. "I think someone swerved in front of Kelsey. She stopped. See those two lines there?" He pointed at what was to him an obvious roadmap to what had occurred earlier. "She braked hard. Those narrow tire marks came from a car the size of hers. The vehicle behind her had also come to a hard stop, leaving a wider stretch of rubber on the road. He left wider marks, and look at the wheel to axle ratio."

Shit. He might have rammed her with a big truck. Gabe took a deep breath, forcing his empathy for what Kelsey might have gone through back to a manageable level, but damn. Her little car wouldn't have stood a chance if her attackers were in some big four-by-four.

"What else do you think happened?" Sullivan pointed to the deeply gouged ruts leading all the way to the river. "It looks like someone might have gotten stuck in the mud. See there?"

Gabe focused on forensics. Not Kelsey's very likely anxiety. "I think she was double-teamed. One guy swerved in front of her. The other hit her from behind hard enough to break her taillights and scare the hell out of her. There might have been a fourth car involved, another jerk who rammed her from the side. Maybe not, but someone shoved a lighter car into the river. Sideways. Look at the mud trail between the road and the shoreline. See how the yaw marks end at the roads' edge? See how the reeds and bushes are mashed all the way to the water's edge? Either that or..."

He gulped at the terror she must have felt in those last few minutes. All alone, and fighting for her life. His heart rate kicked up and his throat went dry. A full-blown panic attack welled up from his gut. He forced it back down. Again. "Either that or someone else was waiting for her."

"I still don't get it. How did your office even know where she was? If you're right, her phone had to be underwater by then. If that's the GPS signal you were track—"

He lifted his cell phone to Shelby's view. "Ever heard of ruggedized cell phones, ma'am? All of our equipment is built to withstand crap like this."

I just never expected Kelsey would need a waterproof cell phone. Shit. What's going on?

Gabe dared Shelby to argue. Instead, she seemed to be honestly trying to understand, her lower lip trapped between her teeth as if she needed a moment to reason through what he'd just explained. "Then she has to be around here somewhere," she said. "We need to look for her."

At last. Sullivan said something worthwhile. He sized her up. Typical California blonde with shoulder-length hair. Slender and petite, a waif-like quality hung around her, as if she needed an arm to steady her against the light breeze blowing off the river. Worry lines crinkled her forehead. She looked east to the Potomac, then west.

The whine and squeak of the winch drew his attention back to the scene. By then, they'd drawn closer to the police tape nearest the tow truck. Gabe leaned into the tape for a closer view of the car dangling out of the water, the rear winched high in the air and water running from the open doors. Show and tell was done.

Sidestepping the tape, he muttered a quick, "Sorry, ma'am, but I've got to talk with this guy," to Shelby.

"Hey. You shouldn't get any closer. It's against the law."

Bullshit. Just watch me.

He left Sullivan standing on the law-abiding side of the tape. Too much evidence stood to be destroyed. He needed to record as much of it as he could, as quickly as possible. So he did. Gabe snapped picture after picture while the tow truck operator worked around him, preparing to winch the car onto the flatbed.

"Hey." The guy cast a furtive glance at the sheriff still at his vehicle and talking with Zack, then nodded toward the front seat of Kelsey's sedan. "I've got something you need to see if you're interested in what really happened."

"You bet. Whatcha got?"

The tow truck operator left his station at the winch and positioned himself between the driver's seat of Kelsey's sedan and the sheriff, nodding his chin for Gabe to take a look. "Just that."

Gabe peered inside. The airbag had deployed, but one long slash left it hanging over the steering wheel in ribbons instead of simply deflated like it should've been. The seatbelt had been cut. Not hacked. The slices were too clean.

"It looks to me like a Good Samaritan might've come along and rescued whoever was driving this car."

"Kelsey Stewart," Gabe said, looking through the vehicle.

Good Samaritan, nothing. This looked like the work of someone who knew exactly what they were doing. Gabe didn't know what to think anymore, but if she'd cut herself out of her own seatbelt like it looked like she might have done, where was she? She would've used that ruggedized cell phone by now to alert Mark or someone. Kelsey was smart like that.

She'd lived long enough with Alex. Hell, she carried a concealed weapon, probably a SIG if Gabe knew Alex's first choice of handguns. He'd taught his wife to shoot. Why not how to carry a trusty blade, too?

Gabe growled at his jumping to conclusions. Maybe he had this all wrong. Maybe Kelsey was that Good Samaritan. Maybe she'd come across someone else in trouble and attempted to help. That would be like her.

Mud and silt from the river bottom mucked up the floor, but it was the windshield that caught his eye. The darned thing was still intact as if nothing had happened. A Saint Christopher's medal dangled from the rearview mirror. The damned patron saint of travelers must've taken the day off.

The fact remained. Kelsey's car was empty and battered.

"Then where is she?" Gabe asked out loud, scanning the river's edge through the passenger-side windows. The only one standing on the edge of the muddy riverbank was Nurse Sullivan. Watching him. What did she want now? She looked away. *Good. This is your fault as much as mine, damn it. We both should've been there when Kelsey needed us.*

The tow truck driver shrugged, a heavy tow strap looped in his hand. "I only know I'm not pulling a car out of the river with a body in it today. That's good enough for me. Hey. Ain't your Mrs. Stewart the lady whose husband was gunned down a few days ago? They had his picture in the obits. Looked like a nice enough guy."

"Yes," Gabe said somberly. "Alex Stewart. He was my boss."

"I was sure sorry to read that. His missus helped my daughter a while back when Crissy ran away from home and was living on the streets. Mrs. Stewart's a real nice lady. Least, she was."

"She is." Gabe met the man's apologetic eyes. *Damn it. She is.*

The awful thought that she might be hurt, lying somewhere in the mud, galled Gabe. There was no reason she should've been out here all by herself. Nurse Sullivan should've stayed with her. *And I shouldn't have let Alex die.*

"Just thought you'd want to see this. Sometimes these guys"—The driver jerked his thumb back toward the deputy—"think they know what happened without even paying attention to little things, like this seat belt. Here." He handed Gabe a set of keys. "You might as well take 'em. These guys won't notice they're gone. Heck, they ain't even looked inside her car yet. Guess they've already decided what happened."

The man was right. For now, the sheriff and his deputy stood with their backs to Gabe, talking with Zack and seemingly uninterested in the vehicle. Good enough. Zack was running interference, giving Gabe time to accumulate evidence before being forced from the scene.

He glanced at the jumble of keys the tow truck driver had handed him.

Didn't it figure?

The heart-shaped, plastic-covered face of Alex Stewart smirked back at him.

Chapter Five

Not again.

The sensation of a five hundred pound weight on her chest squeezed the life out of Shelby. She scanned the river, on the verge of hyperventilating and running for cover. One glance back over her shoulder told her all she needed to know.

Agent Cartwright would rather she left and never came back. Both the guys were too busy to care what she thought— not that she expected them to. Not that she'd ever tell them.

It's your fault. Again.

You should've known better.

What have you done?

The eternal voice of recrimination rang in her head with her words. Her guilt. Her shame. She used to love working in the pediatrics ward at the Northern Virginia Hospital Center. Children gravitated toward her, and she'd loved working there until...

You don't give a child the wrong medication and not expect everything in your life to change.

And change it had.

Her throat closed in sympathetic response to what had happened less than a year ago. She could still see little Rudy gasping for air, gray from struggling to breathe while his lungs nearly shut down.

The hospital didn't even have to fire her. She just quit. They'd wanted her to come back. It wasn't her fault, none of it. Libby Houston had been her greatest advocate, but Shelby couldn't take the chance ever again.

It might've been the pharmacist's fault for sending the wrong medication to her floor, but she, the Certified Nursing Assistant on duty, put the mislabeled inhalant into Rudy's lungs. She was the one who'd nearly killed him. Not Libby.

Everyone said it was an honest mistake, but the terror of watching a two-year-old asthma patient nearly suffocate at her hand resulted in an out-of-control need to micromanage everything and everyone in her care.

They called it *Obsessive Compulsive Disorder*. It might go away some day. It might not. It surely wouldn't with Kelsey Stewart possibly out there in the water, and all because Shelby had insisted on all food groups instead of simply toast for her client.

She turned her back on yet another of her failures, rubbing her biceps to ward off the cold that never went away. Agent Cartwright stood with his back to her, preoccupied with the tow truck driver. Agent Lennox had joined him, but everywhere Shelby turned, she saw Kelsey's sad face and she heard that sad question. *Do you think I'm crazy?*

Shelby lifted her hand to her throat at the thought of that sweet woman drowning. This tributary emptied into the Potomac six or seven short miles to the east. That's where Kelsey would be. Downstream. Floating. Agent Cartwright had to be right. Kelsey had to be alive.

Agent Cartwright's adamant declaration *'Not Kelsey!'* offered her hope. Shelby marched straight back to the sheriff. "What are you waiting for? You need to get searchers on the water and divers in the river. Right now."

Her reflection glared back at her from the shiny barrier of his dark glasses. He nodded, his face a mask. "Already on their way, ma'am. I wouldn't get your hopes up, though. Looks pretty straightforward to me. Seen a few rollovers in my time, you know. The car door sprung when it rolled. The force of the roll ejected the driver. Since there's no body on the road, there's only one place it could be." He nodded downstream. "And a woman in that river isn't going to be found alive. Not anymore."

The need to do something—anything!—spurred her into action.

Agents Cartwright and Lennox were combing the riverbank, Cartwright downstream, Lennox up. Shelby opted to join Cartwright. She didn't have to like these guys to help search. She just had to get to Kelsey in time.

"You were so beautiful," Mark told the picture of Kelsey that Alex kept on his desk. "God, how do we run this place without the two of you? How do we even begin again?"

He and Harley had come back to the office to double check incoming correspondence in the hope something turned up. While Harley scanned incoming calls and voice messages at Mother's desk, and hopefully remembered to call home to check on his long overdue pregnant wife, Mark did the same at Alex's office.

For three long days The TEAM searched, but there'd been no sign of Kelsey. No body. No footprints leading out of the river. Not even a hint that anyone saw or knew where she was.

Nurse Sullivan had proved unstoppable. She'd organized search grids, door-to-door efforts, and a newspaper campaign that kept Kelsey's face in the public's eye. She'd logged as many foot and driven miles as any agent, but nothing mattered. Kelsey seemed to have disappeared, and Mark dreaded the day when someone found her poor body along a lonely river shore. Or in a fisherman's net.

This second blow felt deeper. More personal. Losing Alex was one thing. He'd always been a target. The man rattled more sabers and made more enemies than most, but Kelsey? She'd never hurt anyone. Defending herself against her demented ex-mother-in-law didn't count. Ethel Durrant deserved to die. Kelsey didn't.

At least Alex and Kelsey are together now.

That line of bullshit didn't bring one moment of comfort. Mark lowered his face to his folded arms on the desktop. He needed a moment to think or pray, trying like hell to draw strength from his personal beliefs that taught of life after death, resurrection, and hope. Not today. He plain didn't have the heart for this business anymore. The TEAM was running on empty and so was he.

"Show me a way," he whispered. "God, we do thy work. I know we do, but we can't do this alone. I can't. Not anymore."

The silence in the empty room echoed the hollow feeling in his chest. He ached. There seemed no light left in the world after this double hit. Tears got the best of him. He honestly didn't know what he'd expected. He'd just hoped.

Instead of waiting for an answer that wasn't going to come, he wiped his face and pushed back from the desk. The sheriff might be right. They weren't going to find Kelsey.

"You what?" Harley bellowed from the outer office. "Say again."

Mark scrambled out the door. Hope stirred in his soul at the excitement in Harley's voice.

He stood at Mother's desk, scribbling on a notepad with the office phone in his ear, his eyes wide with anger and his tone filled with authority for the first time in days. "Who are you? How do you—?"

He slammed the phone down. "I know where she is!"

"God, he's an ass." Gabe jammed his cell phone into his front jeans pocket after another hostile confrontation with Harley. "Someone called in an anonymous tip. Kelsey's supposedly at these coordinates. He wants us to check it out. We're closest. Come on. Let's go get her."

Zack didn't have to be asked twice. While Gabe keyed in the coordinates to their vehicle's mapping system, he accelerated to well past cruising speed. In less than ten miles, they were rolling through an upscale neighborhood that boasted manicured lawns and five-acre plots. No children. No pets. Just wealth. That kind of neighborhood.

"Over there." Gabe indicated a white brick ranch-style home sprawled at the crest of a small hill. Sunlight reflected off the enormous picture windows at the front of the house. A low-running hedge lined a wide driveway as well as the telltale motion detector spikes of an outside security system.

The whole neighborhood was quiet. Sterile. No kids played in any of the yards. No dogs or cats prowled, barked or meowed.

Every home within sight declared executive wealth and privilege, nothing like the neighborhoods Gabe had grown up in. Whoever lived here had a good view of the Potomac below. He knocked on the front door, then again harder, while Zack investigated around the north side of the place.

The smallest sound. Gabe cocked his head to be ascertain whether it came from inside or out.

"You should see what's out back. These folks have a full-sized tennis court and a—"

"Shhh. Come here," Gabe whispered, his ear pressed to the door. "Listen. Do you hear that?"

Zack stilled. The murmuring sounded again, so soft Gabe couldn't tell if he'd heard anything or not.

The faintest murmuring again.

"It's Kelsey's voice. She's inside. I know it's her."

"One way to find out." Zack applied his fist to the door. "Kels? You in there? Let us in."

The softest 'yes' this time, and Gabe needed to get inside the damned house.

"Are you okay? Can you let us in?" he asked.

The doorknob jiggled, but no more. "I'm... here," she muttered from the other side of the steel door. "Zack? Gabe? Is that you?"

"It's us," Gabe called to her. God. Finally. He could breathe. "We're here. Open up."

The knob wiggled again, not enough. "I can't. My hands... my fingers... I'm hurt."

All the worst scenarios blasted his logical thought process. What kind of a creep had her stashed away like this? Was she hurt? Abused? Tortured?

Frustration roared to life. He slammed a palm to the door jamb, needing to get inside!

"Take it easy," Zack muttered. "You've got your B&E kit on you, don't you? Use it."

"Yeah, but, the second I pick that lock, every police car in a ten-mile radius is going to be on this doorstep with us."

"So?" Zack barked. "Kels is in there. Open the damned thing."

Gabe pulled his lock-pick kit out of his back pocket and opened the door in five seconds flat. The moment he eased it open so as not to shove her out of the way, his heart sank.

There she stood on unsteady bare feet, her palms flat to the wall behind her for support. Both of her eyes were blackened, one swollen nearly shut, her nose split with a horizontal gash that looked as if it had been stitched but not taped.

Gabe had her in his arms before she sank to the tiled entry.

"Oh thank God," she murmured.

Zack stepped around him and entered the home, searching quickly. Sure enough, a siren sounded in the not-too-distant neighborhood. The police were on their way.

Gabe smoothed his hands over her shoulders and down her arms, diagnosing as he went. Not only were her arms black and blue, but several of her fingers were splinted and bandaged, too. She struggled to breathe, every inhalation ragged and her chest heaving.

"My God, Kelsey. Who did this to you? Have you been here the whole time?"

"I... don't know." Her eyes brimmed with tears. "I just woke up and I was... here."

He looked closer. Her hair was clean. Someone had been taking good care of her.

"No one else is here, but you ought to see what's in the first bedroom down the hall," Zack muttered. "An IV tree with a half-empty bag hanging on it. Plenty of other evidence, too. Blankets. Medical tape. Gauze. A couple prescription bottles. Maybe the police can get a clear print off some of this stuff."

He crouched with Gabe, feeling Kelsey's forehead with the back of his fingers. "You're feverish. Whatcha been doing in here? Do you remember anything?"

She clutched Gabe's shirt as if she needed something to hold on to, even though she couldn't get a firm grip. "You wouldn't believe me if I told you."

"You know me better than that. Come on, Kels," Zack soothed, his voice as tender as Gabe had ever heard. "I'm on your side. Friends to the end, remember?"

"How many days?"

Gabe held up three fingers.

She looked up at him through tears, swallowing hard. "Three? Really? It had to be him."

"Who?" Gabe asked quietly.

"Alex. I think... Alex brought me here."

Gabe didn't gasp, blink or betray one iota of surprise. It must not have been enough to convince her that he believed her though.

"But he did. You have to believe me."

"I do," Zack answered. "Hell, Kels, you're here safe and sound. Who else would've taken care of you like this? We both believe you."

Gabe nodded, going along with whatever came out of his senior agent's mouth. But what kind of a jackass would play a cruel trick like this on someone as sweet as Kelsey? The poor thing trembled against him, inciting every male instinct to protect and guard her—and to kick the living shit out of whoever had hurt her.

"Trust us," he said. "You're safe now. If you believe he was here, then by hell, so do we."

"You do?" She searched his face.

He peered directly into those deep, sad brown eyes. He didn't mean to hesitate. He'd never lie to this woman. Tears brimmed anyway. He hadn't answered quick enough.

"But he did," she cried, melting against him.

Gabe shot a desperate look over the top of her head at his agent in charge. Zack answered with one short shake of his head.

Yeah. No way it could've been Alex.

Chapter Six

It had been a whole day since Kelsey was found. Once again, Mark assigned Gabe and Zack to protect Kelsey—not like he had much of a choice. Her recovery sparked The TEAM's energy. They argued to relieve each other in overlapping shifts, but no way would Gabe or Zack consider it. They stood firm, their hearts on their sleeves and their minds made up. They'd found her, and possession was nine-tenths of their unwritten sniper code.

She's ours. Leave your flowers. Visit for a while, but back off.

The unexpected dilemma of finding Kelsey turned out to be Mother. She'd shown up at the hospital ready to move into Kelsey's hospital room with her, only to be politely rebuffed by Gabe. When Mark agreed with him, things went from bad to worse. She'd left in a huff, a very un-Mother-like reaction at a time when Kelsey needed her most. He chalked her bizarre behavior up to stress. He had more to worry about than the resident drama queen.

Kelsey had slept most of the time since Gabe and Zack found her. She was groggy and exhausted by the time Zack pulled into the emergency room parking lot. Mark had been so emotional just seeing her alive that he hadn't asked enough questions before Kelsey was hustled off to her own room.

The doctors called it fatigue and said it was nothing to be concerned about. It sounded logical, but now Mark wondered. Relieved that she was safe, but damned baffled as to what really transpired that day on the river bank

Some guy named Olsen owned the place she'd been located in. He'd been out of the country with his wife at the time. He didn't know her. Kelsey didn't know him. No friend of Alex Stewart knew him, either. *Curious.*

The anonymous male tipster who'd contacted Harley had to be the one who'd saved her from drowning. Cared for her. Hid her for three long days. Then refused to reveal his identity? *Why?*

Unease prickled up the back of Mark's neck at what might've happened during all those missing hours. Even the authorities were perplexed. *Damn it to hell. What kind of a sicko stashes an injured woman, then doctors her himself instead of taking her straight to an emergency room?*

The facts remained. By the time Gabe and Zack found her, she was already on a strong antibiotic, which her doctors immediately replaced with one of their choosing.

The IV Zack had found in Olsen's home was simple saline. Someone had professionally set and splinted her broken fingers and hands, none of them compound fractures. Her hands were a bruised mess, but healing. Even her broken nose had been correctly straightened, the lateral gash across it stitched with the tiniest stitches to minimize scarring.

The whole thing smacked of Alex, but never in a million years would he have walked away and left Kelsey behind in that kind of condition. Hell, no. He'd have her in the best hospital with the best doctors. Nothing meant more to Alex than his wife. Nothing and no one.

The rumor still spread like wildfire. Harley's nervous energy hit an all-time high. Exhumation took on another dimension Mark hadn't expected—the need to prove once and for all who had been laid in Alex's grave, if only to get everyone past the hysterics of all the *what ifs*.

Alex wasn't Elvis, for hell's sake. Not Lazarus, either. The miracle of resurrection didn't exist in this day and age. Yes, someone had saved her from the river. Kelsey had seen what she'd wanted to see. That was all.

And Harley? Well, he was another case all together. He'd grown more intent on finding Alex since Kelsey had been located. Mark knew exactly what he needed. Or who.

Ember had located the *list of ten* in a folder Alex kept in his file cabinet of all places. The man never utilized technology. For a savvy entrepreneur, he'd still relied on pencil and paper when it came to detective work, that or his razor sharp memory. Taylor and Izza were working hard on the list, but coming up with a lot of dead ends.

The FBI meeting Mark had postponed when Kelsey went missing had finally taken place. Unfortunately, it raised more questions than answers. Mark listened politely with Harley and David while Agent Kenny outlined his forensic evidence. He corroborated the Medical Examiner's finding that three ten-millimeter rounds had killed Alex.

The ME had the three slugs in an evidence locker should the assailant's weapon ever be located. Kenny had pictures depicting the proper-sized holes in a man's chest, plus others that showed corresponding blood spatter inside Alex's car that fit the scenario.

He presented very scientific diagrams that proved the kill shots came from the rooftop across from The TEAM's parking garage exit. The only thing Kenny couldn't prove was who pulled the trigger. The shooter left no casings behind and no fingerprints. The FBI had no leads. While Harley insisted it had to be the gang of ten, Agent Kenny wasn't impressed by unsubstantiated accusations.

"That was odd," David stated quietly when Kenny left.

Harley leaned forward, his hands clutched in front of him on the table, his toe tapping a mile a minute beneath it. "Looked like he was trying to convince us how it all went down, huh? Didn't it look that way to you?"

Mark remained thoughtfully quiet. The FBI had agreed with the ME. That in itself was unusual, but Agent Kenny used the identical phrasing from the ME's report. Harley might be right.

"Their forensic evidence may lead us to the killer," David commented in his agreeable way. He was like that, always willing to see both sides to keep the peace.

Harley snorted. "I don't believe a word of it. The only way we'll know what happened is to get on that rooftop ourselves."

"It will take time. The Bureau cordoned it off as a crime scene." David sighed.

"So? What's the plan then? Sit on our thumbs while—"

"The plan is that we do our job. We go over the evidence as soon as we can and we find the truth," Mark interrupted. "Have you heard from Judy yet?"

"Ah, yeah." Harley glanced at the pager on his belt. "She buzzed me a while ago, but—"

"She buzzed you? And you're still here? Go home."

"Nah. She said her water broke. It's no big deal. She's got plenty of time, and—"

"Get your dumb ass out of here, Mortimer. I'm not asking. I'm telling."

"But I wanted to see if the FBI..." Harley brushed a hand over his head and headed out the door. "Okay. I give. You'll call me if anything breaks?"

"Something's already broken. She's in labor, for hell's sake. You don't work here right now. Get her to the hospital."

"Yeah, but—"

"You're an ass, Mortimer. Judy needs you more than we do. Get the sonofabitchin' hell out of here."

The door shut quietly behind Harley.

David shook his head. "He needs help."

Mark stared at the closed door. "No. He needs Judy."

"Don't say one word to me, Mortimer," Judy warned.

How could he? She clenched Harley's hand as if she meant to snap it off at his wrist. A woman in labor had some awful powerful strength, especially under the influence of one breath-stealing contraction after another. It didn't help she was mad when he showed up. Spitting mad.

She yanked his face down to her nose, her teeth grinding. "This is all your fault."

"Yes, ma'am, it is, b... b—"

"Don't call me ma'am!" Her face morphed into a sweaty Halloween mask that in no way resembled the joys of motherhood. "I hate you! I hate you! I hate you!" she whined in a throaty, threatening kind of way he'd never once heard before.

Birthing rooms weren't his area of expertise, although it felt a lot like a warzone now that he thought about it. The panting woman digging her fingernails into the flesh on the back of his hand did remind him a few hand-to-hand combat scenarios he'd lived through. She grunted the same way his opponents had, only she looked deadlier than any insurgent he'd ever encountered. Maybe the United States Army ought to drop a few women in labor on the Islamic terrorists. That would teach 'em.

Even the kind professional words from the delivery nurse at his elbow didn't soothe the savage beast crushing his fingers. "You're doing fine, Judy. Take a deep breath. Remember how we practiced."

"How *we* practiced? I don't remember you being there, either!"

Harley cringed. Those words were meant for him. He eased his fingers from his wife's grip, but he didn't escape her wrath. She glared at him with the malevolent eyes of a wolverine caught in a trap, ready to chew its leg off and attack anything that moved. "You and your damned job! You're never home."

"I know, darlin', and I promise—"

"Oh, shut up! You know I don't mean it. Arghhh!"

Another contraction stole the nasty words right out of her mouth, and Harley hoped, out of her mind. Since he'd left the office and shown up at the hospital barely two minutes after she'd arrived all by herself—*just two minutes, mind you*—she hadn't said one nice word to him or to anyone else.

The strength of this woman was fierce. He'd no sooner leaned in for his customary *hello darlin'* kiss when she'd pinched his lower lip, pulled him down to her nose and shrieked in no uncertain words, *"YOU'RE LATE!"*

From that split second on, he tried not to say anything, and he was pretty sure his lip was bleeding.

His cell phone sent out a barrage of flute tones. Mother. Great. She probably just wanted to know if the babies were born yet. He scooted the noisy thing out of his tight jeans pocket, and—

Oh, shit. If looks could kill...

Judy glared at him like one of Charlie Manson's girlfriends, her left lip lifted and baring teeth. "So help me, Mortimer, if you answer that phone, I'll get off this bed and kick your ass. God, I feel bad about what happened to Alex. I'm sorry about Kelsey, but I need you to focus for once in your life. I need you in this room with me. Here! Now! Do you hear me?"

He shoved the phone back in his pocket, nodding as fast as his head could bob. *Yes, ma'am, I am so focused right now.*

"Okay. That's better. One breath per second."

The cheerful nurse seemed unflappable. Harley on the other hand was close to passing out. He hadn't eaten or slept in days, and here he was in the middle of a different kind of hell again. What he'd thought would take minutes had stretched into hours while Judy grunted, cursed, and sweated through the—get this—*joys of natural childbirth.*

Next time, we adopt.

"There you go, Judy. Now slow your breathing. Good job. Good girl," the nurse crooned.

"I'm not a good girl and I'm thirsty," Judy snarled before she relaxed into the pillow at the end of an extra hard contraction. And just like that she was her old self again. She turned pleasantly to Harley with a small smile. "I need an ice chip, honey. Could you please... get... a tiny one... for me? Hurry."

He scrambled for the plastic cup of ice on her side table and spooned a single chip out, intent on redeeming himself. By the time he got it halfway to her prehensile lips, she grabbed his fingers again, twisting and clenching and, *oh, hell.* The ice chip sailed. Damned woman had the grip of ten men. Something cracked. Felt like fingers. His.

"Ow. Ow. Ow! Not so hard," he whimpered, trying real hard not to make as much noise as she did.

The contraction eased off. She relaxed her grip. Closed her eyes. Took a deep breath.

He rescued his fingers.

"Big baby." She shoved his hand away. "You wanna trade places?"

He kept his lips zipped. She had that shut-up-and-go-to-hell look in her eye again.

"I'm having a baby here, and... and I want a divorce, and I want you to get a different job, and I want... VALIUM!"

He held his breath. The beautiful, sexy woman he'd fallen in love with had turned into a raging schizophrenic on her way to the divorce court, with or without him. And this two-headed beast would now be responsible for the welfare of his innocent children? To what—eat them alive? How much longer could having a baby take? Is this what women had been doing for thousands of years? *What was God thinking?*

She relaxed with a panting sigh, and even though she'd tied her thick red hair behind her head, tendrils curliqued the edges of her sweaty forehead and temples. He didn't tell her that, though. Instead, he wiped her face very carefully with a damp cloth, steered clear of her clutching hands, and kept his big mouth closed.

The obstetrician finally showed up, another woman with a no nonsense demeanor and eyes like daggers. Dr. Hehrsmann was embroidered on the left breast of her scrubs. *Oh, yeah. That name sounds familiar.*

"Nice to finally meet you, Mr. Mortimer," she said with a definite monotone, judgmental New York kinda accent that made him feel as if he should go to confession and apologize for being a man.

He ignored the barb. "Hey, umm, is this normal, Doctor? Is all this pain and craziness normal for a woman in labor, or is—"

"ARGHHH!" Judy jerked his knuckles to her teeth.

And he forgot his question. She bit him. *Hard.*

The doctor was too busy to answer, or maybe she didn't like him much, either. Whatever her reason for ignoring him was, she pushed the sterile sheeting off Judy's legs and positioned herself on a stool at the bottom of the birthing bed while he extracted his knuckles from his dear, sweet wife's incisors. The nurse handed the doctor a giant pair of ice tongs, or at least that's what they looked like.

"No. I won't need those right now." Dr. Hehrsmann rubbed Judy's huge belly in a slow circular motion. "How are you doing?"

"Just great. I've got a rapid heartbeat, my blood pressure's spiking sky-high, and a freaking smart car's coming out my ass! How do you think I'm doing?" Her sweet melodic voice evolved into the rumbling baritone of one of Satan's minions.

Harley zipped his lips tighter. He wasn't stepping into that bear trap again. No way. Let the doctor find out for herself how much fun this particular patient was. Any second now, his darling wife's head might start spinning around, as nasty as she sounded. At least she had a grip on his full hand right now instead of just fingers. He stiffened his spine. She had to be in a powerful heap of pain to have gone all Freddy Krueger on him. If Judy could do this, so could he.

"Then let's push, shall we?" the doctor asked in the same steady voice. "Come on, Judy. Tuck your chin to your chest. You know how to do it. That's good. Lean forward and—one, two, push."

Harley helped her lean forward. This part he knew. He'd actually attended that class.

Judy clenched his hand with a fierce grip, snorted and pushed with everything she had. He squeezed his eyes along with her, contorting his face at the same time. The contraction passed, but Judy trembled, and in that split second—everything changed.

Her heartbeat pounded in the sweaty fingers tucked inside his hand. She couldn't seem to let him go, though. The little gold hoop earrings rattled against her neck. Her feet shook in the stirrups. He got it now.

She wasn't mad at him. Well, yeah, maybe she was, but mostly she was just a scared little mama, afraid something might happen to her babies. And yeah, delivering them hurt, and... and he'd been a freaking dumb ass, left her alone when she needed him most. With all the stuff going on with Alex and Kelsey, he'd neglected his number one priority: her.

He reached an arm around her shoulders, for the first time overwhelmed with what *they* had done, and what *they* were doing. *They* could get through this—together.

Repentance replaced the pain in his fingers. He pressed her fingers to his lips. Everything else fell away. She needed him now most of all.

"I'm right here, darlin'," he murmured. "I'm sorry I'm so thoughtless and dumb. I promise. I'm not leaving. I love you, Judy Mortimer. Can you forgive me?"

She looked up at him through tears and sweat, and growled, "You're not dumb."

Another contraction gripped her belly. Frightened emerald greens blinked. She whined. Dr. Hehrsmann told her to push again and—

Alexander Marcus Mortimer was born on a gush of blood and water. He uttered an angry baby scream that made Harley smile and cry at the same time. Big alligator tears blurred the sight of his newborn son.

Harley wanted to crow and cry at the same time. The world needed to know. *That's my boy!*

Dr. Hehrsmann calmly suctioned the baby's mouth and nose while the little guy sputtered and kicked. Baby Alex let out another angry wail. Harley winced. The doctor might know what she was doing, but she sure handled his boy a lot rougher than he expected newborns should be handled. She flopped the little guy gently to his back onto Judy's abdomen while she clamped the umbilical cord. Eying Harley expectantly, she extended a pair of surgical scissors handle first. "Are you ready?"

"Yes, ma'am." He released Judy's shoulders and took hold of the scissors. With a nervous clip, he looked at Judy.

God, he could hardly see her through his tears, but what a sweet smile shone through those tired green eyes of hers.

She pinched her lips in a kiss while he accomplished his first official chore of fatherhood. He severed the umbilical cord. Baby Alex flailed under the bright lights, as if the whole world startled him. As if he needed someone to hold him tight so he wouldn't fall. As if he needed his daddy.

An overwhelming need to save his son washed over Harley, but Judy squirmed, arching her back to keep her eyes on her son despite the contraction assaulting her body. "How... how is he? Is he healthy?"

"He's perfect," Harley whispered, his heart literally in his throat at the miracle unfolding.

"His color is good. You can hold him the minute his little brother gets here, okay?" Dr. Hehrsmann said. "You're doing fine. Rest for a minute. Relax. Breathe."

Judy rubbed the side of her sweaty face against the pillow. "I'm tired."

Harley wanted to see his son again, but one nurse had taken the little guy and stretched him out to measure him, while another blackened his feet for footprints. Little Alex hadn't made a sound since the nurses took him, probably because he was under the heat lamp. Harley wanted to hear him again, just to be sure. The poor little fellow had squeezed out of a very narrow tunnel. Damn. No wonder he'd screamed the second he'd shown up.

"We're in the home stretch." Dr. Hehrsmann held her palm on Judy's abdomen. This time she met Harley's eyes with kindness. "Are you two ready?"

"Why not?" Judy asked tiredly. "I'm not going anywhere."

Harley kissed the top of her head. "I'm here, darlin'."

She peered up at him, her eyes brimming and her lips puckered, ready to cry. "I know," she squeaked. "I'm sorry I was so mean."

Another contraction commenced. Within three minutes of his older brother, George Patrick Mortimer slid silently into the world.

"Is he okay?" Harley and Judy asked at the same time. Baby George hadn't made a peep.

Dr. Hehrsmann suctioned the infant's mouth and nose before she held him up with a big smile. "Congratulations. You have two very handsome and healthy sons."

Little George blinked wide-open eyes at the bright lights, his tongue darting in and out like a baby lizard's. The doctor laid him across Judy's stomach. Judy smoothed her hand over the little guy's bald head while Harley wrapped an arm around her, placing a fervent kiss on her forehead.

He choked. "I love you so much, wife."

"I love you, Harley," she said, cupping his jaw with her palm.

Harley stepped forward again to clip his second son's umbilical cord. The nurses took baby George to join his brother. While the doctor attended to Judy, the nurses performed all the necessary assessments to evaluate the twin's heart rates, breathing, muscle tone, and reflexes. Harley watched anxiously while they collected blood samples, took footprints, and finally wrapped the boys in blue-striped receiving blankets.

At last, Harley held his twin warriors, their heads covered with knitted blue caps. Baby Alex squirmed while baby George was fast sleep. The moment was too much. He outright cried, baptizing his sons with tears he couldn't stop any more than he could keep his mouth from grinning.

He sank to Judy's side, nuzzling the top of baby George's head. "Look at us. We got redheaded baby boys. They look just like you. You're the most beautiful woman in the world," he said reverently. "God, I love you."

"Fatherhood looks good on you, Daddy."

His heart turned to mush. He'd never thought this day would come, never thought he deserved it, but here he was, gratitude running out of his eyes like two rivers for the blessings in his arms, and all because of the woman who loved him.

"Do you even remember what day this is?" Her emerald eyes brimmed with moisture.

He had to think. The last two weeks had been one nightmare after the other, the days and dates of the calendar completely forgotten. Guilt slithered in amongst the good feelings. *I haven't forgotten her birthday, have I? Our anniversary? Damn. Just when I thought I got something right for a change.*

Nothing came to mind, so he asked, "What?"

She beamed. "It's Independence Day."

A ton of joy hit him square in the heart. The Fourth of July. Best damned birthday ever.

Harley took a deep breath of fatherhood. And life was good again.

Chapter Seven

"You guys," Kelsey muttered tiredly, finally awake after her long nap. She'd slept the better part of two entire days and resembled a raccoon with her two black eyes and purpled cheekbones. "Don't you ever go home?"

"No, ma'am." Gabe set his magazine aside. "There's no place I'd rather be. I promise. Can I get you anything?"

"A drink," she said. "My mouth is dry. I'm thirsty."

No sooner said than done. He held the water bottle for her while she took a long sip. The simple assignment to guard Kelsey had become everything to Gabe. The image of her underwater in that car still haunted him. No one would hurt her again, not as long as he breathed.

Zack had barely stepped out to take a call from Mark, who anxiously wanted to speak with Kelsey and get her version of what happened.

She had lost nearly all of her privacy. Zack hovered over her as much as Gabe did. They camped outside her hospital room when they weren't allowed inside with her. Doctors and nurses had to prove who they were before they could enter. All she had to do was stir, and Gabe was off his feet and ready to assist. It still didn't feel like enough.

A sad smile breached the corners of her mouth. She pulled herself into a sitting position in her bed, a difficult task for a woman with several broken fingers. Libby had brought her a bed jacket. It helped Kelsey feel comfortable. That was all that mattered.

"Someone tried to kill me, Gabe," she whispered, trying to interlock her splintered fingers on her lap. She gave up and laid them flat on the beige blanket.

He pulled a chair alongside her bed. "Yes, ma'am. Sure looks like it."

Kelsey'd done very little but sleep since he and Zack found her. Mark and the authorities only knew the barest details and some nonsense about Alex finding her, but if she felt well enough to talk, Gabe was all ears.

"The sheriff's wrong. He told Mark that I lost control of my car because I was hysterical, but I wasn't, Gabe. I want you to know that."

"Don't worry about him," Gabe assured her. "He jumped to that conclusion before his deputies even finished investigating the crime scene. But why were you way out there then? It's quite a ways from your house. Were you just tired of being cooped up and decided you needed some fresh air or something?"

"No. Not at all. A man called. He said he could prove Alex was still alive. He asked me to meet him there. That's why I went. I was excited. You know, hopeful."

"Did he sound familiar?"

"No. I didn't recognize his voice."

"Tell me exactly what he said."

She thought for a second. "He said he could take me to Alex."

"Where did he want to meet?"

"On the walking path along the river. He said to meet him at the picnic table. I was watching for the turn-off into the parking lot when I got stopped."

"What happened?"

Kelsey took a slow breath. A shadow shifted over her battered face. "A car slid sideways in front of me. I thought maybe the road was wet, but..." She coughed for a moment and needed another drink before she continued. "But then, another car slammed into my back bumper, so I had to swerve sideways to avoid the first car—you know, the one that slid in front of me. I didn't want to hit it. I might've hurt someone."

"What kind of vehicles? Do you remember?"

"Both were big SUVs, a lot bigger than Harley's Jeep, and both black. I don't know what kind, but I couldn't believe someone would ram an old car like mine with a brand new SUV. The guy behind me could've stopped, but he didn't. I saw him in my rearview mirror. He meant to hit me."

She took another sip from her water bottle and licked her lips. "After he hit me, he backed up real fast and cranked his wheel. I thought maybe he meant to run from the scene, but he rammed into me. He pushed me all the way into the river. It happened so fast. I kept pushing the brake pedal all the way to the floor, but it didn't make any difference. He had one of those ramming bars on the front of his vehicle."

"A push bar? Your story matches the tire tracks and evidence at the scene."

"And I couldn't stop and..." She shuddered, reaching for Gabe's hand, splints and all.

He accepted her broken fingers carefully, wishing he could pour comfort into her through his grip. "But they didn't kill you. They might've tried, but they missed, Kelsey, and a miss is a good thing. Focus on that. Can you describe what either driver looked like?"

She nodded. "Alex taught me how to estimate height and weight. I couldn't see the top of this guy's head, the one who rammed me. I think maybe six-three, six-four. He wore dark glasses, but he had a square-shaped head and a buzz cut, from what I could see of it. He had a scar on his left cheek. I could tell because his skin was puckered under the corner of his eye all the way to his mouth. His eye drooped. Caucasian. No neck. Around two hundred and fifty pounds. And his license plate number is..."

Sweet. She might not be savvy about vehicle makes and models, but the plate number sealed the deal. Gabe jotted every last detail on his cell phone notepad app. Leave it to the wife of a covert operator. She hadn't missed a damned thing.

Now he could dispute the sheriff's claim once and for all.

"Good job. The police need to hear this. They might want you to work with a sketch artist when you're feeling better. Are you up to talking with them?"

"Sure. I hate to cuss. Alex does enough for both of us, but I'd like nothing better than to put this bastard behind bars." She actually smiled—until she realized what she'd said. "I mean... he used to cuss." Her breath hitched. The light left her eyes. The vulnerable woman was back. "Someone tried to kill me, Gabe."

"But I've got his plate number now. It shouldn't take long to track him down," Gabe said, hoping to keep her upbeat instead of dwelling on the attempt on her life.

He lifted her right hand from the blanket and held it extra gently. Kelsey was very fragile, but she needed something to hold onto, and he needed her to know she was safe. "Mark's got everyone working your investigation. Either the police or The TEAM will catch these guys and while they're doing that, old man Lennox and I are moving in to keep you company. Hope you don't mind if we turn your home into Fort Knox while we're there."

"No, I'd love the company."

The door opened behind him, and Gabe expected Zack's heavy smack to his shoulder.

"Hi, Kelsey. You're looking better today." Nurse Sullivan's cheerful voice startled Gabe as fast as the finger she jabbed into his shoulder. "She needs her rest. You should leave."

An unexpected jolt of energy rippled from her meaningless contact straight up the back of his neck. He nearly squeezed Kelsey's fingers at the jolt of energy that shot through his shoulder. What the hell? Nurse Sullivan was annoying in more ways than one. He shrugged her hand off, not wanting her to assume familiarity where none existed.

"Hi, Shelby," Kelsey said. "Yes, I'm feeling better today. I'm ready to go home."

"That would be nice, but how about if we get you showered first? Can I get you anything from the kitchen? A snack? Maybe some orange juice?" Sullivan sat at the opposite edge of Kelsey's bed. "They've got the herbal tea you like. It might soothe the last of your sore throat away. I'd get an extra large cup so you could hold it."

"Some tea would be nice. Thank you."

Nurse Sullivan smiled. "Great. I'll be right back. And I'm bringing you some cinnamon toast. I know you like that."

He had to take a second look. Sullivan seemed— different. Lighter maybe? An air of excitement radiated from her as if Kelsey was more than just a patient. Or something. He couldn't quite place it. Sullivan seemed genuinely happy. It looked good on her.

Gabe let his eyes scroll over her on her way out the door, taking in her tanned legs and the sway of her hips when she walked. Nurse Sullivan had dressed in a silky skirt that clung to her curves and accentuated the hollow of the cheeks of her taut ass. He'd not noticed that very feminine, umm, *aspect* at their first meeting.

As curt as she'd been with him, she seemed genuinely concerned for Kelsey. He couldn't deny that Miss Sullivan had organized an effective door-to-door search for Kelsey, too. She'd put in as many miles as anyone. Maybe there was hope for her after all.

He pulled his attention off Sullivan's backside to Kelsey. "Can you remember anything else?"

A shadow drifted over her face. "I remember water flooding my car. It was cold and I couldn't get out. My seat belt was stuck. No matter how hard I tried, I couldn't break the window. That guy kept pushing me in deeper and deeper. My car tipped sideways, and I... I was really scared." She bowed her head, panting in short ragged breaths. "I was underwater when something broke through the window and hit me. He wanted me to die, Gabe. He kept hitting me with... something hard. He crushed my hands."

"Are you telling me that the guy who ran you off the road walked into the water and shoved something at you while you were stuck behind the wheel?"

She nodded, her breath ragged. "It was like he wanted to make sure I couldn't get out." A tear trickled alongside her nose.

Gabe squeezed the palm of her hand, careful not to hurt her fingers, needing to rescue her again. "Look at me, Kelsey. You're not in that car anymore. No one's going to hurt you again. Come on—look at me. I've got you now."

She did, her eyes bleak. Swallowing hard, she whispered, "I drowned, Gabe. My car filled up with the river and... and... I drowned. It hurts to breathe water. Did you know that? It burns. My head pounded like it was going to blow up. I couldn't get my harness off, and then all I could think of was Alex. I'd join him. I'd lie beside him in the cemetery forever, only..."

Gabe's heart lurched in his chest. He already knew what she was going to say.

"He's not there," she whined, lifting her bandaged hands to her lips, already pinched into a tight line. "I know I saw him at the hospital that day, but..."

What was left of Gabe's heart melted at the anguish pouring out of this fragile woman. She choked on a sob before she could continue. "How do you think I got out of my car, Gabe? Do you know?"

Hurriedly, he pulled his cell phone out of his jeans pocket and brought up the pictures he'd taken at the scene, thankful for the reprieve. "Yes, ma'am. I can show you that. Somehow, the guy must've hit your car hard enough to deploy the airbag. See the airbag and the seatbelt? See how they're cut? Unless you're packing a sharp knife, the evidence speaks for itself."

Wait a minute. Gabe snapped his mouth shut, rethinking what he'd just said. It didn't fit with her version. "Do you remember the airbag inflating?"

"No. It didn't. I kept expecting it to, the way he rammed into me with his SUV, but it never did."

And yet it had. Anger clenched Gabe's shoulder muscles. The bastard. Was that why he'd broken Kelsey's window and shoved a metal bar at her? Was he crazy enough to try to activate the airbag after the fact, thinking it would inflate and keep her or her body trapped? How dumb was this guy? And yet it had worked. The bastard had walked right into the river to make sure she died. So what had stopped him?

Gabe stowed his internal rant. Kelsey didn't need to hear what he was thinking, not until he had solid facts. "The bottom line is that someone got to you in time. Whoever that person was, he cut the airbag and sliced the seat belt to get you out."

"Oh," she said, blowing out a deep sigh. "I'm glad you have pictures. That helps."

"Why?"

Kelsey studied him for a moment before she answered. "It really was Alex," she whispered furtively. "I know it was. I saw him. At least, I think I did."

Gabe didn't know how to respond. She'd said this same thing when he'd found her in Olsen's home.

Mark thought Kelsey was simply overcome with grief and doing everything she could to avoid reality. Gabe just didn't see the eyes of a crazy woman staring back at him. If anything, she looked hopeful, as if entreating him to accept the unimaginable fact that Alex still walked the earth and arrived just in time.

God, if it were that simple. Gabe of all people wanted to believe the man whose life he'd tried desperately to save was still alive. Maybe then he could draw a deep breath without feeling guilty for it. Maybe then he could sleep without waking up in a cold sweat, scared that the life-saving compressions he'd performed had only worked the bullets deeper into his boss's chest. Scared he was the one who'd really killed Alex.

"Let's go back to the river for a second," he said quietly. "Do you remember anything after you... drowned?" *Smart move, Cartwright.* He wanted to bite his tongue off for asking such a stupid question, but speaking with Kelsey was a walk through a minefield. "I mean, tell me why you *think* you saw Alex. What did you see?"

She closed her eyes. "Nothing. It's more like a feeling, like when he held me when I was sick. Like he was mad and sad all at once." Kelsey clutched his hand tighter in her pick-up-sticks fingers before she opened her eyes and whispered, "I'm sure, Gabe. Alex was there in that home with me. He is alive."

"Then he's got some explaining to do, doesn't he?"

She let go of his hand, and damn it, guilt crawled up inside of him. He hadn't answered as she'd hoped. He could tell by the way she bit her lip and studied him.

He pulled her car keys out of his pocket. "Oh, yeah, here. These are yours. Your car's still at the sheriff's impound lot. As soon as Mark can, he'll have it towed to The TEAM's garage so the guys can check it over themselves."

She took one look at Alex's picture and held it to her heart. "Thanks."

He changed the subject yet again—anything to keep her from breaking down. "Can you tell me anything about those three days you were missing? What do you remember?"

"Nothing. All of a sudden, you and Zack pounded on the door, and I woke up in someone else's house. Whose was it, anyway?"

"An older couple named Olsen. Mark contacted them. They weren't too happy you were in there, but they're not pressing charges."

"But Gabe." Her eyes narrowed. "I just thought of something else. When you found me, I was in my own clothes, but they were clean, weren't they? Someone washed them for me."

Say what?

"Are you sure?" That didn't make sense. "I mean, look at you. You're all banged up. You're sick with pneumonia. Are you sure they were clean and not—"

"Not what, Gabe? Dirty and grungy and still wet?" she asked, a bit of a snap to her voice.

Kelsey seemed to be drifting between victim and survivor mode right now, one minute ready to cry, the next sounding a little like—Alex. "I know what I was wearing that morning. Someone cleaned and changed my clothes. Ask Shelby. She'll tell you what I had on that morning. It was the same thing I was wearing when you found me. Only clean. Alex must have done that for me. Who else would have? It's a clue, Gabe. He wants you to know he was there. Please believe me."

"I do," he insisted. "The police will want to hear what you just told me and I'll chat with Sullivan as soon as she comes back. Don't worry. We'll get to the bottom of this. You should rest now."

Kelsey leaned back onto her pillow, her face drawn and pale. "I'm tired of resting. I'm tired of everything, but most of all, I'm tired of no one believing me."

He diverted the downward tempo of the conversation. "I've been by your house to feed your dogs. Whisper and Smoke will be happy to see you again."

"They'll be happy to see Alex, too."

Gabe shifted uncomfortably in his chair. Without a doubt, every conversation with Kelsey would lead back to her dead husband. For the first time since meeting her, Gabe almost wished Nurse Sullivan would return.

Chapter Eight

"She won't stay in the hospital any longer," Libby whispered to Mark before they entered Kelsey's hospital room. "It's been four days. She wants to go home."

"Not going to happen," Mark replied, even as he pasted a smile on his face and pushed the door open. This woman was on her way to a safe house out of the country, if he had anything to say about it. France, maybe. Or Japan. Whether she knew it or not, she'd become the heart of The TEAM, and it just plain couldn't function without its heart.

Alex might not have bequeathed her with the business side of the elite covert surveillance company, but Mark intended to remedy that soon. Legally. Once and for all. Undercover operator or not, Kelsey would soon become part owner, if in name only. Harley and David agreed. They wanted to keep her close to the only family she knew.

Taylor and Izza were about finished with their initial rundown on the gang of ten. The FBI hadn't released the crime scene across the street yet, but Mark had no doubt that was imminent, and the sheriff's department had taken Kelsey's story seriously instead of brushing it off as hysteria. A hint of normalcy just might be around the corner.

Gabe lifted out of his chair as Mark and Libby entered. "Hey, Mark. Hi, Libby. How are things?"

"Better now that Connor and Rory hauled Kelsey's car into our garage this morning. They'll give it a thorough onceover. Where's Zack?"

"Right behind you," he answered, one big hand splayed on the door, the other holding a paper cup of coffee. "I went out to grab my favorite girl a good brew. Here you go, Kels."

She accepted the covered Starbucks cup, but her gaze remained on Mark. "I want to go home."

Damn. She went straight for the throat. Her request melted Mark's heart. Despite the determination in her voice, everything about her spoke of loss, from the missing sparkle in her eyes to the once shiny hair she'd pulled back into an I-could-care-less ponytail. *All the more reason for her to stay.*

"Sure. As soon as you're ready. I've got a few safe houses where you can recuperate. Two on the beach in Hawaii. Would you like that?"

"No, Mark. I said home. I don't need oxygen anymore. I'm getting better. I want to leave today."

Gabe stared at the floor between his boots, not saying a word. Zack was unusually quiet, too. They had to have known this was coming.

"Kelsey, I'm sorry, but I can't risk taking you back to your place. It's too dangerous."

"But my dogs are there. Besides, it would be just like a safe house. Gabe and Zack will be with me, won't they?"

"Of course, but it's not the guards that make a safe house, Kelsey. You know that. It's the secrecy of the location. Whoever targeted you knows exactly where you live and how to get you to do what they wanted."

Her gaze dropped to the cup in her hands. "I still want to go home."

This wasn't going well. Libby stood silently at Kelsey's bedside. Gabe and Zack weren't much help either, not speaking up, as they should've done.

"Harley and Judy had their twins today," he said, hoping to shift the conversation.

"Oh?" Kelsey looked right through him, the joyous news another tidbit she couldn't seem to comprehend, or perhaps she didn't want to. She rattled her splintered fingers on the paper cup. The silence in the room stretched. At last she said, "That's nice."

"I'd really rather you were in one of our safe houses, Kelsey."

"Home, Mark. God, you can't take everything away from me."

Ouch. Low blow.

"We'll keep her under lock and key," Zack offered. "Besides, she lives close to the office. We'll set up so many security cameras in the neighborhood, it will feel like you're right there with us."

Gabe never said a word, just lifted his head and met Mark's gaze with those piercing green eyes that declared he'd give everything to protect this woman.

"Am I the only smart one here?" Mark asked, on the verge of relenting.

"Not so," Libby spoke up. "But you are the only one who can keep Kelsey safe wherever she wants to be, and she wants to be home."

Aw, shit. Logic.

Mark growled. He had no legal right to override Kelsey's wishes. He'd just hoped he could've talked some sense into her. "Then Libby and I will take you home first thing in the morning, but if you get so much as one prank phone call, I'm moving you to the moon whether you like it or not."

Mark leaned in to give her a gentle hug, but Kelsey's breath caught at his small act of kindness. She pulled herself into his neck, and he couldn't let her go. One trembling arm circled him. He held on, careful not to bump her fingers or squeeze her ribs too tightly.

"I miss him," she sobbed.

He closed his eyes against his own tears. "Me, too. We all miss him, honey."

She gulped. "Besides, he might... he might be looking for me, and I don't want to miss him. Just in case he comes back, I mean."

So that's what this is about. Kelsey still believes. That damned anonymous tipster needed to come forward and admit to saving her. Only that would put Alex to rest, once and for all.

Smart or not, Mark bowed to her command. "Then why wait? Let's get you released and on your way home right now. Are you ready to go?"

As quickly as they could get her physician to agree, Mark and Libby took Kelsey home. He sent Zack and Gabe on ahead to ensure sufficient security was in place prior to her arrival. Libby contacted Shelby so she'd be ready and waiting.

Kelsey walked as if she were a much older woman to her front door. Mark followed with her overnight bag, and another full of prescriptions and all the medical supplies the hospital sent with her.

Zack and Gabe stood in the carport, waiting. They'd driven their own vehicles and had completed a thorough security sweep of the neighborhood by then.

"Are you two ready for twenty-four-seven duty?" Mark asked on his way into the house.

"No different than the Corps," Zack answered.

"I'm just about to walk the perimeter. It won't take long. You want to come with and see for yourself?" Gabe asked.

"No. Go on ahead. I trust you guys. You've done enough deployments."

By the looks of the place, Nurse Sullivan had taken charge inside. She'd cleaned the house, placed boot trays at the front door and cleaned the windows, judging the way they gleamed. *Nice touch.*

The moment Kelsey crossed her threshold Shelby took her arm and assisted her to the couch. "Welcome home."

"Ah, it's good to be here."

Mark nodded for Libby to follow him into the kitchen. "Is this in any way a good idea?" he asked once they were out of earshot. "One good breeze and she'll blow away, and did you see the way she looked down the hall? She expected Alex to be here waiting for her. She's so broken. God, she looks like she's been in a featherweight brawl and lost in the first round."

"It takes time," Libby answered gently. "She's still in the denial phase. She's not thinking clearly right now."

"She reminds me of Harley. Neither of them is thinking right.""

Libby slid her arm around Mark's waist while they commiserated together. "Maybe now that the babies are born, he'll settle down."

"He did sound more like himself when I talked with him this morning." Mark pulled his wife close as he stared at the frail woman in the next room. Her splinted fingers sat like crossed pencil sticks on her lap, but at least she'd stopped peering down the hall.

How sad. Once again she had to deal with the disappointment of coming home to an empty house. Mark couldn't begin to imagine the depth of losing his wife to natural causes, but there sat Kelsey, dealing with the murder of her beloved.

Never in a million years would he have used that word to describe Alex, but that's exactly what he had been to Kelsey. Her knight in shining armor. *Damn it to hell. Fairy tales aren't supposed to end like this.*

Mark placed a kiss on Libby's cheek. "She does look happier."

"You've got two of your best men on the job. Zack and Gabe will take good care of her. Shelby, too."

"Then let's go. I've got to get back to work."

Libby gave Kelsey one last hug on her way out the door. "Shelby's here to help with your morning shower and meds, but call me if you need anything, okay? I'm only a minute away."

"I will," Kelsey promised. "It's nice to be home, Mark. I feel better already. Thank you."

He gave her one last look from the front door. Shelby had taken Kelsey's overnight bag to her bedroom while Zack studied the newly installed video camera feeds on his laptop.

Gabe had already returned from one of many perimeter walks he'd no doubt be making. He sat with Kelsey, chatting up the benefits of Whisper and Smoke, her two EOD dogs now turned into fierce watchdogs. Between them and all the other safety precaution Zack and Gabe had taken, Kelsey was in damned good hands.

And paws.

Kelsey might live in a dinky house, but her bedroom and adjoining bath were opulent. It might not explain why Kelsey still lived there, but it helped knowing she wasn't simply content to live in a low-income neighborhood, squalor by any other name.

Whoever had done the remodeling work had enlarged the master bedroom and added an oversized and very lavish bathroom, complete with sunken tub and a glassed-in shower stall. The black tile walls and floor accented the white porcelain tub, sink, and commode. Seashells and candles lined the edge of the tub. Rolled plush black towels rested in a peach-colored wicker basket beneath the frosted window. The room was an elegant mix of feminine and masculine tastes.

A cherry wood sleigh bed situated beneath the window dominated the bedroom. Sheer drapes completed the romantic ensemble. The walk-in closet offered the same balance of masculine and feminine, lined with two bars, both filled with clothes.

Shelby ran a fingertip along the row of expensive men's suits. Instant appreciation rose within. The suit jackets lined the 'his' side in order by color, coordinating slacks on sturdy hangars alongside. A variety of colored dress shirts hung inside the closet door, a cedar shoe rack beneath.

Most closets smelled musty, but this smelled of cedar and men's aftershave or cologne. She sniffed the pleasant fragrance wishing she'd had the chance to meet Kelsey's husband. Alex Stewart must've been quite the well-dressed gentleman. He'd smelled good, too.

Shelby took extra care putting Kelsey's few things away. Gabe had questioned her about Kelsey's clothes, and now that she had the chance to really check Kelsey's blouse, she agreed. She couldn't tell by the jeans Kelsey had worn because they looked like any other pair of jeans, but the blouse had definitely been washed and pressed. Maybe dry-cleaned, not at all the condition one would expect after a near fatal drowning.

She lifted it up to her nose before she dropped it into the hamper. It still smelled of detergent or fabric softener. Not a hint of sweat. Certainly, not filthy river water. And it most definitely was the same pale violet shirt Kelsey had been wearing the morning she disappeared. Shelby prided herself on her attention to details like that. She knew her clients.

Shelby busied herself by refreshing the bathroom towels. She wiped all the bathroom surfaces down with an antiseptic cleaner and folded the corner of the comforter down on what appeared to be Kelsey's side of the bed. The poor woman had to be worn out. Sleeping in her bed would help.

Matching lamps adorned both nightstands, but the alarm clocks were different. Kelsey's was a combination radio, clock, and iPod. Mr. Stewart's was a plain clock radio from Radio Shack. *Interesting.*

Finding Kelsey had renewed Shelby's confidence. She might not have been the one who actually found her, but she'd taken pride in the search efforts she'd organized that had kept everyone looking.

It didn't hurt that Kelsey now had two bodyguards, but that posed another problem. Shelby hadn't realized they were both ex-military until she'd overheard Mark's comment about deployments when he'd brought Kelsey home. That was one detail she wished she hadn't missed.

Both Agents Lennox and Cartwright seemed to think they needed to keep not one, but two weapons tucked into leather holsters under their arms, another thing she took exception to. Army guys with guns. Not her favorite combination.

She should've known. She'd seen Agent Cartwright's weapons tucked under his jacket out there on the river the day he'd explained about skid marks. And that was another thing. Who knew simple skid marks could reveal so much about the events of an accident?

Built of hard muscle and bone, he'd been on the rude side of helpful that morning, but more interesting was the reaction of her body to his. Rude or not, like it or not, the rush of warmth up her arm when he'd cupped her elbow didn't go unnoticed. Neither did her inexplicable tendency to lean into that warm, solid body of his.

That had to stop, and stop it would. She had better sense than to get mixed up with the likes of him. She'd never been around guns, not with intellectuals for parents, her father a university professor, her mother a researcher at the Environmental Protection Agency. They'd raised their daughter correctly. If only the world were as smart as they were. There'd be no need for guns and killing. No soldiers. No wars.

Of all things, she, Shelby Sullivan an outspoken advocate of gun control, was now housed with two guys who'd no doubt killed men, women, and children while they were— wherever they'd been. If her mother could see her now, Penelope Sullivan would've been fit to be tied. She'd faithfully steered her children toward academics, and Shelby most of all.

If you have to marry, marry a doctor or a lawyer. Aim high. People who say money can't buy everything don't know how to shop. And for heaven's sake, steer clear of guys in uniform. They're trouble.

Shelby couldn't stand to live with anyone who believed in war and killing. Nonetheless, she'd come here to do a job, and she wouldn't let Kelsey down again. Kelsey was the important one in this household.

Only Kelsey.

Chapter Nine

"Hey, Whisper. Hey, Smoke. You guys need to stretch your legs?"

Whisper, a black German Shepherd, and Smoke, a silver Malinois, were quiet as Gabe entered Kelsey's backyard through the driveway gate. He'd barely finished another sweep of the neighborhood while Zack attended to lunch. For Kelsey's sake, this guard duty needed to go down as routine and uneventful. Sometimes, boring was damned good.

Located in a sedate, older area of Alexandria, the simple brick home fit Kelsey to a T, but for the life of him, Gabe couldn't envision Alex living there. He'd always pictured his boss in a mansion with servants at his bidding, maybe a couples-only condo.

This little house with a covered carport instead of a four-stall, heated garage provided an entirely different perspective. Alex might have been master of the universe at work, but at home he was just—a guy. He probably raked his own leaves and weeded his own flowerbeds, too. Who'd have thought?

Unlatching the kennel gate, Gabe released the dogs for a run in the fenced backyard. He took off the light jacket he wore when carrying and draped it over the kennel gate. Neighbors didn't know he was armed. At the sound of the back door opening, he looked up to Nurse Sullivan's sour face, her lips in a tight disapproving line. *What now?*

"Come on out," he called, hoping to start fresh with this prickly woman. "They won't hurt you."

She started across the yard. Sullivan couldn't be all bad—not given the way she'd commandeered the search and rescue operation. Blonde and capable. A little on the tense side, though. She needed to loosen up. Maybe a good game of catch with the dogs would help.

She seemed to want instant compliance when she spoke. She'd alienated most of The TEAM during the search for Kelsey, not that it would've kept them from searching on their own. They'd simply worked around her when they disagreed with her telling them what to do and when to do it, as if they didn't already know.

Sullivan seemed not to understand that most military men and women were one-half alpha from the ground up. They'd all been trained to lead. Following a bossy civilian didn't set well. She didn't get that a good leader doesn't command respect, either. They earn it.

It's one of those symbiotic relationships a guy can't learn from a book. If a good first sergeant takes care of his men, his men will take care of him. If not, he got the kind of allegiance that happened too often in the Vietnam War—attempted murder by any other name. An arrogant officer who thought he was better than his men might have woken up to a hand grenade tossed into his hooch. Or worse. He might not have woken up at all.

Of course there were other dynamics at work during that war. Politics. Gabe tossed the rubber bone he'd retrieved from the dog kennel and let the history lesson go.

Whisper bowled Smoke over to get to the toy first. Smoke recovered quickly, but Whisper scooped the bone into his powerful jaws, not missing a step. Both dogs made a mad dash around the yard before they circled back.

Nurse Sullivan picked her way across the yard toward Gabe, watching where she stepped and carefully avoiding the dogs.

He crouched to retrieve the bone. With a spring-loaded cock of his arm, he pitched it high into a steep arc that forced both dogs' eyes upward. While they pranced and scrambled to retrieve it, he snagged another chew toy from their kennel and tossed it to Sullivan. "Here. Play fetch with us."

"Ewww. No thanks." She sidestepped, letting it drop to the grass when the dogs roared back for more.

Goodhearted Whisper bumped his nose against Sullivan's butt, urging her to come play, too. Or saying hello. *It's kind of hard to tell with dogs.*

Sullivan twisted her backside out of the reach of his long muzzle and smacked his nose. "Beat it, dog. Shoo. Get away from me."

"Aw, come on. Don't hit him. Whisper used to be an Army EOD K-9, you know—a military working dog. He sniffed out munitions, bombs and IEDs while in—"

Her hands hit her hips. "I thought so. You're ex-military."

"USMC and proud of it." When her eyes narrowed, he spelled it out. "Sorry. United States Marine Corps, ma'am. Ex-Sergeant Gabriel Cartwright at your service. Whisper's Army buddy over there, the guy on his belly who should've brought me *the bone...*" Gabe lifted his brow with a semi-stern warning in his voice. "That sneaky silver fellow is Smoke. Come here, Smokey. Bring it here."

Smoke glanced at him for one scant second before he turned to the bone trapped securely between his two front paws. He'd been caught red-handed—umm, red-pawed. Even for a dog, he looked guilty as sin.

Poor Whisper still must've thought Sullivan was a friend, or maybe a toy. When he rounded her backside, he goosed her again. Apparently, Whisper liked girls' butts. Didn't all guys?

She let the big dog have it, yelling at him to, "Stop doing that. I mean it. Get away from me."

Whisper ducked his head low, his tail between his legs. He circled around Gabe like the bad puppy he was not.

"Aww, is she being mean to you?" Gabe crouched to one knee, ruffling his fingers over Whisper's furry face and trying hard not to laugh at the way Whisper had welcomed his new friend. "How can you not like these dogs? Look at this cute mug." He turned Whisper's face for Sullivan's viewing pleasure, stretching his lips into a big canine smile. "He's adorable. And he's smart."

"Not if he was in the Army, he wasn't."

"Excuse me? You got something against the Army, ma'am?" Gabe did, too. All jarheads did, but even the be-all-you-can-be grunts in the Army were still brothers at arms. And no one should mess with a guy's brothers.

"Dogs are nothing but hair and germs, the last things Mrs. Stewart needs inside her home." Sullivan sniffed, her nose lifted in the air. "Besides, I didn't come out here to play."

"So what did you come out here for?" Gabe tugged on the end of the rubber bone protruding from Smoke's lips. The rascal slapped both front paws to the ground and tugged back. Whisper crouched low, his tail waving like a happy flag behind him, watching for a chance to steal the prize.

"Would you pay attention?" Shelby snapped with her usual imperious tone, her arms crossed. "I don't have all day."

"So talk. What do you want? I can listen while I play." With a quick flick of his wrist, Gabe stole the bone from Smoke. "Sheesh. What's so important that you don't have time to take a break and play for a minute?"

Smoke's bright eyes followed Gabe's every move.

"I'd like to discuss Mrs. Stewart's clothing, if you don't mind. You were right. They'd been laundered. At least her blouse was. And you need to know I've got her on a strict schedule."

"Kelsey's got a schedule? Hmm, guys. I didn't know that, did you?"

"Woof," Whisper replied.

"Of course, she does." Sullivan's intensity ramped up. Her voice pitched into a higher and more demanding tone. "Especially now that she's recovering from pneumonia. I've organized a medication schedule and a menu for her."

"What's the big deal?" Gabe held the bone over the dogs' heads. "Let her sleep when she's tired. Give her meds when she's awake. There. Problem solved."

"That's not good enough, and you know it. We need to discuss the guns you're carrying, too. And the boot trays. I know you've seen them. Why don't you use them?"

He would've answered if he'd wanted to, but belligerence never motivated him and Sullivan seemed to think she was in charge. He tossed the bone for another round of fetch.

"Will you stop horsing around and listen to me?"

"Yes, ma'am." Gabe got to his feet, rolled the pain out of his neck that was quickly moving down his spine to his butt and faced the agitated nurse. The chain of command that, at least in her mind made her top dog, had worn thin.

"Good. That's better." She smoothed her hands down her pant legs, as if wiping away something repulsive. Must've been those dog germs she'd picked up when she'd smacked Whisper's poor snout. "Now, as I was saying, it's important that we stick to a tight schedule and—"

"Woof!" Smoke slapped the ground, still ready to play.

Gabe tried to look interested in Sullivan, but her tone sparked his trouble-making side, and what the hell? Both dogs wanted to play. He twitched the rubber toy back and forth like a metronome, then a little faster. Two pairs of bright black eyes followed intently.

Tick. Tock. The game was back on.

"As I was saying—"

"Woof! Woof!"

"Stop interrupting me," Nurse Sullivan scolded Smoke. She took a quick couple of steps forward and snatched the toy out of Gabe's hand. She really should've tossed it to the other end of the yard, but she didn't. Instead, she stomped her foot and spiked it into the ground like a linebacker making a touchdown, or—like she wanted to play after all.

The dogs sure did. Both launched themselves to retrieve their prize. They roared over her and knocked her flat to her butt. She hit the still damp morning lawn with a breathy, "Oh, my!"

In less time than it took to say *fetch*, she found herself surrounded by eight canine legs, two slap-happy tails and all those terrible germs. Her glasses ended up perched over her lip.

"Dogs!" Gabe extended his hand to rescue Kelsey's hapless nurse as a black tail swept across her face and brushed over her lips, not once but three times before she finally shut her mouth and grabbed her glasses.

Smoke accidentally stepped onto her lap with one big hind foot, wrestling with Whisper who by now had the trophy raised high.

Sullivan spit and sputtered, wiping her lips with the back of one hand, the other stuck in the ground behind her.

"Dogs. Off," Gabe ordered more firmly.

Both pranced away, but Whisper looked a lot happier than Sullivan. He had the bone.

She clutched Gabe's forearm, tucking her butt as if they might take a bite out of it when she lifted off the grass. She pressed against him, keeping him between her and the dogs.

Silly girl.

She shouldn't have done that, either. It had been a long time since he'd felt a woman's body close enough to feel the warmth of her breasts and thighs at the same time. A wave of prickly awareness washed through him, filling him with heat—and something else he didn't expect. Not from her.

"They won't hurt you," he explained, his voice suddenly hoarse and gravelly, damn it. "They thought you wanted to play. That's all." He stifled the compulsion to wrap a protective arm around her. She might bite it off.

"I don't like them. They're dirty." She peered around him, breathing hard. She had a death-grip on his bicep, her glasses folded in her other hand.

Damned if she didn't have paw prints on her shirt, and damned if Gabe didn't notice how lovely her small breasts were beneath that shirt. A sliver of her lacy bra showed above her collar, another thing he shouldn't have noticed. Or enjoyed.

"Are… are you afraid of dogs, ma'am?" *Damn. I sound like a stuttering fool.*

"Kind of," she admitted, not taking her eyes off the now tranquil animals, nose to nose at Gabe's feet, the bone on the ground between them. "Mom has a teacup poodle. Peewee fits in her purse. He's cute and, umm, controllable."

He got it then. Sullivan needed to control everything. That's why the tedious search grid for Kelsey. That's why the boot trays at the front door. That's why her fear of dogs, too. She couldn't control them. It also explained her snippy attitude and the damned menu and medicine schedule. Gabe didn't really need to know about it. That was her job. She just needed him to know that it was her job and that she was in charge.

Silly girl.

There was a time he'd tried to control everything thinking he could stop bad things from happening. Didn't work.

"Watch this." Gabe held his hand out with the palm down, needing to redeem himself. "Let me show you how smart these dogs are."

Alex had developed his own hand signals when he'd trained his dogs. Whisper and Smoke crouched to their bellies, their eyes bright with this new game. When Gabe clenched his fist, both dogs lifted to their haunches and resumed an identical sitting position. He presented a vertical flat palm. Both dogs backed up until he clenched his fist, at which point the dogs sat again, watching alertly for his next command.

"See? Smart. Alex taught them silent commands in case..." Gabe made a mistake. He looked down at this nervous woman burrowing under his arm where he didn't quite want her to be.

But there she was, snuggled up to him like his new best friend with her hand on his chest. Nurse Sullivan didn't wear much makeup, either. She didn't have to. Thick, long lashes fringed the most incredible violet-blue eyes. A guy could get lost in there.

Her brows were delicately arched for the moment, lifted in wonder and curiosity. She almost looked interested in Whisper and Smoke the way she peered around him at them.

Straight blonde hair hung to her shoulders in a blunt cut that lent a pixyish quality to her. High cheekbones. An upturned nose that was elfin delicate. Lush lips moistened by the pink tip of her tongue. She only needed wings. Violet wings. With glitter.

A good case of nerves rattled her slight frame, straight through his arm and—all the way to his groin, damn it. He didn't want to stop looking. The woman snuggled up against him for protection from Kelsey's dogs was downright good-looking, in a severely controlled way. She needed to lose those ugly men's glasses, though.

His gaze drifted to the peaked mounds beneath her scrubs, dropping lower to take in hips that swelled in perfect proportion to her small breasts.

The faintest hint of rose and vanilla and damp grass wafted up from her creamy skin, now flushed with a pinkish hue. His nostrils flared, pulling the delightful scent in. He took another long breath, relishing the pleasure of her close proximity—the last thing he'd expected. Or wanted.

She glanced up and caught him looking. *Shit.*

That did it. She jerked her hand out of his and stuck those glasses back on her nose with a wicked stab of her index finger. The pleasant warmth of the moment evaporated under her icy glare. Damn. Those pretty violet eyes had turned to cold blue icicles. *All four of them.*

She took a quick step back. "What are you looking at?"

"Ah, nothing. I just thought you'd like to see how good these boys can be when—"

"They're not boys. They're dirty animals that have no business being inside the house with a sick woman. Don't bring them in again, and leave your boots on the back step while you're at it."

"Yeah, but Kelsey—"

"But nothing. I came out here for a serious discussion about our client, not to be treated like this." Sullivan dusted her hands off, rubbed them against her pants again and stepped back. "I should've known. You're no help. Tell your boss about her blouse. I'll post her orders in the kitchen. You can read, can't you?"

"Umm, yeah." He watched the dirty butt prints on her jeans bounce with every step she took away from him. *What the hell just happened?*

Nurse Sullivan might be uptight and rude, but he'd seen her interest in Whisper and Smoke. He'd also seen tension below the nasty attitude she exuded—or thought she had to. He'd lived through enough crap. He'd seen worse behavior in nastier guys. It usually disguised something else.

She wasn't just afraid of the dogs. No way.

Wait a minute. Did I just tell her I'd leave my pistols at the back step?

Chapter Ten

The nerve of that man.

Shelby couldn't get away from Agent Cartwright fast enough. *Humph. As if he knows anything about taking care of a sick patient, much less a sick woman, much less—anything!*

She'd intended the back door to slam behind her, hoping to punctuate her aggravation and let him know exactly what she thought of him. It didn't. No. Some thoughtful homeowner had installed a hydraulic hinge to cushion its closure. Probably the same guy who'd remodeled that exquisite bathroom for Kelsey. Didn't it figure?

It only made her angrier. Shelby rubbed a shiver off her biceps, not that she was cold, just aggravated she'd fallen on her butt in front of Agent Cartwright. And embarrassed. The jerk had laughed. He always seemed to get the upper hand, and it bugged her.

Darn. Who knew dogs could be so smart? She didn't, and of course he'd enlightened her once again just as he'd done with the skid marks. The problem with this more recent enlightenment was the jolt of energy that came with it, an awareness that tickled when he'd taken hold of her hand.

Tickled, nothing.

More like it shocked the heck out of her. He had strong fingers. Hard as rock biceps. Heck, the whole guy was hard and strong. That single touch had all but sizzled up her arm and over her shoulders. And other places. It meant nothing, absolutely nothing, but still…

The scent of some manly body wash that made her tongue lick her lips every time he got too close. He was not at all what she'd expected from an Army guy.

She turned, dusting her pants while she kept an eye on Cartwright and those dogs from the back door, which opened directly off the kitchen. He'd tossed the bone a few more times and of course the dogs loved him. But did he have any idea how the air rippled with every breath he took?

She did. Every time she got close to him, her pulse rate skyrocketed—and she didn't even like him. Not really. Cartwright was minor league good-looking. Nothing to brag about. Athletic. Broad shouldered. The stereotypical well-groomed, mahogany-haired, chiseled-ab kind of guy on the cover of *GQ*, *Men's Health* or *Esquire* and…

Oh. My. Heck.

A sigh sneaked up on her. Those eyes, green and glorious. Deep. Enticing. A woman could fall into them and do it willingly. Deep laugh lines that resembled rays of sunshine bracketed them when he smiled. Everything about him seemed to draw her in. Her heart thumped with another round of palpitations just thinking of those sexy eyes. And that smile.

Yeah. Okay. So he's good-looking. Looks aren't everything, but darn. Her nipples had noticed him, too, pebbling on sight and downright tingling, as if they had minds of their own and knew exactly what they wanted. The pads of his thumbs. Maybe a gentle scrape from his fingernails. His tongue. His teeth.

Stop it. Get your mind out of the gutter!

She very nearly chuckled. The guy did have large hands, though, and long, straight fingers with clean nails. He was gentle with those awful dogs, gentle when he ran his fingers over their heads, tickling their ears the same way he might tickle a woman's—

No.

No.

No!

He's not my type. I hate military jerks who wave their rifles and parade their guns and flags for attention. Not my type at all.

Cartwright didn't have a buzz cut, but he might as well have. All that mahogany hair had been precisely combed and managed with some kind of hair product. Maybe mousse. Or gel. *Do you think it's soft?*

No.

No.

No!

Everything about him smacked ex-military, from the proud way he carried himself to his *ma'am* this and *ma'am* that. But he didn't mean it with respect. Maybe with Kelsey he did. Cartwright seemed to light up around her. The jerk.

You're jealous of Kelsey.

Who me? Oh, heavens no!

Shelby shushed her wandering mind at the very idea. Where did that stupid thought come from, the moon? It might as well have. No. She really liked Kelsey. She'd do anything for her client, even put up with—

"The soup's ready," Agent Lennox said behind her. "Are you hungry?"

Startled, Shelby whirled to face the other problem in the house. She'd been so engrossed in Gabe that she hadn't noticed Agent Zack Lennox across the room at the stove. Also ex-military. Darn it. Had he heard her encounter with Gabe and the dogs? Worse. Had he seen her at the window salivating over his buddy in the back yard?

A tidal wave of heated embarrassment lifted up her body, spilling over her neck and face. *Oh, God. I'm surrounded.*

The man radiated testosterone. All that mocha-colored skin didn't help. He was a big bruiser of a guy with a shaved head. Dark brows lifted over darker eyes on a handsome face. A black polo fit snug across his chest, as snugly as it did over his biceps. At the moment, all that masculinity was quietly offset with a kitchen towel tucked into his belt and the soup ladle in his hand.

At least he was a gentleman. He'd come straight into Kelsey's kitchen after Mark and Libby had left earlier and actually did something helpful, unlike Cartwright. He'd taken off the second his boss left. The slacker.

Shelby couldn't help it. The tantalizing aroma of garlic, basil, and oregano filled her nostrils. Her stomach growled, despite her discomfort.

"I am hungry. Kelsey must be, too, but first I need to make a few things clear," she said, regaining her composure. "If we're going to work and live together, which I guess we are, we need a few ground rules. First, no dogs in the house. They're dirty. We need to keep things as clean as possible for Kelsey's benefit."

She paused in case Agent Lennox wanted to argue, which he'd better not. She had statistics on her side. Animals spread germs and hair everywhere they went. Period. No discussion to it.

He lifted one shoulder, as if he could care less.

"Secondly, please use the boot trays I've placed at the front and back doors. That tiny courtesy alone will keep the floors cleaner and help Kelsey recover quicker."

He rested the ladle on the counter beside the stove, a gentle smile tugging one side of his mouth as he crossed his arms over his chest and faced her. "Anything else, Miss Shelby?"

At last. A guy who listened. Kind of. He didn't seem to remember that part about calling her by her official title, but oh well. Calling her Miss Shelby was a small infringement. She could concede that one small point.

She took a deep breath, encouraged by his compliance. "No guns in the house. I'd appreciate it if you and Agent Cartwright stored your weapons at the front door."

"What is it you think we do?" he asked, his dark brown eyes riveted to hers. "I haven't had time to talk with you yet. I'd like to know precisely what Mark and Libby told you about Gabe and me and why we're here."

"Just that you're bodyguards. You're here to protect Mrs. Stewart in case, I don't know..." She rolled her eyes, ". . . something bad happens now that she's home."

"I take it you don't believe she was run off the road like she said she was? You don't believe she's in danger. You don't believe her."

Of course, I believe her. It's you guys I don't trust.

Shelby opted to keep her opinion to herself. What happened at the river was tragic, but here in Alexandria, things were different. Despite the lower class neighborhood, patrol cars made daily rounds. She'd seen them more often than she'd expected. "It doesn't matter what I believe. I'm here to do a job, the same as you. I'm her health care provider. You keep her safe. I'll get her healthy. Deal?"

"No, ma'am. It's not that simple. Gabe and I aren't just bodyguards. We worked with Kelsey's husband before he was killed. When it comes right down to it, I guess you could safely say we love her. We're family."

Enough with the melodrama. "Next you're going to tell me you'd die for her."

Agent Lennox didn't even blink. "If dying's what it takes."

Darn. This wasn't going well. Honestly, did he think he could impress her with all his military machismo? She stood her ground. At least she tried.

"You gave me your rules, now here are mine," he said. "Until we know who murdered Kelsey's husband, Gabe and I are here to stay, so you need to climb down and back off. We're not here to fight you, but we have a job to do and we'll do it. The boot trays are a good idea, but we're on call twenty-four-seven. Boots and weapon are not optional. They stay. The dogs? They're Kelsey's. If she wants them inside, they'll come inside. Hell, I don't care if they sleep with her if it makes her feel better. As for you, stay indoors as much as possible. Do your job. Things are pretty quiet right now, but that can change. Let Gabe or me know if you need to leave the premises. I'm fine with your menu plan. You already know I'll take my turn fixing meals. The soup should speak for itself."

Great. He only agreed to the menu. Well, we'll see about that.

"Why don't you call the police if you're so worried about Mrs. Stewart's safety? Why do you think you have to take the law into your own hands? Are your guns registered?"

He didn't bat an eye. "Yes, ma'am. We follow the laws of the land, same as you, but we're here because the police can't provide around-the-clock coverage like we can. Kelsey trusts us more than she trusts them, anyway. She might not be thinking quite right yet, but she wants us here."

Shelby leaned against the back door, her hands behind her back. This guy thought he was pretty clever. Not so. Again, she had statistics on her side. "You do know that guns kill hundreds of innocent people every year, don't you? The facts speak for themselves. Guns kill people."

"No, ma'am. People kill people. Guns are tools, like steak knives and hammers. Besides, it's not the law-abiding citizens who register their guns I'm worried about. It's the guys who killed Kelsey's husband and who might still come after her. Do you think they registered their weapons? Do you honestly believe the police could've gotten to her in time to help her that day at the river?"

Shelby swallowed hard. That was exactly what she'd believed. She'd lived a protected life and attended all the best schools. Not once had she doubted what her parents espoused. Law and order. The police arriving in time. Things like that.

Zack made the world sound scary and unpredictable enough that everyone should be armed, something she wasn't willing to accept. She couldn't let him have the last word. Some things could still be controlled. "I'm posting a menu. We will eat healthy while I'm here."

He had the audacity to offer one sexy, chocolate-eyed wink, his face crinkled into a gentle smile. "Why do you think I fixed soup? Nothing helps a person feel better than homemade yeast rolls and chicken noodle. Sit down. Take a load off. You'll feel better once you eat, too."

"Well, okay. Let me see if Kelsey is ready to eat. It does smell good."

"I'll call Gabe. He's been working all day. He must be starved like me."

Shelby squared her shoulders and changed her mind. "Never mind. I'll eat later."

Mark turned his attention to Taylor. "Go ahead. Tell us what you've got."

Most agents had worked through the night. Coffee cups cluttered the Situation Room conference table as information trickled in. Rory and Connor had yet to venture forth from the garage where they'd torn into Kelsey's car.

Ember had located the list. Since then, she, Taylor and Izza had spent hours tracking the whereabouts of the gang of ten. The murder board now sported ten ugly faces, five of them marked through with a black *X*.

Taylor activated the slide presentation on the overhead screen and highlighted each crossed-out face while he explained. "We've narrowed the gang of ten down to five. Hank LaBouche, Alan Townsend and Teddy Whitaker are doing time for armed robbery in Florida. Ruben Ewing died last year of AIDS, and Rick Shuberg's in a nursing home in

Arizona with early-onset Alzheimer's. That leaves us with these guys," Taylor continued, hitting each remaining face with his laser pointer. "Clark Manson, Nate Stevenson, Rick Bukowski, Carlos Echevarria and Ron Fallon. They are definitely the ones we need to worry about."

"What a bunch of losers," Ember commented. "As Harley would say, these guys aren't the brightest bulbs in the box. Which reminds me, any word from the Mortimers? Did they have their twins yet?"

"Yeah. Damn. Sorry," Mark muttered. "The boys were born the day after we located Kelsey. Alexander Marcus and George Patrick. Mother and babies are doing fine. There was so much going on, Harley said he forgot to call, but he sounded good for a change."

"We should throw him a baby shower," Ember said.

"How much did they weigh? How long are they?" Mother asked sharply.

Mark grimaced. "Man, I don't remember. I think maybe he said they were both around six pounds? Twenty-some inches."

"Whoa, they're good-sized for twins," Izza said. "No wonder she got so big. Poor Judy."

"And they'll be tall like their daddy," Ember said.

The feeling in the room brightened, but Mother's expression darkened. She was another one Mark needed to talk with, and soon. She'd grown distant, and he didn't know why. Even his request for her to check into exhumation procedures had gone unanswered—not that he minded. It was just odd for the woman who normally had her fingers in everyone's business.

Taylor advanced to the next slide that listed the expertise of each of the final five, ranging from explosive ordnance disposal to spec ops. Each of the Vets was a trained killer with a criminal record. Ron Fallon looked to be the worst with two charges of attempted murder, but no time served. The others pandered to lesser crimes involving drugs and petty theft once they left the service. All had served in the Army or the Corps, not a good sign by any means.

"Now we're getting somewhere," Mark said. "Are these guys still in the local area?"

"They all are," Izza replied. "What's worse, Fallon, Stevenson, and Bukowski are on the FBI's watch list. They're mixed up with some homegrown terrorist group called *Chaos Now*. It doesn't recognize federal authority and the members believe states have the right to secede. According to their website, terror's a necessary tool in what they call a *righteous revolution against oppression*."

"What's your next step?"

"Taylor and me are making contact with each of these guys today. Thought we'd talk with them face to face, let them know we're watching them." Izza looked ready for a fight. Most of the other agents had dressed casually today, but she wore the uniform of an active operator: black TEAM polo tucked neatly into cammie cargo pants. She also played with her knife while she worked the laser pointer, another sure sign she was ready to engage.

"We're just looking for information, Izza," Mark warned. "That's all. Don't scare them off before we know what they're up to."

"I know. You want to make sure it's them. I got that." She almost sounded sincere.

"No, I want a solid lead. I want motive, means, and opportunity before we blow them out of the water."

"Yeah. Sure," she said, but Mark recognized the signs. Izza wasn't making direct eye contact. She wanted revenge. Mark had no doubt these five guys would do.

The Sit Room door burst open and in walked two men in dirty coveralls. Rory pointed to the screen while Connor went to the computer and keyed in a few quick commands to access his files.

"This the list?" Rory asked.

"Yeah. We've whittled it down to five," Mark answered. "What do you have?"

"Hope you don't mind if we take over for a couple minutes, but you've got to see this. I'm hoping we can whittle your list down some more. Look at this." Connor snagged the laser pointer from his wife with a wink. A security camera photo flickered on the overhead screen. He zoomed in as the shot came into focus. It showed two black Escalades on the highway where Kelsey had been forced off the road.

One man trudged into the water with a baseball bat. He swung hard.

"What's that sonofabitch doing?" Izza growled.

"He's trying to kill Kelsey," Mark said. Gabe mentioned what Kelsey had said about some guy hitting her, but seeing it was something else.

"I ever meet him, he's going to be wearing that bat up his ass," Izza promised darkly.

Mark could barely swallow. The guy stomped out of the water and joined his three buddies on the shore. They lined up like a bunch of gangsters. Every last one of them raised their right arms and pointed at the river as if—

"They're shooting!" Taylor jumped to his feet. Everyone bristled.

"At least they were. Calm down," Rory stated. "Show 'em what else we found, Connor."

Connor dropped a handful of mangled bullets on the table. "Inside the trunk and along the left rear quarter panel. That's why we drove back out to the river first thing this morning. There's a new credit union north of where Kelsey's car was found. That's who gave us this security footage. They've had a couple robberies because they're out in the middle of nowhere, so they'd installed a high-tech digital system. We're lucky they caught it on film. Heck, they weren't even opened for business yet. It was too early in the day. All we need now is to find the guns these bullets were fired from, and we've got the bastards who tried to kill her."

"Another thing," Rory said. "We found a big swatch of black paint on the driver's side, damage consistent with her car being pushed off the road like she said. The sheriff's either one lazy sonofabitch or he's covering for these murderers. Kelsey didn't over-correct and she didn't lose control. She was pushed into the river. No doubt about it."

Mark swallowed his opinion of crooked cops. The local police department had just gone through an extensive housecleaning at the heavy hand of the Virginia Attorney General. A couple detectives and police officers were implicated in a cover-up that nearly cost Taylor Armstrong his life. Liars and cheats were everywhere. Hell, even Alex had to deal with the likes of Charles Oakes, the bastard at the root of this current nightmare.

"It gets better." Connor keyed in another command and the video clip continued. Another man, one dressed completely in black and wearing a covering over his head and face, emerged at the extreme right of the screen, his arm extended at the first four.

"Whoa. Who's he?" Izza's nose scrunched.

"Who do you think?" Connor asked.

Within seconds, three of the first four fell to the ground. The last ran around the nearest SUV for cover. The fifth man peeled the covering off his head and dove into the river toward Kelsey's submerged vehicle. In the meantime, the last of the four shooters assisted one of the other men off the ground. Between the two of them, they dragged the others behind the Escalades.

"It's him," Izza murmured, her eyes glued to the screen. "It's got to be him."

Mark winced. *Here we go again. No, it isn't. Alex is dead.*

The man in the river wasn't visible for several long minutes, but when he emerged, he had Kelsey in his arms. He laid her on the riverbank and rolled her onto her side.

The room stilled while everyone watched Kelsey choke river water out of her lungs while the stranger thumped her back. She lay there unmoving. He disappeared off screen, but quickly returned with a blanket and his head covered again. He wrapped Kelsey in the blanket and lifted her off the ground.

"What the hell is he doing?" Mark muttered, not convinced this stranger was as noble as he appeared, not if he'd also kept Kelsey hidden those three days.

Hidden and cared for, his logical side reminded him.

Bullshit. Kidnapped. Medicated. And all to himself, the bastard. He should've called the police or an ambulance.

"Just wait," Rory said. "Watch."

Connor typed in another command. The close-up shot zoomed out to reveal where the man had taken Kelsey. It wasn't far. He'd placed her in the back of a black sedan, but the way he did it spoke volumes. He climbed inside the vehicle with her, taking his time laying her on the backseat. With his knee to the car floor, it almost looked like he—kissed her.

"Zoom in," Mark ordered. *Who the hell is he? It almost looks like Alex, but this guy is broader shouldered. Bulkier. Isn't he?*

Connor zoomed in as tight and close as he could. No go. The black covering blurred the guy's head. The image was pixilated. The man exited the vehicle, closed the door and ran to the driver's side. In seconds, he drove away.

"Who was that guy?" Mother asked, her brows narrowed and her lips pursed.

"Alex," Taylor murmured. "He sure looked like Alex."

"How could you tell?" David asked quietly. "He had a balaclava on his head."

"You saw him kiss her," Izza argued. "It had to be Alex."

"No," David replied. "We saw a man with a covering over his face and lips lean into her. He might have been making sure she was still breathing."

Mark released a sigh of relief as David took the lead for a change. He needed someone on his side, damn it, someone not emotionally compromised.

"It was Alex," Izza declared, an edge to her voice. "Who else could it be?"

David's sharp eyes met Mark's across the table. He often played the role of Devil's Advocate. It forced people to think better and dig deeper, whether they wanted to or not.

"Good question," Rory answered. "Ember is working on some satellite images for us. Hope we can have a better answer next time we meet, but at least this footage agrees with Kelsey's version of what happened. So does the evidence in and on her car."

"Can you get the footage prior to her car going into the water?" Mark asked, needing to validate Kelsey's version of events.

Ember spoke up. "We did, but it agrees with her story. This footage shows what she couldn't tell us because she was already underwater and drowning. It fills in the blanks. Someone did come to her rescue just like she told you."

"Great work, guys. Anything else?" Mark asked evenly, not going to entertain for one second the fallacy his team seemed to have latched onto. Hope did funny things to people under stress. He wouldn't encourage it.

"Yeah. Let Kelsey know that we're on her side," Connor said. "Right now she thinks she's losing her mind. Let her know we're doing everything we can to prove she's not."

Damn. I can't win.

Chapter Eleven

Gabe stretched out on Kelsey's front room floor, listening to the quiet creaks all houses made in the still of the night. He flipped through several screens of differing neighborhood viewpoints on the laptop resting on his stomach.

The carpet was quite comfortable. He had no problem sleeping on the floor. Not after some of the places he'd slept during operations and deployments. He had a good buddy who cooked, the kindest woman to watch over, and not much going on otherwise. Life couldn't get much better.

Zack's chicken noodle soup had turned out surprisingly good. Right now, the old man was hoofing it around the block and checking the perimeter one last time. He was the only one out there. Good deal.

But Miss Sullivan? What a beast. Kelsey's medication schedule was now taped to the kitchen cupboard door over the sink, along with a menu plan. Go figure.

Zack had laughed it off, but the pushy woman irked Gabe. She had one thing on her mind and it had nothing to do with simple courtesy. *Control freak.*

The TEAM better find what was left of the gang of ten or this was going to be one damned long operation.

A noise from the back of the house caught Gabe's ear. He set the laptop to the floor beside him and shifted to his elbows, his head cocked to listen better.

Zack? Back already? That can't be right.

There it was again, a quiet sound, almost like a murmur. Or a sob.

Gabe pushed to his feet, his ears on high alert. Either Kelsey was talking to herself or someone was in her bedroom with her. He turned the hallway light on and padded to her closed door. Rapping quietly so as not to wake Sullivan, he asked, "Kelsey? Everything okay?"

She moaned, "Miss... you."

He waited and listened, but no other voice responded.

Another sad groan. "Don't... go."

The desperation in her tone pushed him. Gabe knocked politely again. "Kelsey. May I come in?"

"No. I can't do it."

And just that fast he was in the room, his heart pounding at the fear she'd projected. The hall light behind him cast shadows over the tangled blankets. Clutching them to her chest between splintered fingers, she thrashed, whining, "I don't... want to."

Gabe crouched at her bedside and placed one palm to her upper arm to hopefully wake her. "Kelsey. It's me, Gabe. You're just dreaming. Wake up."

"N... no!" She came to with a start, bolting upright and blinking, her sleeveless cotton shift twisted around her in a tangle with the bed sheets.

"There you go. Wake up. You were having a nightmare. That's all."

"He was here," she mumbled, scrambling to her knees, her splinted fingers flat to the sheets. "He came to me. I know he did."

Gabe moved out of her way when she all but climbed under the bed, her fingers splayed and clattering over the carpet, searching for someone she'd never find again. Looking for Alex. *Damn.*

"No, no, no. He was here. I know he was. I... I..." She turned to Gabe. "You saw him, didn't you? Did he walk past you? God, Gabe. Why'd you let him get away?"

He sucked in a deep breath, wishing with all of his heart that what she had dreamed was real. "You were just dreaming."

"No, I wasn't. The bed moved when he got in. It did." She lifted her face, her eyes wild and her voice tightening with hysteria. "He told me he loved me. He said that this all will be over soon. I can still feel him holding me. He kissed me. I can still smell him. *He was here.*"

And Gabe could've cried. Thank God, Zack came back from the neighborhood check. He stood at the doorway, blocking most of the hallway light. "What's going on, Kels?"

"He was here, Zack. I know he was." Desperation crept into her tone. "Please turn the light on. I'll prove it."

Zack opened the door a little wider and hit the switch, illuminating one frightened woman hanging on by a thread. Once again, she made the rounds, crawling onto the empty mattress only to end up on the empty floor, her hands outstretched as if touching the sheets and rug would conjure her dead husband.

Gabe reached for her shoulder, needing to stop her from falling apart. The Alex he knew wouldn't torment his wife like this. And he sure as hell wouldn't hide. If he were still alive, he'd be the one on the floor comforting his wife, not a couple of hired hands.

Breathless and shaking from head to foot, Kelsey pulled away from Gabe's touch. "But he was. I felt him. He was here, and he... he told me he loved me. You have to believe me."

"I do believe he loved you," Gabe offered sincerely. *God, I want to believe he was here, too, but it was just a nightmare.*

"You both think I'm crazy. I can see it in your eyes. Stop looking at me like that!"

"No, we don't, Kels," Zack grumbled, "but we do know you're going through hell right now. Take it easy. Here's the thing. Did you see anyone else in this room when you opened the door, Gabe? Was the window opened? Anything?"

Gabe hesitated. Kelsey needed one glimmer of hope. He wanted it to come from him.

"You didn't, did you?" She pinned him with those big brown eyes, daring him to lie. "Did you hear anyone else in here besides me? Did you hear him tell me not to worry, that he'd be back as soon as he could? Please tell me you did."

Gabe shook his head just enough to destroy all hope.

She sucked in a sharp breath, her gaze still sweeping her room. Her eyes brimmed and the tears spilled over. "It always seems so real. Every night. I close my eyes and he's there and none of this nightmare ever happened. I almost start to believe that... I almost believe him, but then I wake up and..."

Gabe was a goner. He would've gathered her into his arms if it had been proper. If she'd have let him, but she only wanted Alex. She sat there beside him blinking and trying not to cry. "Maybe I am losing my mind."

He couldn't take it anymore. He circled her shoulder with one arm and tugged her into his side. His heart choked on the sheer sadness pouring out of her. "I'm so sorry."

She sagged into him, wiping her face with the backs of her hands, her fingers stiff and as useless as Gabe felt. "I don't want to do this anymore. It's too hard. I almost wish he were dead."

And there it was. It didn't matter what anyone else thought or said.

Kelsey still believed.

The next morning and a good night's sleep brought new energy. Shelby woke early, determined to strike a proper balance with the men she was stuck with in this tiny house. How hard could it be? She'd stay out of their way. They could stay out of hers.

According to the menu she'd organized, it was her turn to fix breakfast. Kelsey had wanted a spinach omelet the morning all this started, and Shelby intended to deliver. Hmm. Breakfast in bed and a nice leisurely start to the day might be just what Kelsey needed to help get her day off to a good start, too.

Only the aroma of coffee already filled the air. A man's quiet voice, too. Great. The guys were already up, and by the sound of the one-sided conversation, Agent Lennox was on his phone with his boss. Darn. Didn't he ever go to sleep?

She wrapped her bathrobe around her and proceeded down the hall. The kitchen light was on at her right, but it was the sight on her left that stopped her in her tracks.

There lay that obnoxious Agent Cartwright, flat on his back and sound asleep in Kelsey's living room. His hands were peacefully interlocked on his chest, his legs crossed at the ankles, and he was completely dressed except for his boots.

Did the man not realize how much room he took up? A person could barely step around him if they needed to get out the front door. His computer equipment and gear bags took up the rest of the room. Things had to change.

Her eyes lingered a moment too long on that long body. His black polo had ridden up, exposing his abdomen and the lightest trail of hair between his navel and his belt.

Oh, mama. What's the thermostat set on?

She couldn't stop watching the way his belly expanded and contracted with each steady breath. The way scruff shadowed his clean-shaven chin. The way sleep had mussed his hair.

A narrow beam of early morning sun lay diagonally on his chest. She stopped walking.

Gabe Cartwright was one long combination of squared-off angles and corners, his chest muscled, his shoulders broader than she remembered. Was this the same guy who'd aggravated her yesterday? She couldn't think. He looked— different.

Her heart pinched in a really annoying way just looking at him, and those darn pesky nipples might as well have been waving pompoms.

It wasn't often a guy made her look twice. Most were immature and needy. Either they still lived at home with their mothers or they wanted to. One guy she'd dated had actually planned to move into her apartment while he was job hunting. *Yeah, right.*

She could smell a loser a mile away. No way was she desperate enough to fall for a line like that. One day she would have her nursing degree. No sense in marrying down. No. Her sights were set on a man with uncommon business sense and a plan for his future that didn't include playing in a band, flipping burgers, or anything law enforcement related. Or military related.

She was about rules and plans, playing it safe and being smart. Still...

Agent Cartwright looked relaxed. Endearing. Cute, in a really annoying way. His long fingers interlocked in prayerful repose set her heart to throbbing. Heck, it set her entire body to throbbing.

She licked her lips, wondering how his mouth tasted. How that morning scruff might feel against her—

Good grief, her breasts tingled with heat and hormones, suddenly alive and—needing to be cupped by those masculine hands?

Uh-uh. No way. Not him. Never.

She crossed her arms over her chest, tucking her fingers in her armpits to control the tremors. How was he able to do that to her? Asleep? She knew biology, but this was more like some kind of sizzling black magic. Unsettling for a woman of her advanced edu—

"You ready for some coffee?"

Shelby jerked out of her tantalizing reverie. Darn it anyway. Agent Lennox kept catching her in the act of outright voyeurism. She nearly couldn't speak, not with her hormones welling up in her throat as they were. Or was it her throbbing libido? *Argh.*

"Umm, sure. That would be nice," she spat out, lowering her hands to her sides, her fingers still clenched, but she was hoping for nonchalance. *Oh, yeah. That was where I was going. The kitchen. Breakfast. Omelets.*

Agent Lennox kept his eyes on the cup in his hand while he poured, the jerk. He had to have seen her gawking at his junior agent like a teenage girl in heat. "Hope I didn't disturb you. Had to make a few calls. Take a seat. Those two won't be up for a while. Kelsey had a nightmare. He stayed up with her for a while."

Shelby glanced into the living room where Agent Cartwright snored lightly, because looking at Agent Lennox made her uncomfortable. *Darn. Kelsey had a nightmare and I slept right through it?*

"You should've woken me, Agent Lennox. I didn't know," she said meekly, taking the proffered cup of coffee and wishing her fingers didn't tremble like they did.

"Darn, girl. Chill. Knock off the formality already. I'm Zack. He's Gabe. You're Shelby. Sound good?"

Gabe, huh? As in Gabriel?

Gabe woke to Zack crouched over him and tapping his shoulder.

"Time to take another look around the 'hood. Miss Shelby's in the shower. Kelsey's outside on the patio. Coffee's on the counter."

"Right. Got it." Gabe stretched the kink out of his neck while blinking himself awake. "How is she this morning?"

"Tired. Said she needed time to think. The dogs are with her so she's not alone."

"You talk with Mark yet?"

"Yeah. Guess Connor and Rory tore into Kelsey's car. They also got hold of some surveillance footage near the shore where Kelsey wrecked, too. They've got definitive proof four guys tried to kill her, but get this. A lone Samaritan showed up at the last minute. He rousted the other guys and pulled her out of the river."

Gabe's heart jumped to the back of his throat. It couldn't be. No way. "Alex?"

Zack shook his head. "You know better. Mark says no. The guy was thicker in the middle. Didn't walk like the boss. Come on. Get moving. We've got work to do."

"Good enough." Gabe pushed off the floor in time to see Zack's backside clear the front door. Yeah. There was no way Alex had saved Kelsey. Why the question sprang to his lips the way it had, Gabe couldn't explain. Chalk it up to hope springing eternal, or something crazy like that.

He checked the view out the kitchen window before he fixed himself a cup of coffee. The sight of Kelsey alone in her backyard tugged at his heartstrings, which were damned tender anyway. There'd always been something about her that got to him. She'd proven herself to be a very resilient woman, but he couldn't suppress his instinct to protect her, even when

Alex was still alive. The feeling only intensified with him gone.

When the day came she took another man in marriage, so be it. Kelsey was sister material. Like Ember and Izza. That was all. But whoever took Alex's place had better be one helluva man because, whether she knew it or not, Kelsey had one bad-assed family of brothers and sisters at her six.

He paused at the back door. Kelsey had knelt to Whisper and Smoke's level. Both dogs sat in front of her with ears forward, listening intently. She rocked forward and backward, one moment with a hand on Whisper's wide forehead, the next hugging Smoke like he was a little boy instead of a loyal hound dog, and damn it. A crying woman with broken fingers made for a pitiful sight.

Gabe ventured forth. Neither the dogs nor Kelsey heard him step out on the back porch, but he heard her. "Everyone thinks I'm crazy, but I felt him. I think you know he's been here, too."

Whisper placed a huge paw on her shoulder.

"There has to be a really good reason he can't come home right now, don't you think?"

Gabe could've sworn he'd heard guttural agreement in the black dog's growly voice. When Kelsey bowed her head, he couldn't bear to keep his presence hidden anymore.

"They look like they'd do anything for you," he said softly as he crouched beside her.

Kelsey turned away, a sob caught in her throat. "Wh... what?"

"I didn't mean to startle you, ma'am. I'm sorry, but these dogs sure love you. They'll do anything for you, huh?" He ruffled Smoke's ears and neck. "I've worked with them before. They're the best trackers around, aren't they?"

She wiped her face and sniffed, the back of her hand to her nose, the splints stiff and straight and stabbing Gabe's heart. "They're not just pets. They're my... boys."

"I see that." By now, Smoke faced Gabe, bright-eyed and ready to play. "So why does a dog bond with one person and not another? Harley's an old Army K-9 handler. He and dogs go together like beer and pizza, but these particular dogs love you more. Anyone can see that."

"They saved me," she whispered. "A long time ago."

He let her sad comment go, stroking the thick ruffle on Smoke's neck. "Where's the ball, Smokey? You want to play?"

Smoke took off with his nose to the ground, but Whisper remained steadfast at Kelsey's side. She pushed up from the lawn and retreated to the garden swing nearer the back door, although now it resembled more of an arbor bedecked with a dense vine. She'd dressed for the day in stonewashed denims and a light blue sweater over a purple button-up blouse. Her eyes were on her hands, her fingers interlocked like awkward knitting needles as she lowered onto the wooden slats.

"You were sleeping when I walked by the living room," she said. "I hope I didn't disturb you."

"Zack rousted me." He stretched his back and ran a hand through his hair, hopefully brushing out the bed-head he no doubt had. "I can pretty much sleep anywhere. You look good sitting there in all those purple flowers. Wisteria?"

"You know your vines."

"Yeah. Mom's got one like it on her patio. The darn thing's a weed."

"They can get out of control." She pulled a fragrant clump of purple to her nose. Just that quickly, a shadow shifted over her countenance. "They're like children. Before you know it, they're into everything."

"Are you warm enough?" He had to ask. She'd shivered talking about children.

Kelsey released the flower and tucked her hands under her arms. "I'm fine. Zack wouldn't let me out the door without my sweater. Aren't you guys tired of babysitting me yet?"

"If you're really asking if I'm tired of your company, that would be a big fat negatory, ma'am. Why? Are you trying to get rid of me?"

"Just seems to me that you guys have better things to do than sit around here all day and wait on me."

"Can't think of anything I'd rather do. I mean, old man Lennox made some darn good soup for us last night. What more could I ask for? I didn't know he could cook, did you?"

"Oh, yes. He and Mei have had us over for dinner a couple times. He's quite the chef when he's got the time."

Gabe rubbed his stomach with a smile. "I've never gained weight on an op before. This might be my first."

Smoky returned with a blue rubber ball and the rubber bone sticking out of his mouth. He sat at Gabe's feet, his hopeful black eyes fixed on Gabe.

"Where's home?"

Gabe snagged both the bone and the ball from Smoke. He tossed the ball to the far end of the yard. "Well, let's see. I was born in Germany when Dad was in the Air Force, but when he and Mom came to the States, they settled in Texas."

"Oh? What part of Germany?"

"Ramstein Air Force Base, ma'am."

"Ah, please don't call me ma'am anymore. It makes me feel old."

"Sorry. You're what, all of thirty?"

By then, Smoke had returned with two balls, his cheeks puckered out like a gopher's.

A half-smile twitched at Kelsey's mouth at her watchdog's silly antics. She nodded. "Thirty-one. How about you?"

"Twenty-seven going on eighty."

"I know how that feels. So you were an Air Force brat?"

"Not that I remember." He tossed the ball across the yard again. Whisper watched with disinterest from Kelsey's feet while Smoke launched off the patio in retrieve mode. "Dad met Mom while he was stationed over there. He didn't re-up. I was two years old when they moved back to the States. His family's all in Texas, so there we are."

"Where in Texas?"

"Dallas Fort Worth. You ever been there?"

"San Antonio." Her voice dropped a tone. "It was April."

"The River Walk?"

"Yes. It's beautiful, isn't it?"

And just like that, Gabe lost her. Her head dipped. She wouldn't meet his gaze. She must've gone to San Antonio with Alex. Death had a way of turning good times into painful memories.

He bounced one of the balls Smoke had retrieved into her lap. Both dogs shifted their gaze to her, bright-eyed and ready to play, but it got her attention, too. She managed to grab hold of the ball and tossed it to Whisper. Of course, he brought it right back to her like the faithful companion he was.

"You feel like taking a walk with me and these rascals? I promise we'll walk really, really slo-o-o-w," Gabe teased.

Her poor fingers clattered against the wooden slats as she stood. "I'll get the leashes."

"Oh, no you don't. Just who's the sickie here? You or me?"

"Me," she said softly, still blinking her emotions away. "I guess."

"That's right, and don't you forget it." He walked over to the back door and reached inside for the leashes. Zack was just coming through the front door. "Hey, Lennox. We're taking the dogs for a walk. You wanna come with?"

Zack walked straight out the back door in a heartbeat. "You bet. Give me that big ol' moose, Smoke. Gabe, you take Whisper. Miss Shelby's in the shower right now, but it's her turn to fix breakfast anyway. We'll be back by then."

Kelsey stood at the swing. "But guys, who do I get to walk?"

Gabe handed Whisper's leash off to Zack. "Me. Here. Take my arm."

"Great." Zack huffed in playful annoyance. "I get the dogs. You get the girl."

"You got that right," Gabe stated proudly. "I'll trim that old wisteria thingy that's taking over your porch swing when we get back, too."

"Oh, you don't need to. I'm just glad you guys are here," she whispered as they started toward the driveway gate.

Gabe clamped his hand over the top of hers, careful of her fingers. "Me, too, Kelsey. Me, too."

Chapter Twelve

"Can we talk?" David stood at Mark's workstation, a black folder tucked under his arm.

That was what caught his eye. *Who the hell's running a black op I don't know about?*

Before long, the two men sat at the small conference table in Alex's office, where he'd debriefed them in days not so long past. It was the place of one-on-one moments with their intense boss. Moments like that built the agent and strengthened The TEAM.

Of course, Alex could also shred an agent who'd fallen down on the job. Heaven help the man or woman who got an innocent civilian killed. He had no tolerance for collateral damage.

"What's up?" Mark asked.

David ran his index finger inside his white shirt collar. "I know you're certain Alex is dead—"

"I know what I saw." Mark heard the sharp sting in his words. He didn't want Alex to be dead, but it was time they dealt with it.

"And you believe you saw him die."

"It's not just a matter of what I believe. I saw it. I saw the blood. God, I saw his body at the morgue. What more do you guys need?" Mark clenched his jaw and waited.

David laid the black ops folder on the table. "Perspective. I'm not your enemy here. I'd like to propose a couple of theories, that's all."

"Then propose away." Hell. Why not? Rumors were flying. He was at a loss as to how to stop the latest fairytale that it was Alex who'd rescued Kelsey. Connor's video coverage was no help. Despite what Mark had told Zack in their morning conversation, that mysterious guy in black sure walked like Alex, but would he have done that, just covered his face and drove away?

Hell, no. He'd have made damned sure he was seen, that whoever filmed him got a clear shot of his middle finger. Or a live round.

"Bear with me. Hear me out. You're the boss here, and—"

Enough! Temper got the best of Mark. "No. I'm not Alex. What the hell, David? Everyone looks at me like I'm the natural-born heir to the Stewart throne. Well, I've got news for you. I'm not."

"But you are."

"No, I'm not. I don't know why the hell Alex left this place to you, me, and—"

"And Harley cannot deal with leadership right now. He's better off at home with his wife and sons."

Mark clenched the back of his neck with one hand, weary with the weight of perceived leadership. Everyone sure saw something different than he did. Despite his USMC training, this wasn't the job he'd signed up for. Plain and simple, he didn't want it. "And that leaves you and me."

Still—David was correct. Harley wasn't capable of leadership at the moment. The TEAM was better off with him at home.

"Yes," David said, still as calm as ever. "That leaves you and me, but you're the one holding everyone together, Mark, not me."

"I am, huh? Sure doesn't feel like it."

"You just can't see it because you're walking point. You're so far out ahead of the rest of us that you can't see who's behind you anymore, but believe me. Everyone's got your back. We're all here."

Mark stared out the ceiling-to-floor window. Alex's ghost was everywhere, his fingerprints on every damned wall and countertop of the company he'd built from the ground up. No matter what any legal document said, The TEAM was his. Still. It always would be.

"Okay, so talk. I do need some help."

"That's why no one went home last night," David reminded him. "We're here to help. All of us."

"Yeah. I know." Mark blew out a big breath and let a fraction of frustration go with it. The TEAM was the absolute best covert surveillance company in town. Hell, maybe on the entire East Coast. He just didn't want to lead it, not this way. "Whatcha got, David? What are you thinking?"

"That maybe we need to set aside everything we thought we knew. To begin again, tell me what you saw when you and Harley accompanied Kelsey to the morgue."

The recollection came back in a flood of nausea and all too vivid detail. Mark's headache kicked up a notch. He'd tried to talk Kelsey out of going, but she'd insisted. That was when all this crazy talk about exhumations and Alex visiting her in her dreams started.

"She could barely stand," he said softly. "When the ME pulled the tray out of the drawer... when he lowered the sheet... I barely caught her before she hit the floor."

"And Harley was upset."

Mark nodded. More like devastated. Anguished. Hopeless. Maybe suicidal. Mark didn't know who'd cried harder that day, Kelsey or Harley.

"I'm sorry. I know this is hard, but did you notice any stitching? Was there a Y-shaped incision on the body?" David pressed. "It would've been visible below the collarbones. The ME had completed his autopsy by then. He would've made the thoracoabdominal incisions in order to determine cause of death. It's standard procedure."

Mark lifted the back of his hand to his mouth. God. MEs and morticians. Ghouls of the trade. "I didn't see any incision. The ME only exposed Alex's face."

And that was enough, because it was his friend and boss on that stainless steel tray, only it wasn't. The macabre image of Alex's gray lips and lifeless, pale skin tortured Mark still. He didn't need to see stitches to know the body had been cut open, every organ measured and weighed, bagged, and replaced.

David extracted two black and white eight-by-ten glossies from the folder. He'd been unusually quiet the last week. No wonder. He'd been running his own investigation on the ME.

From neck to trunk, the photos showed the cleaned-up version of a male cadaver with three entry and exit holes, including the very prominent stitching David had asked about. The label in the upper left corner declared these grotesquely intimate images to be Alex.

Bile lifted up from Mark's gut. The walls closed in, making it difficult to breathe. Why the hell had David ambushed him like this? *God, that's not just a body you're showing me. Alex was my friend. Maybe my best friend.*

"Tell me what's missing, Mark. Do you see it?"

He glanced at the photos, his heart thumping in his chest. "I don't see anything." *And I sonofabitchin' don't want to.*

"Look again," David urged. "You will."

Swallowing hard, Mark did as David requested for all of sixty seconds before he shoved the images back across the table. "Why didn't the ME include the vic's face in the shot? How do we know this is really Alex?"

David pushed the photos back under Mark's nose again. "I know this is hard, but I want you to remember what Alex would say to us right now."

That word. Mark had heard it a thousand times. He could almost hear the impatience behind it when Alex snapped it out of his mouth like a sting at the end of a whip.

Think.

Mark scrubbed a hand over his face and looked at the damned pictures again. And then he looked closer. Alex had lost a kidney after a confrontation with Kelsey's ex. He'd been beaten and knifed. Left for dead. "This body doesn't have any scars. It sure as hell should have."

"Precisely."

"So either the ME labeled the wrong photos or..." Mark bit his lip at the evidence, not wanting to entertain the impossible. Could there be another body out there with three identical bullet wounds like the ones Alex had suffered? "Or what? Or the dead body I saw with my own eyes wasn't

Alex? No, David. This is an administrative error. Call the ME. Tell him to send the right pictures."

"I did. He claims these are the right ones." David's eyes narrowed. "There's another thing that puzzles me. Who called the paramedics the morning Alex was shot?"

"I'm not sure. Gabe maybe? He was first on the scene," Mark replied, his mind still on the pictures of the body that very well might not be Alex's. *Could it be possible? Damn it?*

"I checked with 911 dispatch to verify. They have no record that anyone called."

"What are you saying? That someone intercepted Gabe's call? Maybe the paramedics were just in the right place at the right time for once. It happens." *Was there any damned way Alex was still alive?*

"Maybe." David's quiet agreement spiked Mark's irritation. "Or maybe someone did intercept the 911 call as you suggested."

"What? You think those guys who showed up weren't really paramedics?" This conspiracy theory just kept growing. Now David believed? Mark had just been thankful the paramedics arrived as quickly as they did, but now he didn't know what to think.

He held one hand up to stop this insane line of thought. "Wait a minute. If you're insinuating the paramedics were fake, then you also think the emergency room doctor lied. And if he did, the ME's lying, too. So is FBI Agent Kenny. You're way off base, David. That's just too damned much collusion to be real world. No way could all of those professionals pull off a cover-up that big. The boss is dead. God, let it go."

A frission of unease crept up Mark's spine even as he argued. Kenny *had* lied. Mark knew it in his sniper's heart, which meant the ME and the Bureau were in league for some ungodly reason. *Could David be right?*

David leaned forward on the table, his fingers interlocked in front of him. "I found something on the FBI server. I'll need Mother's help to crack it, but I thought you should know about it first. It's an encrypted file called Eagle Two."

"So?"

"So it's on the Secret Service server, too."

"Why are you inside federal servers?"

"Because I don't believe Agent Kenny and neither do you."

And there it was, the real problem. God, Mark wanted to believe, but facts were facts. He'd seen what he'd seen, damn it.

Bottom line—The TEAM had enough on their plate right now. The last thing they needed was to get between the FBI and Secret Service, both heavy hitters and lethal as hell if you got on their bad side. "Why'd that grab your attention?"

"Would you understand if I told you I have a gut feeling that it's related to Alex? I'd like to investigate further if it's okay with you."

That was Alex's first rule, wasn't it? Always trust your gut?

"Why are you asking me? You're co-owner of this outfit, too. Do what you want."

"We both know why, Mark. Each of us brought a different aptitude to this place on the day we were hired. I may be your equal in title, but there can only be one in charge." David glanced toward the door. "Besides, they're already following you. As am I."

There it was again, the humbling enlightenment that he, Mark Houston, was the top dog now. It rattled him to his boots. "Thanks. I guess."

David offered the barest smile. "I would think a farmer's son would know the cream rises to the top. In ten years, no one will remember caliber or weapon, only that you stepped up to the plate and salvaged a team worth keeping when they needed you most."

"Well, there's an old Marine saying that tells us to shoot everything that moves, too." Mark rolled his eyes at his friend's implied compliment. He, of all people, knew better. He wasn't the cream. He hadn't risen to the top because he was the best. More like in the wrong place at the wrong time. "Grab Mother or Ember, whoever's got the time to help. Let me know what you find. But while we're talking, how's Mother seem to you?"

David's eyes narrowed. "She's grown quiet since the funeral. Why do you ask?"

Mark dug his thumbs into his tired eye sockets. "Maybe it's just the grief talking, but she's been short with me a few too many times. And that scene at the hospital was just plain weird. She'd brought her overnight bag. She meant to move in. It's almost as if she wanted Kelsey all to herself."

"You do know she had strong feelings for Alex."

Mark grunted. Yes, she'd been known to declare she loved everyone on The TEAM, Alex included. Mark just hadn't thought of it as *that* kind of love.

His cell phone interrupted the awkward conversation. It was Mother's snippy voice on the other end of the line. And that was another thing. Why hadn't she buzzed him on the intercom, as she would've done with Alex?

"If you're not too busy, would you mind spending a couple minutes with Steven and me for a change?"

He drew in a deep breath and prepared to be extra patient. "Be right out."

David excused himself while Mark went immediately to Mother's workstation as summoned. Actually the center of the work bay, her station formed command central, a beehive of monitors, CPUs, phone lines and everything else computer related.

She stood behind Junior Agent Steven Cross, her crisp navy-blue blazer and skirt complementing her silvery short hair and cream-colored blouse while she followed his progress over his shoulder.

Mark wasn't worried about the crime scene across the street anymore. He doubted the roof would hold a hint of believable evidence once the FBI was through with it. Thankfully, the lack of hard evidence hadn't stopped Mother or Steven from checking into it.

Steven pointed at his monitor the minute Mark arrived. "Look at this, Boss."

"Don't call me that." Mark didn't mean to snap.

"Sure. Sorry, but you need to see this," Steven continued unfazed.

Mother rolled her eyes. Something was definitely bothering her. She'd taken a stern position behind her poor apprentice, her arms crossed over her chest and her toe tapping.

Mark rested his hand on Steven's shoulder to take the sting out of his rebuke. "Whatcha got?"

Steven reversed the video and ran it forward in slow motion. "The shooter. I think. Watch this."

Mark watched while once again, Alex pulled up to the security gate on the day of the shooting. He extended his left arm through the driver's side window and keyed in his pass code. The gate rolled to the right. The vehicle's left-turn indicator blinked bright red.

Everything looked normal until the car's tires rotated forward.

A flash of bright red followed by puffs of white hit the windshield. Alex slumped forward in his seat belt and Mark's heart hit the floor. Damn. The god-awful empty feeling of losing a buddy never went away.

"Run that again. Slow it down," he said hoarsely, licking his lips to restore moisture.

"Yes, sir." Steven reversed the video and decreased the tempo.

This time Mark knew where to look. There it was again. The flash of red highlighting the front windshield a scant second before the burst of white, only the flashes hadn't come from the same location. One was high. One low.

"Run it again."

Steven complied quickly, and there it was. The flash of red from the rooftop, exactly where the FBI and ME reported the kill shots came from. Hell, they'd even trumped up diagrams to support their so-called evidence. Liars. The kill shots came from a window directly across the street from the parking garage exit, not the roof.

Guys in Afghanistan called it *painting a target*. They'd laser tag a Taliban terrorist's front door or a munitions dump to guide an F-16 bomb strike. Some asshole had painted Alex from the roof while another murdered him. What the hell? Was that sniper so poor of a shot he needed his targets marked? Or—

Damn. David was right. The FBI and ME's reports were bogus. Every word out of their lying mouths was intended to one hundred percent misdirect them. That's why the Bureau refused to release the so-called crime scene. It wasn't one, but as long as The TEAM believed that, they hadn't looked further.

Only Steven had. And Mother. And David.

Another wave of frustration edged up Mark's spine, filling him with the need to strike back. Hit something. Had he had his head in the sand all this time?

He stuck his index finger to the monitor screen, pointed to the dark window across the street. "Can you zoom in right here? I want to see this area closer."

"Already zoomed in and enhanced, sir." Steven brought up the requested image.

At first, Mark could only make out the blurry outline of the tools of the trade—the tripod holding what had to be a sniper rifle, the round lens of a scope that brought targets up close and personal.

Steven worked to bring the image into better focus.

The broad shoulders of the bastard behind the scope materialized. The man raised his head to assess the damage he'd caused. The sonofabitch smiled.

"Who the hell is he?"

Steven handed Mark a printout from their private facial recognition database, a compilation of every national and foreign facial rec database. The sonofabitch in question was

Samuel Becker. Ex-Navy SEAL. Current FBI undercover sniper. Flaming asshole.

"The FBI killed Alex." Mark lowered his voice too late. Every head in the work area popped up and all agents crowded into Mother's workspace.

She stood smugly behind Steven, rocking back and forth on her heels. "Go on. Show him what else you found."

He handed Mark another photo. "Sir, I also ran thermal imaging on this sequence of shots."

"What am I looking at?" Mark asked, his blood humming with a spike of adrenaline and a boatload of righteous indignation. The day Libby lost her sister, Faith, to an FBI protective detail gone bad was the day Mark knew Alex was right. The Bureau couldn't be trusted. Ever.

What had they done now? Taken Alex out because he was their better? Because he and Jed McCormack, the local billionaire, were tight, and Jed had more clout in Congress than the FBI director? Or just because Alex had been a flaming pain in the ass from day one? Because he really could do more with less? God help the FBI the day the American taxpayer found out that little nugget of more-bang-for-your-buck information.

Damn. Was this assassination because of the FBI annual budget? Was this nothing more than the Bureau director's personal vendetta carried out by his in-house snipers?

The wildest scenarios flooded Mark's head until Steven pointed to the video monitor, following the slow-mo trajectory of the kill shots. "See? Right here. There's no heat signature, Boss, umm, Mark. Sorry. Whatever FBI Agent Becker shot into the victim lacked a significant heat signature. It was not a live round."

"Say what?"

"Exactly," Mother purred. She had her smug face on. *I told you so* glistened in her crystal blue eyes, and something else, but Mark simply didn't have time to analyze her bitchy mood.

"So you're telling me Becker's shot wasn't lethal? He didn't kill Alex? Then why did he fire at him? What kind of ammo did he use?"

"Whatever it was, sir, it wasn't the ten millimeter the ME and FBI claimed. That size of round would've lit up under thermal imaging, both from the combustion gases and the friction when the rounds exited the chamber. This, whatever it is, was significantly cooler. It might've been a smart bullet. I need to run more data to be sure."

"Can you enhance it?" Mark asked impatiently, the facts he thought he knew at war with this newest intel. *What the hell is going on? Is Alex alive or not, damn it?*

"I'm still working on that. If I can't do it, I'll find someone who can," Steve answered quickly.

"Good job, Steven. You, too, Mother."

Mark mulled Steven's breakthrough over on his way back to his office—*umm, Alex's office, damn it*. Had Steven just proved Alex wasn't assassinated? No way. They were missing something. They had to be.

I saw the blood. The body. There is a reasonable explanation. There has to be. He is dead, damn it.

Isn't he?

Chapter Thirteen

"Man, Boss. Even up there in heaven, you surprise me," Gabe muttered when he opened the door to Kelsey's backyard shed. A shelf ran the length of the back wall with a pegboard wall behind it that held everything from hedge clippers to garden gloves.

Shovels, rakes, and a hoe hung in their appointed place to the right of the door—a green garden hose neatly coiled on its rack hung at the left. The only thing on the concrete floor was a simple push mower with a grass catcher. Even the damned grass catcher was clean. His OCD boss really was—OCD.

Gabe knelt to retrieve a roll of garbage bags for the wisteria trimming he'd promised Kelsey. Why not? All the video feeds showed normal, and besides, trimming an unruly vine seemed a damned small thing to do. Hell, he would've painted her house if it had made her happy.

Besides, it also kept him out of Sullivan's domain.

Her brows had spiked plenty when he and Zack had returned Kelsey, after her less than thirty-minute walk, to the end of her driveway. The poor thing was exhausted, so Sullivan took over and ushered her to her bedroom. Of course, Sullivan's evil eye was in play by then, which only made Gabe want to laugh in her face.

She thought she looked mean with that skimpy raised brow of hers? Hell no. The thing wasn't even bushy. She ought to meet a few Afghan tribal lords he'd worked with while in the Corps. Those unibrows meant business. Sullivan had nothing on them.

Shaking the plastic bag out, he latched onto a pair of stainless-steel hedge clippers and prepared to tackle the wisteria beast. If it was anything like his mother's, this could turn into an all-day chore. Of course, Alex also had a chainsaw. Gabe deliberated for all of one second, but Kelsey liked the vine. Hacking it off at the roots was probably not a good idea.

He commenced clipping and trimming, pulling long strands of woody vine away from the swing. The wisteria demanded careful concentration. One particular branch turned into a twenty-foot long tentacle that travelled the entire length of the rain gutter under the eaves. He clipped it where it sprouted from the main branch and pulled until the dead wood lay in circles at his feet. As gnarly and stubborn as it was, the massive vine offered a definite blind spot to this corner of the yard.

He stepped around the back of the swing, hoping for easier access to the tangled mass. The sight stopped him cold. Imprinted in the soft soil was a clear set of boot prints.

Only they weren't his. Zack's either. They both wore the prescribed work boots, steel-toed with a zigzag pattern on the sole and a circle on the ball of the foot. Whoever had been standing in this spot of the flowerbed had left a definite elliptical pattern bordered by a waffle-weave of rectangles.

"Hey, Gabe. You ready for breakfast?" Zack called out the back door. "Miss Shelby made omelets. They're good."

"Come here." Gabe motioned him over. "Look what I found."

Zack ambled to the flowerbed. "That explains camera nine. I thought maybe we had a bad lens. All I've gotten this morning is glare." He scanned the backyard. "We've been had. Look at that."

Gabe followed where Zack pointed. A finger-sized metal cylinder on the neighbor's fence post aimed a bright red light at camera nine, the one Gabe had personally situated under the southwest corner of the Stewart's eaves. A laser.

"Mark will want to know about this." Gabe scoped the fence line for additional camera placement to make sure this didn't happen again. "He's looking for any reason to pull Kelsey out of here. That will do it. Someone is definitely stalking her."

"The dogs didn't make a sound, though," Zack said. "They let this guy get in close."

Gabe looked at the kennel. "You're right. I was up most of the night with Kelsey. I'd have heard them. These guys never made a peep."

And she swore someone was in her bedroom with her. Was she right?

Conversation stalled. Gabe wasn't going to say out loud what had to be on both their minds. There was one person who could've easily disarmed this security system. He would've known TEAM protocol, too, and where the new cameras would've been installed. And the dogs wouldn't have made a sound when he showed up.

Nope. Dead men don't visit their widows, not like this.

"Let's eat," Zack said.

"You bet. Let me finish up here and I'll be right in. You mind checking Kelsey's bedroom window the first chance you get? Make sure it's locked and secure like we think it is?"

"You bet."

It didn't take long to bag the wisteria debris, rake the odds and ends, and stow the clippers, but the puzzle remained. Somebody had gotten inside their perimeter and maybe the house.

After double-checking the immediate area around the entire house, then walking the perimeter, which he expanded to five houses just to be extra safe, Gabe wandered inside. "How's the rest of our stake?" he asked.

Zack sat in the front room at the laptop, a mug of his usual flavored cream with a touch of coffee in his big mitt. "Good. Window is secure. Whoever our intruder was, he knew exactly how to approach the house and get under the eaves without being seen. Except for a couple of bright flashes, which had to be that damned laser, I've got nothing. This guy's good."

Just like the boss.

"We've got a clear set of boot prints, though. I'll make plaster casts soon as I'm done eating." Gabe glanced down the hallway. "Are the women in Kelsey's room?"

Zack nodded, one brow lifted. "Speak."

"Why would anyone stand outside her locked bedroom window? It's not like a guy could get in from there without making any noise," Gabe whispered.

Zack lifted one shoulder. "It doesn't matter. That intruder just blew our one and only chance to stay here. Hit the shower. I'll call Mark, but I'd plan on moving before night falls."

"I'm good with that." Gabe rifled through his duffel, grabbed his shaving kit along with another set of the prescribed uniform of the day and hit the head opposite the guest room. A good breakfast wouldn't hurt, but he needed a shower first.

After he turned the faucet to hot, he kicked off his boots and stripped out of his dirty clothes. His holster and weapons went to the top of the hamper outside the shower, just in case. A sniper never let his weapons out of reach.

While steam warmed the glass-enclosed tub, he shaved at the sink, his mind filled with reasons their intruder couldn't be Alex. It made no sense. People didn't come back to life. Good husbands didn't torment their widows. And wishing something didn't make it so.

The fact remained. This encroachment felt like an inside job. Too bad Whisper and Smoke couldn't talk.

Of course, Kelsey wanted to stay in her own home. It made a difference in her recovery. At least she believed it would. Now he wasn't so sure. Was there any way in hell somebody had gotten into bed with her last night, that she hadn't been having a nightmare? That she was right?

Acid pitched up his throat at the thought of an intruder inside her bedroom. Predator or ally, it made no difference. No one would get that close to her again, not if Gabe had anything to say about it. The time had come to button up any holes that might still exist in their defenses and hunker down. Or move the hell out.

When Gabe told Kelsey at the hospital that he believed, it hadn't seemed like a lie at all. He'd meant it as encouragement, but now that he'd seen her fall apart after a dream, he understood exactly what he'd done. He'd tossed her a lifeline, and she was hanging on for dear life. She desperately needed someone to stand with her until... *Alex came home.*

Yeah, right. Gabe pursed his lips to one side as he shaved. His loyalty for Kelsey ran deep. She deserved all he had to give and he would do no less, but if she wanted to stay? That was a tough one. This little home was fast becoming an indefensible position.

TEAM safe houses were out of the question. Anyone with inside intel, like Alex, would know right where to find her again. Hotels were full of innocent civilians, another no-go. That left one place that no one knew about, because it had just been remodeled prior to Gabe signing a seven-year mortgage.

Hell, Taylor and Maverick didn't even know that a one-level rambler on the outskirts of Silver Springs was his yet, and they were his best buds.

He was lost in plotting a strategy for Kelsey's safety when the bathroom door banged open. He thought he'd locked it, but Sullivan stood there with an armful of bath towels and her mouth wide open, her teeth all but falling out of her head.

Silly woman must not have heard the shower running.

"I, umm... ah..." she muttered without saying anything intelligent—or rude.

He grinned at her flustered confusion while those violet-blue lasers of hers zipped down to his feet and back up to his eyes in about two seconds flat. Crazier yet, she finger-stabbed her glasses back up on her nose.

There he was, standing at the sink without so much as a stitch on and she wanted better visibility? Violet-blue settled on his chest and then his stomach, slowly drifting downward, her mouth open in a silent *O*.

He turned to face her. There was no sense hiding what she'd already taken a gander at. "Care to join me?"

Her mouth finally closed, but a lovely shade of rose blossomed up her neck, spilling onto her cheeks. An embarrassed young woman replaced the cool, professional and very stuffy Nurse Sullivan, who'd probably seen it all in her line of work. She took her glasses off, blinking like crazy and shaking her head. This shy girl took a step back and blurted out a squeaky, "No, umm... no."

Her glance dropped to his feet. His prosthetic foot. She shook those blond tresses, glanced at his cock, which by now had stood up and noticed her, too. One more time her eyeballs scrolled up and over his bare chest. She bit her lip right before she blew out an adorably embarrassed sigh and slammed the door behind her.

He chuckled. It had been a long time since any female had seen him in the raw. Women tended to steer clear of guys with fake limbs. He'd learned the hard way. War hero or not, once he let the cat out of the bag that he'd left a part of himself in Afghanistan, the romantic dinner was over. The night was done. They'd taken off. Every damned time.

He'd stopped looking for Mrs. Right months ago and bought a house. Less stress. More equity. As far as his feelings toward his missing foot? He'd dealt with it long ago.

Wasn't much choice, was there?

Modern technology had provided a rugged substitute that would've allowed him to stay in the Corps if he'd wanted, but hell no. The molded plastic served its purpose. It kept him mobile, functioning, and able to stay productive. He had others, like his paddle foot for running, but it drew too much attention. He preferred to look like other guys. Normal on the outside.

It ached when the weather changed, which was really funny, considering the foot wasn't there anymore. Phantom pains, his rehab therapist called them. Ha. Nothing phantom about those aches. Otherwise, a foot was a foot, mechanical or not. It held him upright. He stuck it in his boot and forgot about it. Other things hurt a helluva lot worse. Like losing friends and brothers. *Just ask Maverick, why don't cha?*

But the look on Sullivan's face? Priceless.

He wiped the last of the lather off his grinning mouth and chuckled loud enough that she surely heard it from wherever she'd run off to. Everyone else must have, too.

The steam in her eyes had been unexpected, though. Dark violet—a very enticing color. Simmering. Hmm. Yet another side to the beast.

Well, now she knew. A twinge of regret shifted over the face of the man staring back from the mirror. He'd been down this road before. Never ended well.

Gabe focused on shaving instead of that—*silly girl.*

And I had to push my glasses up? Like I needed to get a better look? At him? Naked? Am I that stupid!

Shelby fled toward Kelsey's room, blood humming so loud in her head she couldn't think. Not only had she embarrassed herself by intruding on his privacy, but the man had a prosthetic foot attached to the bottom of his right leg.

Agent Cartwright was a tibular amputee. How had she not noticed *that* before?

Her flustered mind raced over the last two days. He didn't limp. He didn't even favor the leg. Nothing. But she should've detected the difference, especially when she'd seen him lying on the floor this morning. She should've noticed the difference in his gait yesterday when he'd played with the dogs. She should've noticed something. Anything.

Why didn't I? Am I really that stupid?

No. Simply focused on job number one, Kelsey, like you should be.

Other things bothered her about these two guys. Like their need to always wear those darned holsters, guns included. And their boots. And those dogs. Had she been so irritated with all that stuff that she'd missed really seeing *them*? That she'd never really looked at the men behind the whole professional bodyguard persona?

But wow, a transtibial amputation. Most orthopedic surgeons opted for less of a residual limb, taking a damaged leg off closer to the knee joint and leaving just enough of a stump to attach a longer prosthetic leg instead of a prosthetic ankle and foot. Why had this doctor elected to leave more of Agent Cartwright's leg? Was that what Army doctors did?

Oh, wait. He's not Army. What was that rank he'd tossed at her? USMC, something or other. She hadn't cared enough to listen, but wished she had now. Agent Cartwright might act like any other guy, but he wasn't.

Agent Lennox treated him like he had two normal legs. Surely he knew, didn't he? Or was Agent Cartwright just that good at hiding his... his what? His handicap?

The word didn't fit. Not one bit. Not him. No. The man wasn't handicapped in any sense of the word. Those were oftentimes more of a mental condition anyway. People who'd suffered acute trauma tended to label themselves as handicapped, crippled or divorced, as if that label truly identified who they were. The problem was that once labeled, they'd effectively pigeonholed themselves for the rest of their lives. They accepted less. They believed they were less than whole.

But Agent Cartwright hadn't. He still worked. Walked. Acted like any other guy. He was just—Gabe. Kelsey's protector. The one who had gotten up with her in the middle of the night and took her for a short early morning walk after a night of little sleep. Like he cared.

Shelby pressed her hand to her chest to still the kettledrum beating there.

But the light in those eyes when she'd flung the door open. Sultry green. Downright enticing. Steamy…

Another heat wave throbbed up the length of her body, just thinking about him standing there without a stitch. Nope. Agent Cartwright, umm, Gabe, wasn't like other guys. Not at all.

Missing a foot or not, he still looked—chiseled, like one of those carved Grecian gods adorning half the buildings in D.C. with all their naked splendor. Only this guy was built. Ripped. Muscled from chin to, umm, foot. Tanned. The right sprinkle of dark hair dusted his pecs, trailed down his stomach and from there to—

There.

She should know. She'd just seen all that male splendor, up close a little too personal. He was more—endowed. She licked her lips. Prickly desire filled her breasts yet again, places farther south, too. He was fast becoming an unhealthy fixation, and she needed to get a grip. This uncontrollable feeling was nothing but animal attraction, but—*mama. What an animal.*

She'd almost reached out to touch that six-pack just to know if that abdominal wall was as solid as it appeared. What did the guy do? Live at the gym?

Thank heavens she'd kept her hands to herself, although further examination would've been purely medical. *Yeah, right.* His medical condition wasn't why her heart banged at the back of her throat. Well, kind of it was. Every rare specimen deserved a thorough examination, didn't it? Didn't he?

Shelby composed her nerves as much as she could. She had work to do. This crazy infatuation had to stop. Opening Kelsey's bedroom door, she peered inside.

Kelsey looked up from where she sat at the edge of her bed.

"Can I help you with your shower?" Shelby asked, her voice squeakier and her mouth drier than she'd intended.

Kelsey looked up from where she sat at the edge of her bed. "Thanks, but I'm already done. I have a favor to ask, though. Could you reach the box on the top shelf in my closet while you're here? I can't grab onto it with my fingers like they are. It keeps slipping."

"You bet." Helping Kelsey was easy and Shelby needed someone else to think about. She retrieved the box, and would've made Kelsey's bed for her, but it was already tucked in for the day, the pillows fluffed, the drapes opened.

"You're doing really good for a lady with four broken fingers."

"I manage. The plastic bags you suggested for my hands worked perfectly in the shower. Good thinking, Shelby."

Shelby placed the boxes on the bed. "Is here okay?"

"Yes, thank you." Kelsey lifted the lid off the nearest.

The boxes were full of carefully indexed photographs, each index card dated in black ink with feminine handwriting. She'd just given Kelsey a time bomb of memories.

Oh, no. What have I done?

Shelby sank to the bed. "Are you sure you want to do this right now? Wouldn't you rather sit on the couch or something?" *Play with your dogs. Read a book. Anything but this.*

Splinted fingers tapped over the index cards. "No. This is exactly what I want to do right now."

God, why not wait a year or two until you're over him? Give yourself time to heal, to find someone else. To move on.

"Can I at least help you find what you're looking for?" Shelby asked, her heart in her throat.

"No. I've got it. This. Just this." Kelsey pulled out an envelope of photos, her lips pinched in a thin line of determination. She spilled them to the comforter, spreading them like a deck of playing cards. "I want to introduce you to my husband, Shelby. We took these on our honeymoon. This is the man I love. This is Alexander Bradley Stewart."

Shelby swallowed hard, taking the photo Kelsey offered. She'd used one very definite word: *love, not loved.* Shelby adjusted her thinking accordingly. If Kelsey wasn't ready to use the past tense, neither would she.

The happy couple in the wedding picture melted her heart. Kelsey's smile filled her whole face, but the man standing behind her? Utterly drop-dead gorgeous.

Alex stood at least a foot taller than Kelsey, dark-haired and debonair, his arms around her and his hands interlocked over her stomach, his chin tucked into her neck and his eyes on the camera. They were both dressed formally, her in a long, ruffled gown, her bare toes peeking out from beneath the hem. He wore a proper black tux and shoes, but the light in his blue eyes? Pure adoration.

What a hunk.

"That was taken on the beach at Waikiki. Sunset. We'd just said our vows." Kelsey rummaged for another shot. "Here. Look at this one."

In the next shot, she faced him, her hands on his chest and his heart very much on display in those sexy blues. What a romantic couple. They glowed and it wasn't from the pink sunset tinting her white gown, either. Love and lust emanated from both of them. The perfect couple.

"My goodness, you two look amazing. How did you meet? How did he propose to you? Why did you choose Hawaii?" A plethora of questions filled her head stemming from a need to know this man and woman better.

"That's another story, but this picture..." Kelsey placed another in Shelby's hands. "This is my favorite."

Shelby took the image carefully, a lone shot of Alex walking out of the blue Pacific ocean toward the picture taker, which had to be Kelsey, judging by the smirk on his handsome face. With his athletically sculpted body still wet from the surf behind him, he was the epitome of relaxed. Tan. Sexier than hell, and maybe a little bit hungry for the woman in his sights. Swimming trunks hung off his hips, adding to a truly delicious photo. A snorkel and mask hung off his fingers by a strap. The man definitely had his swagger on.

"That was at Hanama Bay. I was sunbathing—well, kind of. I had more fun watching him snorkel. I swear, the man isn't afraid of anything. Alex can be such a tease. He walked straight out of the surf and didn't stop until he spilled a scuba mask full of cold water all over me." She rubbed her biceps. "We had so much fun acting like kids again."

"You married a very handsome man," Shelby said. "What a cute couple you two were."

A shadow shifted over Kelsey's face, and Shelby wanted to call the word back.

Were. Not are.

"The thing is..." Kelsey's eyes brimmed, ". . . it doesn't matter where he is, Shelby. Maybe he really is gone. Maybe I'll even believe that someday. But Alex doesn't have to be here in this room for me to feel him. Wherever he is, he's thinking of me right now, and he's loving me. Maybe that's what I sense when I finally fall asleep. Maybe that's why I can still feel the man who owns every beat of my heart, every breath I take. You're young, but one day you'll understand. When love comes to you, I hope your man will love you as deeply and as purely as I know my man loves me, wherever he is."

She stilled, her fingers caressing the rugged face of her man in the photo. "Because there is only true love, Shelby. Once it springs to life, it cannot end. No one but you can kill it. There is no 'he *loved* me.' Only 'he *loves* me.' And I'll love him until the day I die."

Chapter Fourteen

Damn it. David again. He was fast becoming another Harley, only calmer. Methodical. And still barking up the wrong tree.

Mark clenched his jaw and hunkered down to listen to more logic. Once again, they were head-to-head in Alex's office, out of earshot. David had come up with some damned convincing evidence that Alex might be alive, but try as he might, Mark knew better.

God, he wanted to believe in fairy tales. So what if the ME and the FBI were covering something up? So what if Sam Becker's clever little bullet carried no heat signature? The FBI had funding. The damned round might have been a smart bullet. At the end of the day, none of these speculations mattered. Eyes don't lie. They don't. Maybe in a magic act in Vegas they did, but not in the damned morgue and cemetery.

David pursed his lips. "Let's assume Alex is still alive."

"So assume. What next?"

"I believe he'd do everything possible to contact us, don't you?"

"At least he'd contact Kelsey," Mark murmured, "and since she believes he rescued her, maybe he's already been in touch with her. Is that where you're headed?"

"Who else would've stayed with her those three days in a vacant home?"

"We're assuming a lot here, but okay. He would've made sure she was safe before he left her."

"He also took very good care of her. Like you would've done with Libby."

"I guess," Mark admitted.

"And he placed an anonymous call that directed us straight to her because he knew we'd protect her. He trusts us, Mark."

This was a lot of guessing and assuming over a man with three holes in his chest, embalmed, and supposed to be six feet under, but okay. If David wanted to play guessing games, what the hell?

"If our first assumption is valid, why hasn't Alex come out in the open?" David asked, still probing and still working on Mark's last nerve.

Because he's dead, Mark thought, but he played along and said, "I guess he would if he could."

"Exactly."

David was a lot like Mark, a behind-the-scenes kind of a man, steady and calm while others, like Alex and Harley, tended to overreact. Not David. He was the rock, not so much unemotional as extremely thoughtful and analytical.

He seemed the steadiest of the three senior agents, and Mark was grateful to have him. But the man was obsessed, and Mark couldn't for the life of him understand why. It seemed he was fighting his team. Every last one of them.

"I've lain awake every night since it happened," David continued. "I know Alex as well as you. He's the sharpshooter we all want to be, but he's also the best ghost out there. I've seen him at work. He can get into places the rest of us wouldn't think of going and never be seen again.

The man doesn't even need a ghillie suit. He just evaporates into thin air."

"But he'd never hurt Kelsey, David. If he isn't dead, this bullshit game he's playing is killing her. Hell, it's killing all of us."

"You're right. He'd never hurt Kelsey or his team—if he could help it."

"So you think maybe he can't help it?"

As much as Mark hated to admit it, David's assumptions answered a lot of questions. The only problem was the truth kept getting in the way.

"But I saw him, David. So did you."

"And it was a very traumatic experience for all of us. We were highly susceptible to misdirection."

"I guess." Mark scrubbed his face with both hands, tired of remembering.

All it did was bring the nightmare back in living, *dying* color, and he wanted to forget. No, he needed to forget because more and more, it forced him into the role of devil's advocate, the one who argued that Alex was dead. The last place Mark wanted to be.

"How is Kelsey?" David changed the subject.

"She's hurting. She looks more like the living dead than—"

"Jesus Christ! What the hell do you want now?" Maverick bellowed loud and angry from the work bay. "The shirt off my back? Every last ounce of my blood? What, you sonofabitchin' asshole? Spit it the hell out of your lying mouth!"

"Get off me, Carson! Back off before I hurt you!"

By the time Mark and David got out the door, Connor had Maverick in an arm lock. Maverick looked lethal, his chest heaving, his face red and his jaw tight. Landon lay flat on his back with Izza's knee in his chest. Lisa Channing stood behind Izza, her eyes bright with tears that hadn't spilled yet.

What the hell? This was a first—a brawl in the office.

Maverick jerked out of Connor's grasp but Landon stayed put because Izza wouldn't let him move, not with her knee at his throat.

"What the hell's going on?" Mark asked.

"Nothing," Maverick said angrily. "Forget it."

"These guys broke my coffee maker." Mother glared at Mark as if that was his fault, too. Wasn't everything?

Mark looked to Landon for an answer, but he was no more talkative than Maverick.

Izza had no problem, though. "They're fighting over Channing, Boss."

"Are not!" Maverick spat, thumbing his chin, still ready to fight. "I couldn't care less that they're sleeping together. They deserve each other."

The guy seemed wound tight, ready to take a swing at Connor. Good luck with that. Connor had grown up with a few brothers in Boston, plus he'd married Izza. He knew a few things about kickboxing and playing dirty.

"Let him up, Izza," Mark ordered.

This kind of foolishness would've never happened with Alex, mostly because he scared the hell out of his new agents. He was taciturn, rude, and downright oblivious to the newbies until they stepped up to the plate and proved themselves worthy of his notice.

Landon rolled to his feet, still silent, but his upper lip lifted in a smirk.

Maverick already stood at his desk, his back to the rest of the office and his shoulders heaving.

"Clean this mess up," Mark ordered.

"I'll get it," Maverick rasped.

Terrific. More trouble.

"Team. Meeting. Now!" Mark barked.

The Sit Room filled with a couple of sullen team members, Maverick and Mother.

She still had an attitude Mark couldn't pin down. She sat in her usual position, which would've put her at Alex's right if he'd been there. Only now that Mark had unofficially taken over, it put her between Landon, who'd taken Alex's chair, and Lisa. Mother's lips were pursed, her arms folded over her chest as if she had some place better to be.

"Team," Mark began quietly, "I've made a mess of things. I've been pushing you guys pretty hard—maybe too hard. With Gabe and Zack on duty at Kelsey's, we're two men short. Guess I need to take a step back and adjust workload."

"You're not telling us everything you know, either," Mother snapped. Her lips stuck out like a petulant high school prom queen's.

"What haven't I told you?" Mark had to ask. He thought he'd been forthcoming with all the intelligence they'd gathered so far. *What have I missed?*

"You didn't tell us right away when Harley's boys were born. I tried to call him all last night, but he wouldn't pick up. You should've told us the minute you knew. Alex would have."

God. How on earth did Alex ever deal with these people?

"You're right. That's important. I should've made that announcement sooner."

She studied her brightly-colored acrylic nails.

"Would you take up a collection for the Mortimer family?" Mark asked, kissing her ass despite his inclination to kick it.

Her face brightened. "Yes, Boss—I mean, Mark. I'd be happy to do that *for Harley and Judy.*"

He caught the jab. Apparently, her problem resided with him. "Have you checked into exhumation, like I asked?"

"Not yet. I've been busy with Steven finding the shooter." She kept pushing.

"Have it on my desk by tomorrow morning." Mark pushed back. "I need to tell Kelsey we're doing what she asked. Anyone else got something to say?"

"Just give us marching orders," Rory spoke right up. "You lead. We follow."

"How's Kelsey's car coming?"

"We're down to loose ends. Nothing that can't keep."

Connor slid a file across the table. "Yeah. Let me know if you need any of these findings explained, but Rory's right. We're ready for another job."

"Good to know. Steven?" Mark turned to the other quiet man in the room, relieved he didn't have to fight everyone.

"Yes, sir. I have further analysis of the weapon and rounds that actually hit the victim." He flipped on the overhead video. The extremely slow motion and close-up clip showed FBI Agent Becker's unusual weapon and the projectile fired from it.

Mark hadn't seen a rifle like it, nor had he seen the oblong rounds tumbling end over end until they hit the windshield and shattered the glass. Alex slumped forward. Becker fired again. The second and third shots caused identical damage.

Ember whimpered.

It was god-awful hard to watch.

"What the hell kind of projectile is that?"

Steven calmly continued. "Not sure, but take a close look at the rifle, sir."

Mark watched while Becker disassembled his weapon. It wasn't the standard issued M-40 rifle, the M107 fifty-cal Browning machine gun, or the M-110 semi-automatic Marines used. This barrel was long, but much too wide, the buttstock compact. Downright short.

Instead of a magazine, Becker detached a rounded canister from the bottom slide. The whole damned thing fit in an ordinary gym bag.

"You ever seen anything like it before?" Mark asked Steven.

"No, sir. I have not."

"What kind of ammo?"

Steven cringed. "I'm still not sure if it is ammo, Boss, umm, damn it. Sorry, Mark."

"Still no heat signature?"

"Not one we'd expect from a 10-millimeter."

"It almost looks like a paintball gun," Rory commented.

Steven's report roused everyone's attention, but Mark wasn't about to send his team on a ghost hunt. There was a logical explanation behind all this misleading evidence.

There has to be, damn it.

"Good work, everyone. Steven, since you discovered the shooter, take the lead in tracking Becker down. Who do you want to work with?"

"Taylor and Izza, sir."

"Sorry. They're tracking the last five suspects." Mark turned to Izza. "How's that going?"

Her brows narrowed. "I can't find them. They're nowhere."

Taylor spoke up. "Right. No physical street addresses. Only post-office boxes. Stevenson has a mother in Oklahoma, but she hasn't heard from him in years. Said she doesn't want to."

"None of those jerks are even married," Izza added. "Every last one of them is divorced. We checked DMV records, too. We can't find anything but the police records we showed you earlier, and even then they have no forwarding."

"All five of these guys are off the grid," Taylor said, "What's worse, they've been virtually non-existent since they left the service, which is downright scary now that we know what they're capable of. It's as if they've been planning revenge on Alex for years."

Acid flooded Mark's gut. Damn Charlie Oakes to hell. He might not have been the mastermind to this *gang of ten* plot, but he should've alerted Alex to it a helluva lot sooner.

"How about you let me and Connor take a shot at finding them?" Rory asked. "That'll free up Izza and Taylor to assist Steven, and you know what they say about a second pair of eyes."

Leave it to Rory to offer a viable option. "Thanks. Good idea. Consider it done. Mother, can you help with Becker's cell phone and GPS, maybe get an angle on him so Steven knows where to start?"

"Yes, Mark," she answered primly, her eyes still on her fake nails. Whatever bug had climbed up her butt, it seemed to have taken up permanent residence.

"Good. The minute we know where the five are, we make our next move."

"What is our next move?" Rory asked.

"Ha. You and Connor go introduce yourselves, whatcha think?" Izza smirked as she gave Rory a high five. "Tell me. I want to go with you."

Rory smacked her open palm. "Trust me. I'm all for that. The quicker we nab these dogs, the better."

"Izza's right," Mark agreed. "Any other questions?"

No one spoke.

"Good. Report in every hour, on the hour. Stay safe. Maverick. Hang back a minute."

The room cleared. Mark blew out a big sigh. No wonder Alex called this business his stupidest idea ever. It only took a couple disgruntled employees to ruin it for everyone.

He faced the angry man to his left. Hands down, Maverick was the better agent. He did a hard day's work every day, while Landon seemed more enamored with Lisa Channing.

Maverick lifted his chin and ground out between clenched teeth, "I don't give a shit if those two are banging each other's brains out."

"Me neither. Wish they'd keep it out of the office, though. You want to tell me what's going on?"

Maverick's nostrils flared. He all but snorted, the cords in his neck as tight as his fists. Mark didn't get the feeling he wanted to take a swing at him. He didn't answer the question, though.

Mark opted for the middle line. "Guess I owe Mother a new coffee pot."

"I'll take care of that, sir. I started the fight."

"That's not like you, Maverick. Come on. I can't help you if I don't know what's going on."

Nothing broke through. Maverick's expression turned to stone.

Good enough. Mark would chalk it up to the stress of two assassination attempts, one fatal. "When this is done, we all need to head on down to O'Connell's and throw back a few. You in?"

Maverick pushed his chair from the table and stood. "Will that be all, sir? I have a mess to clean up."

Mark let him leave. A man wound that tight needed more than conversation and a beer. He needed a friend. One thing was clear. Whatever had happened between him and Landon, it was bad.

Chapter Fifteen

"So where is she?" Zack asked. "She's not in the house. Where'd she go?"

"What? Who? Kelsey?" Gabe jumped up from the kitchen table. He'd made the plaster casts and barely reheated the spinach omelet Nurse Sullivan had left for him.

"I'm right here," Shelby said from the guestroom doorway. "Did you check her bathroom?"

The way the Stewarts' house was built, the front door opened into the living room and then immediately led to the kitchen. The hall branched off the front room with Kelsey's bedroom to the south, the guest bedroom to the north. She couldn't have gotten past Zack, Gabe, or sharp-eyed Nurse Sullivan, either.

"Why do you think I'm looking for her outside?" Zack peered out the back window.

Gabe ran to Kelsey's bedroom, Nurse Sullivan on his heels. The door stood ajar. It was a small enough room, all of it visible from the hall. Photographs littered the bed, but there was no sign of her.

No way. No one could've gotten in or out of here.

"This is my fault. She wanted me to know Alex," Nurse Sullivan murmured. "We were looking at old photographs. I know it wasn't good for her, but she needed to see them, you know?"

The raw anxiety in her voice brought Gabe up short. "What's wrong with you?"

"I'm sorry. I just meant to help. She's so sad."

And then he heard it, the softest murmur. Gabe didn't have time to worry about Sullivan. The closet door was barely open. He peered inside. Kelsey sat on the floor in a heap of clothing. An over-sized sweatshirt swamped her tiny frame with big bold USMC stenciled in yellow across it. She held a crumpled T-shirt against her teary face, breathing deeply into the cotton fabric, her eyes red and swollen.

Gabe sank to his knees beside her, his heart lodged up high in his throat. The poor thing was falling apart. "We thought you ran away and left us."

She offered him the T-shirt. "He was here. He really was. Here. Smell."

God, I know he lived, sweetheart, but now he's gone...

Gabe took the shirt, wanting to hold her instead. "We couldn't find you."

"But..." She hiccupped a noisy sob. "I'm not lying. He really was here, Gabe."

"I know." Tears stung his eyes. "We believe you. Honest, we do."

Zack bellowed from the back door of the house. "Cartwright! You find her?"

"Here," Gabe called out. "We're in her bedroom closet." *With all the ghosts...*

"What the f—?" Zack shut his mouth when he caught sight of Kelsey. He dropped to one knee at the door, the wind knocked right out of his sails. His tone softened. The man could pour on the honey, and if ever there was a time, it was now. "Kels. Honey. What are you doing in here all by yourself? Are you looking for something?"

Dumb question, bro. Of course she's looking for something. Him.

She buried her face in the front of the USMC sweatshirt and cried. "Alex. I just want him back. I don't want to hurt like this anymore."

Nurse Sullivan angled her shoulder past Zack's, reaching for Kelsey's arm. "Let's get you out of there and—"

"No. I want to sit here and... and..."

"And think about him," Gabe finished.

She nodded, her eyes brimming with tears. "Yes. I don't ever want to forget him."

"Then by God, if you want to sit here, that's what you're going to do." He rolled to his butt and sat cross-legged alongside her, fingering the old T-shirt. "We need some tissues in here, Zack."

Distress shifted through Nurse Sullivan's features, but Gabe didn't care. Right then and there, Kelsey could've asked for the moon and he'd have found a way to deliver.

Zack tossed Gabe the tissue box off the nearest nightstand, and Gabe transferred a handful to Kelsey. Nurse Sullivan leaned against Kelsey's bed, watching, her arms crossed over her chest, her spectacled expression nearly as sad as Kelsey's. Something was up with her, but Gabe could only deal with one unhappy woman at a time. Sullivan was on her own.

"Hey, Zack, you ever seen such an organized closet?" Gabe changed the subject while Kelsey sniffed and dabbed her face with the tissues.

The choking sounds coming from the back of her throat were killing him. It was like watching his best friend fall in Afghanistan all over again. There wasn't one day Darrell Carson's bright smiling face didn't show up to remind Gabe of the aching hole in his heart. How much worse to have lost half of that heart, your eternal companion, the one and only one you'd given your body and soul to?

"My gosh, Kels. Did Alex color code everything in here or what?" Zack asked gently.

She took a minute to blow her nose. "Kind of. He... he always wanted everything to be ready... just in case he, umm, had to leave suddenly."

Gabe smoothed his hand over the cuff of an expensive suit jacket hanging overhead. "Very nice. Your man knew how to dress."

"That's cashmere," Zack agreed quietly. "No wonder the boss always looked sharp. Did you help him shop?"

"Ah, huh. He and I... He..." She couldn't finish, the tissue shredded at her fingertips.

"You can feel him in here, can't you?" Gabe asked.

Kelsey nodded. When she leaned into his bicep, he pulled her into a hug. They rocked back and forth together like two little kids, and he was glad the closet was dark. She needed someone to hold onto. She was lost right now, that was all. And he was her protector—one of many, judging by the looks on Zack and Nurse Sullivan's faces.

Hell, if The TEAM had been there, every last one of them would've been crowded inside that closet with him. And they'd all be bawling and trying to act tough while they did it. Like him. He sneaked a hand across his face.

"It's like... it's like I'm on a roller coaster," she whined, the T-shirt retrieved once more and held snug against her cheek and nose. "One minute I'm... I'm doing okay, and the next minute, I'm falling and... and I can't catch onto anything. I can't stop myself. I just... keep... falling."

"That's why we're here." Gabe pulled her close again, his voice tight. "You hang onto me and old man Lennox. We'll keep you from falling, but if you do, we'll keep picking you back up. Promise."

She nodded, but sucked in another trembling breath. "And it's hard to breathe, you know? Sometimes I can't get any air. My lungs squeeze shut as if they don't want to work without him anymore, either."

"Stress," Zack said matter-of-factly. "A lot of guys hyperventilate in times of stress."

"Like war zones," Gabe added. "It's a traumatic stress indicator. Believe me, I know."

"PTSD?" Kelsey asked quietly. "You, too?"

"No, not really, but, yeah. Maybe a little," Gabe admitted in a round-about way. PTSD was one of those monikers that could stick with a guy. He'd avoided the label until now, but if it helped Kelsey, he was fine using it. "It still sneaks up on me sometimes, so if you ever see me on my back gasping for air like a fish outta water—"

"Smack him," Zack finished jokingly.

"Yeah," Gabe agreed, determined to downplay his panic attacks. Kelsey had real problems. She didn't need to worry about him. "Throw cold water on me. Pound me. That usually works."

"It's amazing how fast he snaps out of it when I thump him in the solar plexus," Zack teased.

"I'd never hit you, Gabe," Kelsey whispered.

"I know. You're a lady, but Zack's a guy. That's just what dumb jocks do to each other. I sure as hell wouldn't want him hugging me, would you?"

Zack huffed. "No way I'm hugging a guy, but I'll hug Kelsey any damned time she wants. Can I get you a glass of water, honey? Maybe a cup of tea?"

"Water would be nice," Gabe answered. "I am kinda thirsty."

"Not you. You're no honey of mine. Hell, Gabe. Get your sorry butt out of there and get your own damned water. I meant *her*. I'm here for Kelsey, not you."

The friendly sparring match broke the spell. Kelsey let Gabe pull her up from the floor and in no time at all, they were back at her kitchen table. Zack must've brought Whisper and Smoke inside with him when he'd gone looking for Kelsey. They were sprawled across the kitchen floor, two shaggy fur rugs he had to step over on his way to get the coffee, cream, and sugar.

Instead of joining them in the kitchen, Nurse Sullivan opted to sit in the front room, a magazine in her hand.

"Hey, Shelby. Come have a cup of coffee," Gabe offered, finally using her first name instead of the stuffy title she'd insisted on. This could be their first, no-kidding family-type meal together. Kelsey might enjoy that.

"No. I don't drink coffee." Shelby shot a disparaging look to the dogs, so Gabe let it go. *Fine. Whatever. Dog germs. I get it.* He focused on Kelsey.

"Harley has PTSD, too," she murmured.

"Yes, ma'am, he does. Mine's not that bad," Gabe agreed. "His version's more debilitating when it kicks in. I just get anxiety attacks, but not as often as I used to. Loud noises trigger mine, and, bam. I'm back in the sandbox."

Zack poured three cups of coffee and set them on the table. "It's different for all of us, Kels."

"Does everyone who goes into combat get it?" Kelsey asked.

"Some do, but you don't have to be in combat to get it. I still hate fireworks," he replied as he placed the coffee carafe back on the coffeemaker. "The girls love 'em, but I don't."

"What do you do on the Fourth of July then?"

"I light them like any other daddy on the black. Can't spoil the day for LiLi, Song, or Miki just because I'm jumpy, but I don't buy the noisy kind. Not anymore. Had enough of the real ones."

Kelsey lifted her steaming cup and took a sip. "You have sweet little girls. What about you, Gabe?"

He shrugged, the cup in his hand too hot to drink. "I still hit the dirt every time a car backfires. It's normal. I think every other guy and gal who's been in combat probably does too. No big deal. When you go through tough times, you get a little beat up in the process. Don't feel like you're all alone, Kelsey. Look around. You're in danged good company even if I do say so myself."

"I'm glad you're both here. Shelby, too."

Gabe glanced at the back of Nurse Sullivan's head. Something was still up with her and he was fairly certain it had nothing to do with her control issues, not if that tear in her eye meant what he thought it meant. She'd connected with Kelsey's heartbreak by the look on her face and Gabe empathized with her. The ripple of Alex's death touched everyone, even hardcore Marines and nurses.

Whisper came to sit by Kelsey. Absentmindedly, she ruffled his furry face, but that wasn't enough for the big dog. He put one huge paw on her knee, then the other.

Gabe lifted out of his seat. "Here. I'll put them outside."

"No. It's okay. He's trying to tell me something. Whisper can talk, you know." Kelsey leaned into Whisper's forehead. The black dog leaned against hers, growling softly in his gravelly voice as if he really were confiding a secret. "Tell me, Whisper. What do you know?"

He barked quietly once, spun around in a complete turn and went to the back door, pawing to be let out.

Kelsey followed him. "This reminds me of the game we used to play. Let me try something." She knelt in front of Whisper, her hands in the ruffled mane at his neck. "Find him, Whisper. Find Alex."

And *blam*. Whisper and Smoke went ballistic, howling, prancing, and filling the house with such a racket.

Gabe about choked, those plaster casts and the boot prints first thing on his mind. *Shit. What if Whisper goes directly there?*

The minute Kelsey opened the back door, they roared out with her right behind them. Gabe followed with Zack close on his heels.

Just as Gabe feared, Whisper and Smoke led Kelsey to the location of the boot tracks. They had been safely obliterated, but that didn't stop the dogs from putting those vacuum cleaner snouts to the ground and doing what they did best—scenting. In seconds, both dropped to their haunches right where Gabe had poured the plaster castings, their bright eyes fixed on Kelsey and their mission accomplished.

He gulped. Damned if they hadn't scented Alex like she'd asked them to, which meant nothing, not in the man's own property. Of course they'd scent him. He'd lived there. But why only there? Why not anywhere else in the yard?

"What are you boys doing? There's nothing here." Kelsey looked thoughtfully around the swing.

Gabe followed her eyes. There was no place for a man to hide, not with the wisteria gone. He'd cleaned the mess after the plaster casts were poured and set. Nothing remained.

She peered up at him, concern etched on her crinkled brow. "I don't understand. They've tracked you, Gabe. Why?"

Whisper bumped his shoulder against her leg and sat at her feet. Damn it to hell. Those big black eyes of his focused on Gabe as if the animal dared him to say anything but the truth, which at the moment, Gabe honestly did not know.

Zack shot him a stern look and Gabe meant to obey, but now he wondered. Whisper and Smoke were two of the best trackers around. Zack might not like it, but oh, well. Gabe couldn't take any more meltdowns in the closet.

He cleared his throat. "Are you up for a ride, Kelsey?"

Zack frowned right on cue, his pursed lips twisted to the side and one brow lifted in a *'Don't you say one more word, Cartwright.'*

"Where?" she asked wearily. Whisper's bright eyes still stared at Gabe in that deadpanned way of a good dog that can see right through a man.

"To the river. Let's go back to where it happened."

The depth of her devastation stabbed him. "Why?"

"Because I heard you talking to your dogs before, and I think you're right. There has to be a reason Alex can't come home right now. If you believe he rescued you, then so do I." Gabe crouched and steadied her with a hand to her shoulder, for the first time really meaning every word he said. Something was going on or the dogs wouldn't have both scented their owner as quickly as they had. It was time to put an end to her confusion, once and for all. "Come on. Let's prove he really was at that river. What do you say?"

Zack stood behind her, shaking his head with a definite negatory, but Gabe kept going. Call it insubordination or call it inspiration. This was what Kelsey needed, and she'd keep breaking down until she knew one way or the other.

She pulled Whisper into her arms, a desperate sob climbing up her throat. "But what if it wasn't him?"

Ah. So that's what's really going on. Her poor heart was at war with logic.

"I don't know," he answered honestly.

She groaned, and the pain in her voice took him back to the wailing women in Afghanistan. All the mothers, wives, and daughters who'd lost children, husbands and fathers to a lifetime of war. Always the ones left behind, he was forever amazed at the strength of women to endure—and to suffer.

He squeezed her shoulder. "You know what? Never mind. You're worn out. You take it easy while me and the dogs run the riverbank for you. I'll take a video of the whole thing. We'll pop popcorn when I get back and make a regular movie night of it. Sound good?"

"I don't know." Whisper pushed her to her butt and settled into her lap like a poodle instead of the lumbering moose he was.

"Zack?" Gabe asked brightly, despite the stink-eye he was getting from his agent in charge. "Well? Can you hold down the fort or not? I won't be gone long."

Zack had a way of making a guy think he could kill them just by looking at them. He'd arch his left brow in a damned sharp spike. But not now. He grunted all the way to his toes in definite disapproval, but Gabe saw the hesitation through the tough guy routine.

He pushed the limit. "You said it yourself. If anyone can track Alex, it's his dogs. If we'd done this a few days ago, we wouldn't be having this conversation now, would we?"

Zack stretched both arms behind his head, his forehead wrinkled up to his scalp. "What if they do? What then?"

"Then I'll know he's coming home someday," Kelsey whispered. "And I can wait for him, Zack. You know Alex as well as I do. He'd never hurt me. He wouldn't. He'll come back for me."

This gentle lady only wanted a shred of hope to hang onto. Zack didn't seem too opposed to the idea, either, especially since the dogs had tracked their owner to those mysterious boot prints in record time. It didn't hurt that Kelsey had just pinned him with her sad eyes, either. Who could resist?

He stalled.

Come on, big guy. Loosen up. Let me do this one little thing for her. Right damned now.

Finally, Zack offered her his arm. "Come on, Kels. You need to rest while he's gone or you'll be sick again."

Gabe shot him a quick nod of thanks. One of these days he'd have to tell Zack about that revoked license. Not today. "Should we let Mark know what I'm doing?"

"I'll take care of it. Just don't take all day."

Gabe winked at Kelsey. "Remember? Movie tonight. My treat."

Chapter Sixteen

In one day, this job had turned into one of her hardest.

Shelby couldn't read the magazine articles in front of her nose. She wasn't needed. And she certainly wasn't in charge. Agent Lennox and Cartwright had made that clear. They seemed somehow in tune with Kelsey, and Shelby was the odd man out.

The nerve of Gabe to hug Kelsey while armed with those loaded guns of his. Yet he'd hugged her as if he'd never let her go. And she'd hugged him back and cried into his shirt, the last thing Shelby needed to watch. Everything she'd tried to do ended up being wrong or at least inadequate. Especially letting Kelsey look at all those old pictures.

Gah! I should've known better!

But that wasn't what hurt the most. Listening to Kelsey explain how the simple act of breathing hurt—what should've been the automatic reflexive action of drawing air in and exhaling—brought the true nature of grief and loss home. Kelsey carried an invisible hole in her heart, still raw and weeping.

For that one moment, her pain was tangible, a wave of sorrow, and a wash of lost love that would never be again. If there were any way possible, Shelby would've reversed time and not pulled all those reminders of Mr. Stewart out of the closet. She would've come up with a diversion, anything to forestall dragging her kind patient through the anguish of missing her husband again.

And yet, what would it be like to love a man so deeply that your lungs didn't want to take another breath without him? To be so smitten with your mate that you believed he surpassed all other males in the world, that you only had eyes for him even though he was gone? To ache so desperately, to need so intimately that you wanted to die instead of live without him?

Shelby set the stupid magazine aside. She'd worked hard to be independent, a strong woman in her own right and totally capable. She rented a comfortable apartment in a singles-only gated community in Silver Springs, drove the latest model, a new eco-friendly car, and had a good reputation as a home healthcare provider. True, it was a second chance after the debacle at the hospital, but she'd worked hard and she was good at it. Only—

Kelsey had so much more. She'd loved and been loved. No, make that adored. Any fool could see how much her dead husband had cherished her.

Shelby fingered the magazine cover, not seeing the glamorous starlet sprawled across the gossip rag. What would it feel like to be worshipped, loved so perfectly that living in this little cracker-box house with neighbors who didn't take care of their yards or put their garbage receptacles away after garbage day, was—*enough? Maybe more than enough? Maybe everything?*

What had she said? *There is no loved, only love?*

Shelby stilled. Her heart pinched, constricting all she thought she knew about love right out of her.

The back door opened as the men and Kelsey trudged back in, the dogs, too. Shelby brushed her emotions off her face and lifted to her feet, prepared to get on with the business of doing what she did best. Putting on a happy face. Doing the best she could to make up for past mistakes. Trying harder.

She didn't expect to run smack into the wall of Agent Cartwright's muscled chest while Kelsey and Zack settled at the table behind him.

He and Agent Lennox were the epitome of respect. He dipped his head the way polite men did when they encountered a lady. "Sorry, ma'am. I didn't mean to startle you, but when I asked you before what was wrong, I meant it sincerely. What's going on, Shelby? You're different today. Are you feeling okay?"

Her ears perked up. *He said my name again. Wow. Twice in one day.*

She cleared her throat and stabbed her glasses up high on the bridge of her nose, determined he not see any hesitation on her part. Nurses were decisive, in-charge types of people. She might be just a CNA, but she would be nothing less than the professional he was. "I'm fine. Did you get the omelet I made for you? Was it okay?"

He scrunched his lips, drawing her attention to his mouth and—every darn muscle below her waist clenched. *What is it about this guy?* He was nothing but a hick in combat boots, one of those backwoods folks from who knew where.

"Sorry. I got distracted when Kelsey went missing, only she wasn't. Bet it was good," he drawled. And that was another thing. Gabe Cartwright had a definite western twang to his rumbling bass, the very last thing she cared to hear. It made him sound uneducated. Lazy. Kind of sexy...

"I'll make you another," she offered to get her roaming mind off his tongue and mouth.

"No, that's okay. I'll grab something else. May I ask you something, ma'am? If it's not too personal?"

Shelby shrugged. Nothing had stopped him from bugging her before.

He lowered his voice. "You thought this job would be easy, didn't you?"

Okay, anything but that. Just because he was in tune with Kelsey didn't give him the right to jump to conclusions about her. No one needed to think for a second that Shelby Sullivan couldn't handle a grieving widow.

The self-told lie would've worked if the tenderest glimmer hadn't lit those green eyes of his. There he was, all six-foot-plus tough guy blocking the doorway with broad shoulders, and he was kind and considerate after she'd been nothing but demanding. How could he?

"Yes," she admitted quietly. "I don't know what to say to her sometimes. I've never lost anyone." *And I feel so helpless when she starts crying. I never know what to do.*

"All you can tell her is you're sorry," he said quietly, as if he'd read her mind. "Losing Alex is something we're all trying to wrap our heads around. Death is a sucker punch we don't often see coming. It knocks you down and stomps the hell out of you, but eventually you'll get back on your feet. Kelsey needs a little more time. She'll come around." He paused, his chest expanding as he drew in a deep breath. "We all will."

Shelby's eyes filled. How did she not realize until now? Agent Cartwright was grieving as much as Kelsey. He'd lost Alex, too. So had Zack. Darn. The whole house was full of people with real problems, and she'd been awful to most of them.

"I don't think I can do this." Her inadequacy and arrogance slapped her down. Maybe all those drawling hicks weren't as backward as she'd thought. Maybe she was just as bad and sad as those poor people who'd labeled themselves handicapped or divorced. Maybe she'd been the one doing the pigeonholing.

"You've all... I mean, you and Zack... I mean, Umm, I'm sorry for your loss, Gabe," she offered pitifully, using his name the way he'd used hers. *I'm sorry for everything.*

"Hey." He claimed her wrist with one big hand, and she was snared. His fingers circled her wrist with plenty of room to spare, but he didn't hurt her. If anything, he was too gentle. As if he didn't want to break her. Or scare her.

"Don't worry about me. Kelsey's our one and only mission, remember? We're all here to keep her safe and help her get back on her feet, as long as it takes."

Shelby nodded. Humility wasn't her strong suit, but for once she and he were actually communicating. And that hand. He'd tightened his grip enough that she could feel the pad of his index finger placed precisely on the pulse at her wrist. Had he done that intentionally? Did he have any clue what his close proximity did to her heart rate?

"Listen, I need you to do something for me." He cast a backward glance over his shoulder. His voice had already dipped to rumbling sexy. Any deeper and she'd melt, and darn it, why did he unsettle her? Guys with a redneck drawl and who played with guns weren't her type, and she definitely had a type. Suave. Educated. Upwardly mobile. Tuxedo dapper. Never military. Or blue collar. Or dog lovers. Or—

God, I am prejudiced.

"I'm taking the dogs back to the river where this all started. Can you keep Kelsey upbeat while I'm gone? Don't let her look at any more old photos though, okay? Play Monopoly or UNO or something. Bake her a cake. Just don't let her do anything that will make her any sadder."

An ember that Shelby had ignored for years flamed into a wildfire. She took a step closer to him, trying to see beyond the light in his eyes. Was he toying with her or was he—just. That. Kind?

"I didn't mean to make her sad," she told him honestly, the heat from his body noticeable and—hot. Enticingly hot. Temptingly hot. A whiff of musky men's shaving lotion struck her nostrils. She nearly lost her train of thought. "I, umm, didn't mean to make her cry."

He loomed over her, blocking the view of the kitchen behind him. "Oh, I know. You only meant to help, but it's unavoidable. Kelsey's heart is broken. It'll take time to heal. Might never."

"Why are you leaving?" She bit her tongue for that stupid question. *Let him leave. What do I care?*

"Because if Alex is the one who pulled her out of the river, his scent will still be on the riverbank. His dogs will track him. Do this one thing for me? Please?"

Gah! If he hadn't cocked his head like a little boy pleading for another chocolate chip cookie, she'd have been safe, but no. He blinked those deep greens at her as if he knew it would work, and darn it. It did. Not like she would've refused anyway, but this little game they had going on was working on her last line of defense against this guy.

And those eyes. Gabe had a fringe of eyelashes that deepened the mossy hue of his irises. Pure, clear green, the color of river rocks on the north bank where sunlight didn't shine. The kind of green that made a woman wonder what it might feel like to rest within their serenity for a moment. Or two.

She couldn't resist him, much less his request to keep Kelsey happy. That was the only reason she was there, after all. For Kelsey. Only Kelsey.

But then he made it worse, the tease. He pursed his lips, as if he'd pout to get his way if he thought it would make her smile. The man had some serious charm, but he was one of those types of guys she'd never be attracted to in a million years only—she was.

The darn flirt.

Shelby stabbed at her glasses, not that they'd moved since the last time she'd stabbed them. A knot stuck in her throat. Had to be nerves. Couldn't be anything else.

"Be careful," her hoarse voice croaked out.

"Yes, ma'am, for you, I will." A warm glint flickered to life in those sexy eyes. He reached his index finger to brush her bangs off of her glasses. He only touched the frames, not her skin, but the jolt to her senses frightened her. The guy had his nerve, but—

He didn't touch me. Didn't he want to?

It didn't take long to load the dogs and get back to the scene of the accident. Gabe parked his Land Rover at the edge of the riverbank. He'd worn a light jacket to cover his holstered pistols. It held two extra magazines in the pockets, nine rounds each. He'd also brought his gear bag along with his mini-camcorder and one of Alex's shirts, though he doubted the dogs needed it. Whisper and Smoke knew their master. This wouldn't take long.

With his mini-cam already running in his left hand, he opened the rear gate of his vehicle. Panning to the left to orient his viewing audience, he began the show, "As you can see, we're back at the river. It's a sunny day. Traffic on the highway behind me is light. Feels like a light breeze from the southeast." He panned back to the two eager noses in the back of his ride. "Whisper? Smoke? Are you boys ready to rock and roll? Let's do this. Find Alex."

Like that was hard for them to do. Whisper and Smoke shot out of the vehicle and raced to the river's edge, sniffing through the ruts and mud. They seemed yoked together by an invisible leash, both noses to the ground and working. After following a short trail along the river, they tracked to the edge of the road and dropped to their haunches, signaling they'd done their job.

In less than two minutes.

Damn. That was quick.

He crouched with Whisper, the camcorder capturing both dogs' snouts as well as his fingers examining the ground at their paws. The tow truck had left enough ruts and heavy tread marks to validate this was the correct piece of riverbank. No doubt about that, but the attempted murder had occurred well over a week ago. Could Whisper and Smoke be wrong?

"Was he here?" Gabe asked, wishing they could verbalize what they seemed sure of. "Did you scent Alex?"

Whisper growled. Smoke offered one quick little, "Yip."

If only they could talk.

To be sure, Gabe walked back to his vehicle. He hadn't really expected they'd find Alex so fast, but now that they had, anger smoldered. He jerked his boss's shirt off the front seat where he'd left it and marched back to the dogs. Pressing it to both of their snouts, he told them again, "Find Alex."

Whisper didn't even budge. He whined in a deep, growly kind of voice and slapped one bear-sized paw to the ground, as if saying, *I already did, dummy. He was right here.*

No wonder Kelsey claimed he could talk. Smoke, on the other hand, backtracked to the shoreline before he returned to sit beside his kennelmate.

Gabe rolled the knot out of his neck, getting more and more pissed at his supposedly dead and buried boss. *That sonofabitch.*

"Well, I'll be damned," he said semi-cheerfully for the sake of his audience. "That sneaky boss of mine might just be alive. Good enough. Let's see what else you boys can find while we're here."

He walked the road with the dogs at his side, fuming at the man he used to respect almost as much as his father. How dare that bastard hurt Kelsey? The TEAM? Gabe's fists curled. Alex was alive, damn it, and he wanted to beat the living shit out of him.

And yet...

Who'd gotten shot if not Alex? It sure as hell had looked like him. Whose life did I try so damned hard to save? Who's right—the dogs or my eyes? My hands?

Time for a commercial break. He hit the camcorder's stop button and called Zack. "You're not going to believe this."

"Whatcha got?"

"Either the dogs tracked Alex or someone planted his scent on the river bank. God, Zack, I've run them twice. They keep coming up with the same answer. He was here, damn it."

Zack's voice lowered. "Mark's fighting the same battle at the office. David's convinced the FBI fabricated evidence to match the ME's version of events. Our own security cameras caught footage of the shooter, some ex-Navy SEAL named Becker. Steven claims the rounds that supposedly killed Alex weren't live ammo. Not sure about you, but I'm fast becoming a believer."

"I don't know what I believe anymore, but I'm fast becoming pissed off. Why would he hurt Kelsey like this?" Gabe's anger spiked. Nothing made sense. "God, I'd rip his head off if he were here."

"Settle down. We don't know what's going on yet. All we've got are puzzle pieces."

"The lying bastard."

"Gabe. Knock it off."

"You can't talk, can you? Are Shelby and Kelsey right there?"

"Copy that."

Gabe drew in a deep breath and slowly exhaled. Anger never settled anything, and this was Alex he was angry with, until now one of the few honorable men left in the world. He'd better have a damned good reason for the god-awful deceit, or Gabe would gladly hold him down if Kelsey wanted to kick the shit out of him.

"Woof!" Whisper and Smoke left the edge of the road and trotted up to their bellies into the water. They stopped, but stood staring at something ten or so yards offshore.

"Hey, listen. I've got to go. The dogs found something. I'll check back soon."

"Copy that."

He holstered his phone and switched the camcorder on again. "You guys find a duck or something? Come on, boys. Stop horsing around. Let it go. We've got popcorn to pop and a lady waiting at home."

And a rat-bastard boss to find.

When Whisper growled at the water, Gabe investigated closer. An encounter with a muskrat or raccoon would make for interesting viewing. Kelsey would get a kick out of watching her dogs scramble after a smart rodent, or maybe play in the water for a couple minutes. It sure beat the dark thoughts Gabe was harboring.

He pushed through the few bushes along this part of the shore, fully expecting a splash when the clever creature made its getaway, but something else caught his eye. The water looked darker in this portion of the river. Flatter, as if it swelled over something big and flat beneath the surface. A thin glint of silver shimmered up from the murky depths. Looked like a silver strip of chrome.

The dogs weren't playing. They'd found something and that bigger, flatter *something* just might be a car.

"Sit. Stay."

Whisper and Smoke dropped to their butts in the shallow water while Gabe walked into the river to investigate. Something definitely rested beneath the water. Big and flat, it might be a submerged rock, the silver of a fisherman's lost pole.

He couldn't wade out to it. Any deeper and the water would fill his boots. "I'm probably going to regret this, but since I'm already here, I might as well take a look see at what's got the dogs' attention."

Gabe stripped off his jacket and fashioned a cushion for the camcorder. Once it was in place on the padding, he stepped behind it and removed his holster and weapons. Gabe glanced at the highway behind him, thankful the reeds and brush concealed his stupidity from the road. There wouldn't be any videos of his half-naked ass bouncing all over *YouTube* if he could help it.

He only wished he could conceal this next part from Kelsey. She didn't need to see him in his boxers, but one way or the other, she would have the confirmation she needed by the end of the day.

Pulling his shirt over his head, he tossed it over his weapons and kicked off his boots. Pants went next. Draping them over his already covered weapons, he double-checked his prosthetic and made sure it was secure. Losing this foot wasn't an option.

His dad's watch went next. Gabe peeled it off his wrist and set it on the stack of clothing. Zack would chew his butt for sure, especially since Gabe was filming his own stupidity. He did it anyway, stepped in front of the camera, boxers, prosthetic plastic foot and all.

"Let the Oscar nominations begin," he muttered, the water rising with every step. Splashing the chilly river up high onto his chest and arms to prepare himself for what he planned to do next, he kept a narrative going. "Man, this river's colder than it looks. This has to be the dumbest thing I've done in a long time, huh, Zack?"

Zack's resounding, *Hell, yeah!* came to mind, but so be it. A dive in the chilly river was a small thing compared to what Kelsey had suffered.

With that final thought, he lifted both hands over his head and said, "Here goes nothing."

He dove in.

The river greeted him with a shock of breathtaking cold. Six quick strokes took him to his underwater target. The murky water made it impossible to see much more than shafts of light, so he relied on his hands, feeling the smooth metal surface of a submerged vehicle. Just as he'd suspected.

His oxygen supply exhausted quickly. Gabe surfaced for a gulp of air and submerged again. With steady strokes, he positioned himself to arrive where he judged the side of the vehicle to be. Smoothing his hands along the drowned auto, he came to a door handle. At that point he knew which direction the vehicle faced. He moved along the side until he encountered a partially open door.

With his air depleted, he surfaced again and gulped an extra large lung full. The water was cold, but his body had begun to acclimate to the temperature. This time, his hand struck the edge of the partially open door right away. He yanked it open farther. If nothing else, he planned to retrieve something from the glove box. A vehicle registration would be nice. Maybe a weapon or other evidence. Who knew, right?

But instead of access to the interior, he got something else. An object followed the door's outward momentum and bumped his forehead. A solid object. Big. Like a—body.

Damn! Gabe choked on a mouthful of water.

He flailed backwards, kicking to get away from that thing closing in on him. No such luck. It followed, bumping his thrashing legs with something hard that felt a lot like a—head.

A root reached out from nowhere, snagging his real foot above his ankle. He knew the corpse hadn't really grabbed him. Too bad panic didn't.

Damn it! Another mouthful of river water went down the wrong pipe. Choking, he stroked to the surface, pulling away from the nightmare he'd unwittingly discovered.

Finally! Topside!

"Jesus Christ!" spewed out of his mouth along with a lot of dirty, river water. The bloated dead guy surfaced, too, right on Gabe's six. He kicked away from it, but it spread its arms wide like it wanted a big hug. The disgusting thing wore a ridiculously tight-fitting business suit and a strangling tie.

Gabe flailed backward.

It bobbed and rolled, revealing the milky-white eyes of what appeared to have once been a Caucasian male, his mouth open in a silent, gaping scream. Its fingers were too chewed up to have grabbed him. The thing seemed to want Gabe's company, though, drifting closer with every backward thrust he took.

Gabe dog-paddled to keep afloat and his distance. *Holy, goddamned shit.*

With a final bubbling snort, the body faced the sky before it rolled face-down, its left palm slapping the water with a pathetically weak smack. The partially eaten scalp with strands of long black hair declared there were fish in the river. *Hungry* fish.

Gabe half-staggered, half crab-walked to shore, choking down a scream. Cursing was manlier, so he ripped off his most tame expletive instead of what he'd been thinking. "Damn it to hell! Damn it! Damn it!"

He wiped the river off his face, still spitting the river out of his mouth, the same river that he now knew held a rotting corpse. "Blah! Damn! Blah. Sure didn't plan on... that," he said to the dogs and the camcorder.

Whisper and Smoke turned to look at him briefly, but turned right back to the corpse bobbing its way to shore. It didn't come to a rest until its face scraped the shallows, as if it knew right where Gabe had gone. Of course it was simply the current he'd created by scrambling out of the water, but still. The dead guy creeped him out.

Goose bumps lifted up his back and over his shoulders. Huge. Really big, goose bumps.

Whisper and Smoke took a few steps toward it to investigate, their noses to the water.

"No. Come on, guys. Stay away from... that."

The dogs complied, sniffing him up and down instead. Smoke licked the water off his face while Whisper planted his big butt right on top of Gabe's bionic foot. Good enough. He brought the camcorder up and aimed it into his face for one final curtain call in his best Porky Pig voice. "Th... th... that's all, folks."

Fumbling to get his cell phone out of his nice dry jacket pocket, he rang his Senior Agent. "Is Kelsey sitting with you?" he asked, shivering uncontrollably.

"No. She's taking a nap, and Shelby's baking cookies. Why? What's wrong? You okay?"

"Yeah. Yeah, I'm good." Gabe flopped to his back, gulping in a deep breath of clean air and thankful for the sunny blue sky overhead. Good was the last thing he was, but no guy admits that. "You know that video I was making? Sonofabitch turned into a horror flick."

Chapter Seventeen

Mark made a quick trip home to grab Libby and his two little girls before he headed over to visit Kelsey and the guys. JayJay giggled with excitement and baby Faith giggled simply because her big sister did. Before long Mark and Libby were letting themselves in through Kelsey's front door. The two girls ran with happy squeals to snuggle with their favorite aunt on the couch.

"Hey Kelsey," Mark said while JayJay clamored onto the couch for Kelsey to read to them. Ah, the innocence of youth. His girls knew their Aunt Kelsey was sad, but their enthusiasm at seeing her overrode her gloom. She gathered them both into her arms with a contented sigh.

Libby joined Shelby in the kitchen.

Zack caught Mark's eye and nodded toward the back yard, where they could talk out of earshot. "You're looking tired, ol' man."

"Aren't we all? How's Shelby working out?"

"Good. Real good."

For now, she sat chatting with Libby while Kelsey read to Mark's little girls. She kept a ready supply of children's books in the end table. JayJay took three-year-old charge of page turning while her baby sister oooh'd at the pretty pictures. Kelsey seemed happy with her arms full, a bittersweet scene. It had to be difficult to hold other's children the same age her boys were when they died. If it was, her sadness didn't show. Baby Faith pointed to the brown rabbit on the page and cooed while Kelsey snuggled her close.

"Where's our boy?"

Zack frowned. "Out taking videos. I thought he'd be back by now."

"Out where?" Mark asked, but his cell phone rang. No wonder Alex was prone to throw the damned things. They were a mix of ball-and-chain and steady interruption. "Houston," he answered, the pleasant scene in the other room already forgotten.

"Were you coming back to the office tonight?" David asked.

"Yes. Libby and the girls are visiting Kelsey right now. Why?"

"I've discovered something you need to see. It's about Eagle Two."

"On my way." He signed off and faced Zack. "I've got to run. Where's Gabe, damn it?"

"He took the dogs back to the river to prove once and for all who rescued Kelsey."

"Don't tell me she's got you guys convinced Alex is still alive?"

Zack hedged. "Possibly. Why don't you come back later and see what Gabe turns up? Face it. He's right. One way or the other, we'll know if Alex was on that riverbank."

"I guess," Mark agreed reluctantly, "David's certain he's still alive, too. Hell, it seems everyone is. You'd think the dogs would've scented Alex when we had them out searching for Kelsey, though."

"Not so. You and Harley told them to find Kelsey, not him. Dogs don't do multiple choice."

Damn. More logic. Mark lifted two fingers to his right temple. A migraine. Just like Alex used to get. "But what about you? Can you handle these two all by yourself?"

"You mean Kelsey and Shelby?" Zack asked, his brows lifted on his forehead.

Dumb question. Zack? Not able to handle two women?

"There is something else, now that you're here." He lowered his voice. "Gabe found a set of boot prints in the backyard this morning. I meant to call, but we've had our hands full keeping Kelsey cheered up."

"Boot prints? Where? Never mind. It doesn't matter. You guys are out of here. Gear up and get ready to move to a more secure location—wait. What do you mean, you've had your hands full keeping Kelsey cheered up? How did you guys make her sad?"

"Now hold on. Before you go all *Alex* on me, hear me out. Kelsey's had a bad day. That's all. She's hanging on by a thread. Let's see what Gabe turns up before we turn her world upside-down again."

Mark closed his eyes and began counting to ten.

Around number three, he knew damned well he was right, and that Zack better snap to and follow orders.

Around seven, Kelsey started singing *Over the Rainbow* to his girls. His baby Faith giggled. Kelsey always did have a way with kids. She almost sounded like her old self.

Around eight, he reconsidered. Zack and Gabe were the best, even if one of the boneheads was not at his post at the moment. Around ten—*aw, shit.*

He caved. "One more incident, just one, and you guys are moving. Count on it."

"Whatever you say, Boss."

Yeah, right. Lip service, Lennox. Too little. Too damned late.

"Come on, girls," Mark called to Libby and his daughters. "We're leaving. Daddy's got to go back to work." *Damn it.*

Libby offered her usual understanding smile, but JayJay grumbled. "Aww. I wanna read more stories, Daddy."

Libby gathered the girls, shushing their opinions of a short visit. "Aunt Kelsey needs to rest, but when she feels better, us girls are going to the zoo. Maybe Aunt Kelsey can come with us. Would you like that?"

"Yeah," Faith blurted. Problem solved. She loved Kelsey and she loved the zoo. Her child-like enthusiasm almost made Mark smile. *Almost.* He owned another problem. Running the business took everything from him, even his precious little family time. Not good. He sounded more and more like Alex, too. Always swearing. Curt. Impatient.

Damn. I need a break.

He dropped Libby and the girls at home before he headed back to the office. The place felt as if it had barely opened for business, everyone busy and focused despite the late afternoon hour.

David already sat in the Sit Room, his findings spread on the table in front of him. Everyone was running on empty, but it seemed even the glare off David's bald head was somehow subdued. He looked as tired as Mark felt, his eyes shadowed and his head in his hands.

"Whatcha got?"

David looked up. "Another puzzle. I couldn't get Mother's assistance with the encrypted file. She said she's too busy with other things, but I've taken this as far as I can."

"Tough encryption, huh? Ember's good at that kind of stuff. Have you asked her?"

"She's busy with Connor and Rory, but she said she'll take a look as soon as she can." David showed Mark what he'd discovered. "It looks like our FBI sniper is involved with our group of ten. Remember Ron Fallon? If what I'm seeing is correct, Mr. Becker is also part of *Chaos Now*. Look what I took off their website. This was taken at their national convention last month right here in D.C."

Mark studied the screen print, a group of men dressed in camouflage pants and shirts. David had enhanced the photo enough that Sam Becker's face was clearly visible while he talked with Ron Fallon. Both men carried assault rifles over their shoulders, as well as pistols at their hips. Fallon sported fully loaded bandoliers crisscrossing his chest. More concerning were the smiles on both men's faces.

"Looks like a bunch of survivalists to me. So talk to me about *Chaos Now*. What else do you know?"

"They also have a link named Eagle Two."

That perked up Mark's ears. "Is it the same file as the FBI's and Secret Service's?"

"I'm not sure, but I came across this timetable on their website."

Mark took the paper from David's hand. It showed a timeline all right, with the word **REVOLUTION** bolded in bright red letters at the top. The next words weren't any better. Chaotic Disorder. Mayhem. Military rule. Chaotic Order.

"A timeline from chaotic disorder to chaotic order? Makes as much sense as Army Intelligence."

"They might not be rocket scientists, Mark, but they're arrogant and they can put our country in great danger."

"Let's get Ember and Mother on this. We need to know exactly what these jokers are up to."

"There's something else," David murmured. "I know who Eagle Two is. It's Vice President Frank Winston."

"How can you be sure?"

David pointed to the small print beneath the bright red heading. Mark had to squint to make it out, the font so tiny. Damned if David wasn't right. These guys were arrogant as hell. There in print so small—but there nonetheless—were the words: *Winston first. Then the world.*

Gabe dressed while he waited at the riverbank with the dogs. The sheriff's cruiser finally arrived, followed by the coroner's van and a tow truck. Despite the warm summer day, he'd developed a chill. The only saving grace was that the sheriff was not the same one who'd *investigated* Kelsey's accident.

The corpse still bobbed in the shallows, face down. The gruesome thing hadn't gone far, and for that, Gabe was thankful. He didn't need to be strolling out into the river to make sure it stayed put.

The sheriff climbed out of his cruiser to survey the scene while the coroner hooked the floater and dragged it onto shore and the sheet of black plastic he'd laid out. When he stuck a probe in the corpse's extended abdomen, Gabe jerked his eyes off the proceedings. Time to go. He'd seen enough. Besides, he'd been driving on a revoked driver's license. Wouldn't that be something to explain to the sheriff or Zack?

The tow truck operator came prepared with a diver who had no problem going into the water. Once he hooked a tow strap onto the rear of the submerged vehicle, the tow truck driver winched a large black SUV out of the river. An Escalade.

The day got worse. Another bloated corpse flopped out of the rear passenger door and hit the ground with a gruesome, squishy splat. When something long, black, and slimy wiggled out of the dead guy's left eye, Gabe's stomach lurched up the back of his throat. He pivoted on his good heel. *Shit. Definitely time to get the hell out of there.*

The sheriff's brows arched. "Did you know these guys?"

"No, sir, sure didn't," Gabe replied through chattering teeth. He lifted his jacket, displaying his holstered pistols while he pulled out his permit to carry and forced his gut to calm. "Before we go any further, you need to know I'm carrying. Here's my permit and my employee ID badge authorizing me to do so. I came out here to take my friend's dogs for a walk. They're cooped up in their kennels most of the time, so I did her a favor and brought them out for a run. That's when they got spooked. I made the mistake of swimming out to see what was going on. Not my brightest decision today."

"No, it wasn't, but thanks for telling me you're armed. Who's this friend of yours?"

"Kelsey Stewart."

"Alex Stewart's widow?" the sheriff asked, a spark of recognition glimmering in his eyes.

"Yes. These are her dogs, Whisper and Smoke. I thought they might help me locate some more evidence in case we missed something before. You knew him?"

"Yes, I had the chance to work with Stewart on a child smuggling ring a few years back. Damned good man. You find anything else?"

Gabe nodded his chin toward the corpses. "Only those guys."

The coroner interrupted with his preliminary findings. "Excuse me, but you'll want to see this." He handed over two waterlogged wallets. "I need to run more tests, but I'd estimate cause of death at ten to twelve days ago for both of these guys. Looks like they were shot before they drowned."

"Well now, who do we have here?" The sheriff peered at the driver's licenses in the wallets. "Huh. Clark Manson and Carlos Echevarria. Let me know what else you find."

Gabe damned near choked. *Two of the gang of ten, now reduced to five at last count according to Mark. And they'd died around the same time of Kelsey's attempted murder. Holy hell.*

"You need me for anything else? I'd really like to get home and out of these wet clothes."

"No, I think I've got enough. I'll be in touch if anything comes up."

Good enough. Gabe turned to his Land Cruiser, loaded the dogs and waved goodbye with one quick salute. He'd gotten more than he'd bargained for during this impromptu swim, but knowing the corpses were two of the guys Mark was looking for made it worthwhile. Ten was now down to three.

It took all of twenty minutes to get back to Kelsey's. Shelby met him at the back door after he'd kenneled the dogs, concern bright in her eyes. She latched onto his arm and pulled him inside. "Your boss was here. What on earth have you been doing? You've been gone so long. I thought you were just taking a walk and a video."

A round of sneezing delayed his answer. Zack strolled into the kitchen, his arms crossed over his chest. "You couldn't leave well enough alone, could you?"

Gabe sneezed again. "I made a darn good movie," he said, surprised his voice had gotten hoarse on the drive home. He shrugged out of his jacket and unlaced his boots. "Mark was here?"

"Don't worry. He'll be back. Tell me about the body you found."

"A body?" Shelby hitched her glasses up with her index finger again.

"Bodies," Gabe corrected, holding up two fingers. "Both male. Manson and Echevarria. Both shot. They'd been underwater a while, maybe as long as Kelsey's accident."

"Are you sure?" Zack asked.

"Yes. Weren't those two of the guys Mark's looking for?"

Zack pursed his lips and nodded. "Yeah. Mark didn't have names, last I heard. Our mystery Good Samaritan must've hit two of the group."

"And his buddies drove their vehicle into the river with them still in it. Wonder if they were dead then?"

"Don't care one way or the other," Zack muttered. "They're dead now."

"What are you guys talking about?" Shelby demanded. "You guys know who tried to kill Kelsey?"

"Shh," Gabe cautioned, his gaze on the hallway again. "We didn't have names until today."

"And someone really did save her, like she said?"

"Yes. Only you've got to understand. I was there the day her husband was shot. I tried to help Alex and I've got his blood all over my clothes. I know damned well he's dead, so..." Gabe snapped his mouth shut at what he'd said. He looked at Zack. "Damn it. I've got evidence. My bloody shirt. My pants. We can prove if it's Alex's or not. That will support my video."

His brain drifted to the day in the parking garage. The bright red blossoms in his boss's chest. The lack of blood pouring out of those three gunshot wounds. It all came back. So did the questions. "I tried to keep his heart pumping, you know, massaging it through his shirt until the paramedics got there, but there was so little blood."

"What are you saying?" Zack asked.

Gabe honestly didn't know. He'd been panicked, so scared he hadn't thought about what happened within the turmoil. His brain replayed the images now. The sound of gunfire. The bile creeping up his throat when he saw that Alex was shot and dying. The anger. The fear. But other details pierced the fog. He'd attributed the lack of blood to internal hemorrhaging, but was it? And the feel of that blood wasn't right.

"I need to get back to my place, Zack. The blood's all wrong."

"What do you mean?" Shelby interrupted.

Gabe focused on her face. She was a nurse. She should know about physical trauma. "It was thick and cold. I remember thinking how strange it was for a man as hot-tempered as the boss. I thought it would've been warmer. Thinner, too."

Shelby grabbed hold of his forearm. "Are you sure you're remembering right?"

"Yeah. I was right in the middle of his chest. Believe me, I'm sure, but the whole damned thing was a nightmare, and I got caught up in the commotion. I hadn't thought about it until now. There was so little blood. I barely got my hands wet, just enough to make them sticky."

"He had to have been losing a lot, being shot like that. You would've been covered in it," Shelby said. "Was it all over your clothes?"

"No. That's the thing. I had some on my hands, but not much. I wiped it on my pants, but there's something else now that we're talking about it. It was like he was shedding his skin. You ever see a gunshot victim do that?"

"Shedding his skin? What do you mean?" she asked.

Gabe brushed his thumb and index finger together to demonstrate. "It's like his skin peeled or something. Every time I'd push on him, you know, to see if I could get him to keep breathing, I could feel my palms slid over his shirt, like his skin was bubbling off of him in tiny patches."

Now he had Shelby's complete attention. "Was his car on fire? Did he get burned?"

"No fire. He just got shot."

"Wait a minute." Zack held both hands up for silence. "You're confused. It was an awful day. None of us were in our right minds."

"I was there, Zack. I saw three red splotches on his shirt. That's all. Even at the hospital, I never saw the actual physical damage on his body. Just bloody packing and rags on the floor. Medical instruments. I never saw the actual holes. Neither did Kelsey."

"That's not right," Shelby murmured. "The hospital would've never allowed Kelsey to see her husband like that. Someone would've cleaned the room before they let her in."

"And that's another thing. You ever hear a man talk after he's been shot dead?"

"I've seen dead patient's lips move, like they were trying to say something, but... why? Did Alex say something?"

"Yes, but he had to have been dead by the time I got to him, right? I mean he'd taken three to the chest." *Shit. Here I've been blaming myself instead of questioning what really happened. Shit. Shit. Shit!*

"Okay," Shelby said calmly. "Exactly what did you hear him say?"

"I lifted the windshield out of my way. I reached in over the dash to turn the car off. He was blinking real hard at me, as if he was surprised. And he turned to me, and he says, *'I'm shot?'* You know, like he couldn't believe it. Then he wanted me to tell Kelsey he loved her and, God, I lost it. I mean..."

The morning stormed over Gabe again. Once more, he'd arrived too late to save his friend. His heart thumped while he relived Alex's last gasping breath. The blood that might not have been Alex's blood. The death that might not have been real, either.

Gabe lowered his aching head, his mind rejecting all arguments as too hard to figure out at the moment, and that damned snaky feeling of a hand at his throat. Suffocating him. Triggers nagged at him to succumb to panic. *Not now, damn it.*

Shelby's hand still rested on his arm. "But he was shot three times, right?"

Gabe nodded. His throat had gone sore and dry. "Yes, and then he slumped over, and he—"

Died.

Name it or not, admit it or not, PTSD had a sneaky way of elbowing the mission out of the way when it showed up. Like that day in the garage. Like thinking about Darrell. Or Alex.

"Three to his chest. Are you certain?"

"God, you don't forget something like that." *At least not for long.*

The prettiest violet-blues drilled him. "Alex wouldn't have been talking by the time you got to him, Gabe—not if he sustained three mortal wounds, like you described."

"I think you're right," Gabe whispered more to himself than to her, aware of the calmness flowing from her body to his.

Shelby frowned that beautiful *of-course-I'm-right* frown of hers. Did she have any idea how much he needed her touch on his arm right now? "Where's Kelsey?" he asked, needing to be sure she was out of earshot.

"I gave her something to help her rest. You're not going to tell her about the bodies, are you?"

Gabe looked to Zack for that answer. "I'd as soon tell her everything we think we know, but it's up to you."

"Let's talk to her when she gets up," Zack replied. "Kels is tougher than she looks right now. She might be able to take it."

"Good. Since she's sleeping, I'm going to take a quick shower. Be right out," Gabe muttered, needing to be warm again. He couldn't stop shivering.

Zack and Shelby followed him to his duffel bag in the front room like two overprotective mothers. "Will you two back off? I really can dress myself," he said, between chattering teeth. "It's not like I'm dying here."

"No, but you're coming down with something." Shelby eyed him intently. "You're flushed and your eyes are red. Is there anything I can do to help?"

"No, ma'am. Probably got river water in my eyeballs is all. I'm good."

"You should've let the sheriff handle it," Zack drawled. "You didn't need to go swimming. They have trained divers for that, you know."

"Yeah. I know, but Kelsey needed peace of mind, and I think I've finally found some for her. Least, I hope. I'll call Mark soon as I'm done showering. He needs to send someone over to my place to get my dirty clothes."

"I'll call him," Zack answered. "Get changed. You'll feel better after a shower."

Gabe pulled a dry pair of cammie pants, a couple of pullover shirts, and some clean socks out of his bag before he headed to the bathroom. In no time at all he was under the shower, his pistols once again on the lid of the hamper.

The hot water felt good, but he still shivered. His muscles ached. Head ached. By the time he'd dried and dressed, congestion had settled into his chest and everything else ached, too. *Damn, I've got the flu.*

He took extra care drying his bionic foot, but he was more worried about Kelsey's reaction to what he'd found than he was ensuring his spare parts were in good condition. Traces of Alex. Two bodies. It didn't get more bizarre than that. And the blood evidence on his clothes? He opted to keep that from Kelsey until he knew for sure it didn't belong to her husband. Damn. Had she been right all along?

Zack had a cup of coffee waiting for him at the kitchen table and Shelby stood there with a blanket in her hand by the time he exited the bathroom. Gabe stuffed his dirty clothes into his rucksack. He brushed the notion of the blanket aside and grabbed a kitchen chair instead, but Shelby thought she knew better. She wrapped the blanket around his shoulders the minute he sat down anyway.

"You're sick," she said firmly. "And you're feverish. I made lasagna for dinner, but I'll get you something for that fever first."

He would've argued, but a coughing fit ensued. *She might be right.* "I got news for you. That river's cold in the summer. And it's dirty. No wonder Kelsey's as sick as she is."

Shelby returned with a glass of water and three tablets in her hand. "Here. Ibuprofen. Take them."

He obeyed, not able to ignore the tender touch of her cool fingers on his cheek. Nurse Sullivan had changed. Her fingers lingered longer than if she were simply diagnosing a sick guy.

"Not sure I'd have gone into the river if I'd known who else was in it," he admitted. Her gentle smile caught him by surprise.

"No kidding," Zack said.

Gabe snapped his gaze away from Shelby.

Zack glanced over his shoulder toward Kelsey's bedroom, but not before Gabe caught the glint of curiosity in his eye. Zack was no dummy. He'd picked up on the subtle change in Shelby, too.

"Do me a favor, kid," he said, without looking Gabe in the eye. "Mark said Rory and Connor located security footage from the day Kelsey went missing that confirmed someone who looked and acted a lot like Alex was at the riverbank that day, I hear her moving around back there. She'll be out here soon. Let's take it slow with her. Let her draw her own conclusions. Shelby, would you put a couple bags of popcorn in the microwave? Gabe, let's get your camcorder hooked up. We're having a party, remember?"

Kid. The standard nametag for any jarhead with less military time under his belt. It had nothing to do with age, but Gabe caught the drift. Zack was the old dog in the room. He meant to protect Kelsey, even from the good news.

"You bet. Let's not tell her about the blood evidence yet, either. Not until we know for sure." Gabe doffed the blanket, but rising to his feet brought a moment of dizziness. He paused with his hand on the back of his chair to let his head settle down.

Man. What was in that river water? Oh, wait. Two dead guys. Yuck.

He latched onto his gear bag and joined Zack on the floor in front of the television set, another indication of the kind of man Alex had been. The set was cheap and small. "You're kidding me, right? How am I going to hook up a camcorder to this? What is it? Co-axle?" he asked as he pulled the mini-cam out of his bag.

"You'll manage." Zack turned the set sideways on its matching small wooden stand while Gabe pulled his mini-cam and cables from his bag. "The thing is, Alex used to have a nicer television. Used to have me over for football games and dinner with him and his girls way back when. Guess he purged all his good memories after they died."

"They what? He's been married before? His *girls* died?"

"Shh. Keep it quiet, but yes. Car crash took them both. The video line goes here. See?" Zack tapped the video input. "Yeah, Alex hooked up his old TV when my little LiLi wanted to know why she couldn't watch Big Bird and Barney at her grandpa's house. She's a pistol. Always called him Grandpa. Funny thing, I think he liked it."

Gabe's gaze drifted to the mantle. He'd only given the family pictures lined up there a cursory glance, but the younger guy in the family portrait was his boss? Gabe thought maybe a brother, because that smiling guy resembled Alex, but it really was him? Wow. He was a lot happier then. Carefree.

Two other photographs displayed two smiling brown-haired boys not included in the family shot. "Who are they?"

"Joey and Tommy," Kelsey said from the front room entry.

Gabe snapped his neck, ashamed she'd caught them discussing what had to be another damned painful time in her life.

"It's okay, Gabe. You can ask. They're my sons. I lost them before Alex and I ever met. The picture on the left is Alex with Sara and Abby. They were his first family. I'm his second."

Embarrassment flamed Gabe's cheeks. He wished he'd kept his big mouth shut. "I'm sure sorry, ma'am."

"Don't be. I'm glad you asked. It helps to talk about them. It keeps them alive in my heart. And this guy." She adjusted the portrait of another man who had to be unrelated. The guy had a serious unibrow on a forehead that hung out over two light-blue eyes like a cliff, resembling Frankenstein. "This is Raymond. I met him last summer when I was kidnapped. He helped me get away, but he died in the process. We adopted him after the fact. Kind of. I had an artist do this pencil rendering. I don't want to forget him, either."

"Popcorn's ready." Shelby smoothed a hand over Kelsey's shoulder. "How was your nap?"

Gabe was thankful for the distraction. More than ever, Kelsey needed the proof in his camcorder. "Ready to watch what me and the dogs found?" he asked, his cold and flu symptoms insignificant compared to what she'd survived and overcome.

Her eyes lit up. "Him?"

Chapter Eighteen

Gabe and Zack were very smooth operators. They'd both brightened when Kelsey appeared, not telling her anything she didn't already know, but honestly. Gabe's version of events on the day of the shooting was either inaccurate or Mr. Stewart wasn't dead. No way. It couldn't be. That handsome man in the pictures wouldn't pretend to get killed. Not Alex. He wouldn't hurt Kelsey. Heck, he had everything most guys wanted—well except for a decent house.

But darn. Kelsey had lost her first husband and sons, too? A shiver skated up Shelby's spine, raising a rash of goose bumps across her shoulders at what she'd overheard. She brushed her hands over them, trying to dispel the chill.

Here she'd thought she'd be bored spending a few quiet days with a grieving widow, but the simple job had changed. She was up to her ears in more intrigue than she'd ever known. And now they were going to sit down and watch a movie with dead bodies? She rubbed her biceps, unable to chase the goose bumps away. *Brrr.*

"Hey, Shelby," Zack called from the front room. "While you're up, would you grab a couple beers?"

She complied, which was really weird. Her? Taking orders? Even her family knew better than to ask her to *'get something while you're up.'* She wasn't staff or anyone's gopher. But Zack wasn't so bad. A drink might do everyone some good.

She snagged four bottles and stepped over Whisper and Smoke on her way into the front room. Another weird thing. She did not approve of animals in the house. Ever. Until now. Kelsey's dogs made her happy, and that, Shelby discovered, made her happy, too.

She took her place alongside Kelsey on the couch and doled out the icy cold bottles. Gabe and Zack twisted the tops and Zack took a long pull on his. She twisted her bottle cap and took a sip. Here she was, surrounded by a definite military lifestyle complete with two soldiers. Her world was changing in a lot of weird ways.

Gabe and Zack sat cross-legged on the floor, Gabe near Kelsey, his arms on his knees. He twisted the top off Kelsey's beer for her, but she placed it on the end table instead of taking a drink. When everyone was seated, Gabe started the video. He'd managed to get fairly smooth footage following the dogs while they did their thing. He'd done good making them track Alex twice. But watching him stroll into the river as if it were no big deal? Scary.

Shelby looked closer. The guy was lean, but well-muscled. Those green and black plaid boxers were kind of sexy. A smile tweaked her lips. She'd seen what was beneath them. Glancing at the guy in question, her heart set to fluttering. He'd caught her looking. He winked a sly wink. The flirt.

She looked away, but couldn't resist. One quick glance back and there he was again, still smiling. Still winking. She rolled her eyes back to the screen in time to see him dive into the river, and hopefully before Kelsey or Zack noticed their innocent exchange.

"Not smart, Cartwright." Zack chuckled. "Only an idiot would've done that."

"We're lucky he's still here," Shelby murmured, her heart in her throat. "Ah, I mean, yeah. What were you thinking, Agent Cartwright?"

Zack gave her a look. She offered a glare in return but he'd either heard the emotion in her voice or the foolish attempt to disguise it. His left brow arched giving him a truly devilish look.

She focused on the television screen and took another sip of that icy cold beer. At this rate, her bottle would be dry in no time.

Bubbles surfaced. Minutes stretched. But no Gabe. The camcorder silently recorded the ever-widening ripples. Only Whisper and Smoke's panting from the riverbank broke the silence.

"I'm actually impressed the kid could hold his breath this long," Zack teased.

At last, Gabe splashed to the surface, but only long enough for a gulp of air before he dived again. Then again. Shelby cringed and clenched Kelsey's hand. Darn, he was seriously one crazy guy.

At last, he erupted out of the water with a splash and a sputtering, "Jesus Christ!"

Kelsey pointed to the screen. "What's that floating thing? Right beside you. It looks like a log."

"That, my dear, is a body," Zack announced as a corpse bobbed alongside his very frantic junior agent. "Gabe found one of the SUVs that ran you off the road. This guy was in it."

Shelby couldn't look away. Every powerful stroke Gabe took seemed to compel the corpse to follow. It looked like a scene from a living dead horror flick. She took another drink, her lips dry and her heart pounding despite the fact that he sat less than six feet from her. Darn him. Hearing about it was one thing, but seeing it? He'd taken too much of a risk. He could have died out there.

"There were actually two bodies. Their buddies must've ditched them and their ride when they got shot," Gabe explained. "This guy couldn't wait to get out."

"But who shot them?" Kelsey asked.

"That's right. You haven't heard the whole story yet, have you?" Zack asked.

Shelby cringed, needing another swallow of beer. Kelsey was fragile right now. Should they be telling her all this?

"The same guy who saved your life shot these two jerks," Gabe muttered. "Actually, there were four jerks to begin with. They shot your car after they ran you off the road and into the river. Connor and Rory found some security footage that shows a guy in black shooting back at them. Once he chased them off, he jumped in after you."

Kelsey sat in a daze—just what Shelby was afraid of. The video showed too much and too fast, and this new information was more than the poor thing could absorb.

"Can I watch my boys find him again?" Kelsey asked quietly.

"You bet." Gabe dropped to the front of the TV and set the video to replay.

Kelsey leaned forward, her elbows on her knees. First Whisper sat, his sign that he'd located the scent he'd been told to find. Then Smoke. Then Gabe made them do it again.

"You took such a risk jumping into the river," she said. "You were all alone. What if something happened?"

Gabe pushed off the floor. He set his beer on the end table and sat beside her. "Something did happen. You saw the dogs track Alex, didn't you? They found him. Twice. That's good enough for me. He is alive. You were right."

Shelby downed the last of her drink. Kelsey seemed to have stopped breathing. She stared at the paused image on the screen. Gabe had caught both of the dogs' faces when he'd paused the replay. They smiled with black licorice lips. At Kelsey.

"It was him," she whispered. "I knew it. Thank God. He's alive."

Gabe tugged her into his side. The man looked as if he needed a long rest, but Shelby couldn't stop looking at him.

"Come on, Kelsey," he murmured, squeezing her tight. Tears brimmed those gorgeous green eyes of his. "This was supposed to make you happy."

She leaned into her hands, covering her face. "I am. I'm really... so happy."

"But happy isn't supposed to leak out of your face like this," he teased, a tear tracking down his cheek. He brushed his face against his shoulder.

Shelby couldn't pull her eyes away from the tender scene. The man loved Kelsey. There was no other way to put it. They really were family.

Zack had taken up position in front of his computer screen instead of watching the replay. Both brows descended into a *V*. His forehead crinkled with worry lines and his cell phone tucked against his shoulder and cheek. "Yeah, Kels. You're supposed to be dancing off the ceiling right now and drinking a beer."

"I'm happy." She wiped her eyes and glanced up at her ceiling. "Believe me, my heart's up there. It really is. I'm just afraid to believe it."

"Yeah. Me, too," Gabe said. "We were with you at the hospital, remember?"

Shelby reached for the box of tissues on the end table beside her. She offered it to Kelsey, then Gabe, before she snagged one for herself. Nothing about this job was easy.

"Wow," Kelsey whispered. "I haven't cried like this in years, huh?" She turned to Gabe, cupping his jaw in the palm of her slender hand. "You poor thing. You could've drowned out there."

Shelby turned away. It really was true. He would die for Kelsey.

Eagle Two became top priority and Mark was glad. For once, everyone focused on something besides proving Alex was alive. Steven had located Sam Becker. Izza, Taylor, and he were staked out at a warehouse next to the Gangplank Marina off Water Street in D.C.

Becker had gone inside with another male. Izza had already forwarded a couple of photos of them when they'd entered the warehouse. His takedown appeared imminent, but for now, it was a game of wait and see.

"Hey, Boss," Rory said. "We're running some traffic cam footage through Ember's facial rec program to see if we can spot our suspects, but check this out. Connor's been busy."

Connor turned on the overhead screen in the Sit Room. "These are kinda choppy because I had to piece a few downloads together, but watch."

The Sit Room was filled with the remaining agents and Mother. Connor's satellite footage tracked the man in black after he'd driven Kelsey to the vacant summer home. Once there, he picked the front door lock and carried her inside.

"He's got a lot of nerve." Mother summed it up for the group. "Who was that guy?"

Connor keyed in another command. "You tell me. This guy must have disabled the security system, too. It sure went off when Gabe picked the lock to get to Kelsey."

The overhead screen now showed three enhanced close-up shots of the man when he arrived on the scene, when he dove into the river, and again as he worked to resuscitate Kelsey. Dressed entirely in black, he'd kept his face concealed with a balaclava. All except for when he'd dived into the river.

"That's not much help," Mother exclaimed petulantly.

"No?" Rory asked. "Look closer."

Connor zoomed in again until it became obvious this person was indeed a Caucasian male, around six feet tall, give or take an inch or two, and whose body shape looked as if it weighed around two hundred pounds. He moved like a man who knew exactly what to do, but what cinched the deal was the tender way he handled Kelsey as he carried her from the water and administered first aid on the riverbank. He stroked her cheek once she started breathing. He knelt over her on hands and knees, so close that it looked as if he'd kissed her forehead. Only then did he replace the black mask over his head.

Mark sat back with a gasp of denial. "It can't be. I saw him die."

Rory stared at Mark across the room. "Then who else is it?"

"Wait. Not done here," Connor spoke up. "You all know the airbag and seatbelt in Kelsey's were sliced. Who always carries a blade with him? I mean, besides Taylor and Izza?"

Maverick and David answered at the same time. "Alex."

"Anything else?" Mark asked evenly, his logic card overloaded by this additional evidence. Until now, Connor and Rory hadn't been able to bring this portion of the video into sharp enough focus. They'd all seen this stranger place Kelsey inside his sedan. It had looked as if he'd kissed her then, but as David had pointed out, he'd been wearing his balaclava. He could've simply been checking to make sure she was still breathing. But now?

Mark gulped. Could this guy be Alex?

"One more thing. Watch this." Rory signaled Connor. The video came to life again, showing an aerial shot of the Olsens' home on the day of the anonymous tip.

Exactly two hours before Zack and Gabe roared up to Olsens', another black sedan rolled slowly into the driveway. Two men exited the vehicle and entered the house. Moments later they reappeared, escorting another guy to their vehicle, this one with his head covered again.

One of the men drove Kelsey's rescuer's sedan away from the home, while the other drove their vehicle, leaving her completely alone. It appeared her rescuer had been apprehended, but by whom?

Dead silence met the end of the video. Even Mother had nothing to say.

Rory pointed to the overhead. "I'm telling you. He's alive. I don't know how, but this guy has got to be Alex."

Mark bolted. He had to get the hell out of there. The man he used to respect as much as God, couldn't—wouldn't!—hurt his wife, not like that. It couldn't be him, despite all the evidence. *It. Can. Not. Be. Alex!*

"Mark," Mother snapped behind him. "Izza's on the line. You want me to take a message or what?"

God, she'd gotten nastier with every passing day. Mark returned to her counter, surprised she'd left the Sit Room when no one else had. He lifted the receiver out of her hand striving for courtesy and wondering if she'd followed him. "Thanks. Houston."

"Mark!" Izza shouted. "Becker's headed toward Kelsey's. Get over there right now."

"Where are you?"

"Fixing two flat tires," she hissed. "The ass is good. We never even saw him."

Mark dropped the phone and ran, but even that didn't let him escape the tangled mess of leadership.

"Hey," Mother called behind him. "Where are you going?"

"Becker's on his way to Kelsey's," he answered over his shoulder, his cell phone chirping away in his belt holster. "Tell David to follow me. Hell, tell everyone! Do it. Now!"

He stabbed the elevator call button while he lifted his cell to his ear, needing to be at Kelsey's instead of answering another damned phone call. "Houston."

"Hey, Mark." Zack's quiet voice rumbled over the line. "Gabe's back. He's got proof you need to—"

"Gear up. Becker's on his way to you."

The elevator doors slid open. *About damned time.*

"Let him come," Zack purred. "Me and Gabe will be waiting."

Chapter Nineteen

"Hey, Gabe. You want to come over and check something for me?"

"Sure." He eased away from Kelsey to join his Senior Agent. "What's up, old man?"

"Not much. Might have a low battery in camera seventeen is all." Zack pointed to the laptop screen that showed a black sedan rolling past Kelsey's home, its windows too dark to determine how many people might be inside. The car slowed at the curb.

"No problem," he said to keep this new development from the ladies. No sense ruining their evening. "I can do batteries. It's time for a perimeter check anyway."

"Keep your ears on," Zack warned quietly enough that the women couldn't hear him.

"Copy that. Be right back." Despite feeling like crap, Gabe headed for the back door. Might be Alex out there. Might not. Didn't matter. Whoever was in that car, they were in for a surprise.

Gabe pulled his jacket off the kitchen chair before he slipped out the backdoor and around the side of the house. Inserting the blue-tooth earpiece in his ear, he slipped his jacket over his shoulders and took quick stock of the backyard.

Both dogs looked at him from their kennel, their big, old German Shepherd ears pitched forward like radar dishes. Neither offered any signal that they sensed an intruder, but he made sure the home was secure before he left. He loved them, but he didn't trust them—not anymore. Not Alex Stewart's dogs.

"Comm check," Zack said quietly.

"Loud and clear. Looks like our company moved on."

"I called Mark. Becker is on his way to us. Watch your six. That could be him out there."

"Copy that. Good to know." Gabe replied. *Damned good to know.*

The late summer evening had turned dark. Nothing stirred. Kelsey's street ended in a cul-de-sac five doors north of her front door. Gabe swept through there in case Becker had decided to park. Nothing.

Walking back gave him a complete view of the rest of the street, including the T-intersection four doors south of her place and to the east. The driver of a mini-van tapped his brakes at the stop sign and proceeded south before turning into a driveway.

"I've got a silver van three doors south of the intersection. Anyone we know?"

"Saw it. Cromwell's van. They usually go out for dinner. Must have called it an early night. Proceed."

"Checking west perimeter next." To do that, Gabe had to walk through two of Kelsey's neighbors' backyards to reach the street behind her house. This was the blind spot as far as he was concerned, so he'd mounted a couple of extra cameras on the street lights in front of those homes.

While Mark and Libby dealt with the administrative side of getting Kelsey released, Gabe and Zack had vetted their security perimeter with all the neighbors prior to trespassing and posting any off-property security cameras. It had been a good morning spent meeting Kelsey's neighbors. She was well respected and loved. Not one person had argued with the extra precaution.

Gabe kept to the shadows, half-listening to the conversation back in Kelsey's living room. It turned to healthcare, with Zack targeting Shelby for specifics. She was a Certified Nursing Assistant, a CNA, who preferred home-care to the stress of hospital work. She wasn't married. No big surprise there, given her air of superiority.

"Hope you're not doing this for my benefit," Gabe muttered, his throat tight and sore.

Zack seemed not to hear so well. "You look too young. When did you graduate?"

"I'm old enough. I've been in private care for three years now."

"That makes you all of what? Nineteen?" Zack teased Shelby.

"Twenty-three, if you must know."

"What? No way. You engaged?"

"Knock it off." Gabe didn't even want to hear the answer to that one. "You're so far off base, old man. Put a sock in it."

"Not looking," she responded lightly. "I'm dedicated to my patients."

Don't fib, little girl. You were certainly looking in the bathroom this morning.

"Why are you in private practice if you're an RN?"

"Well, you see..." She hesitated. Gabe's ears perked up. "I'm not actually a registered nurse. Not yet."

Excuse me all to hell?

"I'm just a nursing assistant. I'm going to go back for my nursing degree one of these days."

Then why the hell did you want us to call you Nurse Sullivan, Miss Smarty Pants?

Gabe shook his head at the nerve of that woman. Damn. The extent people go to for control.

Zack kept on not minding his business, as if that last revelation didn't bother him. "You still live with your parents?"

"Oh, no. I have an apartment in Silver Springs. It's in a very nice gated community with all the amenities."

"Really? Well, isn't it a small world? I know a guy who just bought a real nice home in Silver Springs."

"Don't do it, Lennox," Gabe growled. His nosy senior agent was treading on thin ice. Shelby didn't need to know Gabe might be her neighbor. Ever. Unless... could the old blabbermouth mean someone else?

"You don't live far from the hospital then." Zack artfully changed topics yet again. Sort of. "You live there all by yourself?"

"Not far, and yes, I live alone."

"All alone? No dog? No cat?"

"No goldfish, either." She chuckled, a pleasant sound in Gabe's congested head.

That was a first. The old man must know his way around prickly women. He spoiled it by turning the conversation to second amendment rights. "You don't think anyone has the right to carry guns though, do you?"

Great. That ought to get her stirred up.

Gabe coughed quietly into his sleeve. He stopped listening for her answer at the sound of a car engine idling. A sedan sat parked six car-lengths down the street to his right, its light off. "Target in sight," he advised Zack.

"Copy that. You know what to do." His answer came back soft and sure, while Shelby and Kelsey chatted in the background.

No problem. *Watch the enemy and learn. Apprehend if necessary. Eliminate if push came to shove.*

Gabe dropped behind the cover of a neatly trimmed privet hedge bordering the corner residence, a brick home with all lights blazing. Rock music bellowed from an open second-story window, signaling that at least one of the Browns' three teenage boys was home.

Gabe liked these kids. They were hot-rodders, like him. The '63 souped-up, two-door Nova in the driveway gave them away. It looked a lot like his, only this one needed a paint job to cover the primer-gray. Their father's pristine candy-apple red Ford Fairlane caught his attention, too. *Gear heads. Gotta love 'em.*

Still out of sight, Gabe retrieved the pistol tucked under his left arm, racked the slide and slid a laser scope onto the top rail. Sometimes that little red dot was enough to make a man think twice.

Just in time. A single guy, dressed entirely in black, his head and face covered as well, stepped out of the driver's side of the sedan, quietly shutting the door behind him. Six feet tall, body shape hinting him to be close to two hundred pounds. Ramrod straight posture. He walked between the two homes behind Kelsey's. The bulk at his hip and the thigh holster spoke for themselves. This was no cat burglar.

Gabe swallowed hard. Now directly in front of Gabe's position, but still on the street, the intruder glanced from left to right, his head cocked. He looked just like Alex. Walked just like him. Had to be him.

Undetected, Gabe waited. The soft rubber soles of his boots were designed to absorb the impact of sharp terrain, which also made them extra quiet. Given the right conditions, he could get the drop on this guy with no trouble.

Alex must've thought things were clear. He advanced to the sidewalk and between the homes, neither fenced. He stepped over a child's plastic trike and other toys littering the joined space as if he knew exactly where he was going.

God, he had balls of brass.

Gabe followed, sticking close to the edge of the home to the north, his weapon aimed and ready. The guy seemed to know where he was going. Oddly, Whisper and Smoke remained quiet. That cinched it. *Has to be Alex, the bastard! How could you do this to Kelsey! Your wife!*

Gabe followed less than ten feet behind, his emotions running as high as his fever, until the stealthy man came to a halt at the Stewarts' fence line. With one jump, he'd be out of reach and next to the dog kennel.

Not going to happen, you lying ass. Gabe closed the distance and pushed the barrel of his weapon between the guy's shoulder blades before the jerk could make another move.

"What the hell are you doing out here, Boss? What's going on? Turn around and knock off the black op routine."

The man lifted his hands but didn't turn around. The time to be nice was long gone. Gabe snatched the balaclava from guy's head.

Damn it to hell.

It wasn't Alex.

Her ears perked up at the thump against the back door. And then her heart. Already in the kitchen, Shelby looked out the window. Gabe had a man at gunpoint, cuffed with his hands in front of him, on the step.

Zack's hand clamped her shoulder. "Get away from the door. Go sit with Kelsey."

"Why? Who is that?" She needed more than an order to comply. If something was going on, she wanted to know.

Zack twisted the knob to the left but didn't open the door, his voice stern. "I said now, Miss Shelby. Sit with Kelsey. Don't open the front door for anyone. Stay put."

"You need to—"

"Now! That guy's the reason we're here. Now go. Do what you're told."

She stepped back, swallowing hard. Whoever Gabe had cornered, he must be dangerous for Zack to be so blunt. He let himself out to the porch and shut the door behind him. Shelby did as he'd asked.

"What's going on?" Kelsey had actually smiled tonight, but worry lines etched her face now. "Is Gabe hurt?"

"No, he's got some guy on your back step though." Shelby peered over her shoulder, frightened for the man she didn't want to have feelings for. Gabe was sick. He shouldn't have been outside in his condition, much less working.

In came Zack again. "Kels, I hate to ask, but this guy says he knows you. Says he worked with Alex. I've never seen him before. Can you come to the back door and give me a yay or nay?"

"Sure." She lifted off the couch and followed. Shelby, too.

Zack only let the women peer through the back-door window. Gabe didn't even look up, his eyes dark, bent on the stranger. And darn. His chest heaved, probably from all that dirty river water. He kept blinking, as if he were exhausted.

The stranger looked up, his rugged face lit with a cheerful smile when he spied Kelsey. He could've passed for the Marlboro man. Thick, wavy hair. Mustache. Scruff on his chin and cheeks, but his neck clean-shaven. Handsome. He tipped his head in friendly greeting, like a cowboy might touch two fingers to the brim of his hat.

Honestly, Gabe looked meaner, sick as he was. Shelby relaxed. What was there to worry about?

"I've never seen him," Kelsey told Zack. "Why would he say such a thing?"

He grunted. "To get close to you. Look again. Are you sure?"

"Pretty sure. I've met a lot of people since I married Alex. I might be wrong. Do you want me to talk to him?"

Zack hesitated. "Only if you stay on this side of the door. Gabe won't let him get to you. He's already disarmed this joker, so don't be afraid."

"I'm not afraid. Let's see what he thinks he knows."

Disarmed? Okay, so maybe he wasn't so harmless after all.

Zack opened the door, but kept his arm between Kelsey and the screen.

"Mrs. Stewart," the stranger greeted her amicably enough. "It's nice to see you again. You may not remember me, but I remember you. You're as pretty as ever. Hayden Carell, at your service, ma'am. We met in Seattle when you and Alex were headed up North to Alaska for halibut fishing. Remember?"

She pursed her lips thoughtfully. "Which cruise were you on?"

A big smile cracked his rugged face. "Now you know better than that. Alex leased a private rig. The Frigid Wind. Remember?"

Hayden Carell didn't look dangerous, but Gabe did, his elbows cocked, his pistol aimed at the man's chest. Gabe was sick and breathing hard, but fierce. Angry. His lips were set in a thin hard line that brooked no discussion. His eyes had changed from puppy dog adorable to the feral glitter of an alpha wolf protecting his pack.

So this is what he looks like when he's ready to lay down his life. Or take one.

"Is he right?" Shelby asked, pushing her glasses up on her nose to see more clearly. "About the fishing boat, I mean."

Kelsey huffed softly. "I don't know. The name's right, but I can't place him."

"I'm sure sorry to hear about Alex," the stranger said contritely, as if he really cared. "And I'm sorry I got your boys here all riled up for nothing, too. The truth is, Alex asked me to check in on you if anything ever happened to him. I'm only following up on my good buddy's last request. That's why I'm here."

"You call creeping around her house checking up on her?" Gabe snapped. "Was that you standing under her bedroom window the other night, too?"

Kelsey gasped. So did Shelby. *Darn. The secret was out.*

Hayden Carell, if that's what his name really was, shook his head, releasing a hank of wavy hair over his forehead. He smoothed it back with a big hand as his gaze zeroed in on Gabe. "Kind of hard to walk up and knock on her door with you goons on patrol every hour on the hour. I didn't think I could get in to see her the way you've got the place buttoned up and locked down. Hell. It's a might safer than Leavenworth."

"I don't know you," Kelsey stated firmly, drawing his attention off Gabe.

"It's okay. Don't worry about it. You do remember me pulling you out of the river though, don't you? You can't have forgotten that."

A tiny yelp burst from her throat. "That was you?"

Shelby put a protective arm across Kelsey's shoulders. With one breath, this jerk had ripped the last shred of hope from her.

"Yes, ma'am. Glad I could oblige. My buddy, Craig Olsen, said I could use his summer place if I ever needed it. Sure glad. You were in mighty bad shape that morning. I needed to get you somewhere safe."

"Listen, buddy. *IF* that was you, why didn't you take her to the hospital?" Shelby demanded. "Why take her to some guy's house and hide her away for three days, huh? You want to explain that?"

"Someone needed to keep her safe," he drawled, extra slowly, as if he needed to make a point.

"Not good enough, Mr. Carell, or whoever you really are." This guy was lying through his straight, white teeth. He'd manipulated Kelsey, and she wasn't strong enough to see through him. Well, Shelby could, by heck. "She was badly hurt. You should've called an ambulance. You should have had her transported to the emergency room. Instead, you let the people who love her go crazy with worry. We searched for three days while you played hero. She could've died."

He lifted one shoulder. "Guess after your guys let Alex die, I wasn't convinced you could keep her safe."

"I didn't let him die," Gabe spat. He closed in on the guy, but Zack lifted a hand to stop him.

Gabe's emotional outburst caught Shelby short. *Oh my. Gabe. You poor thing. You didn't let anyone die. He just—did.*

"But my dogs," Kelsey murmured. "They scented Alex on the river. I know they did. I just watched them do it. Twice."

Hayden Carell had the good grace to offer a truly sad face. Even his mustache drooped. "Sure sorry 'bout that. Your husband gave me a good pair of boots when he came home on emergency leave from Iraq. They were nearly new, so I kept them and used them. Must've been what the dogs caught wind of."

Oh, my God. Shelby shuddered. All along Kelsey had insisted that Alex had climbed into bed with her. Was it really this guy? Had he gotten inside? Had he held her in his arms and—

Ewww. The thought that this guy might have taken that extreme liberty with a medicated and unconscious woman creeped Shelby out, but it made sense. Kind of. She shot a lightning quick glance at Gabe, wanting to ask, but not willing to frighten Kelsey any more than she already was.

Kelsey stepped away from the stranger, shaking her head. "No. It wasn't you. Not you. It was Alex."

The front doorbell rang.

"Don't let him out of your sight," Zack growled.

Gabe shifted his weight, his pistol still aimed at Hayden Carell's head, while Zack pulled the ladies inside before he locked the rear door. Striding through the house with Kelsey and Shelby at his side, he pointed at the couch. "Sit. Now."

Shelby knew better than to argue, but damn. Carell seemed to have an answer for everything. Maybe Alex really was dead.

Mark Houston burst into the house. "Where is he? I want the bastard before the police get here."

"He's all yours." Zack nodded toward the back.

"He hurt anyone?"

"Settle down. Hell, he didn't get the chance. Gabe intercepted him at the back fence line. He's cuffed and disarmed. Not going anywhere. Calls himself Hayden Carell. I've got to tell you, he sounds authentic."

"Like hell. He's Sam Becker, the FBI bastard who killed Alex."

"Oh, no," Kelsey murmured as she sank deeper into the couch, her face as pale as the day she'd come home from the hospital. She clutched one hand to her mouth.

And Shelby had had enough. Jumping to her feet, she blocked Kelsey from Mark's view. "Stop it. Right now. You guys need to leave. I won't have you hurting her. She's had enough and so have I."

Mark shot her a menacing look, but Shelby didn't back down. She took another step forward, her finger pointed into his chest. "You're as bad as that guy out there," she bellowed, her index finger stabbed in the direction she meant Mark to go. *Away, damn it!* "You're hurting her! Go outside and break someone else's heart!"

He nodded, his anger restrained. His gaze flickered over her shoulder to Kelsey, but it was Zack who dropped to one knee at Kelsey's feet. "I'm sorry, Kels. For a minute there, Gabe had us all believing, didn't he?"

Kelsey broke down. She dropped her face into her hands and Shelby came unglued. "I still believe, damn it. Gabe's telling the truth. Trust him, Kelsey. Not Hayden What's-his name. He's a liar."

Kelsey's shoulders heaved, and Shelby melted onto the couch beside her. She took her sad friend in her arms and pressed her to her chest, stoking her head. Shelby's eyes brimmed as Kelsey's pain became hers. This nightmare had to stop.

"Your husband is alive, Kelsey," she crooned, rocking back and forth and giving Kelsey all she had to give. Kelsey had become more than a client. She was family.

Chapter Twenty

The police showed up after Mark questioned Hayden Carrel, alias Samuel Becker. The liar. The entire interrogation took place on Kelsey's back step to keep her out of further confrontation. He admitted no complicity in Alex Stewart's, despite being caught in an outright lie, and Mark's statement that he held video evidence to the contrary. Steven had caught Becker red-handed. He was going down.

"I've got you dead to right," Mark hissed, his nose an inch from Becker's. "You're lucky the police have you in custody, but I promise. My team's damned good. Make one wrong move and they'll jump down your throat and rip your heart out."

Becker shrugged, not intimidated or concerned, by the looks of him. The man had an easy attitude, as if he were untouchable. Off he went in the custody of two of Alexandria's finest.

David, Rory, and Connor had shown up shortly after Mark's arrival, but were already headed back to the office. Gabe restored his pistol to its holster under his left arm. "The bastard's lying."

"You get anything out of him before I got here?"

"Just the crock of shit he told Kelsey about knowing Alex, but damn. I thought we finally proved the boss was alive."

"Sonofabitch!" Mark roared. "When the hell are you going to give it up? Dead men don't come back to life. Every last one of you guys is fighting me on this, but you, of all people should know better. You were there, Gabe. Jesus Christ, you watched him die."

Gabe hated that Kelsey might be able to hear the angry tirade from inside. He hadn't seen Alex die. Not really. He'd gone to get Kelsey while the ambulance went the other way, but now was not the time to bring that detail up.

"You're right," he said, more to get Mark to calm down than because he agreed with him. "It was stupid. I give." *But I'm still glad I did it, and I'd do it again.*

Mark stabbed an index finger in the direction of Kelsey's bedroom window. "Look what you've done. You got her hopes up for nothing. It stops now or I'm pulling your ass off this assignment. Do you hear me?"

"Yes, sir," came quickly to Gabe's lips.

"Settle down," Zack told Mark. "Becker's caught. Maybe the police will let you talk with him in the morning. You've got all the evidence they need to put him away. It doesn't matter what he said tonight. He'll go down for murder."

Mark faced the house, his eyes dark and angry. "This bullshit's killing her, guys. Get her out of the country and the hell away from here until we know who's after her. Spain. Take her to freaking Spain if you have to."

And Gabe was done kissing Mark's ass. Mark didn't have a clue how fragile Kelsey was. He hadn't been in the closet with her while she clung to her dead husbands T-shirt. She needed to be here. Her dogs were here. Her memories. Her heart.

"No, Boss. She stays here. Making her leave is what'll kill her. Listen. The bodies in the SUV that I found in the river were Manson and Echevarria. They were on the riverbank that day. I can prove it. It's on the video. Come watch."

"And that's another thing, *Junior Agent*."

Damn. *Junior Agent* never started a good conversation. Gabe couldn't win. He sucked in a deep breath, wishing it didn't hurt as much as it did, and prepared for a Hellfire missile strike.

"You ever pull that kind of a stunt again, and you're fired. I tasked you to guard Kelsey Stewart *IN her home*, not to traipse out to the river to indulge a grieving woman's misguided wishes. Shit. If it isn't you guys, it's the rest of the whole damned team!"

"Hey, calm down. What's really going on?" Zack asked, his voice level and firm. "You're usually rock solid."

Mark raked his fingers over his head, huffing short, angry breaths. "Nothing. Don't worry about it. Just do your damned jobs. Can you handle that or not?"

"We are. That's why you're here. Gabe did exactly what you're paying him to do. He found two more of your gang of ten, didn't he? And for a few hours, we thought we'd found positive proof the boss might be alive, too. Hell, you can't blame us for trying."

"Well, how'd that turn out for you?" Sarcasm poured out of Mark's mouth.

Gabe stepped clear of the showdown neither he nor Zack seemed able to win. He'd never seen Mark so nasty or ill-tempered. Only when he dropped to the single step at Kelsey's back door and gripped his forehead, did Zack re-engage. "Spill, buddy. What's really going on?"

"Shit. What isn't?" Mark rubbed three fingers back and forth over his forehead, his thumb pressed to his left temple. "God, now I know why Alex had migraines all the time. Just never realized how much crap he put up with. If it's not the stink-eye from Mother, it's Maverick and Landon going after each other in the office. Every time I turn around, I'm shoveling more shit."

"It's tough being lead dog," Zack agreed.

"Yeah." Mark grunted. "Believe me. I get that."

"Maverick and Landon fighting? I'd pay to see those two go a round," Zack teased.

"No, you wouldn't," Gabe argued. "Maverick would as soon kill Landon as look at him."

Zack's brows lifted. "Oh, yeah? Why's that?"

Gabe paused, unsure how much to share. What the hell? Mark deserved the whole story.

"Because Landon's a sonofabitchin' liar. He had the balls to tell Alex he'd worked with Maverick in country, only the bastard never did. Yeah, he was in Afghanistan, just didn't serve with Maverick or us when everything went bad. That's how he got the job, though, by making it look like he was tight with Maverick, Taylor, and me. Now he's stepping out on Maverick's ex with Channing."

"With Lisa?" Mark asked. "Shit. That explains a lot."

Gabe crouched to Mark's level, one knee to the patio. "Listen, I hate to talk about my buddy behind his back, but you need to know what's going on. Maverick's fiancée was a gal named Kimberly. They had their wedding all arranged and invitations in the mail. Hell, he'd asked me to be best man until Landon went home early. Next thing Maverick knew, he got a Dear John letter. Kim said she'd found someone else. She said a lot of other crap, too, but the real kicker is her bullshit letter came the day Maverick's brother was killed in action. It messed Maverick up good. That's why Taylor and I recommended him to Alex. Maverick's a time bomb, but he's a damned good operator. Don't be too hard on him. He needs the job or he's going to blow."

Mark closed his eyes, stress etched into the wrinkles on his brow. "He's tight, I'll give you that. No wonder."

"Then he's right where he needs to be," Zack said. "Keep him busy. Hell, send him over here to assist us. We'll keep his ass buried so deep in work he won't have time to worry about Landon. Who knows what other bastard Gabe will apprehend?" He nudged Gabe. "Huh?"

Gabe sneezed, not the best answer he could've given his senior agents. At least now they were talking together instead of swearing at each other.

"I might do that," Mark said. "Are you okay? Sounds like you're coming down with a good stiff cold."

"I'm good," Gabe replied, despite the nasal twang he'd developed. He sucked in a raspy breath, hesitant to bring up what he'd just taken a verbal beating over. "Umm, I need a favor, though. Could you ask someone to run over to my apartment and retrieve the pants and shirt I wore the day Alex got killed? They're in the hamper in my bathroom, maybe on the floor. I'm not trying to be obstinate, but Zack and I were talking, and I'm not so sure it was blood coming out of Alex that day. Maybe I'm remembering things wrong, but could you at least get Mother or Ember to get it analyzed?"

Mark offered a bleak smile. "I guess. Why do you think it's not blood?"

"It didn't feel right and there wasn't as much as there should have been. I think." *And I should have thought of this in the first place.*

"No problem. Maybe then everyone will stop looking for ghosts."

"You know me and Zack are behind you, don't you?" Gabe retrieved his keys from his jeans pocket and handed Mark the one to his apartment. "We just need to be sure what really happened. There are too many unanswered questions."

"Yeah. I get it. I understand." Mark slapped his palms to his knees, aggravated but resigned.

"You never know," Zack said. "Gabe might just have solved the whole case for you."

"God, I wish." Mark shrugged both shoulders. "Zack's right. Maybe the police will let me interrogate Becker tomorrow. Who knows? Maybe hell will freeze over, too."

Gabe pushed up from the patio and offered his boss a hand up off the concrete step. "It already has. Now we just need to figure out how to live through it."

"Kelsey. What's wrong?" Shelby bolted down the hall, following Kelsey, who ran to her bathroom and slammed the door behind her.

Shelby came to a dead stop. The wretched sounds coming from beyond the door explained everything. Kelsey was not only sick at heart, but also sick to her stomach as well.

Tears flooded Shelby's eyes at what this sweet woman had gone through.

Damn Mark for upsetting her.

Damn that Sam Becker.

Damn everyone who'd hurt Kelsey!

She would've damned Alex too, if he hadn't just been declared dead again. God. How much could this poor woman take?

Shelby knocked at the door, listening for any sound from the other side. Only the toilet flushing answered. "May I come in and help you?"

The saddest voice answered with a squeaky, "No. Please. Leave me alone."

Shelby didn't have the heart to walk away. She turned the knob and peered around the door. Her heart melted. Kelsey sat cross-legged by the toilet, her head in her hands and a wad of toilet paper at her feet.

"You poor thing." She knelt at Kelsey's side and pulled her into her arms, tears falling over her cheeks.

Kelsey buckled. She had no words. She just held onto Shelby while the storm let loose and sobs shook her. Gabe was so right. Death was a hellacious sucker punch, only it kept knocking Kelsey down and stomping her into the dirt every time she got to her feet. It never let her get a handle on living without the man she'd loved.

It came as easy as breathing. Shelby held Kelsey to her heart and began rocking back and forth. "I don't know what to say, Kelsey, but I'm here, and I'm not going anywhere. And I'm so sorry."

Kelsey nodded, her forehead on Shelby's shoulder. "I just... miss him," she finally said, her voice cracking. "He's the kindest man I've ever known. He loved me when I wasn't worth loving. When I made the worst mistakes a mother could make. When I..." her voice broke, and Shelby kept rocking. She couldn't cure grief but she would sit with Kelsey for as long as was needed.

"You've taught me a lot while I've been here, and the greatest thing you and Alex had was your love for each other. Don't let it go. Don't ever stop believing in him."

"But everyone says he's dead," Kelsey cried, her tears a river she couldn't seem to stop. "What if they're right? What if I really am crazy?"

"Don't listen to them." Shelby kept rocking, surprised at the conviction she felt. "Listen to your heart. That's the only thing that will last. Your heart and his. No one and nothing else counts. There is no *loved*. Only *loves*. Remember?"

Kelsey murmured something Shelby couldn't understand, but it didn't matter. She rested her chin on Kelsey's head and held on. She'd come to the Stewarts' house expecting a couple of weeks of easy employment. Instead, she'd found one of the greatest truths.

Love like Kelsey's love for Alex transcended time and space, and maybe eternity. The day might come when she could finally stand alone and face the hard facts, whatever they were, but until then, Shelby planned to stay with Kelsey for as long as necessary. And beyond.

At last the tears ceased. Kelsey wiped her face and the women got up off the floor. Shelby gave the toilet one more flush.

"Thanks, Shelby," Kelsey said, her face drawn and her eyes red again. "I'm going brush my teeth and go to bed. I've had enough."

"I'll help you get ready."

"No. That's okay." Kelsey lifted her chin and eyed the face of grief in the mirror. "I'll feel better in the morning."

"I'll come check on you in a little bit."

"Thanks, Shelby. Good night."

By the time the guys decided to come in from the back porch, Shelby had a full head of steam. Things had to change, but one look at Gabe and her anger dissipated. The guy was seriously sick. His cheeks were flushed and his lips dry.

"Are you hungry?" she asked. "I could warm up some chicken soup."

"No. Just tired. Mark's sending another guy over to assist tomorrow. I'm going to take a nap until the next perimeter check."

"Hit the sack," Zack said. "I'll walk the 'hood tonight. You get feeling better."

"But you should eat first," Shelby persisted. "You haven't even had breakfast. At least get something to drink before you lie down."

"No. I'm good." Gabe headed toward the front room floor. With a flick of his wrist, his sleeping bag unfurled, followed by two pillows. He dropped to his knees, still fully dressed and stretched across his bed for the night—the floor.

Shelby cringed. It hadn't dawned on her. Gabe and Zack endured sub-standard accommodations to protect Kelsey. And her. Yet they'd never complained.

I'm such a bitch.

She opened Kelsey's cupboards and fixed a hot toddy with an extra shot of whiskey from the Stewarts' bounteous liquor cabinet. She recognized some of the labels. Jamison Irish whiskey. Jack Daniels Single Barrel. Grey Goose vodka.

Bacardi Oakheart spiced rum. Interesting. Alex must've liked his drink at the end of a hard day.

Crouching beside Gabe, she said, "Here. Take this."

The poor guy had his arm covering his eyes from the kitchen light. "No, thanks. I'm not hungry."

"It's just a hot drink. It will help you sleep."

He lifted to one elbow. "What is it?"

"A hot toddy. I figured you could use one tonight."

Exhausted green eyes regarded her carefully before he accepted the cup, downing the drink in one long gulp. His Adam's apple bobbed, drawing her attention to the ragged edge of the black polo he always wore. Everything about him seemed like he needed someone to look out for him. Someone to care.

He handed the empty cup back. "Thanks. That was thoughtful."

When he leaned onto his pillow, she smoothed a hand over his forehead. "I'm worried about you. You're burning up."

He closed his eyes with a sigh. "Of course I am. I've got a hot chick's hand on my face."

She pulled her fingers back, startled he'd taken her compassionate service for something else, and hoping he hadn't noticed what her nipples were busy doing—standing up and begging for attention like cheerleaders with pompoms. If this kept up, she'd need a padded bra.

"Do you want more ibuprofen?"

"No, ma'am. Just sleep. I'm dogged."

"Get some rest, Gabe. Good night."

"Good night, Shelby."

Chapter Twenty-One

The pictures on the mantle haunted Gabe. Kelsey had an easy way with children. Giggling. Happy. He'd seen her with Zack's girls in the past. She should have a house full. Why didn't she? Kids would make her happy. Like she used to be.

Damn. So much death. Nothing seemed fair. Not Darrell. Not Alex. Not those cute little brown-haired boys on the mantle. *Sure as hell not this lumpy bedroll.*

Gabe tossed. He turned. Did all the things a sick guy with muscle-aches that felt more like he'd been run over by an eighteen-wheeler did. He stripped down to his boxers and polo, covered his head with a pillow, and wished the hot drink Shelby had given him would kick in and let him drift away. He brushed a sweaty hand over his face, wondering who the hell she really was—bossy or kind. Both?

She'd surprised him, the way she stood up to Becker for Kelsey. The girl definitely had guts and the hot toddy was a nice surprise. Kind of like her. It went down sweet with a burn.

Rain and wind hit the front window. A stab of lightning lit the room, a flickering strobe that ended with a distant peal of thunder. Zack walked the line tonight. In the dark where murderers skulked and insurgents lingered...

One minute, Gabe was uncomfortable. The next, he fell into a dream where little boys giggled and teased. That blonde little gal squealed about spiders. Whisper and Smoke joined in a game of tag. Round and round they ran.

He played along, counting to ten in a game of hide-and-seek that in some way transported him back to that stinking hillside in Afghanistan. *That* day. *That* nightmare. *That* other little dark-haired boy.

WHOOSH!

Incoming! Run for it!

The ground shook. Men screamed and bellowed. Confusion reigned. Black smoke filled the bunker, burning his nose with the rank smells of burning diesel, raw sewage, and blood.

He scrambled out of the line of fire, groping for his weapon. *Gotta find that kid. He was just here. Sonofabitch! Where's my rifle? My helmet?*

Incoming! Night turned to day. *Run, for God's sake! Don't just stand there, kid. Run!*

Thunderous detonations sucked the air out of the night and—he couldn't breathe.

Someone grabbed his neck. *Where's that damned kid, for Christ's sake?*

Panic clawed up his throat. Not even it could find a way out. No scream. Just the sucking rattle of a man running out of air and time. The gasp of a guy who couldn't draw one... damned... breath.

He blinked. The kid. He'd just materialized out of the smoke and confusion and he still wore that same haunting smile. He put a hand on Gabe's shoulder and patted him. No words. Just that brown-eyed smile that beckoned Gabe—back into Hell.

No! No! Never again! God! Help me. I'm dying here!

Someone pounded his shoulder, but he couldn't see who it was through the smoke. Taliban maybe? Enemy? Friend? Taylor? Darrell? Names flooded back.

"Gabe! Gabe! Stop it. Oh, my gosh, you're hurting yourself."

A woman? Here? No way.

A man needs air to speak. To scream. His lungs tried to suck in a breath. They wheezed, shutting down even as he needed them to open up wide and let him live.

The shoulder pounding shifted to his chest. Dead center. *Like the bloody body shots to Alex. And Darrell.*

Outright fear cranked up the noise inside his head. He kicked, writhing away to escape the stranglehold at his neck and the deadening touch of that little boy's hand. Always the same damned question. *Why look for him? The little guy always shows up and it never ends well when he does. He's the bringer of death. Every. Damned. Time!*

Adrenaline swamped what was left of Gabe's thin control. *Get off me, you sonofabitch! Let me go!*

"Gabe. I'm here. Stop it." The voice reached into the murk and pulled him apart, unraveling the nightmare strand by freaking strand. The grip at his windpipe lessened.

"You're hurting yourself. Stop it."

At last! *Air.* He sucked in one long pull of it. Oxygen flooded his head. Another life-saving gulp replaced the last. He stilled, letting it fill and replenish until his mind cleared. The little boy had vanished.

"Where's... where's... the kid?" *Thank God, he's gone, but where'd he go?*

"What kid?" A shadowy figure loomed overhead but... he... she... wasn't... *them.*

The black smoke of the Afghanistan battlefield evaporated into the soft light of Kelsey's front room. Someone peeled his fingers from their death grip at his throat. *Damn. It was... me. I was choking myself. Shit.*

He fingered the oxygen mask that had suddenly appeared on his nose, pulling in more of the sweet, soft air. *Good. I can... breathe... again. Good. I'm not... there.*

His vision cleared. *Damn it.* He'd backed himself into the corner by Kelsey's brick fireplace. He'd torn his polo shirt in the struggle, the buttons scattered to who knew where. A lamp lay on the floor beside him, its light bulb still on, but somehow, unbroken. Some magazines. His bedroll, upside down and kicked to hell.

The shadowy figure emerged while he sucked in gulps of oxygen, trying to clear his head and still his quaking body. A medic? Zack? Bright inquisitive eyes peered down at him behind horn-rimmed men's glasses. *God. Not Shelby.*

Yes. Shelby.

He closed his eyes so he wouldn't have to look at her. The ostrich in the sand routine didn't work. Her fingers remained light on his forehead. "Gabe? Can you hear me now? Are you okay?"

Tenderness. Not what he needed. Hell, no.

Her voice sounded frightened, kind of squeaky and tight. He must've scared her. Hell, yeah. He'd scared himself, too, more than he could ever explain.

The kid seemed so real. The kid with the grenade launcher. That damned kid. The one his subconscious soul kept trying to save...

Hyper-vigilance. There was no understanding it until a person lived it.

"I'm fine." Sweat trickled down his neck and belly. *Damn. I need more air.*

With one big grunt, he pushed himself out of the corner and flat to his back. He needed lung space now, room to breathe and time to get back to normal, whatever the hell that was. God, this panic attack was worse than most, probably because he was sick, but shit. *Not in front of Shelby. Go away. Please, just pretend none of this happened and go away.*

She readjusted her position. Her hands moved to the center of his heaving chest and he honestly didn't care. He covered his eyes with his arm and inhaled steady, slow breaths to prevent hyperventilating any worse. That much he knew for sure. He had to regain control while he could. He set to counting deliberately and slowly.

One. Shelby could wait.

Damn it, she did.

Two. She removed the oxygen mask from his face, and like it or not, he was glad she was there. Waking up alone after an attack sucked big time. He covered his eyes again once the mask was gone.

Three. Damn, she was quiet. She must've gone to the kitchen or bathroom, because all of a sudden, she came back and knelt at his side again. A damp washcloth skimmed over his brow.

Four. Stinking panic attacks. They wreaked havoc on his lips. He ran his tongue over his bottom one, mostly checking for blood or bitten flesh. Parched or chewed, he never knew how they'd end up. *Damn. Fat lip again.*

Five. Shelby eased one hand under the back of his neck, lifting his head enough to place a glass to his lips. "Drink this and breathe easy. I'm here and you're safe now."

Six. He gulped in one long swallow and quit counting. Yeah, right. Safe. Bullshit. A guy's never safe from his nightmares.

Funny thing. Panic attacks used up every last ounce of strength. Dainty little Shelby could've had her way with him right then and there if she'd wanted to. He wouldn't have been able to fight her off. Wouldn't have mattered in the long run, though. He had nothing to give her, not physically spent like he was. Wrecked. Wasted.

He heard the glass bump the end table. At least he hadn't knocked *that* over.

Her hand came right back to his chest, her fingers splayed as if counting his heartbeats—not like it was hard to do. They still sounded plenty loud to him, but her touch helped.

It had been months since a woman had touched him as gently. It probably meant nothing to her, but those slender fingers moving in small, slow circles over his pecs soothed him in ways he couldn't explain.

She didn't know it, but that simple contact went a long way to holding him together. God, he craved it down to the deepest recesses of his soul. Stupid tears welled up in his eyes, and he was damned if they'd well up and drip over the sides of his head. A woman's touch. Nothing like it in the world.

"It's just thunder and lightning," she said. "You aren't in battle and those weren't bombs. There is no little boy to save. You're in Kelsey's home. It's okay."

He squeezed his already closed eyes tighter, wishing he could do the same for his ears. *Not bombs, Shelby. Rocket-launched grenades. That's what took my foot. And that boy? A little brown-eyed kid with a worried smile and no shoes. A kid who had no business toting that heavy grenade launcher on his skinny shoulder. A kid I didn't want to have to kill. But I did.*

Gabe pushed the ghost away. How embarrassing, a full-blown panic-attack in front of Attila the Hun. Shelby sounded really kind, but he knew better. She could change on a dime. Any second now that gentle hand would lift off, and she'd revert back to herself. Besides, he didn't want her seeing him like this.

"I'm fine," he croaked, rolling to his side, away from her.

She stayed with him, her hand soft on his bicep, squeezing just enough so he'd know she hadn't left.

"I'm fine," he insisted again, wishing she'd take the hint and leave. He knew how it worked. Date once or twice, but in the long run, this close encounter would end like all the rest. He'd wind up alone. And he just plain didn't want to risk what was left of his heart one more time.

"You are fine, Gabe," she stated gently. "And you didn't let your boss die, either. That Sam Becker guy is an ass. He said a lot of mean things."

Yep. Still staying. Damn it.

Shelby had just stepped over the line, though. Gabe had no intention of talking about Alex's death with her, or what happened in country. His head knew better, but that old rascal guilt still poked its head up now and then. She needed to stop helping.

"It'll soon be over. It's just a panic attack, isn't it?"

"Yeah," he admitted. *Just a freaking full-blown, green Hulk, rip-your-clothes-off kind of attack. The thunder and lightning must've triggered it. Stinking fever, too. Here he sat in his underwear and a half-ripped off shirt, sweating like a pig. Could this night get any more embarrassing?*

Yes. It could. He wiped the drool off his chin. *Great. I look like an ass.*

"I get them, too. Only no one knows. Well, not until now. You're the only one I've ever told."

He cocked his head to face her and finally opened his eyes. That was a revelation he hadn't expected. "You?"

Something sad flitted behind those geeky glasses she kept pushing up her nose.

"Umm, why? How come?"

"I'll tell you about it sometime. Not now."

"Okay," he whispered back. "I'll hold you to that. You tell me about yours and maybe I'll tell you about... mine." Then again, maybe not. Marines didn't share that kind of crap. War stories were a definite downer. Not meant for civilian consumption. Especially not women. Ever.

"You were injured over there."

"Lots of us were. No big deal."

"A transtibial amputation is tough."

"Nah." He sucked in another slow breath, clenching his fists over his stomach and biding his time. She really needed to leave. "There's guys lots worse off than me."

Like Darrell. Like Maverick. Like everyone who came home in a box.

"There's always someone worse, but every loss of a limb is still difficult," she said more firmly. "It's the same as a death. You need to grieve for the loss of a limb as much as the loss of someone you loved. And I'm... I'm sure sorry, Agent Cartwright. I mean, Gabe. I've been, umm, kind of oblivious to a lot of things since I've been here. I was so focused on Kelsey and protecting her. Then she went missing. I never should've let her out of my sight, and—"

"Settle down. It wasn't your fault," he corrected, thankful for the diversion. "She's not a little girl. You can't make her behave."

"I know, but she would've been satisfied with toast and jelly that morning, but no. I had to make her my special omelet. That's why everything went wrong. I had to have everything my way."

Gabe mustered a small smile. "Like the boot trays?"

"Yes, okay, like the boot trays, but—"

"And the menu schedule?" Focusing on her drew the attention off him. *Good thinking, Cartwright. Keep her talking.*

Shelby pushed her glasses back up her nose again. "See what I mean? I lost control the second you and Zack arrived, and every time I turn around, things fall apart a little more. How am I going to keep her safe and healthy when you guys are always in my way?"

She asked that more as if she were perplexed instead of angry. Was this the real Shelby finally peeking through? Was she trying to figure him out as much as he tried to understand what made her tick?

Gabe breathed deeply. The more he listened, the more he relaxed until one thing got through his embarrassment. Her hot damned elegant black nightie. Spaghetti straps. Silky thin material that showed her thighs and a hint of her ass. The pink bow curled between very perky breasts. Ribbons trailing down her front.

He shifted onto one elbow to see better. And more.

The skimpy nightie he could've dealt with and possibly ignored, but the jiggle beneath it was deliciously distracting. So were the two hardened nubs of her nipples beneath the thin material, all perked up and begging to be touched. Fondled. Licked.

Now she'd done it. He pulled the corner of his bedroll up from behind him to cover his, umm, lap. Running his tongue over his fat lip, his mind shifting to other ways he knew to make a woman happy. This woman.

She lowered her head, peering deeper into his eyes. Closer. Maybe too close for her own good. He didn't mean to look down her cleavage. But he did. Luscious did not begin to describe the fruit hanging nearly within reach, nor the tender valley between.

"Are you even listening to me?"

Busted. He jerked his gaze back to her eyes. "Yes. Sure, you're worried about keeping Kelsey safe and, umm..." *Damn. What was she saying?*

"So? How are we going to work together? I'd like to think we still could. I know I've been unreasonable. All I saw at first was two guys in my way. I didn't realize how much you really cared for Kelsey, both you and Zack. I get it now."

For the first time, she actually smiled. Damn, her smile lit up the night. Shelby meant well. He'd seen her in action on the riverbank when she'd all but accused the sheriff of not initiating a search fast enough. And her outspoken rebuke of Becker? Ballsy.

He captured her hand on his chest. "Has anyone ever told you how beautiful you are?"

"You're changing the subject," she murmured, her eyes averted, her lashes fluttering against the soft swell of her cheeks. "And I'm, umm, not exactly dressed appropriately. I got up so fast when I heard you out here that I, umm, gosh. I need my robe. I should go."

"No. Stay." He tugged her closer. "Talking to someone after an attack always helps."

Especially—you. Feelings he didn't want to admit surfaced with a rush. He lifted the glasses off her nose and set them on the carpet, craving more of her touch.

Shelby's breath caught. She didn't remove her hand from his, and she didn't leave. Instead, she leaned into him. Over him. Closer. Loose chunks of blonde fell over her face as she edged downward.

He shifted his left hand to her waist, then to the small of her back to hold her in place. Easing to the carpet again, he cupped her jaw, his fingers splayed at her neck, the pad of his thumb on her chin. Tremors shivered through her the nearer she came, exciting every last male nerve in his body. A tiny whimper lifted from the back of her throat.

"May I?" he asked, because that was what he'd been taught. *Never assume. Always be sure you're on a two-way street before you rev those engines, son. Once you're off the line, there's no going back.*

"Yes," she breathed, her eyes wide and the sultry color of lavender fields on a dark spring night. She fell those last few inches between them.

And that was enough for him. He cradled her face between his hands, drinking in the delicious scent of vanilla and rose petals. God, she smelled like spring combined with that distinctly feminine fragrance of a woman who wanted a man.

He paused, a breath away from daring to hope again. A woman hadn't been in his life before. Shouldn't have been. Military careers were tough on relationships, so he'd purposefully avoided the complication before he'd been deployed. Then came Afghanistan. Then his injury. After that and one too many rejections, he'd quit looking.

Shelby was right. It was damned tough losing a limb, and a damned tough man gets lonely enough to buy a home all by himself.

But this was no experienced woman in his hands, no *Sex in the City* bed jumper who traded men like the latest fashion heels. This woman was different. Bossy as hell maybe, but rare, and if he was right—pure. That's the impression he got from their bathroom encounter. She'd been so flustered. Curious, but genuinely embarrassed.

She'd closed her eyes. The hole in his chest opened up, that one deep inside the heart he'd closed off years ago. He pressed his lips to hers. She stilled the moment he touched her mouth with his. Her hair fluttered over his cheek as her breathing quickened.

He took time, letting his tongue trace the seam of her closed lips, tasting and teaching, offering sensations just in case she wanted more. His instincts told him this woman hadn't been here before, which meant this might be her first kiss, or at least one of few.

Was it possible?

The notion that she might be a virgin let loose a firestorm Gabe hadn't expected. A groan crawled up from his heart. He'd done what most guys did with girls and girlfriends. He was no saint, but here he was holding something unusual, maybe even endangered.

At last, she relaxed with a sigh onto his chest, her hands soft and warm on his shoulders. And then it happened. She let him ease between her lips, so tentatively, as if she wasn't sure if she should.

He took it slow. Her breath filled him with hunger that he forced himself to control. But God, offering manna to a starving guy in the middle of his own self-made desert was a difficult temptation to refuse. Every last molecule in his awakening male body craved her.

She didn't seem to want to take it slow, either, her luscious curves pressed against his thighs, her round plump breasts planted against his pecs like two clusters of delectable grapes on a platter, as if they were meant to be right damned there.

Blood thrummed through his body. She was small enough. With one good heft, he could have her straddling his hips. Hell, he could have his hands all over her, and he wanted to. God, how he wanted to.

It took what resolve he had left to allow common sense to rule. He and she were both on duty. Kelsey deserved the best they had to give. Now was not the time, and this floor sure wasn't the place. Their risky adventure into heaven had to end before Zack returned and interrupted them.

"Shelby," Gabe growled, his mouth still full of her lips, his hands still cupping her head. Even his fingers were big and ugly in her hair. He opened his eyes to take in the view.

"Uh-huh," she answered, her eyes still closed and the sweetest expression on her face.

He couldn't help smiling. This woman glowed with pure unadulterated pleasure, and he'd put that glow there. He'd given her something that, hopefully, no other guy had before.

"You're something else, you know that?" He concluded their close encounter before Zack spoiled it.

Steamy violet-blues poured heat and desire onto him, and damn it. Gabe wanted his own bed in his own room. *Now.*

He nibbled her lower lip despite the need to release her. Innocent, that was what she was. The oddest mix of innocence and belligerence and compassion, rolled up in a five-foot tall goddess with a major dash of sass. Did she have any idea how close he was to ignition and red lighting on the line?

He smoothed his right hand over her head, lifting her golden locks away from her face. With one last kiss to her forehead, he eased her off his chest and back onto her butt.

"I should go, huh?" she asked, shy again. Her gaze drifted to her clenched fingers.

"No." His fingers lingered in her hair, wanting to pull her back to his mouth for another go around. "You should stay, but not like this."

Zack's hand hit the back doorknob.

Shelby dropped to Gabe's surprised mouth, planted one last wet kiss on his lips, grabbed her glasses and bolted down the hall.

He pushed onto one elbow in time to watch her disappear into the dark, his heart pumping up high in his throat. Shelby had long legs. Her barely covered backside looked way cute in matching black panties as she scampered out of sight. The girl was full of surprises.

Gabe scrambled to stand the floor lamp back where it belonged.

"You're still awake?" Zack asked surprised, shrugging out of his jacket. "Thought you'd be dead to the world by now.

"Just waiting for you. See anything?"

"Yeah, lightning and thunder in the middle of a downpour. Hail, too. Crazy weather tonight. How about you? Feeling any better?" Zack's gaze trailed down Gabe's wide open polo and those missing buttons. He scanned the floor next. "You sure you're okay?"

Gabe took a deep breath and relaxed into the back of the couch, the panic attack gone. Let Zack think what he wanted. "I'm good."

Real damned good.

Chapter Twenty-Two

"Are you guys trying to drive me crazy?" Kelsey asked, her shoulders squared. She'd showered and brushed her hair, maybe even curled it. It had been pulled high on her head, where a few chocolate strands escaped the clip.

Gabe had been on his way out the door to scout the neighborhood and give Zack a chance to catch some shuteye, but damn. This woman sure wasn't the same one who'd gone to bed heartbroken the night before. Kelsey Stewart was back in the house, and ready to fight.

The fire in her brown eyes caught Gabe's attention—until she slapped a long-stemmed red rose on the kitchen table, splinted fingers and all.

"Did you put this on my pillow last night, Gabe?" Her toe tapped the linoleum floor, her Irish obviously up.

"No, ma'am. I most certainly did not," Gabe said, not believing what he was seeing. He raked a hand over his head. When had that happened? "Hey, Zack. Are you seeing this?"

Zack hoisted his tired butt off the computer chair and sauntered into the kitchen. "This was on your pillow, Kels? Really?"

"Yes, it was." She had her nose in the air, and her comeback was full of attitude. "I don't care what that Sam Becker man said. I don't know him, and neither does Alex.

And another thing—I'm tired of you guys hovering over me like I'm going to fall apart every time something bad happens. I'm not, and it's not my imagination, either. Alex pulled me out of the river and took care of me those three missing days I can't remember. He's not a ghost, and he's not dead, do you hear me? And he's not Sam Becker, either."

Gabe couldn't wipe the surprise off his face. Wow, what a change. No wonder Alex loved this woman. She might not have made the most logical argument, but Kelsey had her swagger on.

"And another thing." She paused to draw in a deep breath, her fingertips tracing the petals of the rose. "I'm not some helpless little waif who needs a big tough hero to come to my rescue. I've already got my hero. It's time we start thinking about him for a change. What if he's the one who needs help this time? Have you guys ever thought of that?"

"Kels." Zack's voice turned to honey in that soothing way he had. "Let's not jump to conclusions. You've been on a lot of meds and—"

"That's another thing. I'm not taking any more prescriptions. They make me tired and fuzzy until all I want to do is sleep. They make me dream too much. I'll never feel good at that rate. Explain that rose, Zack. It's real. If you guys didn't sneak into my room and put it there, who did?"

"Shelby must've gotten it for you."

"She better not have," Gabe muttered. That meant breaking protocol by leaving the premises without letting him or Zack know. Speaking of which, where was Miss Shelby? Gabe had been extra quiet to let the ladies sleep, but now he ran to her bedroom and knocked. "Open up, or I'm coming in."

He gave her two seconds before he followed through. Her bed was made, but no Shelby was in it. "Not here." He stormed back to the kitchen, his anger up.

Zack was already at the back door, so Gabe hit the front in time to see her little red car pull to the curb on the other side of the street. Sure enough, Shelby's long legs slid out of the driver's side.

The second her shoes hit the pavement, he couldn't get to her fast enough, his rage ignited at her damned stubborn streak. "Where have you been?"

The happy-go-lucky smile on her face dropped. She extended her right hand and the small white paper bag that was in it. "I ran to the pharmacy for some medicine. You were so sick last night and—"

"Get inside," he hissed, scanning the street for anything out of place while he hurried to her side.

"Oh, stop grumbling." She aimed her key fob at her car. "You caught the guy last night, didn't you? What's the problem with me running one little errand? I came right back."

He grabbed her elbow, intent on dragging her if necessary. "Do you ever do what you're told?"

She twisted around to her cutesy excuse for a car, hit the remote lock and—

BLAM! It blew sky high.

The earth shook.

Gabe teetered. Blinding light and searing heat flashed over him and Shelby in a wave.

She shrieked. He pulled her into his side, shielding her as the blast body slammed them backward to the ground. Gabe rolled, covering her, his arms and hands around her head and face to protect her. Just in time. A piece of burning plastic zipped by her head. She whimpered, but he had no time to worry if she was hurt. Not yet.

A black SUV roared out of the cul-de-sac, gunning for them, its engine at full throttle and its tires screaming. Gabe pulled the pistol from his holster and prepared for battle.

The front plate on the vehicle was covered. Automatic gunfire strafed Kelsey's yard and house. Bullets thudded all around. Plugs of dirt splattered. Windows shattered.

Zack ran straight out the front door and into the line of fire, swearing a blue streak and returning shot after shot. With Shelby planted firmly under him, Gabe offered the same.

The fleeing vehicle screeched on two tires at the T-section and screamed away. Gabe let out a deep sigh of relief, staring at the frightened woman staring up at him. She blinked rapidly, her glasses gone from her face. A huge part of his male soul needed to turn her over his knee and spank the shit out of her for her blatant disobedience. Fear will do that. It will make a guy think things he's never thought of before, but damned. She sure as hell had a whooping coming.

"You get the bastard's plate?" Zack bellowed, lowering his weapon but his gaze still fixed on the direction the assailants had gone.

"No. They were blacked out. Front and rear." Gabe pulled himself and Shelby off the still rain-dampened lawn, his heart pounding at the near miss. He jerked her into his side, his free hand at the back of her neck while he holstered his weapon. "Two men. One driver. The other guy in the rear seat. One of us hit him. He was bleeding."

"Doesn't matter. They're gone." Zack glared at Shelby. "What the hell were you thinking?"

"I just went to the pharm—"

"I don't give a shit where you went!"

"But I—"

"You're insubordinate! I told you what the rules were and you ignored them. Look what you've done!"

"But Gabe's sick, and—"

"Bullshit! In case you haven't notice, Sullivan, Marines don't get a sick day. They hump every stinking day, tired, hungry, or crying their eyes out. Gabe isn't sick. He's on duty!"

Shelby wilted. It was one thing to get an ass chewing, but another thing all together when an ex-Marine did it. An odd need to protect her from Zack skittered up Gabe's spine. If anyone was going to chew her ass, it needed to be him.

"Lay off." Gabe secured Shelby into his side. She trembled from head to foot. Her glasses were gone and those violet blues were brimmed and glistening. The damage was done. Raining crap on her wasn't going to help.

"Don't start on me, Cartwright." Zack stabbed one angry finger at him with a clenched fist to back it up. "Get your gear. We're moving." He stomped into the house, not waiting for agreement or argument.

It was a good thing he did, too. The oddest inclination to kick Zack's butt had just bubbled to the top of Gabe's mind. His fingers curled had into a fist. One more word and there'd have been a different kind of showdown.

"I'm... I'm sorry," she whined. "I thought the coast was clear. I made a big mistake."

He couldn't bring himself to look at her yet, not if she was close to crying. "Yes, you did. We don't have time to talk about it now. Are you hurt?"

"My glasses," she whined, looking down but obviously not seeing them.

Gabe swooped them off the ground, pissed at Zack and mad as hell at Shelby. He tucked them into his shirt collar and ushered her to safety, his nerves still on high alert. Whatever ordnance demolished her car came from nearby. Or some bastard had rigged the car her pretty butt had just been sitting in with a bomb.

Gabe pulled her tight against his hip, needing to keep this hardheaded woman safe despite herself and the panic attack poking at him.

Shit. The bomb might have been stashed under the hood and ready to blow when she drove home. He could have been picking up pieces of her instead of wanting to pound some real world caution into her. He quelled the rising darkness in his head and focused on getting her sweet little ass inside.

"Someone tried to kill me."

"Damn it, Shelby. No shit. That's why Zack's smoking hot. You scared the hell out of him. Me, too." Gabe blew out puffs of air through pursed lips, needing to get in control. *She could've died. What do I have to do? Sit on her to make her listen?*

He couldn't have been more surprised at the front door. There stood Kelsey, a single-carry shoulder holster slung over her left shoulder and a pistol in her hand. A nine-millimeter SIG. Of course. Alex's conceal-and-carry weapon of choice. *What else?*

She might have trembled a little when she rammed its magazine home. Her splintered fingers made it lock all the more surreal, but the sight of a woman who knew the business end of a weapon? Nothing like it in the world.

"Who were they? The same guys who tried to kill Alex?"

"No ma'am, these guys were different." Gabe aimed Shelby at a kitchen chair. "Sit. Stay." *Sam Becker is behind Alex's murder. If he's really dead.*

Surprisingly, she did as she was told. He almost felt sorry for her as pale as she'd gone, but there wasn't time to play nice. Not now. She'd screwed up. Big time. Zack had a right to be nail-spitting pissed.

The front of the house had taken the brunt of the assault. Glass and debris littered the front room. The plate glass picture window was shattered. Bullet holes pockmarked the ceiling and walls. The oil painting over the couch hung askew.

"Pack what you need to travel. Keep it light. Do it now," Zack ordered. He'd already tossed his and Gabe's sleeping rolls and gear to a pile by the door. "We leave in five."

"But Zack..." Kelsey planted her feet in defiance.

Gabe held his breath. Did she honestly think she could stay there now that her home was shot to hell? She'd never win that argument, not with the enemy's open declaration of war and Zack's dander up.

She lifted her chin and stared him in the eye. "I can be packed in two." With that, she retrieved another magazine from the gun safe, removed her family pictures from the mantle and marched to her bedroom. *What a gal.*

Zack went back to packing, but Shelby was the problem. Tears rained all over that bossy façade of hers.

"We don't have time for this." Zack nodded his chin at her. He'd already stowed the laptop and computer equipment in their respective bags, and his cell phone was clamped between his ear and shoulder to notify Mark. "Get her ready to roll or I will."

"I've got it handled." Gabe flipped the chair next to Shelby backwards to sit and face her. She wouldn't meet his eyes, and he understood. The ambush was one of those come to Jesus meetings, when a guy's whole perspective gets changed, whether he's ready for it or not. Gabe had seen it happen plenty overseas. Being shot at tended to shake a person up.

Until now, Shelby had believed in law and order. Truth. Justice. All that crap. She'd thought all she needed to do was call the police and they'd run to her rescue. That honest, hard-working citizens didn't need to protect themselves. *Yeah. All that crap.*

He laid a hand over her trembling fingers. The woman breathed hard, her eyes wide, the pupils big and black. Shelby was well on her way to coming undone.

"Hey," he said softly. "We need to move. Come on. I'll help you pack."

Wordlessly, she lifted out of her chair, but froze again. He tugged her into her room and stuffed everything he could find into her roller bag while she stood, white knuckled at the door. "Anything I'm missing?"

She shook her head, still not meeting his eyes.

He crossed the room to her, the roller bag trailing behind him. Gabe lifted her glasses out of his collar and set them on her nose. "These will help."

The poor thing didn't seem to notice. She gulped, still shaking so hard she could barely stand still.

He cupped her chin to get her to look at him. "Hey. Settle down. We've got work to do."

She flung herself at him, her arms wrapped around his waist and the rest of her squeezing him like her life depended on it. "They blew up my car. They really wanted to kill me. *Me.*"

He dropped the suitcase handle and wrapped her up good and tight against his chest. "Yes, but you're safe now. Stop thinking about it."

"You saved me." Her body vibrated with adrenaline, her face pressed into his shirt.

There was no sense sugarcoating what she'd done. "That's why there are rules. Zack and I can't keep you safe if you don't follow orders. We shouldn't have humored Kelsey by staying here in the first place. This house was never safe or smart."

Shelby pressed closer, burrowing against him as if she wanted to crawl inside his body and hide if she could. Her tears spilled onto his shirt, warming his skin. "You saved me."

"And now we have to leave," he said firmly. "You need to listen up."

"It's not that easy."

"Yes, it is." He cupped her chin to draw her face upward, needing Shelby to open those eyes behind the smudged lenses and re-engage. "Kelsey needs you. You're still alive, and I'd like to keep it that way. Are you working with us or against us?"

Shelby lifted her gaze, blinking through her tears, but hot damn. The strangest thing happened. "Do you have an extra gun?" she asked.

A smile tweaked his lips. Hell, it tweaked his whole face. "That's my girl."

Chapter Twenty-Three

Gabe was right. Kelsey needed her, although it seemed the other way around as they made their getaway in his Land Rover. Kelsey dragged a small roller bag behind her with two pillows and a navy-blue travel blanket strapped to the top of it with a red bungee cord. Shelby hurried to keep up.

Gabe knelt on all fours, peering under his SUV. The sight of his butt on display, his head down and his knees slightly spread should've done more for her libido than it did. Tears sprang to her eyes instead.

Mom was wrong. Guys in cammies who played with guns were good men, too. They knew things most people didn't, and the world wasn't safe. Any minute now the police would be there, but they'd still arrive too late to change what had happened.

"What's he looking for?"

"More bombs," Kelsey answered.

Shelby shivered. *Gabe could've died today. It would've been my fault.*

Sirens screamed in the distance. It wouldn't take long. By the time the police arrived, the Stewarts' home would be empty. According to Gabe, Mark Houston would arrive in time to pick up the pieces and deal with the authorities. That was his job. Hers was to accompany Kelsey and do what she was told.

She took the seat behind the passenger seat, mostly to avoid Zack. He couldn't see her if she sat behind him. Kelsey sat with her in the back seat, directly behind the driver's seat.

Her dogs were loaded in the rear of Gabe's Land Rover, a wire partition between them and the passenger seat. Shelby was almost glad to see them, but she'd rather have a gun like everyone else. The need to defend herself had surfaced with a powerful vengeance. No one would shoot at her again and get away with it.

Gabe said he'd give her one, but he hadn't. For now, his and Zack's guns were holstered, but darn. Both guys had gone straight after the shooters. Not once had they hesitated or flinched. She'd never witnessed a display of bravery before. It literally overwhelmed her.

She couldn't get warm enough, despite the summer sun shining through her window. The memory of Gabe's hard body stretched over hers on the front lawn lifted goose bumps up the back of her neck. Her nipples hardened at the thought of him in that very intimate position on top of her.

Excitement was a powerful aphrodisiac, but the awful reality of what could've happened stilled her physical reaction. He'd been pumped full of blood, every inch of him hard as a rock and taut with rage. He'd fired round after round, ready to protect her. To die for her. But she'd heard the thunder in his chest. She'd felt it beneath her fingertips. He'd turned primitive and deadly, but he'd been scared, too. *All because of me. I did that to him. I put everyone at risk.*

Zack opened the front passenger door and ducked his head inside, still not looking at her. "Change of plans, Kels. You're coming with me. Get your bag. Bring the dogs, too."

Ouch. That hurt. Apparently, he'd decided Kelsey wasn't safe in the same vehicle with her?

Gabe opened his driver side door and climbed in. "I'm not a chauffeur, Shelby. Come up front and ride shotgun."

She unfastened her belt but waited for Zack to leave before she changed seats.

"You know a place we can hunker down?" he asked, his strong hand clutching the seat back.

Gabe retrieved a card from his wallet and handed it to Zack. "It's nearly off the grid, and it's still got that new home smell. Dogs are welcome."

Zack's brows lifted. "Sweet, but are you sure? This could get ugly."

"No problem. Haven't even put in a change of address with Mother yet."

"How'd you do that? You still own your old place?"

"For now. Still got some boxes to move."

"Good enough. You lead. I'll follow." Zack closed the front door, beckoning Kelsey to the other vehicle. She leaned into Shelby for a quick hug. "See you soon."

Zack transferred the dogs and their gear while Shelby scrambled for the front seat and secured her seatbelt. And her nerves.

Gabe's head swiveled back and forth at what had once been a quiet neighborhood. "You ready?"

"Yes," she answered, acid pitching up the back of her throat.

"One rule. If I tell you to get down, I want your ass on the floor with no questions asked, you understand?"

She nodded, her throat dry. God, if she could just stop shaking.

He eased the vehicle out of the driveway and slipped away from what had once been a quiet neighborhood. It looked different now. Still shabby, but with too many places to hide. To stalk. To ambush.

Shelby closed her eyes, the suspense of getting away from danger more than she could bear. *Why did I ever take this job?*

Gabe drove for blocks before Shelby looked behind her. Flipping the sun visor down, she angled it to keep Zack's vehicle in sight. Gabe squeezed her hand on the console between them.

"How are you doing?" he asked, his eyes drifting to her and then back to the road.

She blew out a deep breath. "This is all my fault. I'm sorry."

"Yeah," he agreed a little too quickly, but without malice. "You blew it, but things happen on every undercover op. When they do, we improvise. Stop beating yourself up. It's done."

"But Zack's ready to kill me."

"So what are you going to tell him when we stop?"

"That he's right. I screwed up. I'll do KP or whatever he wants to make things right with him."

Gabe chuckled, a welcome sound on her stretched-too-tight nerves. "The old beg forgiveness routine, huh? Don't do that. Just tell him he's right. That's enough. He's mad now, but he's fair. He won't chew you out if you don't argue with him."

"I'll bake him a cake. What kind does he like? Do you know?"

"Ha. That's easy. Chocolate. Zack's got a sweet tooth the size of his hollow leg."

"What kind do you like?" She had to ask.

Gabe shrugged. "I'm not much for sweets."

"Meat and potatoes?"

"Yeah. I guess. Real food. Chicken enchiladas with roasted habaneras are good, too."

"You like spicy food. You should've told me. Is that what you missed while you were overseas?"

"Nope. I missed my mom's homemade pizza," he said without one second's hesitation. "Greasy, cheesy combination with ten kinds of meat and extra sauce and peppers."

She shuddered at the cholesterol levels this guy had to have, but the conversation calmed her last frazzled nerve. "Ten kinds of meat?"

"Hey, girl, I'm from Texas. What'd you think I want on my pizza? Spinach? Tofu?"

Now it was her turn to chuckle. He had an easy way about him, as if he held no grudges. "Okay, then. Greasy, cheesy pizza with a side of beef and chocolate cake it is. My treat."

He squeezed her fingers. "I know you were only trying to help when you went to the pharmacy. Did you see anything, though? Were there any other vehicles on the street when you left the house? At the pharmacy? Were you followed?"

She gulped, thinking back to the pharmacy parking lot. She'd tried to be careful and quick. It was early. Only she and the clerk were there. "No. I was only gone about fifteen minutes. What do you think happened?"

"Simple. Either someone planted a bomb under your car while you were inside the pharmacy or they hit it with an RPG after you'd parked. Hell, a bomb might have been in your car the whole time. We'll have to wait to hear back from Mark to know what really happened."

She cringed. "He's going to scream at me, too."

"Yeah, probably." Gabe's cell phone vibrated at his belt. Pulling it off his holster, he tossed it to her. "Answer that for me, would you?"

She did. *Ewww. Zack.* "Hello?"

"Tell your boyfriend to pull over. Now."

"He wants you to pull over," Shelby said, tapping the speakerphone on so Gabe could speak for himself. Zack still sounded plenty irritated, especially with that boyfriend crack.

"Why? We got trouble?" Gabe asked.

"Just do it." Zack hung up, so Gabe pulled to the curb within minutes and retrieved his phone. Both men climbed out, leaving the vehicles running. Gabe handed his phone over to Zack. Shelby caught it through the side mirror.

Zack crushed Gabe's and his phone beneath the heel of his boot. "Be sure you discard Shelby's before we take off," he ordered. "If anyone's tracking us by GPS, let this be where the trail ends."

"Copy that," Gabe replied. The men leaned against the Land Rover. Their conversation turned to short concise questions and answers.

"You're sure just two?" Zack asked, his arms crossed over his chest.

"Positive. Both using ARs." Gabe scuffed his boots, crossed his ankles and looked at his senior agent.

"The driver, too?"

"Through the passenger-side window."

"Sullivan has to go," Zack growled, not seeming to care she might overhear.

Shelby lowered her head and closed her eyes. He was right. She'd been nothing but a liability since she'd shown up on Kelsey's front door.

"No. She stays."

"She goes, Cartwright. The sooner the better. The girl doesn't listen."

"Understood, but she thought the op was over when we snagged Becker last night. Honest mistake for a civilian to make. Besides, Kelsey needs her."

"Bullshit. We've been fighting her ornery ass since day one."

Shelby reached for the door handle. She could settle this by walking away. Then they'd all be safe. Kelsey was obviously doing better. She didn't need her help anymore.

"I seem to remember hearing a story 'bout some guy who blew another operation to hell and back," Gabe muttered, his head lowered, his gaze on the ground. "Seems to me that moron put his senior agent at risk then, too. Could've gotten them both killed. David, wasn't it?"

Shelby's ears perked up. *Someone else messed up as bad as me?*

"That was different and you know it," Zack shot back.

Oh, my gosh. Zack? What'd you do?

Gabe elbowed Zack's thick bicep. "You can't blame her for being naive. 'Sides, she asked me for a gun. We might need another shooter on our side before this is over."

Zack lifted his shoulders, but Shelby couldn't decide if that meant he couldn't care less or that he might forgive her. He stared straight ahead. "Sons of bitches."

"Damned straight," Gabe said. "They are son of bitches and they've got us on the run."

"You got a plan?"

"Always," Gabe responded. "Same as yours. Snag a couple cheap burn phones. Contact Mark again once we get to my place. Lay low. Eat pizza and chocolate cake. Let The TEAM do their job while we do ours."

Zack grunted. "Mark needs to step up his game and catch these punks."

"You do realize we could've lost her this morning. She could've died in that explosion before she ever got back to the house."

"Stop with the guilt routine already. She had a good butt reaming coming."

Gabe winked slyly at her. "Maybe, but she's not one of us, and you're scaring the hell out of her."

"Do you and me need to chat about cozying up with clients, Cartwright?"

"Maybe."

Shelby could've kissed Gabe for defending her when she least deserved it. Kind of like Libby had done after the accident at the hospital. Shelby breathed a deep breath and pulled her phone out of her purse, ready to hand it over and be obedient to the bitter end if needed.

Zack slapped the side of the vehicle. "You got chocolate cake at your place?"

Gabe grinned and his whole face lit up, the laugh lines deep and long at the corners of his eyes. Like rays of sunshine. Her body hummed with appreciation for the easygoing way he'd just handled Zack and her. There he stood, facing his senior agent and looking as if he enjoyed it.

Her heart welled up with—what? Not just appreciation. Not anymore. Every part of her wanted another close encounter in the dark. Her body. Her heart. Maybe even her soul. A wave of need rippled up from her toes for another taste of that man's sexy, smiling mouth. Those lips that very well could have chewed her out but didn't.

He seemed at ease, as if they weren't in the middle of a getaway. "I'm pretty sure I'll have chocolate cake by the time we're done with the pizza."

Zack grunted. He actually smiled. A little.

Chapter Twenty-Four

He hadn't had time to think about the rose until now, but damn. How had Alex gotten inside his house and right under their noses, too? The man had his nerve, but there was no denying the rose. Someone who cared about Kelsey had left it on her pillow. The only guy who fit the bill was dead—or supposed to be.

Zack didn't seem convinced, but Gabe gave up fighting Kelsey's conviction that it was Alex. There had to be a better explanation than resurrection. Gabe just couldn't think of one, and he didn't believe a word out of that lying Becker's mouth.

He caught sight of the tail in his rearview mirror when the black Escalade swerved out of its traffic lane and increased speed, but damn. They were on a bridge over the Potomac, headed northwest with heavy traffic and no way to contact The TEAM for an assist.

Gabe slowed until he was alongside Zack, motioning for him to watch his six.

Zack offered a thumbs-up and one quick nod, indicating he'd already seen the tail.

And the race was on.

Gabe ducked in behind Zack and Kelsey, running interference with whoever was in that Escalade. When the guy sped up and tried to refuse Gabe's change of lanes, he twisted the wheel sharply to the right and cut him off. "Back off, jerk."

"What's going on?" Shelby asked, ducking to follow the action in that tiny sun visor mirror.

"Remember what I said earlier?" He tightened his grip on the steering wheel, his eyes glued to the rearview. "Now would be a good time to get down on the floor."

She unfastened her seatbelt and slid to her knees without one word of argument. *Nice.*

"Keep your head down and stay out of sight. Hang on tight. Things might get bumpy."

No sooner said than done. He slammed on his brakes, forcing the tail to do the same, but with no warning and less stopping distance. They locked bumpers. More like smashed bumpers, but the second they made contact, Gabe stomped the gas pedal and disengaged.

The Land Rover responded with a jolt of speed, while Zack's vehicle was long gone, dodging traffic and changing lanes somewhere up ahead. The tail responded, but the collision had caused no major radiator damage as Gabe had hoped.

Once he recovered from the sudden stop, the guy in the Escalade punched it and jerked his ride two lanes to the right. Gabe countered with a similar maneuver that put him alongside a twenty-foot long UPS truck, blocking the tail directly behind him.

For some reason, the UPS truck driver swerved to the right, bringing Gabe's focus forward. He hit the brakes, narrowly missing Zack, who'd slowed due to traffic. That mistake cost. Another Escalade came from out of nowhere and closed in behind him and Zack.

Damn. Two tails.

Gabe hit the brakes again. Jerking his wheel to the right, he cut off the rear Escalade and slid in directly behind Zack, close enough to kiss his rear bumper.

The time had come to change the game plan. He unholstered the pistol under his left arm. "Shelby. Get up. You see the guy in the UPS truck beside us? When I speed up alongside him, wave this weapon at him. Motion him to back off. Act like you mean it."

She climbed onto the seat and took the pistol gingerly out of his hand and into hers. "Just wave it?" she asked breathlessly? "That's all you want me to do?"

Gabe lowered her automatic window. "Yes, ma'am. That ought to work. Don't aim it at him, though."

She extended her arm out the open window and waved the weapon, but when the driver didn't pay attention, she got creative. She knelt on her seat and leaned out the window, waving the gun wildly. "Hey! Would you please move over?"

Somehow *please* and gun waving didn't quite go together, but it did the trick. As soon as the driver spotted her antics, he stepped on his brakes and created his own traffic jam in the slow lane.

Zack took advantage of the break in traffic and veered into the clear lane at the right. Before Escalade Two could follow suit and change lanes, Gabe unholstered his other pistols and fired into the tail's left rear tire. Direct hit. The vehicle swerved into the lane Zack had just vacated, but because of tire damage, it swerved just as quickly out of control to the left.

One down.

"Go, Zack. Go," Gabe prompted. "Get the hell out of there."

Zack was no dummy. He and Kelsey were already car lengths ahead.

The end of the bridge loomed close, but traffic into D.C. was steady. And in the way.

Shelby leaned on her butt back onto her seat, the gun still in her hand. "What's next?"

"Put the gun in the glove box. Get back on the floor and hang on."

Escalade One came up fast behind them. The fool. As soon as Shelby hit the floor, Gabe did what he'd done the first time. He slammed on his brakes, only this time there was no speed-up-and-follow-Zack routine. This was one of those now-or-never moments when hell had to be stopped in its tracks, and not the other way around.

He slammed the Land Rover into park and ordered Shelby to, "Stay put."

Jerking his door open, he rolled one knee to the pavement and fired before the tail knew what had hit him. The round went into the radiator as planned, eliciting a healthy plume of steam. The second round went into the Escalade's right front tire and Gabe was on his feet, ready to fire again. The quicker this went down, the better. Zack needed time to get Kelsey to safety and Gabe intended to give him plenty.

What he didn't expect was Shelby at his left, the pistol he'd given her extended between two shaking hands.

"Get the hell back in the car," he ground out, needing not one more damned distraction. Oncoming traffic was bad enough.

"I can help," she replied, blowing her blond locks out of her face. The stiff Potomac breeze messed with her tough girl, gun-toting attitude. The one Gabe didn't know she had.

He zeroed back on the guy behind the wheel of the Escalade. Whoever the bastard was, he hadn't fired yet; he just sat there, waiting.

Gabe hurried forward while sirens raced toward him from north and south. Damn. This wasn't the way he wanted to waste the day—explaining to Metro PD why he'd stopped traffic on the Arlington Memorial Bridge.

The tail opened the Escalade's driver-side door and placed one damned familiar cowboy boot to the pavement. Gabe couldn't have been more surprised.

Sam Becker stepped out with a big, shitty grin. "Agent Cartwright. Looks like you caught me again," he drawled in that annoying lazy way he had, both of his hands raised in submission. "We keep bumping into each other like this, and there's going to be hell to pay."

"There's hell to pay now. Why aren't you in jail?"

Becker shrugged, his eyes twinkling as if he did this kind of thing every day. "Guess the police didn't believe your story."

"Bullshit. You were stalking Kelsey Stewart and you were armed. I can attest to that. And Mark's got video evidence that you killed Alex Stewart, you fraud."

Again, the shrug. Becker cast a casual glance over his shoulder at the approaching police cruiser, their blue lights flashing. "What I'd like to know now is how you're going to explain the mayhem you've caused. Metro police don't take kindly to wild west shootouts this close to the White House."

"Hands up where I can see them," Gabe ordered, wishing Shelby wasn't out in the open and exposed like she was. What a target she made, but ordering her back to the car wasn't an option. Becker didn't need to know she'd never fired a weapon before. He needed to believe his time on earth had run out.

"You see, Junior Agent Cartwright." He lowered his hands and tucked his thumbs into the belt loops of his jeans, like a cowboy who had nowhere to go and all day to get there. "You don't have a clue what kind of a hornet's nest you just stuck your nose into. You should've let me intercept Mrs. Stewart. I could've helped her. Now you'll be the one going to jail."

Gabe's gaze hit the silver glint at Becker's belt. Damn. An FBI badge.

An inkling of awareness slithered up the back of Gabe's neck. That's why Becker got out of jail free. He really was FBI, and if the FBI was behind Alex's death?

The TEAM didn't stand a chance.

"We had no choice," Zack's voice was hard as steel. "What'd you expect us to do? Stay on site and wait for the shooters to come back?"

Mark bit his tongue, not up for yet one more damned confrontation. He'd been at home when he got the call and come as quickly as possible, but just missed Zack, Gabe, and the ladies.

Shelby's car still sat in the street, smoking from the pipe bomb that had gone off under its hood. The police found pieces of a cell phone in the debris, no doubt the detonator.

Zack was on high alert at a secure location somewhere, though he'd declined to say where, and that angered Mark. The Alexandria police were at the scene at the Stewarts' home, now a massive crime scene. Who knew where Gabe and Shelby were? Every attempt to gain control of this damned team was met with resistance. Now Zack. What else could go wrong?

The local volunteer fire department had barely rolled on scene when he'd arrived. First responders sprayed fire retardant over the smoking carcass. Kelsey's neighbors were curious, but no longer alarmed. A tow truck was backed into position to haul the wrecked car away when the police released it.

"Did you see who did it?" Mark tried like hell to infuse calm authority into his voice. Zack was the older and more experienced agent. He should have been the senior. Challenging a superior and more talented operator never was Mark's strong suit. "Did anyone?"

"Gabe got a good look at the shooters and we both got some shots off. He thinks we might've hit one. I double-checked our security footage of Kelsey's place, now that we've stopped. Mother's checking traffic cams to locate the shooters. It sure as hell seems to me we've got two things going on. Think about it. Who the hell uses pipe bombs and ARs?"

Mark rolled his eyes. His migraine spiked at the dumb question. "Shit, Zack. Everyone."

Kelsey muttered something in the background. All Mark caught of her comment was, ". . . if Alex comes home, what will he..."

"What if Alex comes home?" Mark roared. "Is that what I'm hearing? You tell her that if and when Alex decides to bless us with his presence again, I'm gonna kick his ass!"

He turned away from the crime scene in sheer frustration. Damn it to hell. This wasn't one of his prouder moments. He'd yelled at a grieving woman who wasn't even there. To make it a hundred times worse, it was Kelsey.

Zack sucked in a deep growl on the other end of the line. "Shit, Mark. Calm down, will you? Let me rephrase. I only meant that Sam Becker isn't the kind of guy who'd use a pipe bomb, for hell's sake. Think about it. You've got the evidence yourself on video back at the office. He'd use something subtle, like that fancy rifle you told me about. The guy's no hack. Hell, if he's the one behind the rose—"

"He very well might be," Mark muttered, his eyes back on the activity on the street and the tow truck, its flatbed tilted and winching Shelby's sad little heap onto it. Rivulets of gray water streamed to the blackened pavement. "When I called the police department from home this morning to see if I could speak with him, they had no idea what I was talking about, not even the police chief."

"What? You mean they lost him?"

"I mean they claim they never had him. Whoever intercepted my call to the police department last night must've been in league with him. Did you think Becker might've planted that rose just to keep us spun up and jumping through our asses?"

Zack growled again, his conversation skills disintegrating with every additional piece of bad news. "Listen, Mark. It sure as hell fits. The bastard's a pro, especially if he's really working with the Bureau, but the guys who bombed Shelby's car are not. I'm telling you, there are two very different things going on here. I think we're caught in the freakin' middle of a high-tech operation and terrorist wannabes."

Mark raked a tense hand over his head of hair, fighting the urge to pull it out. Every day The TEAM fell apart a little bit more, and they were no closer to locating Kelsey's assailants or Alex, *IF* the sonofabitch really was alive.

"So you're telling me we've got two different guys after Kelsey?" Mark asked bluntly. "How is that supposed to convince me you can keep her safe now that Gabe's missing?"

"He's not missing. He just hasn't caught up with us yet. But think about it. Whoever hit Shelby's car was most likely out to kill Kelsey, but whoever left the rose is out to save her. At least to help her."

"I can't believe the FBI cares enough to send flowers."

"Then who do you think did it? Because I'm here to tell you, Mark, the flower's the real deal, and Kelsey's a new woman today because of it. You should've seen her after the bombing. She was ready to kick ass. You'd have been proud. Even had her pistol strapped on."

Damn. Mark honestly didn't know how to answer his friend. Alex alive? No way. But a rose to wake up to after Becker sucked the hope out of her last night? Mark scrubbed a hand over his face, glad that Zack couldn't see his mounting doubt. Did Alex even do sentimental crap like bring Kelsey flowers? Mark buckled. "What now?"

"Like you said," Zack reminded him. "We do our jobs. I'll keep Kelsey safe and off the grid. You guys go after Fallon. Becker too. Alex will show up when he's able. You'll see."

Zack made it sound simple.

"Where are you?"

"Somewhere safe. That's all you need to know. Kick ass. I'll be in touch."

The second he disconnected Mark's cell vibrated at his hip holster. *Mother. Just great.* He still hadn't had a free second to chat with her, and his to-do list grew longer every day. His migraine along with it.

"Are you still at Kelsey's?" Impatience edged her tone.

"Just leaving. What's up? Did you get an update from Steven and his team?"

"Don't worry. They're safe, but I'm patching Connor and Rory through to you. They've intercepted your shooters. Shots have been fired. Two police cruisers are in pursuit and D.C. Metro already set up a roadblock." She transferred the call to his cell before he could say yay or nay, dumping Mark into the middle of screeching tires and mayhem.

"Boss, you there?" Connor yelled over the din.

"Here," Mark answered, gripping the back of his neck with his free hand, scrubbing it up and over his head.

"We've got 'em in our sights. The guys who hit Kelsey's this morning. They're traveling east, doing over a hundred. Just like the Escalade Gabe found in the river. Wait! The bastard's shoot—"

A loud BOOM vibrated through the connection. Mark pulled his cell from his ear.

"Hell! Rory! You good?" Connor's voice came back shrill and angry as more shots were fired, hopefully from Rory or Connor's weapons. Screeching tires told Mark the race was still on. Another shot sounded, but Connor halted his progress report.

Mark strained to hear over the wail of sirens and gunfire. Rory uttered an expletive, unusual for him, then nothing. Mark didn't know what he was listening to—the deaths of two more of his team or a rollover. Acid pooled in his gut as the racket reduced to silence.

Finally, Connor came back on line, out of breath. "Boss. You still there?"

"Yeah. Speak."

"Police are here with us. We've got... wait a second. Who is that?" Connor hollered away from the phone. "Looks like we've got Stevenson and..."

Mark listened as yelling and racket ensued on Connor's end of the line.

"Mark? You still there?"

Shit! I'm here already!

"Copy that," Mark replied, exasperated at being asked the same question without getting enough intel to picture the mayhem on the other end of the line.

"The police have Stevenson and Bukowski in custody. Stevenson just knifed an officer, so he's not going anywhere soon. Found a couple pipe bombs in the back seat of their vehicle. Looks like they weren't done terrorizing folks yet."

"You guys okay?"

"Yeah. We're good. Found a box of rat poison, too. You know why they'd have something like that?"

Shit. Were these guys cruel enough to have poisoned Kelsey's dogs? Her boys?

"Yeah. They might have used it on Whisper and Smoke. Give me the brand name. Step on it."

Connor came back on the line in seconds with the requested information. "There's something else you need to know."

"What?" Mark snapped.

"We were kinda in the middle of defending ourselves when a black car bumped us out of our lane. You probably heard the racket. The driver nudged into us nice and easy like, forcing us out of his way. He shot out the Escalade's tires. They lost control. Flipped the SUV over a couple times, but that was who stopped 'em. Wasn't us."

"What'd he look like?"

"Couldn't see through the black window tint. Couldn't see a thing."

"Coupe or sedan?"

"Sedan, just like Becker's last night. Hey listen, I gotta go. The police need to talk to me. Later."

Mark hung up and scrolled through his recent calls. He hit Zack's burner phone number, his heart in his throat. Hell. Losing Whisper and Smoke would destroy Kelsey.

"You called?" Zack asked quietly.

"Check the dogs, Zack. Check 'em now. They might've been poisoned."

Zack dropped the phone, bellowing, "Son of a bitch! Kelsey! Come help me."

Mark closed his eyes at the sounds of tragedy and heartbreak coming over the line. God, she'd lost so much already.

"Smoke!" she shrieked. "Help me, Zack. Please. They're dying!"

"I am, Kels. God, there's so much blood."

"I know. I know!"

Mark clenched his eyes and prayed. *Not them, too. Not Whisper and Smoke.*

More phone bumping and racket ensued until Zack came back on the line. "They're heaving blood. I've got to get a vet here. Sorry, Mark. I've got to go."

"Tell the vet it's rat poison," Mark named the brand so the vet would know how to treat the dogs.

"Right. Later." Zack disconnected, and Mark was as angry and as weary as he'd never been during all of his combat tours combined. Nothing compared. The ugly morning had gone from bad to worse. He'd barely stepped out on the front walk when his cell rang again. *David.*

"Did Connor and Rory apprehend the SUV? Everyone okay?"

"Yes. They caught up with Stevenson and Bukowski. Sounds like Rory and Connor had help intercepting them from some guy in a black sedan," Mark muttered, hating that this info bite would add fuel to the spreading Alex myth.

"Good. The gang of ten is down to the last man then. Fallon."

Mark scrubbed a hand over his face, glad for the accurate assessment, but the continual interference of that joker in the black sedan was a problem he didn't need. Who the hell was he? Alex? Then why didn't he come out and admit he was alive?

"There's something else."

"What?" *Of course there's something else. There was always some-goddamned-thing else!*

"Mother just tendered her resignation."

"She what? But I just spoke with her. She didn't say a word about quitting when she transferred Connor's call."

"And then she left. Sorry. I know this is the last thing you need to deal with right now, but she didn't want to talk about it."

Mark hung up without another word, his phone clenched in his hand so tightly that it hurt his fingers. *Sonofabitch! How did Alex wake up every single day and want do this damned job?*

Chapter Twenty-Five

And here I am, sitting in a police cruiser in the middle of the Arlington Memorial Bridge. What would Mom say?

Shelby growled to herself. Two police officers had Gabe in custody, his feet kicked wide and his cheek to the trunk as if he were a common criminal. They'd frisked him twice, but Gabe was smart. Before that Becker guy could stop him, he'd pulled stuff out of his pockets and dropped it over the bridge railing as quick as if his pants were on fire.

Shelby would've dropped her weapon over, too, but Becker was faster. He'd caught her by her wrists and pulled one arm behind her back. Then the police officers took Gabe down, scraping his cheek to the pavement before that jerk, Becker, stopped the rough handling. "Easy, boys. He's mine."

Shelby had to give him credit. He'd very courteously removed Gabe's pistol from her hand like a gentleman and escorted her to the patrol car.

"Howdy, ma'am," he'd said, as if he were at a Sunday social instead of the middle of a crime scene on the bridge. "Why don't you take a seat and rest awhile, while I have a little talk your boyfriend?"

Shelby hadn't said a word because that was probably what he'd wanted—her to spill her guts or something like that. She worried for Gabe out there and surrounded by police, but what could she do? Escape? The notion intrigued her. She could run. That might give Gabe time to get away, too. Or something. But no. He looked pretty indisposed at the moment.

Sam Becker, the liar. She didn't trust him. Not one bit. He was dangerous. Gabe had said he was. The only guys he'd said anything to were the four police officers. A tow truck had already hauled the Escalade with the flat tire, away. One officer had escorted that driver to another cruiser, not in cuffs though. What was going on? Becker had caused all the trouble. Not Gabe.

At last, the authorities must've believed something Becker told them. They let Gabe stand up straight. He arched his back, but then everything went from bad to worse. They cuffed his hands in front of him.

A white van marked with the bright gold insignia of the FBI on its side panel rolled onto the scene. Becker said something to that driver, nodding toward Shelby, and oh my gosh. Her heart pounded. *He thinks I'm a criminal?*

Becker took hold of Gabe's elbow, ushering him toward her. Gabe turned and leaned his butt against the side of the car. Becker opened the door and ducked his head inside. The darned guy smiled, as if he held all the cards. "Miss Sullivan. Are you currently associated or in any way in collusion with Gabe Cartwright?"

She nodded quickly. Nervously. "Yes. I am. He, umm, saved my life."

Becker winked. Dang, his eyes sparkled with mischief. "Then maybe you'll be the smart one here today. Where is Kelsey Stewart going? Do you know? Where did Zack Lennox take her? Some place safe, I hope."

Shelby froze. Becker sure sounded friendly, and he certainly seemed to know everyone involved with Kelsey. But Gabe didn't like him, and that was reason enough not to cooperate. She swallowed hard, fighting for enough saliva to make her vocal cords work. "I don't know."

Honestly, the guy had a smile as big as the sky and eyes as blue. He scrunched up his nose, arching one bushy brow. "Now how did I know you'd say that?"

He shut the door and crossed his arms over his chest, his legs spread wide, facing Gabe again. Shelby stilled to listen, but couldn't make out one word.

Gabe kept shaking his head.

At last, Becker opened the door and ducked his head inside again. "Miss Sullivan, I'm going to take you and your friend to another location where we can discuss a few things before I decide what to do. I'm not going to have any trouble with you, am I? Tell me now, because I can certainly put you in cuffs if you'd prefer."

She shook her head, trembling from head to foot. This was her first time in a police car, and her first time in trouble with the law. *Me? In cuffs?*

"I didn't think so," he purred. He opened the door wider and nodded for Gabe to enter. "You know the drill."

Gabe ducked his head into the vehicle and dropped to the seat beside her. "You say anything?"

She glanced over her shoulder to keep an eye on Becker, still chatting with the police officers. "No. Nothing."

"Good girl. Follow my lead. Stay close. Can you do that?"

"Y... y... yes." Her eyes widened. The cuffs rested loose on his wrists. He'd escaped them already? Pure adrenaline pounded in her chest. He meant to make a run for it? *Okay, but—darn. I'm going with him.*

"Kiss me," he ordered, and she didn't think twice. Not anymore. He had a plan. All she had was a bad case of nerves. Her lips were on his mouth and her hands on the side of his head in less than a heartbeat. She offered everything with that kiss, her lips parted and her tongue seeking his.

A groan lifted out of his throat, along with muffled words she had to actually ease away from him to understand. "Sorry 'bout this, Shell," he mumbled, "and we are definitely going to do this again later, but if you keep kissing me like that, I'm going to take you seriously and we'll never get out of here."

She tilted her head back, pleased to her toes with the rumbling baritone in his chest but needing to see his eyes. He was still licking his lips. And hers. *You called me Shell.* "Sorry. You said kiss, so I kissed."

"No problem, but listen up, and do what I say. Your door isn't latched tight. Kick it open. Let's get the hell out of here."

"Escape?" She hissed against his lips, her eyes wide and searching for any sign of Becker, afraid he might overhear.

"Don't stop kissing," Gabe urged, leaning forward. "Make it look good. They'll think we're off our rockers, but when I say go, let's bust out of here."

"Isn't that breaking the law?" she asked, mumbling around his lips and tongue. Dang. If the guy wanted to escape, he needed to stop nibbling on her bottom lip like he was. Just his close proximity threatened her thin hold on composure, but all this mouth-to-mouth contact had her body on overload. Him being cuffed, and kind of, sort of, at her mercy, messed with her head, too. But running from the law with him right behind her from real live police officers and an FBI agent who had guns? Hottest damned thing ever.

"We can't help Kelsey if we're stuck in some FBI jail, can we?" Gabe gave her one last gentle bite. He slid the cuffs off of his wrists and dropped them to the floor between his legs. "Do it. Now. Go. Go. Go!"

She pivoted on her butt, placed one foot solidly to the door and gave it all she had. Adrenaline pounded every nerve. With her feet barely on the pavement, and Gabe's right hand between her shoulder blades, he all but pushed her out of the vehicle.

And they were off. He had longer legs, but she had a head full of fear. Shelby couldn't sprint the rest of the bridge fast enough. Her feet flew.

Thank goodness they were closer to the Lincoln Memorial end of the bridge, and they headed straight into the Fourth of July crowd of tourists. She dodged people and bicyclists. Gabe stayed beside her. Everyone stepped out of her way, probably to avoid the police officers behind them. Becker had to be right on their heels, too. The terror of being caught added speed to her feet.

I'm not going to jail for helping Kelsey!

"Head for the tour buses," Gabe ordered.

I can do that. Shelby dodged into a gaggle of elderly passengers who'd just disembarked their tour bus south of the Lincoln Memorial. She ducked low and out of sight, blending in with the silver-haired crowd and ready to board that bus if it kept her out of the reach of the law.

But, no. Gabe grabbed her wrist, spinning her into his arms behind a huge tree in front of the bus. Her heart stopped again. Here they were on the run and he wanted a kiss? Like they did in the movies? Did this stuff really work?

"Aw, isn't that sweet, Becky?" an older gentleman asked. "Young lovers. Hmm."

Shelby got lost in the hubbub around her and the sudden change in direction. There was no asking permission this time, only the heat of Gabe's mouth clamped onto hers, his heavy breathing fanning her lips and in her nose. One big hand trapped the back of her head while he buried his fingers in her hair, his mouth opened wide. Not asking. Taking. Demanding. Devouring.

She couldn't breathe, much less think, so she gave. And gave. Feet thundered by, but she didn't even look to see who it might be. It might have been all those sweet, elderly tourists. Or the police. But honestly, with her hands clinging to his neck and his pulse throbbing beneath her fingertips, the cops could wait. Heck. The whole world could wait.

For this single moment in time only, she was no longer Nurse Sullivan. She was Wonder Woman. Natasha Romanoff, the Black Widow of the Avengers. Hell, she was—invincible.

Gabe tilted her head to the side for better access to her mouth, but when she opened her eyes, expecting to melt under the heat of smoldering greens filled with lust, the jerk had his eyes wide open all right. Only all of his attention was focused behind her. Not on her. She froze.

He smiled into her lips when he noticed she'd caught his indiscretion, but he didn't let her separate from his mouth, not one bit.

"Stay," he ordered gently, his tongue tracing a line of sparks over her now-pressed-very-tightly lips. "They're looking for two people on the run. Not us. Come on. Open up. Don't stop."

Oh, yeah. That. She came to her senses. Embarrassment warmed her cheeks, and of course, immediately flooded those darned pesky breasts, too. Gah! And here she thought he'd kissed her because, well, because he liked her. She stilled her out-of-control emotions for this guy who obviously had better control of his emotions than she did of hers.

Her nipples needed to stand down and turn off, too, the damned cheerleaders.

"What next?" She tried to keep the petulant whine out of her voice. *Men are such jerks. You give an inch. They take a mile.*

"This." He leaned backward to the tree trunk, her head clamped between his gentle palms. He lifted her glasses off her nose, tucking the stem into his shirt collar before he pulled her to his lips once more.

This time she made sure he closed his eyes before she succumbed to the crackling energy between them. He had no trouble breaching the trembling barrier of her lips, his fingers twined through her hair, his mouth hot on hers again.

Oh, mama. Want to or not, a moan escaped up her throat, mingling with the groan rumbling from his. The minty taste of his mouth sparked an appetite she'd not given into with any other man. And the feel of his whiskered chin. The smell of him, part clean sweat and part some men's cologne. She tightened her grip.

"Mmm," he mumbled, licking her lips softly enough to ignite her libido all over again. "What was I saying?"

"I think we were evading the authorities."

"Oh, yeah. That." Easing away from her mouth, he tucked her head below his chin where she wanted to be, against his pounding heart. She lowered her hands to his waist, thrilled at the feel of his hips and the sharp edge of his belt in her belly. Gabe was the first real man in her life. He knew what to do and when to do it. Capable. Ready. Willing. And he wasn't afraid to take on the world.

Relief turned her knees to jelly. She could only hang on tight, listening to the banging beneath his ribs, an oddly comforting beat.

Wow. For two traumatically stressed people, they had a lot of cardiac tension going on between them. The musical rhythm of their two hearts beating together was hypnotizing. It was a wonder she could stand at all.

His breath scorched the back of her neck, weakening her more. Gradually, she thought to open her eyes. Tourists. Vendors. Bicyclists. Mothers and fathers with strollers. That was all. No police. No smirking FBI agent, either. *Whew.*

"I think we lost them."

"We should move," he said, but he made no effort to disengage. "Soon."

"Where?"

Gabe stroked her shoulders, warming her in ways she'd not allowed before. Petting her. Gentling her. Easing comfort and something else she was afraid to name into her body and mind with his fingers and palms. She relaxed into the friction of his touch, wanting more of the luxurious feeling sweeping up from her toes.

At last, he set her back another inch or two, enough to peer into her eyes, and she was smitten. His sexy greens were dark with lust. Standing in his arms took her breath. Heck. He could take everything. If he only knew. If he only asked.

Gabe traced his index finger along her jaw, ending with a gentle pinch to her chin. "You're a surprise, Shelby Sullivan, but I've got to warn you. I like it. I like it a lot."

Chapter Twenty-Six

Time to fade into the busy D.C. tourist scene. Gabe secured Shelby under his arm, walked her up to a street vendor and purchased a couple of light summer hoodies that brightly declared *Washington D.C.* for the world and any local authorities, to see. Hers was in pink, his in gray. The vivid purple lettering convinced him. There was more than one way to hide from police on the prowl. In plain sight.

He snagged matching baseball caps, making sure the brim shadowed his eyes. Hers went on next, but his damned heart stalled looking down into her sweet face. He returned her glasses to their proper place on her nose and adjusted the band on her cap so it fit tighter.

Standing there all compliant like she was didn't help, but when she rested her fingertips on the front of his shirt, she might as well have attached jumper cables. Defiance didn't glint once in those violet pools of his new companion agent. But something else sure did—something more deadly. *Trust.*

"You surprised me when you pulled your weapon on Becker."

Her eyelashes fluttered. "I wanted to help you."

"But you don't know how to shoot."

"I know, but I held it right, didn't I? Besides, he didn't know I was a beginner. I could tell. For a whole minute there I think I had him worried."

"Did you flip the safety lever up before you aimed? You know, so the weapon would actually fire a live round if you needed to?" he asked, knowing damned well she hadn't.

Those pretty eyes widened. "Umm, no. I pointed it like you did with yours. Was that wrong?"

"So you were basically helping me by standing there and looking deadly and dangerous." He couldn't help the smile tugging at his mouth. She didn't have a clue about gun safety, but she did have guts. At least the thing was safe while she held it.

"Umm, I guess. I don't know anything about them, remember?"

"Girl, you and I need to spend some serious time at the range." *Some serious time in bed with me wouldn't be so bad, either.*

He took a step back from the kiosk, but she stopped him with a hand at his wrist. "Wait. You thought I looked good?"

He looked down at her slender fingers barely wrapped around his wrist. The heat of a man who'd gone without female companionship for months roared to life at her touch, scorching his common sense. Gabe grabbed two bottled waters and slapped three twenties on the counter before they stepped out of line and headed to safety.

"Yes," he answered truthfully. "You looked damned good, but let's get out of here."

Glancing over his shoulder, he headed for a cab before his cock took control of his brain. The zipper on his jeans was already tight and uncomfortable.

"Where'd you get the money to buy these?" she asked once they were in the backseat of the cab, with her tucked under his arm. "I thought you threw everything in the river?"

"Just tossed my wallet and my new business cards. They had my new address. Didn't want the FBI to know where Zack went. But yeah, I always keep a couple get-out-of-jail-free bills tucked away," he murmured, his lips in her hair.

The feel of her slender body sparked a fire in his blood. She smelled of flowers and the sun. His hands wandered inside the open zipper of her hoody along the curves of her ribcage until his fingers touched the side of her breast. He caught himself from wandering further. He hadn't anticipated how good it would feel holding her, or knowing how inexperienced she was. Shelby needed more than target practice, and he wanted to be the man she practiced on.

The first. The last. *The only.*

The cabbie's brown eyes beamed through the rearview mirror, winking at him like guys do. Well, let him look. The old fart. Gabe couldn't care less. He'd found something rare in his life, and in the last place he'd expected to find it. Better yet, she seemed to feel the same way.

Shelby snuggled into his side, sparking impossible feelings he'd long since ignored. "Are we going to your place?" she asked, her hand on his chest.

"No. My office. Mark needs to know about Becker."

She stiffened. "But I should be with Kelsey. Let's go to your place. Now."

"Mark first. Then Kelsey. Maybe."

"No, Gabe. You don't understand." She twisted to face him. "She's my patient. Not Zack's."

"Why can't it wait?" Something else was going on. "Zack's real good with Kelsey. He can cook, and you know he'll keep her safe. Trust me."

"But..." Shelby held her breath for a long couple of seconds. "I have to control everything for Kelsey right now. She... needs me."

"That's kinda impossible, isn't it? The whole 'control everything' routine?" *I should know.*

"No. She's my patient, not Zack's. I have to be there for her."

"Okay." Gabe conceded the argument. He didn't want to spoil his pleasant feeling. "Whatever you say. We'll catch up with Zack and Kelsey right after we talk with Mark. Deal?"

"No, Gabe. Now. I have to go now." She leaned out of his arms, her eyes filled with tears. "It's just that... it's just that... Oh, God. I haven't even told my mother this." Tightening her arms around herself, she drew in a deep breath, letting it release slowly, her gaze fixed on the traffic moving by them in a blur. "I almost killed one of my patients, Gabe. It was an accident, but I gave him the wrong medicine."

Gabe blew out a big sigh as the puzzle that was Shelby fell into place. This explained why she fought so hard to be in charge. He knew the feeling, but trying to do the impossible was no way to live. "That's why you have panic attacks."

"Yes." She lowered her head as the story spilled out. "Rudy was only two years old when I gave him an adult inhalant. He stopped breathing and—" She unfastened her seatbelt and withdrew closer to the window. "The pharmacy labeled the wrong can of inhalant with a child's dosage, but I should've known better. I should've double-checked everything. Rudy almost died because of me."

Gabe studied the hard line of her shoulders, the tight cords in her neck. She carried a lot of guilt for a woman of her small stature, and she wouldn't look him in the eye anymore. He turned her around and pulled her stiff back into his chest. Clutching her shoulders, he began a firm massage with the pads of his thumbs along her upper spine.

She responded to his touch, ducking her head into her neck and rolling her shoulders. This woman liked a neck rub, and it was no wonder. Headache bones. That was what his chiropractor called the neck vertebrae where the shoulder muscles got hooked up nice and tight when a person felt stressed or guilty.

"You can't change what happened yesterday." Even through the hoody, he could feel the tremendous stress she carried. "Relax. I'm here to help. We'll get through this together."

A knot let go. Snap. Pop. She cocked her head to the left, then the right. But when she lowered her chin to her chest and moaned, a different kind of therapy for her—and him—came to mind.

"I have to keep anything bad from happening to Kelsey. It's my job."

"No, Shelby. You can't, and it's not." He let his thumbs dig deeper into the tension above her shoulder blades. "Do you think you're responsible to save the whole world? It's an impossible task. I'm here to tell you. Let it go."

She crumbled, sniffing back her emotions, her face in her hands. "I could've killed him. It was all my fault."

"Maybe it was. I don't know. I wasn't there, but are you going to let it define you for the rest of your life? Hell, Shelby. Don't cripple yourself before you even get started. In the Corps, we get told a thousand times a day to *keep on keeping on no matter what*. You need to do the same thing. Prove to yourself and the world that you can rise above that one, damned accident. Get that nursing degree you want so bad. Don't ever quit."

She scrunched her shoulders under his hands. "You know I'm not a real nurse?"

He shrugged. "Yeah. I do, but I think I know why you passed yourself off as one. It sounds a little more impressive than nursing assistant, huh?"

"But it was still a lie."

"Ah, not exactly. A wish, maybe. That's what you really want, isn't it? To be a nurse?"

She nodded. "I thought you guys would respect me more. The minute I saw you guys, I knew I had to do something to keep control. Not very smart, huh?"

"It's a symptom, Shelby. A symptom that you want to make something better of your life. That's all." He opted for sharing time. USMC or not, it was time she knew. "My inner control freak showed up early morning in Helmand Valley. We'd dropped in, quiet as death. Just after one guy. Should've been quick and easy. Wasn't." He paused, the door to that far off valley reopened and the sights and smells of another world filling the cab.

Shelby twisted under his hands, but he wouldn't let her turn around. Not yet. He kept massaging, working his fingers and thumbs into her muscles while the story unfolded.

"I honest to God didn't think that little kid knew how to fire it. The grenade launcher had to weigh twenty-five, maybe thirty pounds loaded like it was." Gabe closed his eyes and wished the tiny ghost away. "Kids over there are so small. He looked like any other, who would've really rather had a piece of candy in his hands, maybe an extra MRE. We always carried extras. Not my idea of a killer. Maybe ten years old. Maybe not. But the way he smiled..."

Shelby leaned into him, so Gabe relented, pulling her back to his chest, his arms around her neck and shoulders so he could bury his nose in her hair. Green apple shampoo smelled so much better than what his mind had kicked up. The blood. The sweat. The damned smell of the real fear that he'd die in that stink hole of an excuse for a village. The phantom pain of a foot too blasted to hell to be surgically reattached.

The flutter under his ribs kicked up. He inhaled deeply, not sure she'd want to stay with him when he finished, but sure as hell going to give it a shot. It was time they both came clean. If she left, well, she wouldn't be the first. Plenty other women had taken off running.

"Little guy just stood there looking at me. I kept hoping. He kept smiling. Funny thing is I knew he'd do it. Had a sick feeling. Just didn't want to believe that I'd gone halfway around the world to kill a kid. Me. A big Marine all armor plated and geared up to fight men. Not babies."

Gabe closed his eyes, fighting to swallow. To this day, he didn't know which hurt worse—killing that smiling boy or losing Darrell in the same fight. Both seemed so damned unfair. Losing his foot paled in comparison. It honest to God did.

"A bullet goes faster than an RPG. Twelve hundred meters per second beats two hundred ninety-four meters a second any day. Damned truth is that it came down to him or

me. Not sure who fired first. It's all one steaming pile of f—"
He bit the ugly word back. *Fuck. It still hurts.*

A gentle, warm hand lifted to the side of his face. He closed his eyes, not deserving her kindness, wanting to forget. Once and forever.

"That's how I lost my foot. Same day I lost Darrell Carson, best damned friend in the world." He paused, his heart lodged high in his throat. Damned sneaky and wrong how the mind hides a shitload of hurt behind four words. *Darrell Carson. My friend.*

"So yeah, Shelby. I get it. I do. I'm right there with you, trying to control the world. It just doesn't work that way. Things still happen, and there's nothing we can do to change them. The only way to live through crap that happens is to keep on keeping on. Get that damned degree. Thumb your nose at regret. Do something with the mistakes you've made. Learn from them. Hell, girl. Be all you can be."

Shit. He mentally shook his head at that last one. Sounded like something out of a recruitment poster. *For the damned Army.*

She twisted around to look at him, cupping his jaw as if she still cared, and once again, he got lost in her eyes. This time was like no other. His breath hitched. Hers did, too. Violet blues blinked with deep dark wonder, just a kiss away.

"You make it sound easy," she said.

"You know better than that. Life's hard, and there isn't a one of us who's going to make it out alive. You think I don't get a little backed up sometimes, that memories don't sneak up on me?" He shook his head at the unrealistic image she might have of him. Civilians always want to see a hero. He was anything but. Just a lousy survivor. "Hell, I could've sworn that little kid was sitting in Kelsey's living room during that thunderstorm last night. There I was, all mixed up and looking for him, and all of a sudden he's right there beside me, patting my shoulder. Smiling that sad smile. Kinda like he knew I had to kill him again, even in the dream. And you know what? I would have."

"You did what you had to do."

"So did you. Don't let one mistake define the rest of your life." He lifted his fingers to her hair. "God, Shelby. Here you are trying to save everyone else and you could've gotten yourself killed. Did you think of that when you left the house this morning? Did you think about what I'd do if you'd died?"

He bit his lip, half-wishing he hadn't blurted that last thought out loud, but glad he did. Shelby's world had changed whether she liked it or not, and he wanted to be part of it. He needed her to see him as more than just Kelsey's annoying bodyguard.

The corners of her mouth lifted into a small smile. Pink colored her cheeks.

He leaned slowly down. Her chin tilted up to meet his. Their lips met hesitantly. He would've settled for a chaste peck if that were all she wanted. It wasn't. Shelby wrapped her arms around his neck, drawing him into her body. The quick peck evolved into a breathtaking, needy explosion of passion he hadn't seen coming.

He lifted her onto his lap while she raked needy fingers through his hair, her tongue urgently asking for more. Deftly, he slid a hand beneath her shirt, needing to feel her warmth. Her willingness. Her fire.

The instant he touched skin, the need to have her naked beneath him engulfed his common sense. One touch wasn't enough, and he'd been so damned hungry for too long. His blood boiled, his body on fire and every muscle taut with need. He wanted her. All of her. Now.

Her fingers on his cheeks offered encouragement. He pressed her backward to the seat, wishing this were another time. Another place. Their breaths mingled until they breathed the same air.

The gentle arch of her body into his encouraged him, but Gabe knew better than to treat a lady like this. He wouldn't demean her by taking her in the back seat of a cab. Hell, no. He was a better man than that, and she an infinitely better woman.

There would come a time.

And it would be damned soon.

Chapter Twenty-Seven

"I still want to talk to her," Mark insisted. He had Ember on the line. Judging by the edge to her voice, she was more than a little overwhelmed since Mother quit without saying a word, much less goodbye to her girlfriend.

Up until Alex's death, Mother was the nosey, but usually calm, information technologist who supplied everyone with lightning-speed computer research and over-the-top admin support. Her workstation was command central, her fingers in everybody's business maybe, but also on the pulse of all operations. So why had she quit?

He pinched the bridge of his nose, fully aware that he sucked at management. The TEAM needed someone stronger at the helm. Someone meaner. Like Alex.

"Good luck with that. I've been trying to reach her since she left, but she won't pick up. She took a lot of stuff with her, too. Her office laptop's gone."

"Do you know why she quit?"

"I don't. Sorry. She's been acting weird lately."

"Like how?"

"Secretively, kind of like she didn't want anyone to overhear her telephone conversations. Wait. My other phone's ringing."

Still at Kelsey's, Mark waited on the front steps while Ember took the other call. He'd already boarded up the front windows while the police gathered evidence and posted the crime scene. As soon as they left, he'd lock the place and take off. Hopefully, Zack would call with an update on the dogs. God, Mark hoped they'd still be alive.

The fire department had handled the hazardous waste from extinguishing Shelby's car before they'd rolled out of the neighborhood. Only scorched pavement remained.

Just as the last of the police officers waved on their way to their cruiser, Ember returned to the line. "Hey, guess what? Dispatch from one of the local cab companies just called with a message from Gabe. He's on his way in. Sullivan's with him. When are you coming back?"

Mark allowed a sigh of relief now that Gabe was accounted for. "On my way, but listen. Kelsey's dogs were poisoned last night, maybe early this morning. I think we caught it in time, least I sure as hell hope so. Zack's handling it. Kelsey, too. Do me a favor and rally The TEAM. We need to strategize."

Ember whined. "Whisper and Smoke? Oh, no! Poor Kelsey. Sure, Boss. I mean, Mark. I'll tell everyone to wait for you to arrive. You got one more second?"

Damn. Now what?

"Whatever you told Maverick must've worked. He came to my desk and sat down and talked to me. He just needed help with a server error, but he's never given me the time of day until now. I think he's coming around."

"Thanks. At least he didn't quit, huh?"

"Aw, Mark. We're not quitting on you. You're stuck with us." Ember had to be smiling. He could hear it in her voice. "Hurry back. A cup of coffee's waiting for you."

He did hurry back, after sweeping the mess and securing the Stewarts' bullet-sprayed home. He'd no more than stepped up to Ember's counter and taken a good long pull on that promised cup of coffee when the elevator chimed. Out marched the agents he'd assigned to track down Becker.

They didn't look happy. Especially Izza. Steven and Taylor strolled out of the elevator behind her, but she looked ready for a fight, her fists clenched at her side, her chin tucked into her neck and her brows furrowed, like a ledge she needed to keep between her and the first person who crossed her path.

Mark truly enjoyed working with Connor's spitfire wife, but for now, he kept any hint of a smile off his face until he knew why she radiated death. When pushed to her limit, Izza's knee-jerk reaction was always to come up fighting, something she'd learned growing up with an alcoholic father. The last thing she needed was for anyone within reach to not take her seriously.

"What the hell's wrong with you, Houston?" She slapped her gloves to the counter, her normally brown eyes shiny black and full of sparks. "You're supposed to have our backs when you send us out on an op."

"We do. What's wrong?" he asked, opting for calm instead of confrontation.

She pursed her lips. Not a good sign. "What's wrong is I've been flat on my face with my wrists tied to my ankles for a couple hours now. I want to know why you guys didn't follow through. Why didn't you check on us when we didn't call in? Hell. You should've come looking!"

"I did. The minute I left Kelsey's last night, I called Mother to tell you to stand down." Mark snapped his mouth shut. Mother's words came back to him. *Don't worry. They're safe.* How would she have known, or did she? Was she in collusion with Becker and Fallon, too? "Who'd you talk to the last time you checked in?"

"Mother. Every hour on the hour, like we're supposed to do when we're on an op."

"So Mother didn't tell you that Gabe intercepted Becker last night? That you guys were supposed to come in?"

"No, she didn't mention that, did she, Steven?"

He shook his head. "No, sir, and we've been on stakeout all night. When I called her last night, she said to sit tight. A relief team was on its way."

Words Mark wouldn't allow to slip past his lips filled his head. *Mother. The bitch.* She'd actively compromised this operation and his team. No wonder Izza was fired up.

Connor sat quietly watching from the safety of the Sit Room, a lopsided smirk on his face at his wife's very loud attitude. Smart man. They were quite the pair, a blonde, blue-eyed and very laid back Irishman married to a kickboxing, passionate, and volatile Latino woman with a giant chip on her shoulder.

"Mother doesn't work here anymore," Mark stated for the record. "Be mad at me, Izza. You're right. I should've come looking for you the minute she walked out on us this morning. I'm sorry you had to go through that. Are you okay?"

"Am now." Izza wiped her nose with the back of her hand, the way a prizefighter in the middle of a brawl might. "What do you mean she doesn't work here anymore?"

Mark let his suspicions out of the bag. "I think she's working with Becker and Fallon. She deliberately lied to you and me. You guys should've been sleeping in your own beds last night. She knew damned well what was going on when she fed you that bogus intel."

"Mother?" Izza about choked. "Our Mother? Sasha Kennedy? That Mother?" She shook her head, her ponytail flipping from side to side. "No way. She wouldn't help Becker kill Alex. She's been to our house, Mark."

Connor didn't seem as surprised as Izza. He'd stretched one long leg under the conference room table, his chin cupped in one fist. "That explains why we couldn't get her to help us. After Steven exposed Becker, she got all sorts of goosey. Like she didn't want to talk to us anymore."

"Like she had something to hide," Rory piped up.

Mark blew out a rattled sigh. He should've talked to her when he'd first noticed her attitude. Mother. His first failure as a boss. Damn. "Let me worry about her. We need to strategize. Do you need a drink or something before we get started? Coffee? Something to eat?"

Izza still needed someone to fight, but he wasn't going to be that person. Let it be Mother, Becker, or better yet—Alex.

"I just want the sucker who knocked me out, you know what I mean?" That was another perk to working with Izza. Her West Coast accent developed a definite Hispanic pitch when angry, turning her words into a lethal promise with south-of-the-border flair. "I'll show him. I want a piece of Mother now, too."

"Come on. Sit Room. Let's get started."

She finally stalked into the room and sat beside Connor, but not before she delivered a good smack to his left bicep. "Quit laughing at me," she growled even as he draped an arm across her shoulders and planted a kiss to the side of her face. "You never even called."

"How could I?" He winked over her ornery shoulder at Mark. "You were working. We don't do personal calls on the job, remember?"

"You didn't even miss me."

He pulled her close for a quick peck on her ornery lips. "Izza, I always miss you."

That seemed to do the trick. Mark let everyone get settled before he dropped his bombshell. "Kelsey woke up to a red rose on her pillow this morning."

He watched that news settle before he continued. Either he was the dumbest supervisor on the planet, or just tired to death of fighting his team. "From this point on, we operate on the assumption Alex is alive and involved in what looks like a terrorist plot. I honestly don't know which side he's on. Again, assume he's working with us." *God, I hope.*

Izza's gaze darkened while Connor winked again. Rory gave Mark the thumbs up sign, and David nodded appreciatively. Only the newest agent appeared shocked.

"Who's in the coffin then?" Lisa asked, her eyes wide. "I mean, umm, we were all at his funeral. Who'd we bury if it wasn't him?"

"I don't know, and right now, I don't care," Mark answered. "We have something more serious on our plates. David? Is there something you'd like to share?"

"Only that I'm completely at your disposal, *Boss.*" David's quiet eyes said a lot more, but the way he'd used *that* title hit a bull's eye.

Mark inhaled a deep cleansing breath and finally looked *his* team in the eye. Alex might have built it, but it wasn't his anymore. Mark settled in to finally lead them where they seemed determined to go.

Landon chimed in with a cocky, "A flower, huh? Clever old dog. She buy it?"

Maverick huffed, but before he could get a nasty word in, Mark pulled rank. "Can it, Truman. I've had enough from you." He left the comment hang and let Landon stew, the smart ass.

"This is what I know, team. Somehow, Alex got into his place last night and left Kelsey a rose. Gabe also believes there's some pretty convincing blood evidence on the clothes he wore when he gave ALEX first aid at the scene. It might not be Alex's blood. Rory might be correct with his paintball theory after all. Ember? Do you know someone who can run a thorough forensic examination of those clothes so we can determine if it's Alex's blood or not?"

"You betcha," she said with a smile.

Mark tossed Gabe's apartment key to Connor. "Soon as we're done here, go get Gabe's dirty clothes. Bag them and bring them in for Ember. The sooner the better."

Connor snagged the key midair. "Will do."

"Okay then. David's got some news on a little FBI project called Eagle Two."

David came to the head of the table. Immediately, the picture of Ron Fallon and Sam Becker at the *Chaos Now* rally flashed onscreen. "We've linked FBI sniper Sam Becker to a local subversive group known as *Chaos Now* operating in Alexandria. It appears they intend to initiate a revolution."

The next slide displayed the *Chaos Now* timeline. "As you can see, these terrorists have no definite dates, but with the increase in their activity, we must assume it will occur soon. It appears their first target is Vice President Winston."

"Why don't we go to the FBI with all this crap?" Landon piped up. "Why are we always doing their job for them?"

Mark met the challenge head on. "Are you serious? Were you not there the day we pegged their top sniper, Agent Sam Becker, as the assassin who killed your boss?"

Landon shrugged. "But he isn't really dead now, is he?"

Maverick cut Landon off. "Just tell us what you want us to do."

Mark chose to act on Maverick's loyalty and let Landon's smirky insubordination go. "We're up against at least one pretty tough black ops guy. Maybe two. Becker and Fallon."

Steven interrupted. "Before you continue, look at this. One of these was stuck to each of our foreheads while we were tied up."

Mark accepted the yellow sticky note Steven offered. A smiling face had been scribbled in the middle of the small square of yellow paper.

"That guy's a jerk," Izza muttered. "He made us look stupid."

"I have to ask." A smile tugged the corners of Rory's mouth. "How'd the three of you get overpowered by one guy?"

Taylor grunted. "Gee. Thanks for asking."

"So?" Rory persisted, his eyes full of amusement as he scrolled his gaze from Taylor to Steven and Izza.

Taylor ran a hand through his hair. "It's like this. He seemed to know precisely where we'd be laying for him. Before we knew it, he was behind us. Steven was out cold, the guy had his boot on my neck and Izza in a choke hold."

"Shut up, Taylor," Izza ordered. "You make it sound like we were sleeping on the job, and we weren't. Least, not 'til he got hold of us."

Taylor chuckled. "There I was, gasping for air, and this guy's turning Izza into a ragdoll. You guys should've seen her. It wasn't funny then, but if that guy really was Alex, it's a whole different story. Man, he got us good."

"I'm gonna kick his ass." Izza faced Connor, her eyes narrowed and her lips pursed. "You just wait."

"And I know you will," Connor answered obediently, like any good husband would.

"But he was dressed in black again? Like the last time?" Mark asked, a creepy sensation tiptoeing up his spine.

"Yes, sir, he was," Steven replied, "and another thing. Yes, he tied us up, but he left enough slack that we were comfortable, not hogtied like gangsters would've done."

"Speak for yourself," Izza said. "I've got rope burns."

Mark listened to his team. It had to have been Alex, but the smiley face? That was definitely not a typical Alex Stewart memento. Mark set the sticky note aside.

"Listen guys, let's focus on *Chaos Now*. We're not going to waste time worrying about Alex, but Becker and Fallon—"

"So if these guys are part of *Chaos Now*," Maverick interrupted, tapping his pen on the table in front of him, "maybe we need to look at their recent activities a little closer. Like what purchases have they made lately? Who are they talking to? Where do they eat? Shop? Bank?"

"And do they own any storage sheds or garages where they could hide fertilizer or gasoline?" All heads swiveled to Lisa Channing's direction. She gulped at the unexpected attention. "I mean, umm, these guys might be planning something like the Oklahoma bombing, couldn't they? Shouldn't we look for stuff like that?"

Mark watched her self-confidence plummet. She dropped her gaze, blinking rapidly. She gulped. Poor kid. This was the first time she'd spoken up during a team meeting. For an ex-Army grunt, she'd arrived with zero confidence, and he had yet to learn why. He needn't have worried.

"Good thinking, Channing," Izza exclaimed. "I hadn't thought of that."

Lisa nodded at Izza. "It makes sense."

"It does. We should also be looking at large, out of the ordinary purchases of nitro methane," Rory interjected. "Plain gasoline for that matter. Let's see if anyone's been stockpiling fuel. Maybe one of these jokers knows how to fly. Do we know that?"

"No, but I can find out," Ember replied.

"Anyone got a black market confidential informant?" Maverick asked.

Mark breathed a *no kidding* sigh of relief. The TEAM's synergy had flashed back to life. He caught David's nod of approval while everyone else pinged ideas off each other for the next several minutes. All except Landon. He'd pushed back into his seat like a spectator at a tennis match. Just watching.

When the meeting finished, every other agent went to their workstations with a self-appointed list of things to track down, verify, and investigate.

It hit Mark. It would be damned hard giving *his team* back to the man who'd created it.

He didn't make it back to his desk as he'd planned. Steven had located Sam Becker again. The brazen FBI agent was back at the warehouse near the Gangplank Marina, exactly where they'd located him the day before. Mark stood over Steven's desk as he followed the traffic cam footage that revealed the same black sedan parked alongside the marina.

"Are you sure it's the same car?"

"No way to know for sure until we're boots on the ground, but look at this." Steven zoomed in on the grill of the car when it turned the corner to the warehouse. A black cover lowered to conceal the front license plate. "Have you ever seen anything like that?"

Mark huffed. "In a James Bond movie. Let's roll."

"Are you coming with me?"

"No. I'm going with you, Taylor, and Izza. Grab your gear, guys."

Steven drove with Mark, while Izza rode shotgun with Taylor.

"This isn't a stakeout," Mark informed everyone over their tactical Bluetooth earpieces. "We go in hot with no introduction. No knock on the door. Nothing."

"Copy that," Taylor answered.

Both cars rolled to the side of the warehouse and parked directly behind what very well might have been Becker's sedan. All four agents scrambled from their vehicles. The corrugated sheet metal building was a long, one-story structure with plate-glass windows in front, none at the side.

It offered two visible points of egress—a wooden door at the top of two concrete steps at the side, and a garage door at the front. Mark motioned Taylor and Izza to enter the side entrance while he and Steven took the front. He tapped his earpiece on. "On three. One. Two—"

CRASH! Another black sedan roared through the front garage door, its tires burning rubber. What the hell? Which belonged to Becker? Didn't matter. The TEAM gave chase.

"Don't lose this guy!" Mark ordered.

Taylor and Izza charged back to their vehicle, in hot pursuit, while Mark and Steven followed in theirs.

"He's headed for the interstate," Taylor said as he accelerated alongside the black sedan. It swerved onto the right shoulder and roared around traffic.

"Box him in," Mark ordered Steven. "Let's get this sonofabitch."

Steven hit the shoulder and stuck to the sedan's rear bumper. In another minute, the vehicle would be on the busy interstate and more lives endangered. The chase had to end now.

"Come on, guys. Taylor! Steven!" Mark urged his junior agents to trap the fleeing sedan between them. "Izza!"

No sooner wished for than done. Izza all but climbed out her window and pointed her weapon into the driver's window, her ponytail whipping in the wind. "Pull over! Now!"

The sedan jerked forward yet again, but Steven and Taylor had both anticipated the countermeasure. Izza, too. She leaned farther out the window, the barrel of her weapon clattering against the driver's window glass. "Do it. Over! Now!"

He slowed.

Taylor and Steven matched the sedan's speed until it nearly stopped. When Taylor angled to block it in, it lurched forward, pushing his vehicle out of its way. A cloud of smoke poured from the sedan's tires.

The collision nearly knocked Izza out of the vehicle and to the ground. She dangled from the window, cussing a storm of invective into everyone's earpieces until Taylor stepped on the brakes and jerked her back inside.

"Don't let him make the on-ramp!" Mark yelled, but the sedan had a jump-start and a healthy lead. It swerved dangerously around traffic and up the on-ramp that fed the interstate, swerving while it dodged vehicles. Horns honked and cars pulled to the left or right to avoid the reckless driver.

Mark blew out an exasperated sigh. "Let him go. Damn it. Let him go. We can't risk other lives. Head back to the warehouse." At least they had the other vehicle.

Taylor and Izza were already there by the time Steven and Mark returned.

Damn it to hell. That sedan was gone, too.

Mark's cell phone rang out from its hip holster. *David. What now?*

"Yes?" Mark answered it, hating the sense of doom that pervaded every phone call and the migraines that had literally moved inside his skull and set up their throbbing shop.

"I just got off the phone with the police chief. He wanted you to know about Stevenson and Bukowski, the guys who bombed Sullivan's car."

"What about 'em?"

"They've both got severe radiation poisoning."

Chapter Twenty-Eight

The cab dropped Shelby and Gabe at an impressive five-story brick building in Old Town Alexandria, Virginia, near the King Street metro station. Gabe hurried her through two glass doors that opened automatically at his approach. The small lobby offered nothing but an elevator door and a beautifully crafted tile mosaic of the American flag on the entire wall opposite the entry. *Never Forget* blazed in crimson red script beneath the rendering.

It stole Shelby's breath. She had to stop to absorb the masterpiece. With clever use of light and color, the artist captured the regal spirit of the flag towering over her, its colors aloft and rippling as if it were caught on a stiff wind before the gathering storm clouds behind it.

"Just who exactly was Alex Stewart?" she asked, suddenly feeling small and insignificant.

Gabe held the elevator door for her. "USMC scout sniper. Good guy. Why?"

"He loved his country, didn't he?"

"Yes. He did. You would've liked him. He was quite the gentleman with the ladies. Respectful, like men used to be."

"So tell me again. You were USMC, too? Right?"

"Yes, ma'am. Sergeant Gabriel Cartwright, at your service."

The heat of her arrogance crept over her cheeks. She'd not paid attention when she should have. She wished she had. "What did you do in the military?"

"In the Marines," he corrected as the elevator door slid closed. He'd automatically assumed a stiffer posture, his back erect, his shoulders squared like he was back in the service of his country. "I served like thousands of other good men and women."

The elevator pinged at the second level. Gabe placed his palm at the small of her back, escorting her onto a red carpet that led to the center workstation.

The blonde woman at the center desk glanced over the edge of the counter circling her space. Her soft green eyes lit up. She was nothing short of stunning.

Statuesque and full-figured, she was perfectly proportioned with a gold-white topknot drizzling spirals of curls down her neck. Her skinny black jeans with rhinestones running up the side seams shouted 'Designer!' The tiny jacket in no way concealed her cleavage, not squeezed into a tank top with horizontal gray and black stripes like it was. The only break in the gray/black color scheme was the teardrop ruby dangling between her breasts. Oh yeah, and the red lipstick on her full lips, an identical match to the gemstone.

"Gabe. Hi," she exclaimed, a smile warming her face. "Where's Zack and Kelsey?"

"Someplace safe. Ember, this is Shelby Sullivan. Shelby, Ember Dennison, our resident genius. Where's everyone else?"

"Mark should be back any minute. He had a lead on Becker so half of the office went with him. Connor and Rory took your clothes over to my friend at Crystal City." Ember reached across the counter, offering her hand. "Hi, Shelby. We're so glad you're staying with Kelsey."

There was no pretentiousness behind Ember's greeting, only admiration.

"I hope I was helpful." Shelby glanced over her shoulder at the others in the office. A handsome guy leaned over the desk of a pretty girl. He'd glanced up at Gabe's introductions, his gaze scrolling up and down, ending at her breasts. She reached for Gabe's hand, intertwining her fingers between his.

Gabe dipped his head to her level. "You okay?"

"Yes. Sure." *Much better now.*

"So where's Mother?" he asked. "She didn't go with Mark, did she?"

"She quit." Ember tossed her head, sending a quiver through the cascade of tangles down her back. "Do you believe that? After all this time with Alex, and she quits when Mark needs her most?"

"You're kidding me. Why? What's wrong with her?"

Shelby listened to make sure she'd heard right. *Gabe's mother works here, too? That's kind of weird.*

Ember wrinkled her nose. "I don't know, but she's off my Christmas list. Mark thinks she's working with Becker and Fallon."

"No way. She wouldn't do that."

"Okay, wait a minute." Shelby lifted her hand for attention. "I'm sorry, but who's Mother?"

Gabe grinned. "Sorry. It's a nickname. Mother was our lead techie. I used to think she was a genius, but now that she's quit I'm not so sure." He turned back to Ember. "Hey. We ran into Becker over in Arlington not more than an hour ago in the middle of me trying to protect Zack and Kelsey from being run off the bridge. Somehow, that ended up being my fault, but I thought he was supposed to be in jail. What happened?"

"I don't know, but if you just saw him in Arlington, who's Mark chasing?"

"Can't be him unless he's in two places at one time."

She nodded at the two empty chairs beside hers. "Since you're both involved, let's bring you up to speed. Oh yeah, those guys who blew up your car also poisoned Kelsey's dogs. Zack's taking care of them and Kelsey at the moment."

"No shit?" Gabe asked as he escorted Shelby past the customer service counter and into Ember's workspace. He offered her a chair and held it until she settled. He grabbed another chair and swung it around backwards and sat, his arms crossed over the chair back, his green eyes shining.

"Stupid, mean people," Ember hissed. "I hate anyone who hurts animals."

Shelby didn't know what to say. Kelsey loved those two dogs, called them her boys. Whisper and Smoke needed to pull through this poisoning if only for Kelsey. They had to!

"I know what you mean," Gabe agreed, "but Zack knows dogs. He'll move heaven and hell to take care of them. Kelsey, too."

"I now, but I can't get in touch with him to get a progress report. It's killing me."

"Ember." Gabe tapped the counter top to get her attention. "Trust Zack. What else have I missed?"

Ember's head bobbed. "You're right. Sorry. Let me show you what's been happening."

While Gabe and Ember chatted, Shelby took stock of Ember's very technical-looking workstation. The sleek black granite counter tops lent an elegant touch. CPUs and other equipment lined a portion of the cabinet to her left, with more on the floor beneath to her right. A bank of monitors lined a half-wall rising out of the floor. It didn't reach the ceiling, but supported more computer equipment than one would expect in a normal business office. Looked more like command central than a secretary's desk.

Eww. All the overhead screens relayed camera views from Kelsey's home, even capturing the burned spot on the street where she'd parked her car. Her heart pinched. Had Ember seen her earlier transgression? Her car blowing up? Probably not, or she wouldn't be so nice.

Ember rolled her chair to another monitor. With a tap of her fingers, a keyboard lifted up from the desk, then another alongside the first. Her fingertips flew from one keyboard to the other. The screen flickered on. She cocked her head and stilled. "Yes, Mark. He and Miss Sullivan are here now. They're okay."

"Tell him I ran into Becker," Gabe urged Ember. "Arlington Memorial Bridge. Zack and Kelsey are at my place in Silver Springs."

She nodded and relayed the intel. "Understood. Check when you leave the hospital. Copy that."

"She's wearing a Bluetooth earpiece," Gabe explained to Shelby. "We all do."

"You all do? Even at Kelsey's?" Shelby asked, a catch in her throat. That little Bluetooth nugget of information didn't sit so well. So Zack and Gabe and Mark and Ember were all connected. All the time? *Even when you kissed me?*

"Yes, but only on active ops, like when Zack or I walked the perimeter or were out of touch with each other," Gabe said. "Keeps our hands free for weapons. No need for twenty-four-seven communication otherwise. It would drive Ember nuts listening to everything we said."

Whew. Big sigh of relief. I mean BIG sigh of relief.

"Oh. Okay," Shelby mumbled, miffed at herself for missing this little detail, too. She should've taken a good hard look at her roomies at the beginning of this affair.

Gabe leaned his elbows to his knees. "So whatcha got?" he asked Ember.

She must've gotten another call. She stilled again and lifted her hand with one finger extended for silence. Her brows raised. "Thanks. I'll tell him. Yes, he's here. You're a peach. I owe you. Big time. Let me know about the rest."

Swiveling to face Gabe, her eyes glowed. "Mark called. He and David are at the hospital. The two guys who bombed your car this morning, Shelby, are sick with radiation poisoning. The second call was Malcolm, my guy over at the forensics lab. And guess what? Cow's blood. That's what you had on your hands that day, that and something else Malcolm can't identify yet. He thinks it might be some kind of a designer drug."

"What the hell is Alex up to? Or Becker?" Gabe hissed, and Shelby honestly felt like a ping-pong ball, contributing nothing but trying her darnedest to keep up with Gabe and Ember's elusive back-and-forths. "He shot Alex with pellets of cow's blood? The other substance had to be some kind of a knockout drug then. You were there, Ember. Alex went down like he was—"

Ember winced. "Dead. I know. I was there, but wow. Who knew the FBI would do something like this to a civilian contractor, huh? You think they needed him out of their way?"

"Hard to know, but it's no wonder the boss hated working with them. Do you think maybe he knew Becker was going to shoot him?"

Ember shook her head adamantly. "No way. Not Alex. It would mean that he hid all of this from Kelsey. No." Ember clicked the mouse at her fingertips through screen after screen of information, some of which Shelby understood. Some, not so much.

"Although we do think he is involved with *Chaos Now*," Ember murmured.

"Who? Alex?" Gabe asked. He seemed to have no trouble following the screens Ember scrolled through.

"Yes. Somehow, he'd gotten himself involved with *Chaos Now,* just like Becker. I'm just not sure they're on the same side."

"Hell. We've got more players in this mess than we know what to do with," Gabe muttered. He leaned forward, his chin on his clenched fists, silently following Ember's breakdown of all he'd missed while Shelby watched and listened. Ember wove into the conversation bullets that didn't really kill, something called a gang of ten, inconsistencies in the Medical Examiner's conclusions on Alex Stewart's COD, and more intrigue and drama than Shelby had ever seen or heard before. Nightshift at the emergency room seemed tame in comparison.

Little by little, anxiety crept up her throat. *Chaos Now*? FBI trickery? Revolution? Who were these people who called themselves The TEAM, anyway?

Thank God, Alex learned how to work well with the police. It was a relationship built on trust, and Mark found himself the lucky recipient of his boss's good rapport with the current local police chief. Unfortunately, the interrogation with Bukowski and Stevenson had to take place in the hospital, since both men were critically ill.

Police Chief Darrin McDonald escorted Mark and David to the gentlemen's joint hospital room. "I'm sure sorry to hear about Mr. Stewart's passing away like he did. What a shame."

"Thank you," Mark replied.

"He was a good friend. We'll miss him. I worked with him on the White Hawk case. Damned shame he's gone."

Mark searched McDonald's eyes for any hint of insincerity. He hesitated revealing what he knew about the *Chaos Now* group, or his suspicions concerning FBI sniper Sam Becker's involvement in Alex's murder. It had become damned hard deciding whom to trust.

Chief McDonald filled the awkward silence, his hand on the door. "I'll be interested to see if these guys talk to you, Agent Houston. The hospital is overcrowded or we'd have them in separate locations, but given their condition, it probably doesn't matter. They're pretty sick. We're not getting much out of them. About the only thing we've heard is Stevenson telling Bukowski to shut up."

"We'll give it a try. Will you join us, sir?"

"Yes. Is that a problem?"

"Not at all. I'd rather you witnessed everything."

A pitiful sight met Mark's gaze when the police officers standing guard opened the hospital room door.

Stevenson was the typical jarhead, muscle bound and thick-necked. His hair was shaved high and tight. Big chin. Square jaw.

Bukowski, on the other hand, was Stevenson's complete opposite. Extremely overweight, he sported a shaggy salt-and-pepper beard, with a spit-polish shine on the top of his bald head. Their only commonalities seemed to be their extremely swollen hands, gaunt faces, and deathly pallor.

"You guys feel like talking?" Mark asked quietly as he stepped to Stevenson's bedside.

Neither man replied, but their doctor did. The elderly, white-haired physician arrived seconds after Mark and David. "I am Dr. Amin Jitar. What are you doing here? These gentlemen are in no condition for visitors. I'm sorry, but I insist you leave immediately."

"We're not going anywhere," Chief McDonald replied crisply. "We need answers, and whether they know it or not, these guys need our help."

Dr. Jitar's eyes flashed with anger. He pointed to Stevenson. "Acute radiation isn't to be treated lightly. The only reason they aren't able to speak now is because of the poisoning. I'm sure of it."

Chief McDonald turned to Stevenson. "Not so. This guy's been talking plenty. So has Bukowski. They're just selective about who's in the room when they do."

"Are they only presenting with gastrointestinal distress, Dr. Jitar?" David interrupted the confrontation. "Are you seeing any neurological degradation, or is it too soon to tell?"

Dr. Jitar's brows lifted as he turned his focus on David. "You are familiar with radiation poisoning?"

"I understand it enough to know that specific symptoms are associated with different doses. For instance, the burns on their hands indicate they've been in contact with a radioactive isotope without wearing proper protection. Is that correct?"

Dr. Jitar nodded. "Yes, they both display skin trauma indicative of recent severe exposure. Intestinal distress as well. I'm not seeing the neurological degradation you asked about yet. However, if they only came into contact with a reactor-level isotope, say caesium-137 or strontium 90, nerve damage wouldn't present for days or even weeks."

Mark watched David's clever strategy as he very gently picked Dr. Jitar's brain while Stevenson and Bukowski listened intently. David had a knack for storing vast amounts of useless trivia. For once, Mark was glad he did.

"You don't think cobalt-60 or iridium-192 then?" David tapped his index finger to his chin.

"It is too soon to tell," the doctor admitted. "It may not be a reactor type of isotope at all. It could be medical or commercial. I simply don't know, but I had to initiate some kind of treatment. If these poor sick men could talk, I could treat them more effectively. It's unfortunate. Their families need to be notified. Arrangements need to be made before it's too late."

Mark glanced from Bukowski back to Stevenson. By the time David got through with them, they were going to regret playing their doctor for a fool by pretending they couldn't speak.

"They could still present with aplastic anemia?" David covered his lips as if trying to keep the conversation confidential. He blew out a long sigh. "That would be tragic."

"Oh, yes. Without a doubt. It's just a matter of time. Hematopoietic syndrome, the extreme drop in white blood cell counts, will eventually compromise every aspect of their recovery. I haven't seen such a case since the Chernobyl reactor failure. I'm giving them vast quantities of fluids and antibiotics, but without knowing the source of their poisoning, it's difficult to determine the best treatment."

"You were at Chernobyl?" David's brows lifted. "During or after?"

"Much later. I studied the long-term effects on the immediate population with the United Nations Task Force. Most unfortunate." He shook his head. "Tsk, tsk, tsk. Such an unnecessary waste of lives."

David blew out a big sigh as he turned away from the patients, presenting his back to them while he lowered his voice. "What you're telling me is this could turn from simple nausea, headaches, and diarrhea to seizures, lethargy, and death within a matter of hours? Is that right?"

Dr. Jitar shook his head sadly. "You know as well as I do that a dose as small as 6 rad will still cause cognitive impairment. Anything larger than 30 rad, and they'll be dead in two days."

"I'm afraid this is very bad, Mark," David stage whispered across the room. "We're too late. Radiation destroys soft tissue first. It's already in their blood. Maybe their bones. Obviously their throats and vocal cords. Maybe we can locate their next of kin. That's about all—"

"The hell I can't talk," Bukowski said hoarsely. "Catch that sonofabitch before he gets away. He never said nothing 'bout that crap being radioactive. Not even once!"

"Shut up," Stevenson hissed from the other bed. "These guys are playing you and you're falling for it. You're an ass."

"No, I'm not. You are. I ain't gonna die for his stupid revolution. Not anymore."

"I'm telling you for the last time. Stow it."

Mark stepped over to Bukowski's bedside, blocking his view of Stevenson. "Who did you handle the radiation for?"

"Fallon. That sonofabitch told us to move it down to the warehouse to where they're—"

"Shut the hell up," Stevenson ordered, leaning forward as far as his restraints would allow. "He'll kill you if you say anything else."

"In case you ain't noticed, he's already killed us," Bukowski bellowed at his cohort in crime. "Did you hear what the doc said? Man, we're gonna die and it's gonna hurt when we do."

"You're playing right into their hands. For hell's sake, why do you think they said all that stuff? They're trying to scare you. They want you to talk," Stevenson ground out, his voice edged with exasperation. "Shut up."

"I don't care and I ain't gonna shut up, neither. I'm sick of laying here puking my guts up and filling a diaper. I don't wanna die." Bukowski's rant descended into a desperate whine. "I need help, Doc. And you, guys. What do you want? I'll tell you everything."

"Where's the warehouse?" Mark asked.

"Across the street from the Gangplank Marina."

"Okay, I know the place. What's the radiation for?"

"So help me. The minute I get out of here, I'm gonna cut your fat neck," Stevenson threatened.

Bukowski's eyes darted from Stevenson and back to Dr. Jitar before he settled on Mark. "Can you really help me, man? I mean, really? You won't let Stevenson or Fallon get to me, will you?"

"No," Chief McDonald stepped forward. "I'll contact the FBI as soon as we're done here. We can offer witness protection if you cooperate."

"Bukowski," Stevenson growled. "Not one more word."

Dr. Jitar stepped over to his bedside with a roll of white surgical tape. "You must be quiet, sir. Your friend is trying to speak." He placed a wide piece of the tape over Stevenson's mouth before he turned back to Bukowski. "Now. What is it you needed to tell these good men?"

Mark nodded at the doctor in appreciation. At last, the man understood what was really going on. Stevenson too. He growled and grumbled, but he couldn't threaten his buddy anymore.

"Fallon's got a dirty bomb," Bukowski blurted.

God, no. Mark's stomach dropped. "Are you sure?"

"Yeah, I'm sure. It's how he's gonna kick off his revolution. With fireworks and lots of dead bodies."

"When?"

"Today. Umm, tonight, I think. Hell, I'm not real sure. Fallon don't talk to me much."

"Where's the bomb now?"

"I don't know. Fallon's making it. Him and this other guy. Them's the only two who know exactly where it's gonna blow. I just delivered the stuff to the warehouse like I was told to."

"What stuff?"

"SEMTEX, C4, and all that damned radioactive crap I been packing for weeks. I'm screwed, ain't I?"

Mark pressed for more information. "How much plastic explosives?"

"Oh, gawd, I hauled crates of that crap. I don't know how much there is. A couple hundred pounds maybe?"

"Surely Fallon can't fund a revolution by himself? Who's financing him?" Mark asked.

"Don't know, but he's got some rich guy jerking his chain. I think it's the same guy who's been sending the money. I don't know who he is, though. Ain't nobody else talked to him but Fallon," Bukowski replied, his eyes wide with concern. "Oh, gawd! I ain't gonna die, am I?"

Mark stepped closer to the frantic man's bedside. "How'd you meet Fallon?"

"In the Army. A bunch of us were in Iraq back in '91. I should've known he'd do something like this to me. He was a mean bastard back then, too."

"Do you know anything about the radioactive isotopes you handled?" David asked. "Were there labels on the containers? Did you wear any kind of a dosimeter?"

"Damn it, man. What the hell are you talking about?"

David tapped his cell phone screen a few times before he lifted it where Bukowski could see. "It would've looked like this. A dosimeter measures exposure to radiation. Anyone handling isotopes should wear one."

Bukowski took a quick look and dissolved into whining. "There weren't nuthin. Oh, gawd! They just looked like big plastic boxes to me. Didn't have no danger signs or nuthin' on 'em." He writhed under the sheets. "Man, he's done killed me, and I helped him do it. Oh, gawd!"

David placed a hand on the worried man's shoulder. "The faster we find the bomb, the quicker Dr. Jitar can help you. Time is of the essence. The radiation your body absorbed is eating away at your nerves and muscles as we speak. Is there anything else you can tell us?"

Bukowski rolled his eyes, blinking furiously and panting hard. "Wait. I heard Fallon talking to this new guy one time. They was talking real low and quiet, but all a sudden, Fallon blows up. He tells this new guy to mind his gawddamned business and go to hell. Said something about how the Vice President's got a thing or two coming to him, too."

"The Vice President? As in Vice President Winston?" Mark asked to be sure. David's daring hack into federal servers was spot on. *Chaos Now*'s target was Winston.

Bukowski nodded adamantly. "Yeah. That's what he said. Oh yeah, he said something about Constitution Avenue, too. It was all gonna happen on Constitution Avenue. I remember now."

"That's where Fallon intends to start the revolution?" Mark asked, shaking his head at the magnitude of this new information.

The poor man's head kept bobbing.

"When?"

Bukowski glanced at Stevenson before he shrugged his reply. "I don't know. He don't like me and Stevenson enough to share what he's doing. We're just grunts."

Mark jerked his head at the door, signaling to David they needed to go. "Mr. Bukowski, you do what Dr. Jitar tells you, and we'll find the bomb, okay?"

"Yes, sir, I sure will."

That seemed to calm the big guy. Stevenson still strained and grunted, but his partner in crime appeared to have found some measure of peace.

"Hey, you," Bukowski called to Mark. "Would you do something for me before you go?"

"You bet." Mark came back to the bedside. "What do you need?"

The big man had tears in his eyes. "I know I don't deserve any kind of help from you guys. Not after I blew up that little gal's car like I did, but if I give you my boy's number, would you please tell him to get my grandkids outta D.C. for me?"

"I'll do my best," Mark answered, his cell in his hand. "What's the number?"

Bukowski rattled his son's number off, and Mark placed the call on his way out the door.

The time had come. Trust them or not, the FBI and every other federal agency in D.C. had to be involved. Mark and Chief McDonald both notified the proper authorities the minute they hit the hallway.

"Contact Ember," Mark whispered out of the corner of his mouth when McDonald stepped out of earshot. "The FBI will be at our office in minutes, and they'll want everything. Tell her to give them only what's related to the car bombing. Nothing more."

"Not what we have on Becker?" David asked as they strode swiftly from the hospital.

"Nothing that relates to Alex's murder investigation." Mark's mind flew over the wealth of evidence they'd accumulated, all the enhanced satellite images, the illegally obtained references to Eagle Two, and Steven's spot-on analysis of Becker's peculiar sniper rounds.

"Anything else?"

"Tell her to secure Steven's workstation and your conclusions on the ME's report. Tell her to put everything in the vault on level three. No one is to talk with the FBI. Only me."

Mark's angst rapped into high overdrive. He couldn't get out of the hospital fast enough. The FBI would sweep through the office like a horde of locusts, devouring anything and everything in their path, possibly conducting intimidating interrogations as well. The competent men and women of The TEAM would be shoved aside and trampled underfoot as the very arrogant Feds took over and stole every last bit of intel, relevant or not.

They'd want Kelsey next. *Not going to happen.* Just the thought of her in their custody spilled more acid into his gut. Mark speed dialed Zack's burn phone.

Zack answered promptly. "What's up?"

"FBI is now actively involved. They'll be looking for you."

"What? Why?"

"Fallon's built a dirty bomb. Maybe more than one. You need to move. Get Kelsey out of the city."

"But, Mark—"

"No!" Mark roared. "Protect Kelsey. Get her out of here. Now!"

Chapter Twenty-Nine

Gabe looked up from Ember's monitor into the cold eyes of a man in a cheap black business suit, a shiny Federal Bureau of Investigation badge in his slimy palm. Damn. What'd the FBI want? More blood on their hands? Another bogus execution?

The man extended a hand over the counter by way of introduction. "Where's your boss?"

Gabe kept his hand on the desk and didn't return the courtesy. The Feds. Big deal. They caused more trouble than not. After what Ember had revealed, these guys were as guilty as sin. "Who wants to know?"

"Agent Benson."

"What do you want?"

"Every. Last. Thing," he hissed as he scanned the vacant office.

"As in what *everything*?" Gabe pushed out of his chair, his arms crossed and *hell no* in his heart. These guys were the bastards behind Alex's murder. Fake or not, it made no difference. He was willing to bet they owned Sam Becker, too. Probably paid him a bonus to bring Alex down. Gabe didn't owe them squat.

Ember glanced at him, her eyes wide though she didn't speak a word. Not even hello. Must be Mark in her ear again. She ended the clandestine conversation with a barely noticeable tap on the device in her ear to signify *copy that,* the way covert operators communicated when they couldn't risk speaking out loud.

Lifting to her feet, her shoulders squared and her head held high, she met Benson head on. Her chin might have been lifted up, but her fingers were hard at work below the edge of the counter, tapping away at the keyboard beyond Benson's view.

His dark gaze skimmed over her upper body from the top of her head and stopping at her cleavage the way most men's did. The girl had it. She flaunted it, and she knew how to use it to distract stupid guys, too.

Gabe couldn't help that his fingers curled into a fist. Ember was another sister. Like Kelsey. She deserved to be treated with respect, no matter her cup size. Benson was an ass.

"You'll have to be more specific, Agent Benson. I'm not giving you anything without a warrant," she declared.

His upper lip lifted in a weak smile. Oatmeal had more spine. "I don't need a warrant when I'm dealing with terrorists. Give me everything you've got on the pipe bomb at Stewart's home this morning for starters. In fact, everything on Stewart's murder, while you're at it. His wife's attempted murder, too. We'll go from there."

"We haven't been investigating Alex's murder," she asserted patiently as only Ember could do. "Your buddy, Agent Kenny, clarified what happened to Alex. The ME agreed with him. Why would we dispute those expert conclusions? And as far as Kelsey Stewart's accident, the sheriff ruled it closed. It wasn't attempted murder. She over-corrected and her car went into the river. That's all. Sheesh.

Don't you FBI guys ever talk to each other? Go to lunch together? Anything?"

Benson stared her down and resorted to bullying. "Liar."

Gabe stifled the rising need to knock this guy on his ass. No need.

Ember could hold her own. Despite the nasty insult, she didn't miss a beat. "Excuse me? Why would I lie to the FBI? You're here, aren't you? And if you're here, you've already got someone inside my server, digging into anything and everything. What could I possibly have to hide and how would I do it?"

Gabe steeled his expression, sure her tapping fingertips were doing just that, securing The TEAM server before the Bureau's finest hackers got in too deep. Damn. They didn't stand a chance. If they were good, she was ten times better, and she looked good doing it.

"I'll tell you what," she offered. "Why don't you have a chair while I copy all files activated since the date of Mr. Stewart's murder. It will probably be just on the pipe bombing, though. Will that make you happy? That way you can tell your boss you got exactly what you came for."

"Paper copies."

She frowned. "Sorry, but no. We only work with digital. You'll have to kill your own trees when you get back to your office."

"Paper," he demanded, his badge tapping the counter with sharp staccato emphasis. "I want both paper and digital copies, and I want them now."

She folded her arms over her ample bosom, covering her cleavage and the red ruby. "Just because you Feds are digitally challenged, doesn't mean we are. You'll make do with what I give you or nothing at all."

He puckered his lips, as if he wanted to argue. "Fine. Make it quick."

"Yes, sir," she replied as cheerfully as if he were the pizza delivery guy. "Gabe. Can you and Shelby help me? I know David has some files on his computer. Steven and Mark, too. Let's give this guy what he wants so he can L. E. A. V. E."

Gabe nearly smiled at her insolence. He pulled Shelby to her feet and followed Ember to Mark's office, the one that used to belong to Alex.

"Shit," Ember murmured the moment they cleared the office doorjamb. "Fallon's built a dirty bomb and it's in D.C. The revolution begins tonight. That's why Benson's here. He wants all of our intel, including what we know about his buddy, Becker. Leave the door open. Let him watch. We don't want to give him a reason to come back."

"Are you sure?" Gabe sat at Mark's desk while Shelby hovered over his shoulder. "A dirty bomb?"

Ember inserted a USB drive into the port on the side of the keyboard. "Oh, sure. Sixty-four gig's big enough to keep our FBI friends happy. While you download these files, I'll take care of everyone else's. Move all files onto this USB drive. Can you do that for me?"

She ducked closer to Gabe, her face hidden by the curtain of her hair. "Yes, and it's supposed to go off somewhere on Constitution Avenue. Mark thinks Benson is after Zack and Kelsey. I'll give him what we know about *Chaos Now,* but nothing on Alex, Kelsey, or Becker," she whispered.

Gabe complied, keeping his head low and an eye on Agent Benson, who now stood outside Mark's office door and looking impatient to be off. Gabe brought Mark's document files on the pipe bombing to screen, sorted them by date and performed a mass copy while Ember strolled past Benson and into the work bay. More like sashayed. The woman definitely had confidence and she knew how to distract a guy.

Benson's cocky head swiveled to watch her backside. The elevator pinged and he turned his back to Gabe. "Mr. Houston. How nice."

Gabe completed the transfer. Good. Mark had returned. Connor and Rory were back, too. Sounded like Taylor, Maverick, Izza, and Steven, too.

"Senior Agent Houston," Mark corrected. "What do *you* want?"

"It's about time." Benson nodded at Gabe. "Your office is occupied. Is there some place we could chat?"

"Here's fine." Mark planted his feet, his hands on his hips while the other agents went to their desks.

Chat? An interesting euphemism for browbeating.

Gabe nodded to acknowledge his boss. Mark nodded back.

One of the smartest things Alex did when he'd designed the work bay was to locate Mother and Ember's workstation and customer service desk dead center of everyone else's. The wagon wheel layout served a purpose. Every agent was now acutely focused on the unfolding power struggle between federal agents and private contractor. If there ever was a need to show these men and women exactly where Mark stood, it was now.

Give 'em hell, Boss.

"I'd prefer a more private—"

"Here's fine." Mark cut the FBI agent off. "You want to chat? Chat."

"Have it your way." Agent Benson glanced around the office. "Might as well let everyone know what happens when guys like you break the law."

Mark didn't respond to the implied threat, but Gabe wanted to knock Benson down and out. *Guys like you?* He lifted out of Mark's chair and went to stand with his boss, transferring the USB drive to Ember's waiting fingers.

"When did you become aware of Mr. Fallon's association with *Chaos Now*?" Benson snapped.

Ah ha, so he suspects one of us has been inside the FBI's server, but maybe he can't prove it. Gabe's eyes scrolled to Ember. Had to be her. *Good girl.*

"With what? Who?" Mark asked.

"*Chaos Now*," Benson repeated with a nasty twang to his voice. "Don't play around with me, Houston. I have every reason to believe you've been investigating Mr. Fallon as a terrorist."

"Fallon's a small part of an ongoing investigation. You think he's involved in terrorist activities? Care to share?"

Benson didn't blink. "Where's he got the isotope?"

"What's he need an isotope for?" Mark countered as quickly.

"I'm not here to answer your questions."

"Then ask better questions. You and I both know the guys who handled the isotope are in FBI custody by now. Go ask them. They're the culprits here, not us."

Benson danced around the real issue. Gabe had no doubt he wanted to know if Mark had an agent inside *Chaos Now*. He'd come fishing for information and determined to get into

The TEAM's psyche. And close to three strikes at the rate he badgered Mark. The man couldn't win.

"You know damned well they're too sick to talk."

"That's strange. Bukowski was talking plenty when I left. I called FBI Headquarters and told them everything he and I discussed. You ever think to check with them before you come barging into a private business?"

"You talked to Bukowski?"

Mark shrugged. "Why not? The police chief asked me to."

"Guess I need to chat with McDonald about proper protocol—not like it matters. Bukowski's not the brains behind any of this. Neither is Fallon."

"Good to know," Mark replied.

Gabe's ears perked up. *If Fallon's not the brains, who is?*

Benson shifted tactics, his sneer still in place. "If I was a betting man, I'd say you and your guys are running your own counter-terrorism operation. You've got Stewart's wife stashed under high-security somewhere. You've been involved in two high-speed chases in one day. Now you're caught chatting up a couple guys with severe radiation burns from weapons grade plutonium. Yeah. If I was a betting man, I'd say it's not looking too good for you, Senior Agent Houston."

God, Gabe really wanted to pop Benson. Just once. Bully tactics. Pure unadulterated bully tactics. So far, he'd done nothing but threaten.

Mark must've felt the same. He took a step toward Benson, his right fist curled and ready. "You haven't caught shit, and you damned well know it. Want to put your money where your big mouth is?"

Benson didn't flinch. "That's why the pipe bomb, huh? You guys were getting too close to Fallon for comfort, weren't you? He's trying to scare you off, isn't he?"

"So. Weapons grade plutonium, huh? Are you sure of that?"

Benson stood his ground, radiating hostility and maybe a hint of regret for bragging and giving Mark intel he hadn't already known.

Gabe let a cautious grin split his face. Round over. Benson never had a dog in this fight.

"Let me make this perfectly clear, Agent Benson," Mark said calmly, his fist relaxed. "The pipe bomb that exploded this morning at Kelsey Stewart's home in Alexandria was delivered by two ex-Army regulars. We discovered the extent of their involvement with Fallon only when we talked to Bukowski at the hospital less than an hour ago."

He took a step closer to his adversary. "I called the Bureau the minute I knew Fallon had a dirty bomb. I don't know how or where his men got the isotope, neither do I know the strength of it. And until now, I didn't know it was weapons grade plutonium. End of story. Check with Police Chief McDonald, but you'd better hurry. Bukowski and Stevenson are sloughing skin and muscle. They'll be lucky to last the night."

Benson's brows spiked. Maybe he believed. Maybe he didn't have enough evidence to prove otherwise. The showdown ended when he turned on his heel and beelined to the elevator without a word.

"Excuse me, sir. Umm, sir," Ember called after him, the USB drive in her raised hand. "Did you forget something?"

She would've gone after him out of the goodness of her heart, but Gabe lifted his arm to block her from being too damned nice. "No. He wanted 'em. Let him come get 'em."

Agent Benson had his dark glasses on by then, but Gabe stared him down anyway as he retraced his steps. The guy was a total jerk-off. Rude. Dismissive. Downright disrespectful to Ember and Mark.

The second the elevator doors closed behind him, Gabe stepped into the inner circle of Ember's workstation, raised his hands and clapped. "Yeah. Give it up for the Boss."

Mark downplayed the moment of appreciation, but every other agent had already joined in by then. Connor thumped his back. Izza whistled, two fingers to her lips. Yes! The TEAM was back, ready to rock and roll.

"Listen, guys." Mark lifted his voice over the applause. "Sorry. We don't have time to celebrate. Not yet. Fallon's really built a dirty bomb. It's somewhere in D.C. We're running on borrowed time. I need eyes on the Gangplank Marina. We've got to find Fallon and the bomb. Or bombs. There could be more than one."

"What else do you need us to do?" Gabe asked.

Mark leveled his gaze, making eye contact with every single agent. "Get your loved ones out of the city."

Chapter Thirty

She wanted to cry.

Shelby left messages on her parents' phone as well as her brother's, frustrated she couldn't talk to them in person. Gabe's friends had barely taken time to arrange for their own families' safety before gathering around Mark in tight military formation. Gabe wanted her to leave too, but she'd flatly refused. If he was staying, so was she.

Mark had sent Shelby an evil, arched brow when he'd first spotted her in his territory, but he seemed okay with her now. Maybe because there wasn't enough time to argue, not if the bomb was really going off tonight.

A couple agents were at their workstations, but everyone else stood at the wall-sized map of Washington D.C., studying it for centralized locations where Fallon might place a dirty bomb for maximum impact. There were so many. Constitution Avenue alone provided a wealth of possibilities, running as close to the White House as it did.

From what Shelby knew, the building was an armed fortress complete with snipers on the rooftop and the ever-present Secret Service lurking in every shadow and behind every column. In no way could anyone get close to President Adams.

Getting within range of any other federal building was just as difficult. The bombing of the Alfred P. Murrah Federal Building in Oklahoma City in 1995 made certain of that. Concrete barriers and balustrades prevented vehicular access everywhere.

"Why kill the Vice President?" Shelby whispered to Gabe. "That doesn't make sense. Why not the President?"

He shrugged. "Why do any terrorists do anything they do? It's all about power. Fallon must have a reason for wanting Winston instead of Adams. He doesn't have to plant his bomb close to his target to make his point, whatever that is. Hell, we don't even know if it's in a vehicle."

"But a vehicle makes sense. A bomb would be easier to relocate on wheels," Mark said, his index finger tapping the location of the White House on the map.

Shelby winced, still not sure she had any business standing with Gabe's team and listening in, much less offering her opinion or asking questions. No one seemed to mind, though, so she stayed close to Gabe.

"You do know a dirty bomb isn't an effective weapon of mass destruction," the Chinese-looking man added.

"True, but any bomb in D.C. will be devastating, David," Mark said. "It's summer. Tourists are everywhere. Congressmen and women. Ambassadors. Dignitaries." His index finger slid across the map to the Mall. "Hell, the Veterans of Foreign Wars is holding a service at the World War II Memorial this coming weekend. Thousands of people will already be there. The vets' families. Friends. Ember—"

"I'm on it," she said, already headed out the door. "I'll check the VP's schedule, see if he's supposed to present anything tonight before the VFW service. The President's schedule, too."

"Yes, but Mark, *Chaos Now* wants a revolution, not just a crater in the middle of D.C. They want mass terror for an extended period of time," David said, his eyes fixed on the map as well.

"Right," Gabe intervened. "It's the long-term effects these guys are looking for. Public fear. Radiation poisoning. That's what this is really about."

"Who stands to benefit?" Mark asked quietly.

"Who else? Fallon," one of Gabe's fellow agents, the tall guy with dark hair and deep blue eyes, answered. "We've linked him to Kelsey's attempted murder."

"True, but I'm afraid I agree with Benson. Fallon's not the mastermind. Then who is?"

And there the conversation stalled.

Shelby analyzed the problem along with everyone else. Until her car had exploded, she hadn't thought anything could happen to her—certainly nothing like this. Her life had been orderly and controllable because she made certain it was. She'd double-checked everything. Played it safe. Never took chances.

"You know, when this all started, I thought maybe Fallon was just one of those malcontents who needed to destroy everything related to Alex," Gabe said, his gaze riveted to the map, his arms crossed over his chest and his right hand cupping his chin. "Like the cold-blooded law of the wild. Eliminate everything dear to the man you hate. Murder his wife. Kill his children. Burn his house to the ground, preferably while he watched. But no more."

He shifted closer to the map. "You're right, Mark. Fallon's nothing but a cold-blooded bastard like Charlie Oakes. He's the go-to guy to get the dirty jobs done, but he's not the brains. Someone more powerful has gotten hold of him and his goons. Someone with a plan we haven't uncovered yet."

"Correct," David agreed, "and that someone has the means to facilitate an attack on the country."

"And we still don't know who it is," Mark muttered.

Shelby shuddered. These people should be on their way out of Washington D.C., too, yet there they were, crazy enough to think they could stand between good and evil. Gabe's arm snaked around her waist, and *oh, yeah. I'm in the company of snipers. That's what heroes do. They jump in over their heads without thinking. They save people—like me.*

"So what now?" she asked, half-afraid to ask.

"Now we do what we do best," Gabe said. "We find Fallon and hope he leads us to his Maker. Come with me."

Shelby found herself swept up in the mechanics of a military-style operation. Mark dismissed everyone. Gabe ushered her into his work area and introduced her to Taylor Armstrong and Maverick Carson. They barely acknowledged her they were so engrossed at their computers.

"Are you the one watching the marina?" Gabe asked Maverick.

He nodded. "That and a couple other things. Hey, Boss," he called out to Mark. "Fallon's made some hefty purchases. Five brand new Cadillac Escalades seven months ago. Three F-150 cargo vans. One helicopter."

"A helicopter?"

"Yeah. I thought that was weird, but it could do the trick."

"Find out which airfield he hangars it at. Track the vans."

"I'm on it."

Shelby's head spun with the information flying back and forth. She leaned into Gabe. "Pretend I'm new here. What exactly is a dirty bomb?"

He turned, bumping his knees with hers. "Sorry. I should've explained. A dirty bomb contains both conventional explosives and a radioactive agent, which in this case is weapons grade plutonium. You heard Agent Benson. With a regular bomb, you've got the initial blast zone. Anyone within range will die when it detonates. But add a radioactive agent to blow with the explosives, and you get a contamination zone that can reach out and touch a helluva lot more innocent people. How far it spreads depends on the force of the initial blast."

She could almost feel the blood drain from her face. Her heart leapt into her throat. "Oh, my gosh. Like a nuclear bomb? We're all going to die?"

He shook his head. "No. Atomic bombs depend on nuclear fission, not conventional explosives. They're a helluva lot more powerful. The primary intent of a dirty bomb isn't mass destruction. It's fear and ignorance. Sure, in a city like D.C., thousands still might die from the initial blast, but the radioactive contamination is the real killer. After the fires are out, the whole District will be under a containment order. It'll take years before anyone wants to visit again."

An icy finger of dread walked up her spine, frosting each and every vertebra on its way into her scalp. *This is so bad.*

The semi-cute guy who'd creeped her out earlier with his less-than-discreet scrutiny jumped up from his chair. "Until three months ago, Fallon received fifty thousand in his bank account every week. Then the real money started to pour in. Someone's dropping big bucks on this guy."

"How much are we talking about, Landon?"

"One hundred thousand plus. The latest was five hundred *K*. Look at the date on that one." He handed Mark a sheet of paper, pointing to the center of it. "See what I mean?"

Mark scrutinized the findings. "That's the day Alex was shot. Where's it coming from? Who's bankrolling him?"

"Don't know. Ember's supposed to be tracking the donor," Landon jerked his head in Ember's direction. He sure had a snarky tone to his voice all the time.

She piped up from her workspace, not fazed in the least by Landon's offloading the focus to her. "Sorry, Mark. No luck. Each transfer originated from an offshore account under the name Smith. John Smith."

"Figures. Thanks guys," Mark said. "Keep looking."

"What can I do to help?" Shelby asked Gabe. "Everyone's busy but me."

He tugged the brim of her D.C. cap. "Sit there and keep me company."

The sexy blond guy from the adjoining workstation stalked over to Ember. "Can you run these photos through your facial rec program? They're from the traffic cams by *Raymond's Kids* shelter."

Her brows lifted. "Kelsey's shelter?"

He shrugged. "Sure. Why not?"

She accepted the papers from his hand. "Okay, Connor. It makes sense. Take a seat. It won't take long."

"I need to do something," Shelby insisted. "What if I ordered pizza or sandwiches? I'll bet everyone's hungry. Aren't you?"

Before Gabe could answer, Connor called out. "Got him! Mark. Everyone. Come see. You won't believe who's been stalking Kelsey."

Shelby jumped up along with Gabe to go see what Connor and Ember had found. It was him. That guy from the bridge. FBI Agent Sam Becker.

Mark ended up beside Shelby. "So Becker was watching Kelsey before he took out Alex? What the hell for?"

"And get this." Ember zoomed in on the right chest area of Becker's shirt. "He's been using your name. See that?" She pointed at the nametag. "He's Mark Houston."

"No shit?" Gabe asked, leaning over Ember's shoulder to get a closer look. "My hell. He's been masquerading as you?"

"Then why the hell didn't Kelsey recognize him?" Landon asked. "You'd think she'd know who worked there. God, it's not like she works at *RFK Stadium* or something. How dumb is she?"

"Who cares?" Shelby's hackles lifted as her mouth engaged before she meant it to, but Kelsey wasn't there to defend herself, damn it. He needed to watch what he said. "Maybe she didn't know everyone at the shelter, but why would an FBI agent stalk her?" *That doesn't make sense. Unless...* "Oh, my gosh, guys. What if he was there to protect her? What if he's been keeping an eye on her this whole time?"

A shiver wiggled up her spine. That actually made sense, and it fit with Becker's demeanor last night on Kelsey's back step. He might not be the most honest guy, but he hadn't struck Shelby as mean enough to hurt a defenseless woman.

"Protect her from who?" Landon had an annoying habit, as if he always needed to top whatever the last person said, and it was really starting to bug Shelby. "Give us a break, girl. Becker stalked her so his buddy, Fallon, could kill her. That's all. You need to sit down and be quiet. Let us do our job."

Shelby bit her lip. *Girl? Who does he think he is?* Landon was a jerk, but he was right, too. She had spoken up when she probably shouldn't have.

"That just takes us back to the same question. Why Kelsey?" Connor asked. "I think Shelby's onto something. Let's hear her out."

All righty then.

Shelby elbowed Mark, her head spinning with what she thought she knew. "Think about it, Agent Houston. Mr. Becker was polite with Kelsey last night, like he didn't want to hurt her feelings. You weren't there yet, but I was, and I know what I saw. He didn't get belligerent with her at all, and he wasn't rude. At least, I didn't think so. He kept calling her ma'am like you guys do." *Just like you guys.*

An unsettling idea popped into her head. *Becker wasn't a bad guy. He was like Gabe and Zack. Ingrained with a deep respect for women.*

Mark stood so close to her that it was like peering up a sheer rock wall just to look him in the eye. Shelby blinked, stabbed her glasses back to where they belonged and took a half-step away from him to shake off a sudden case of nerves. His size intimidated, darn it.

She found herself needing just a little more space to speak to this guy, despite the fact that she'd just overstepped her bounds and elbowed him like he wasn't Gabe's boss. She gulped at her audacity, but kept on going. "What if he's on our, umm, I mean, *your* side? What if he's been trying to protect Kelsey all along, like he said? Just like you've been trying to do?"

"Doubt it. He's FBI." Mark crossed his arms over his broad chest like that ended the argument. "You saw Benson. I've met very few FBI who can think outside their bureaucratic box."

Okay, so Mark didn't like the FBI. She couldn't blame him, but still...

"I just know he was polite when he arrested me," she said. A frisson of insight connected the dots of her last encounter with Becker like a lightning bolt. She turned to Gabe. "Oh, my gosh. You got out of those cuffs quickly. And why was the door to the police cruiser left unlatched? It's almost as if—"

"He wanted us to escape," Gabe finished her thought, his green eyes lit with approval. "I think you're right. I don't like the guy, but Shelby makes sense."

Mark seemed to be listening. He glanced at Ember. "Where's Winston now?"

"The last press release placed him at the National Security Counsel. White House," Ember replied.

"And Becker?"

"Ah, Senior Agent Houston?" A timid blonde woman stood behind Mark, her hand lifted as if she needed permission to speak. "I've been watching him. He's parked on Constitution Avenue."

"You have? You're sure it's him?"

"Yes, sir," she said quietly. "As you know, there are a lot of traffic cams in that area. Another man just joined him. They're both inside the vehicle."

"Same black sedan?"

"Yes, Boss."

"Let me guess. This other guy have a black hood over his face?"

"Yes."

Mark growled. "Figures."

"Has to be Becker and his buddy. Let's go get them," Izza exclaimed eagerly.

Shelby liked her instantly, and not just for her gorgeous dark eyes. Izza eyed Landon as if she wanted to smack him, too.

"Not yet. We need all players on the board first." Mark turned to the timid blonde. "The minute Becker or his friend move, I want to know, Lisa. You understand?"

"Yes, sir." She went dutifully back to her desk.

Gabe and Shelby returned to his.

"Izza and Steven, check FBI and Metro PD activity in the area. See if they're watching Becker, too," Mark ordered.

"Got it." Steven and Izza returned to their computers. He worked his keyboard for a minute before he answered. "No D.C. units in the vicinity. It's quiet. Too quiet."

"No FBI, either," Izza added.

Maverick called out, "I've got Fallon."

The excitement of the hunt spurred Shelby. So this was what Gabe did for a living. Scary, but exciting. She stuck close to his side, peering over his shoulder while Mark stepped in beside her at Maverick's desk. A live satellite feed showed a black Escalade parking alongside the marina's dry dock.

"Fallon's got a boat?" Mark asked. "Can't be. Zoom in. It's not the right shape."

Maverick took the satellite image in tight and close. No rocket or missile, like she half expected. Just some guy stripping a canvas cover off a white vehicle.

"Zoom in closer," Shelby ordered, nearly elbowing Mark out of her way. Again. She caught herself just in time. Graciously, he made room for her.

"Yes, ma'am." Gabe's friend took the satellite image to a higher magnification, just enough to make out the words **FBI SWAT** on the side of a van.

Mark hissed. "Damn. That's one of those F-150 cargo vans. He's repainted it. That's where the bomb is. He'll be untraceable once he decides to transport the bomb. Any other vans in that lot?"

"I'm not seeing the other two," Maverick answered. "I'll keep looking."

Shelby caught that timid woman out of the corner of her eye again. Lisa didn't seem to fit with the rest of the agents. Everyone else acted with authority, but she tiptoed around as if she needed permission to speak.

"What?" Mark snapped when he noticed her.

"Ummm, Becker is moving again, sir," she said softly.

"You need to speak up, Channing." He stepped past her, snapping his fingers at Gabe. "Sit on Becker. I want to know what he's doing before he does it."

"Got it." Gabe commandeered Lisa's computer while she sat meekly beside him.

Shelby moved out of Mark's way and joined Gabe. Irritation shuddered off Mark. He didn't seem to have patience for Lisa's inability to speak up anymore.

"Is Fallon moving yet?" Mark called to Maverick.

"No. He's in the van. Still parked."

"Is he alone?"

"Yes. In the driver's seat."

"Any sign of the Vice President? Anywhere? Anyone?" Mark called out, the aggravation in his voice rising with every question.

"No," Ember shouted at the same time that Maverick and Taylor responded with the same answer. Apparently, everyone was searching for Winston. It made Shelby's head spin how these men and women worked in tandem with each other.

"Mark," David interrupted. "Don't ask how I know, but the FBI just intercepted a message from a burn phone. Short and sweet. POTUS. WWII. 1900. Go."

Shelby glanced at the clock on the wall, the same as Mark. *What the heck did that mean?*

Mark raked a hand through his hair. "Shit. President Adams will be at the World War II Memorial at seven? Tonight? Is that your take?"

David nodded. "It's a go. *Chaos Now* intends to kick off their revolution in less than two hours."

"Damn it. There must be some special program there tonight, then. But where is Winston? If this is supposed to be about him, where the hell is the guy? Team!" Mark bellowed. "Everyone. Front and center. Now!"

Shelby stepped back from the fierce energy radiating off Gabe's boss. Despite his loud call to order, Mark stood with his head bowed, his shoulders heaving and his back rigid. His fists clenched and unclenched. He seemed locked in indecision.

She held her breath. For a second, she thought maybe he was—*praying?*

Everyone circled him in silence. Gabe, too. She interlocked her hand with his while the seconds passed.

When Mark lifted his head, sparks flashed from his eyes. He'd changed and his people had changed with him. A veritable current of electricity crackled from agent to agent.

"David, take Conner, Steven, Maverick, Channing and Landon. Intercept Fallon. Shoot him if you have to, just take him down. Call the FBI en route. Advise the situation and demand an immediate assist. Tell them you need EOD on site, that he has the bomb." Mark turned to the rest of his people. "Rory, Izza, and Taylor, you're with me. Ember, you're command central. Call the FBI and tell 'em what we know. Homeland Security, too. Get them the hell out there on the streets with us. Keep us informed. Keep us safe."

"Yes, Mark." She settled into her position in front of the bank of computer monitors. Everyone else scrambled for their gear bags and the elevator. The room emptied.

Shelby stood stock still. *Holy cow. What just happened?*

Eerie silence filled the work bay. Gabe didn't look too happy being left behind.

"Why aren't you going with them? You have a city to save," she asked.

"No, ma'am. I don't. I'm already on duty."

"What? Me? Am I your duty?"

He nodded, his eye on the elevator.

"But we can't just sit here while a crazy guy blows up Washington D.C."

He took a seat at Ember's elbow and nodded to the chair at his side. "Yes. We can. And we will."

Chapter Thirty-One

He said the right words, but damn. Gabe couldn't sit still. Those were his guys out there. His team. Watching and listening to them in action wasn't much help for the odd man out who could only twiddle his thumbs while everyone else engaged in what very well could be doomsday.

When Ember turned the squawk box up so Shelby could listen in, Gabe removed his earpiece. No need for an annoying echo in his head when he was already sidelined and pissed. He pulled his chair in beside Ember and hunkered down to watch the game unfold. Shelby took the chair next to him.

Dread pervaded the nearly empty office. Gabe struggled to get a grip, but too much depended on The TEAM, and they were so few. How could they conquer on two fronts and do it without loss of life? Acid pitched into his gut. Plain and simple, they couldn't. Another one of his friends would die tonight. Maybe all. Once again, all he could do was watch. *Shit!*

"Becker's circled back around the block." Ember's very patient voice went out to all team members. "He's parked on Virginia now, due north of the World War II Memorial."

"Still in his car?" Mark's disembodied question came back.

"Yes."

"David? Any law enforcement in sight? FBI? Anyone?" Mark again.

"If they're out here with us, they're in ghost mode. I haven't sighted anyone yet. Not even a vehicle which is unusual. My team and I are proceeding to the marina. ETA in twenty."

Gabe watched the traffic cam feeds that caught David and his team's steady progress. Two other cameras captured Becker's sedan parked at the curb on Virginia Avenue. Still others tracked Mark's approach. Rory drove.

No damned Metro PD or FBI vehicles in sight. Where the hell was everyone? How did the FBI and Metro *not* know the President would arrive at the World War II Memorial shortly? The usual gaggle of press vans and media vehicles were there. Why not the nation's most lethal watchdogs?

It made no sense. They had to be undercover, not like that made Gabe feel any better. Was everyone walking into a trap? Sure as hell felt like it, but what else could this band of patriots do? Walk away from the President in his time of need?

Gabe grunted at his dismal thoughts. The TEAM might be a ragtag mix of soldiers, sailors, Marines, but none of them would turn their back on their country.

"Ember. Contact Metro PD and FBI again. I'd at least like their concurrence before we proceed," Mark ordered, his voice tight.

"Copy that." She turned in her seat to connect another line.

"Park here," Mark instructed. "We go the rest of the way on foot."

Rory eased the SUV alongside the curb, facing Becker's parked a ways north on the street. Weapons were racked. Rounds chambered. Pistols returned to holsters.

Showdown.

With each passing second, Gabe's conscience pricked. *I should be there.*

Vehicle doors opened and closed. Boots were now on the ground, his team fully engaged. The traffic cam caught sight of them en route to Becker's sedan.

Damn it to hell! I should be there.

"Switching to video cam," Mark muttered.

Damned time. Gabe leaned forward as the scene from Mark's cam unfolded in jerky, boots on the ground transmission. These cameras were smaller than the normal helmet cams. They snapped to the side of a ball cap or the stem of dark glasses. Mark must have his TEAM cap on. He panned to the opposite side of the street, then to the black sedan. Similar feeds came from Izza, Taylor, and Rory.

For now, all agents had concealed their weapons beneath their jackets. The only thing that might give any of them away was The TEAM's gold logo on the left chest of their jackets. Unfortunately, that was the only *tell* a Secret Service sniper needed to bring down anyone they deemed suspicious.

"Mark," Ember said firmly. "Metro PD is unaware of any altercation in your vicinity. Said they'll get back to me. FBI requests you stand down."

"Not 'til they step up to the plate," he shot back at her. "Tell them we're out here doing their job for them."

"I'll tell them." She relayed the message and blinked a few times in surprise. "Hmm. They hung up on me. Go figure."

Shelby latched onto Gabe's hand, whispering to him what he already knew. "You should be out there."

No shit. He blocked her advice to focus on the video and audio feeds. With every step his friends took, Gabe's heart rate increased. Like the good, dumb jarheads they were, they just kept pushing forward until he wanted to scream at them to *STOP!* Everything felt wrong.

Mark requested status, still on point and as calm as ever. "David?"

"Fallon just pulled the FBI van out of the marina. He's headed your way. We're on him."

"Ember. Metro PD?"

"Nega—"

"Mark!" David called out. "FBI's everywhere. They're here. They're—"

Gabe jumped to his feet. *Shit! I knew it!* A legion of FBI vehicles and FBI SWAT had come out of nowhere, surrounding David and his team.

"Ember!" Mark barked. "What's happening?"

"David's team is completely boxed in by three FBI vans. SWAT, too. They've got him on the ground. They're cuffing him, Maverick and—everyone."

Gabe watched helplessly while FBI SWAT manhandled his teammates and effectively took them out of the game.

"David and his guys lost their comm links, Mark," Ember said quietly. "The FBI was there all along."

"Shit," Gabe bellowed. "Get the hell out of there. It's a trap."

"Not going to happen," Mark replied grimly. "We finish this. Tonight."

"They're dragging them into vans. Wow, they're awful rough. One of those FBI guys just punched Connor in the stomach," Ember added in disbelief. "Mark, are you there?"

He blew out a deep breath. "Here. Damn it. What else?"

"Well, umm, umm," Ember stuttered.

"Ember! Where's Becker?"

"Coming straight to you," Gabe answered for her, the tight grip of panic settling in at his throat. "He and his buddy are on foot. Right behind the tree on the sidewalk. Between you and the sedan. See them yet?"

"Copy that. I see them now."

Mark and his team continued toward Becker.

"Three ambulances approaching from the west on Constitution," Ember advised more calmly.

"Say again? I don't hear any sirens," Mark said.

"They're running silent on your six. Wait. There's four now."

"Get your ass out of there," Gabe urged. "I'm telling you. Something's not right."

Mark ignored Gabe's prompt to retreat. "Got Becker and his buddy in my sights."

Becker and his friend approached with long, confident strides. The other man's face was as indiscernible as before, this time shielded behind dark glasses, the upturned collar of his jacket, and a ball cap with the brim pulled low.

An ambulance rolled by, temporarily blocking Gabe's view. "Move, damn it."

Mark grunted. "What the h..."

"Boss?" Gabe asked. "Say again."

Mark never came back. When the ambulance passed by, he and Rory were on their hands and knees. Taylor and Izza, too.

"Rory! Oh, my God! Mark! They shot Rory!" Ember came unglued. "They shot all of them!"

Gabe jumped to his feet. "No," he ground out. "They couldn't have. I heard no gunfire."

"But... But..."

He dropped his hand to her shoulder. "Knock it off. They're not dead, damn it. Watch."

He gulped as the worst-case scenario unfolded before his eyes. Mark's earpiece would have relayed the loud pop of gunshots. Hell, Taylor, Rory, and Izza's headpieces would all have caught the same report, but none of them had. *What the hell was going on?*

Becker pointed to the now prone figures on the sidewalk. Two men who Gabe assumed were medics hurried out of the nearest ambulance to the men. Becker crouched near Mark and tugged his earpiece out of his ear.

The last thing Gabe heard was the drawl, "You won't need this anymore."

The bastard had the gall to smile up at the traffic cam as if he knew exactly where to look. As if he knew Gabe were watching.

"No!" Ember shrieked. "God, No!"

The scene got more bizarre. Paramedics appeared out of nowhere. They lifted Mark and his team onto gurneys in no time.

None of the agents resisted. Not once. They all certainly looked dead.

Wait just a damned minute.

Gabe brushed Ember out of his way, needing to see two of those medic's faces up close and personal. He captured a still shot and zoomed it. *Sonofabitch!*

"That's the same guys who showed up when Alex got shot. They were here. In our garage. It's them! Damn it to hell. What's going on?"

The medics applied blood pressure cuffs and oxygen masks to each agent before they loaded them into separate ambulances. In the meantime, Becker's buddy in black set a brisk pace eastward on Constitution. Straight for the White House.

"They killed him," Ember whimpered. "They killed Rory and my guys."

"No," Gabe corrected. "There was no gunfire, Ember. This is a set-up. Mark and David walked straight into an FBI dragnet. Shit. Becker knew they'd be there. He knew we'd be watching.

"We need to do something," Shelby insisted.

Gabe looked down at her hand in his. He hadn't remembered grabbing onto it, but there it was. She was right, damn it.

The Marine in him snapped to command. "Gear up, ladies. We're going to war."

If Mom could only see me now.

Gabe had made good on his promise. Not only did he entrust Shelby with two weapons she had no idea how to shoot, she also now toted a backpack loaded with a bunch of stuff she didn't know how to use, either.

Gabe was a man on fire. He'd had no other choice. They'd literally hit the ground running with him in the lead. How Ember could keep up in three-inch glam heels was another thing altogether. But the woman had changed from competent techie to kick-ass warrior. *Warrior-ess? Whatever.*

The backpack slung over Ember's shoulder, combined with the holster on her hip, made her a blonde version of Lara Crofts, the heroine of the *Tomb Raider* mystique. The sharp staccato of her heels made her intentions clear. She meant business.

Gabe commandeered a SUV in the lower-level parking garage. They crossed the Potomac in no time. Shelby rode shotgun with Ember belted behind her in the center seat.

"Keep an eye out for any FBI van." Gabe peered to the left and right as he drove. "Fallon's probably parked it by now."

"Just to be clear, where's our first target?" Ember asked.

"World War II Memorial. To the President."

"But Rory and Mark aren't—"

He gritted his teeth. Tonight was about saving more than just their teammates. She had to have known that when she'd geared up. "Ember. President Adams is our number one priority until we know where the Vice President is. I'm sorry."

"No, I get it," she replied softly, but all Shelby heard was the hurt in Ember's voice and another metal on metal sound. A gun being racked. A round chambered.

And there she was, Shelby Sullivan, a darned good healthcare provider when Gabe needed a weapons expert to cover his back, someone like Ember.

She fingered the leather strap, tracing the outline of the weight concealed beneath a light TEAM jacket and over a heavier tactical vest as her mind went back to that moment in The TEAM vault. The armory. The tender look in his eyes when he'd slipped the holster over her left shoulder had startled her, but more startling—the regret she thought she'd detected.

He'd called it a vertical holster, so much different than the one he wore where the barrel rested horizontally in the pocket, its grip aligned for quick access.

The barrel of her weapon was aimed downward, the end of it snug in the holster's pocket. To draw it, she'd have to wrangle the heavy thing up and out of the holster, then bring it into horizontal position in order to aim.

It wasn't like he meant for her to actually use it. He'd set her straight on that point.

"Don't pull this weapon unless you intend to kill someone, Shell," he'd said, his breath heavy in her face. "Promise me. This isn't the time to bluff or play chicken. People will die tonight. I don't want you to be one of them."

She'd nodded quickly and obediently to prove she meant what she'd said, but mostly she couldn't speak because of the pounding inside his chest. Gabe might've looked fierce and protective, but electricity had crackled around him. His heart had to have been lodged in his throat, the pulse of it throbbing at the hollow of his neck. An unspoken sadness had lingered in his gaze, and she'd known instantly. He was thinking of his friend, Darrell. That little boy with the grenade launcher. And he was scared he'd lose her before this night was through.

Her fingers had ached to cup his chin, her lips to kiss the mouth that had driven her to the brink of abandonment earlier, simply because he'd looked so forlorn. Undecided. Like Mark Houston had looked earlier. Like it had taken Gabe's powerful boss a moment of anguish before he'd decided to send his friends into war.

The reality stunned her. This wasn't the news or a reality show. She got it. Mark had truly been scared that he might have to send his team to their deaths. They weren't just soldiers, nameless faces on news reports she'd never cared about enough to watch.

They were Ember's handsome husband, Rory.

The stoic Taylor.

Brooding Maverick.

That cute blond guy, Connor. Izza, his gorgeous wife.

They were all—*Gabe.*

She'd seen it in the depth of his green eyes in that armory, so dark and black they frightened her. *He loves me. He wants to kiss me, too, but he won't. Because he might die. Because I might die.*

That did it. Even with Ember nearby and strapping on her own array of weaponry, Shelby had cast caution to the wind. If that was to be Gabe's and her last moment together, she meant to grab hold and hang on tight for once in her pathetically controlled life. The second she'd reached for him, he'd clutched her to his chest, squeezing the air out of her, but also squeezing life into her with a fervent kiss. And she'd surrendered, because that was what she'd wanted more than breath itself. *Him.*

The lights of the glorious city ahead drew her mind from that reverent moment in the armory. *That kiss.* She lifted her fingers from the holster at her side to her bottom lip, savoring the only taste of eternity she'd experienced. The only one she wanted.

A melancholy energy filled the vehicle. Ember had to be worried sick for Rory. Gabe's jaw was hard set at a sharp angle, his chin jutted forward. He'd turned himself to stone.

So that was what soldiers did. They shoved their humanity aside to do what needed doing.

Shelby swallowed hard, her throat dry. She pushed her glasses up her nose one last time.

I can do stone.

Chapter Thirty-Two

God, this is the most idiotic thing I've ever done—drag a complete novice, a pacifist at that, into what may turn out to be Hell. But what choice is there?

Gabe purposefully approached the Mall from the southeast. He jumped the curb and parked due east of the Washington Monument. Crowds were heavy, but security seemed lighter than usual, not that he could trust the usual array of Metro PD uniforms anymore. Lack of a good visual hadn't stopped the FBI from swarming David's or Mark's teams.

Palming his cell phone he checked the time. Forty-two minutes and counting, IF the FBI intel David had intercepted was correct.

Not enough time to find the bomb.

Not enough time to save the Vice President.

Not enough time to do anything.

Too bad. He meant to try.

"Move it," he ordered, his boots already on the ground, and damn it. Ember should've worn work boots, not stilettos. Shelby scurried to his side, nearly looking the part of a covert agent, but Ember? *Well, so be it. How the hell do women walk in those things?*

He set a beeline to the World War II Memorial, angling through the crowd, his impossible mission to save everyone falling behind with every step. Shelby and Ember stayed close.

Within minutes, the lighted southern Arch of Triumph, the one commemorating the war in the Pacific Theater, came into view. And God, the sight of the memorial at night robbed Gabe's breath.

The semicircle of fifty-six granite pillars, each representing an American state, district or territory, stood in muted honor to the thousands of men and women who'd given their lives for the sake of freedom. Due west stood the lighted Lincoln Memorial, the silvery reflection pond stretched in between like a regal carpet from one monument to the other.

Reporters were everywhere. A wealth of elderly veterans, too. This was a reverent place for heroes, not the site for a smoldering hole in the ground, a burial place for all these poor people.

The gall of the impending disaster spilled more acid into Gabe's stomach. He scrubbed a hard hand over his chin and kept his panic to himself, but damn it. *Where the hell is Fallon? His van? Becker? Shit, where's the damned VP?*

The impossible mission turned more hopeless when President Adams stepped onto a raised platform within the elliptical circle of the sacred monument. The summer crowd pressed around the edges of the inner pond, vying for a better view. Some had their shoes in hand, wading into the shallow water to see their President.

Sweat trickled down the sides of Gabe's head at the sheer enormity of the challenge before him. *God. I'm just one man. I can't fail. Not this time. Not tonight.*

Cameras flashed out of the corner of his eye. Applause sounded as the military band played *Hail to the Chief.* A roar went up when President Adams stepped to the podium, and damn it! Despite what damned well better be transparent bulletproof panels between him and the crowd, he'd just put himself in mortal danger.

It was happening. And if Adams was there, Winston had to be close by. Where?

Gabe strained his neck in all directions to see over the crowd, searching for the VP and his accompanying entourage of Secret Service. Wasn't that what Mark suspected? The Vice President was the one in danger? Then where the hell was he?

"Look." Shelby tugged Gabe's right sleeve. The poor thing wasn't tall enough. She couldn't see over the crowd.

"What?" He didn't mean to bark at her.

She pointed across his chest to his right. "Is that him? Is that guy by the wall over there him?"

He followed the break in the crowd to where Shelby pointed. And sure enough. Becker. The sonofabitch was cocky as sin to think he could get this close to the President.

Well, no more. It ends here.

"Keep up," Gabe growled to his rag-tag pair of ladies, following Becker up the walk east of the monument. They might not be as rough and tough as the guys, but he was damned glad they were at his six. Glad for Shelby's sharp eyes and Ember's weapons experience. Maybe liberty and D.C. stood a chance after all.

They ran to keep up with their quarry, jostling through the crowd. Becker kept his right index finger pressed to his ear while he walked. The bugger was either relaying intel to Fallon, or who the hell cared anymore? Gabe honestly did not know which side the man was on anymore, and this late in the game, he didn't care. Let him talk. He wouldn't get far.

Gabe picked up the pace. Taking Becker down his number one priority. Then maybe he could get some answers.

Shelby all but ran beside him to keep up. Ember, too. He kicked it up a notch when Becker glanced over his shoulder at the President, now offering opening remarks over a booming PA system to the milling crowd. Becker hadn't spotted Gabe and his team, all the motivation Gabe needed. The asshat knew something or he wouldn't have been running away from the scene of the crime like he was.

Gabe left the ladies behind, and gave it all he had. He sprinted forward to intercept the sonofabitch. If nothing else, Becker would die along with everyone else on this god-awful night. He'd started it. He'd damned well see it through to the smoking bitter end.

Becker pivoted on one foot, and Gabe skidded to a stop. He'd been caught. He brought his pistol to bear on Becker with a curt, "Take one more step and I'll shoot you where you stand."

"Damn it, Cartwright. I don't have time for this." Becker rolled his eyes. "You might as well join me. Get up here." He turned his back to Gabe and headed southwest despite the threat.

Gabe meant to shoot the arrogant jerk, FBI or not, but he didn't shoot people in the back. He concealed his weapon inside his open jacket and followed.

"Why should I go with you?"

"Because you'd die to save the President. Come on. Your lady friends, too. Move it."

He crossed the lawn south toward Independence Avenue, still speaking into his earpiece. "Roger. Ten minutes to Eagle Two. I should be done by then."

"Eagle Two? You mean the Vice President?" Gabe growled.

Becker held his hand up for silence while he continued talking to that other person. Had to be Fallon, didn't it? Gabe wasn't so sure anymore. *Chaos Now* had targeted the VP. *Right?*

"That's why we needed you and only you," Becker continued. "Call when it's done. Hope I'll be around to answer my phone."

Who the hell's he speaking with, Goddamnit!

Becker pocketed his phone and broke into a jog. "Your call, Cartwright. Keep up or shoot me, but I've got someplace to be."

Gabe nodded at Shelby and Ember to keep up with Becker. The farther from the Memorial, the lighter the foot traffic, but the more apprehensive Gabe became. He holstered his weapon, none of his questions answered. "Where are you going?"

"If we do this right, it won't matter. No one will ever know. Maybe it's a good thing you guys showed up after all."

"Oh, no. Look." Ember pointed to an FBI van parked at the curb on Independence Avenue. "There's a van. It might be him."

So that was the deal. Becker needed to move the van closer to the President. That was why the countdown. He'd been stalling, and Gabe had fallen for it.

Well, no sonofabitchin' more.

He lunged, knocking Becker to the ground in a half-nelson hold, his arm caught under Becker's armpit, his other hand pushing the assassin's head into the ground. Gabe brought both fists together and interlocked his fingers. "Now I've got you."

Becker growled, his face mashed in the dirt while he struggled to level a punch that never could've connected.

"You're done," Gabe spat. "The bomb blows, you go with it. Now talk. Where's Fallon? What have you guys done to the Vice President? You kill him already? Is that why you're going after the President?"

"We don't have time for this," Becker ground out, his face still in the wet grass. "You've got to trust me. We've got five minutes left to diffuse the bomb. Maybe less."

"We what? Diffuse?" Gabe loosened his hold a little, not ready to trust. Both Ember and Shelby had their pistols drawn. That alone ramped up Gabe's adrenaline even farther. Shelby really had no business with a loaded weapon.

"You heard me. *We* for Christ's sake, Cartwright. *We.* Let me up so I can do my job. You're wasting time."

Gabe eased back and let Becker go.

The FBI sniper scrambled to his feet. "Shit. I'm not here to kill the President. Not unless I screw up and can't diffuse it."

"The dirty bomb? You're on our side?" Shelby asked, holstering her weapon as if she already trusted this guy.

Gabe glanced over his shoulder at his sole companion. Ember must have gone off to find her husband, and Gabe couldn't blame her. He'd want to be with the one he loved at the end of the world, too.

Becker sprinted toward the van. Gabe grabbed Shelby's hand and followed. At the rear gate of the vehicle, Becker put a finger to his mouth for silence, then jerked both doors open simultaneously.

And '*Holy shit!*' didn't come close to describing what *Chaos Now* had brought to D.C.

In place of the rear bench seats, bricks of orange SEMTEX and off-white C4 had been carefully arranged. The plastic explosives nearly filled the van to capacity, along with an array of blasting caps, fuse igniters, and detonators. A large silver canister stood in the center of the plastic explosives like a buried missile silo.

Gabe clutched Shelby's fingers tighter. "That's the isotope," he muttered, his throat thirty-grit kinds of dry.

"Welcome to the twisted world of *Chaos Now*." Becker fingered the multi-colored bundle of wires leading from the bricks of explosives to the detonator. He pulled a pair of wire cutters from his pocket, handing them to Gabe. "Sure hope you're calm under pressure, Cartwright. Fallon set this up with two hot wires. One for the SEMTEX. One for the C-4. You'll need to make your cut at the precise same moment that I make mine. Understood?"

Gabe accepted the pliers, every last drop of saliva gone from his mouth and throat. *Shit.*

Becker pointed to the wire in question with the tip of another pair of pliers he'd pulled out of his shirt pocket. "You ready?"

Gabe would've replied, but the earth bucked beneath their feet. People over at the World War II Memorial screamed. Something fucking big had just blown up. A blinding white light illuminated the northern sky. Gut-wrenching panic stopped his heart. *God. What have I done?*

He grabbed Becker's shirt collar, damned well not going to be an accessory to anymore lying shit! He had a weapon in his hand. He could stab Becker right there and put an end to this dastardly plan to end the United States. "Was that another one of your dirty bombs? Answer me! I won't betray my country, you asshole!"

Becker blew out a breath between pursed lips, his eyes dark and so damned serious. He glanced at the hand fisted in his shirt before he leveled his gaze on Gabe. The grayest eyes met Gabe's head on. The man didn't even blink. Not once. "To be honest, I'm not sure what that explosion was, but this is the only dirty bomb in D.C."

"But there are two other vans and a helicopter out there somewhere," Gabe spat, his hands shaking.

"You're right, but only one bomb. Shit, Cartwright. I'll explain everything later, but right now, help me save the city. Maybe the world. Trust me, Gabe. We're running out of time."

Icy cold tiptoed up Gabe's spine, coming to rest in a death grip at the back of his neck. Panic loomed, but God. Everything rested on him? A one-footed hot-rodder who'd shot a kid to save his own life? *Me? How can I be sure?*

"I don't know you," he ground out, caught at the edge of nowhere with nothing but trust to rely on. *Shoot too late. Shoot too early. Cut the right wire at the right time. Die anyway?*

How does a man know for sure? How does he trust with so little factual information to base a nation-altering decision like this on? He wavered, his throat parched. How could he trust the man who might have assassinated Alex and who had personally put Kelsey through a living hell?

Shelby pressed into Gabe's side, carefully not bumping him. Her arm slid around his waist, her slender fingers dipping under his belt like a teenage girl might have done with a boy she liked. *Maybe loved.*

Becker gritted his teeth. "Damn it, Gabe. Either you're the man of honor I thought you were, or give me the pliers and I'll do it myself. Decide. Now!"

He'd just voiced Alex's sentiments exactly. *Lead. Follow. Or get the fuck out of my way.*

Somehow that helped.

"I'm here. I'll do it."

Becker acknowledged the impossible decision Gabe had made with a curt nod. "Good. On three."

Gabe lifted his pliers to the designated wire.

Time stopped. He noticed everything. The factory black paint on the barely visible floor of the van. The scrapes at the tailgate where the explosives had been loaded. The darkened windows concealing the weapon of mass destruction from public view.

"One."

A silent prayer is still a prayer. Gabe flung it heavenward, a simple *please God.* No other words. God sure knew what was going on tonight.

"Two."

The simple mechanic's tool rested deadly in his hand, jaws at the red wire, ready to make the biggest mistake of his life. Or save the world. *Shit. How can I be sure?*

"I trust you," Shelby murmured.

It all came down to right there and then. That split second. That terrible pivot point in history. There'd be no wishing it away, only doing what thousands of leathernecks had done before him. *Believe in America. This Republic. This innocent woman at my side.*

"Three."

Gabe held his breath and cut the red wire.

Chapter Thirty-Three

Shelby peeled one eye open to see the most glorious green eyes beaming down at her, the biggest grin cracking Gabe's happy face.

"We did it," he said, his body shuddering under the impact of Sam Becker's hearty slaps to his back.

"No, *you* did it," Becker corrected, blowing out breaths so big his cheeks expanded with every gulp of air. He brushed the back of his right hand over his brow, wiping the sweat away. "I can't tell you how happy I was to see you and your girlfriends in that crowd tonight. I'd prayed for a miracle. Wasn't exactly sure how I was going to stop Fallon. Only knew I was going to try my damnedest."

Shelby giggled she was so relieved, but the moment didn't last.

Becker's eyes scanned the crowd behind them, most of them more interested in the loud explosion than the celebration taking place behind the FBI van. "Listen, guys. We're not out of the woods yet. Do me a favor and fade to black before my guys and the Secret Service get here. They might not be so understanding, and I still need to find out what that explosion was. Sure as hell hope it wasn't President Adams."

"We'll go with you," Gabe declared, and Shelby would've gone, too. In a heartbeat. Oh yeah. She was beyond stoked. Shaking like a leaf maybe, but ready to take on anyone who got in her way. She might not have clipped the wires like these guys did, but saving the world? Nothing like it!

"No thanks." Becker's gaze darkened with concern. "This is my job. You ought to be safe at Stewart's house, so get back there now. Take Miss Sullivan with you and kick back. Drink a tall one for me. Who knows? Maybe I'll show up later and join you."

"What'd you do to Mark and the guys?" Gabe asked. He had to know. "To David?"

"Nothing a good night's sleep won't cure." Becker's feet pointed in the direction he meant to go. "Agent Houston and the rest of his crew are home by now. Don't worry. They're safe. I promise."

"If you didn't shoot them, what'd you give them?" Shelby asked.

"A dose of VEC. That's all. Just enough to get them out of our way. You guys are too damned good. Every time I turned around, there you were like a Wild West posse. Had to take your boss and his team out of circulation before they screwed the pooch on the whole operation."

"What the hell's VEC?" Gabe asked.

Shelby explained. "It's a muscle relaxant used on organ donors to keep them from twitching while the surgeon removes harvestable organs. Mr. Becker's right. Your friends will be mad, but they'll feel better in the morning."

"Where's Alex then?" Gabe asked outright. "Did you use that stuff on him, too?"

Becker paused, his tongue poking the inside of his cheek, as if he didn't yet want to admit to anything yet.

"I know he's alive," Gabe insisted. "Isn't he?"

Shelby stilled to hear Becker's answer, but the glint of excitement in his gaze faded. He thumped a hand to Gabe's back and left it there. "I honestly don't know, but I'm going to find out. Now get out of here before the rest of my guys show up and lock you in jail. Go on. Take care of Miss Sullivan. I'll be in touch."

He turned away from the van and ran off.

"Let's follow him," Shelby insisted, tugging Gabe's wrist to do just that. She craned her neck to see above the crowd, wanting to be off on another adventure. "Come on. He's getting away. I can't see him anymore. There are too many people."

He didn't budge. Not an inch. Gabe bowed his head while he sucked in breath after breath. "Let him. Whatever he's doing, wherever he's going, I trust him now. He's right. We need to get you back to safety before something else happens."

"But I can help." Now wasn't the time to step back and let someone else take over. Heck, no. She had a gun. She might not know how to use it, but... but...

Gabe simply stood there drawing in deep breaths, his palms flat to the open tailgate and his head down.

"Let's at least go find Mark and Ember and all your guys." Shelby wished he'd snap out of it. At least, do something.

All he did was turn his face from her and spit to the other side of the van.

"Are you okay?" she asked, finally tuning in to what was really happening. "Gabe? My gosh, you're pale. Are you okay?"

"Yeah. I'm good, but Becker's right." He circled an arm around her shoulder, tugging him into his side and still breathing hard. "Let's get out of here while the getting's good."

She planted a palm to the center of his chest, needing to be sure he'd told her the truth, that he really was okay instead of on the verge of another panic attack. "Your heart's racing."

"I know." He covered her hand with his and pulled her across the street, headed toward the Arlington Memorial Bridge, the scene of their previous close encounter with Becker. "SWAT's on their way. Come on. We're at ground zero, Shell. Let's get back to Kelsey's where it's safe. We've still got some cleaning up to do."

She relented. Cleaning she could do. Anything to help Kelsey. And Gabe. Shelby fell into step alongside the man who had just saved D.C., if not the whole world. It had taken a lot out of him, but he'd done it without firing a shot.

Emotions she couldn't identify swelled inside for the gentle warrior walking away from the scene, content to fade to black. Content that no one would ever know his name or his role in the miracle. Content in the knowledge he'd done his job.

His hand on hers still trembled, but he walked with his back erect, his shoulders squared and his arm protectively around her. If ever there was a right time, it was then. She had to tell him before the moment slipped away. He needed to know.

"I love you, Gabe. I really do. I'm so proud of you."

He stopped walking, his brows lifted in surprise. Twisting her into his arms, he planted a kiss in the middle of her forehead, and she didn't want to move from his side.

Her fingers rested at his throat, directly over the pounding pulse of her man. Her hero.

Shelby sighed. She knew exactly how Kelsey felt.

Instead of backtracking to the vehicle he'd parked to the east, Gabe hailed a cab. He didn't want to deal with the crowd between him and there. He and Shelby arrived at Kelsey's in no time. They entered through the rear door. The empty dog kennel seemed bleak without Whisper and Smoke sitting at the gate waiting for them.

The scene inside was no cheerier. Mark had done a good job sweeping the glass and debris, and yes, the windows were boarded, but the cute little bungalow where Alex and Kelsey had made a home and a life together felt hollow. As if its heart were missing or something. It had to have been pretty bad for a guy to notice.

Easing his gear to the floor behind the back door, Gabe unfastened his tactical vest and let it slide out of his hands to the table while Shelby did the same. Of course, she headed for the hallway closet where Kelsey kept her vacuum and cleaning supplies, but really? Did she honestly believe his line about cleaning the house when they got back? Now? When they were finally alone? When she'd blurted out the feelings of her heart?

Oh, hell no.

He let her get a couple of steps away from him before he grabbed her hand and swung her back into his arms. "Where do you think you're going?"

A rosy hue crept over her cheeks. Yeah. This woman had to know what he'd been thinking on the taxi ride. It had nothing to do with Pine-Sol. Certainly not Mr. Clean.

Shelby came easily against him, her body warm and willingly pressed into his. He traced his index finger along the soft swell of her heated cheek. The sweet girl blushed, but she didn't meet his eyes long enough to answer the question in them.

He let the pads of his fingertips absorb the feel of her skin, the new texture of silky soft in his life. That now familiar fragrance of rose and vanilla lifted into his nostrils. He'd already tasted her mouth and found it addicting. He wanted a whole lot more.

She might not know it, but he'd seen this same look of adoration on other women's faces before. Libby Houston's when she thought she was alone with Mark in the hallway at the office. Mei Lennox's when she came by the office with her little girls and a plate of cookies for Zack. Kelsey Stewart's when she'd danced with Alex at Taylor's wedding.

"I meant it," Shelby said breathlessly, her index finger tracing some kind of a design on his shirt below his right collarbone. "I do love you."

Enough said. With one scoop, she was off the floor and headed for destiny. Shelby weighed next to nothing, not compared to all the gear he'd carried in the Corps. Her arm around his neck felt perfect, her fingers combing through his hair more than enough motivation.

He angled her through the door of her bedroom. Laying her down, he stepped back. Like most traumatic stress survivors, she had a nightlight in her room. Sweet. The time had come for show and tell.

"How much do you love me?" He teased her with the most juvenile question he could think of. With one quick tug at the back of his collar, he pulled his shirt over his head and off, kicking out of his boots at the same time.

Her eyes widened when he discarded his belt and unzipped his cargo pants. Socks and pants went next, and there he was, a nearly naked man with a spiffy prosthetic foot that usually made women turn tail and run. *Right about now.*

It was time to put her words to the test. That was all he'd meant by that stupid *how much do you love me* question. Yeah, he might've meant for her to prove it, but not by sex.

By staying.

Sexy violet-blues scrolled over him, her lashes fluttering. She gave no more than a cursory nod to his foot, but his boxers? The *hello darling* spike beneath the gray and black plaid had definitely gotten her attention.

He crawled up the bed to where she sat, a little wary. The more he advanced, the more she tilted backward, the uncertainty shifting over her lovely face replaced by stark appraisal. Her tongue slipped over her bottom lip, licking it as if she was hungry. And he wanted it on him. He was hungry, too.

His confidence soared. His foot had passed Shelby's seal of approval. Now—for the rest of him.

He kept advancing until he was directly over her core, and she knew it.

Not once had she shifted out of his way.

The glasses had to go. He lifted them off her nose and set them on the nightstand.

"Shelby Sullivan," he said, his voice hoarse and deep. "Say it again."

Just once more.

She transformed from shy girl into her alter ego. Bossy. Controlling. Nurse Sullivan. Her hands went straight to his manhood, shocking the hell out of him that she was brave enough to touch him there.

"Is this what you want to know, Agent Cartwright?" Her chin jutted forward in a dare. "What? Did you think you could scare me with that funny foot of yours, huh? Did you think I'd run because you're kind of a bionic man and I'm just a woman?"

"Yeah. Something like that." The conversation had taken an incredibly tender turn. This amazing, complicated woman had seen right through his bravado, the same way that he was looking through hers.

With one hand in his boxers, the other gripping his neck, she pulled him down to her mouth, nipping his lower lip with a good pinch. "I love you, Gabriel Cartwright. I love your bravery and your courage. I love your body and your feet. Both of them. You don't scare me."

Her clothes flew somewhere. So did his boxers. He needed to feel and to taste every inch of the soft sweet body beneath his. There was only one problem. The bold woman who'd surprised him with her audaciousness at the get-go had suddenly demurred back into the real Shelby Sullivan.

She might have known how to get his attention, and his erection, but this woman had no skills when it came to the real art of making love. His heart pinched at the sight of the brave lamb in bed with him. Yeah. She was all he'd hoped for.

Gabe stifled the need to bend her over and take her hard. Not for a first time. Not for this woman. The first time had to mean something more, so before he lost control, he eased away from her lips, capturing the greedy hands that seemed intent on exploring his body.

He stretched her arms over her head, pinning her wrists with one hand, the rest of her with his hips. The tender thing didn't spread her feet, much less her knees to accommodate him.

He burrowed one kneecap between her legs until she parted them. Damned if she didn't clench up on him the second he sank between her knees.

"Shell," he said, his intentions for her body crystal clear. She had to know by now. There was no mistaking the happy part of his anatomy now resting solidly against her stomach. He released her hands. "You've never done this before, have you?"

That might not have been the smartest question. She pressed her lips into a thin line and shook her head. "No, but I want to. With you."

"Why?" He cupped the side of her face, his fingers in her delightfully cool and soft blond locks. Was making love enough? Or was he a fool to be thinking beyond the incredible gift she'd offered? Did she want that same elusive *more* that he did?

"Because I've never cared for anyone like I care about you," she said quietly. Timidly. "You're not like other guys. I want to get to know you better. And I really like it when you call me Shell. It's sweet."

He gulped, the tantalizing scent of her arousal overcoming his decision to take it slow and easy. Maybe this wasn't such a good idea.

"Why?" she asked. "Don't you, umm, want me?"

And there it was, the real question of the night. God yes, he wanted her, but not in a one night, *slam, bam, thank you ma'am* kind of way. That wasn't him.

He rolled his eyes, teasing her, needing her to smile again. "Would I be laying here buck-assed naked if I didn't want you?" His heart climbed up his throat, the rest of him hardened and craving her touch. "But you need to be sure this is what you want. I'll go slow, and I'll use a condom, but if you want me to stop, say the word. Just know that once we do this, there will be dating and there will be rules. There might even be sleepovers."

Her breath caught with one short sharp "oh" at his ordering her around. Apparently, she liked it. The lady melted, her face lit with a glow that was his undoing.

"God, I love you, Shelby," he promised with all his heart, wanting her more than ever. "I know it's soon, but I'm not a patient man. I've lost too much already, and who knows what will happen tomorrow. I don't trust time anymore."

He cringed. *Crap.* That sounded an awful lot like the line guys going off to war used to get girls into bed. But some of them came back, right? Some of those hasty proposals turned out okay, didn't they? Must have. The baby boom of the fifties was legendary.

"Are you going to talk all night or are you going to kiss me?" she asked, her voice all sexy and sultry and, hot damn. Gabe sheathed himself and sank to do her bidding, his knees now comfortably between her legs and the stiffness gone from her body.

See? A little talk never hurt anyone.

He captured her mouth and set the feelings he'd controlled loose. There wasn't one part of her body not begging for release by the time he'd tasted, feasted, and run his tongue over her. Every tantalizing nub had been sucked, nibbled, and slathered, every luscious curve and fold blessed by his teeth, tongue, and fingers.

He tempted and teased until she snared his chin, angling his lips back to her bossy mouth. "Stop playing around, Gabe. You're killing me."

He obliged his lovely lady with a quick "yes, ma'am," sliding into her gently, despite the urgent thrust of her hips to meet him. Short little gasps coming from the back of her throat announced yet another new sensation to Shelby's world.

He meant to ease back, but those fingernails digging into the cheeks of his ass added the heightened sensation of pain to their lovemaking.

Yet he knew the exact moment he'd breached her innocence. He froze to give her time to adjust to the gentle plundering of her body. Once again, Shelby proved she wasn't like other woman. She stiffened from the sensory overload of her first orgasm.

"Oh, God. Oh, Gabe. Oh, God," she moaned, gripping him tighter.

Tears filled his eyes at the gift of a lifetime he'd just been blessed with. Nothing could compare. His woman was so damned sweet.

He leaned back from her to watch the writhing woman beneath him, the one with her eyes closed and the sheer glow of ecstasy on her face. She smiled. She frowned. But mostly she pushed against him, wanting more.

So he obliged again.

Chapter Thirty-Four

Oh. My. Gosh. That was out-of-this-world amazing. Why did I wait so long?

Because then it wouldn't have been with Gabe.

Oh, yeah. Oh, wow. So, this is what I've been missing. I'm so glad I waited.

Shelby lay snug in the crook of the arm of the only man she'd felt so in tune with, awed by the nature of the beast and his handsome body. The guy was built. He had broad shoulders, and was solid from stem to stern. She would know. She'd checked out that tight backside of his, *hands on.* He didn't seem to mind her fingers or palms on any part of him. She now had favorite Gabe parts, and she liked to touch them all.

His stomach, for one. It was relaxed now, but still muscled, firm beneath her questing fingers. She was on a Gabe quest, filled with an insatiable need to explore every facet of this magnificent male specimen.

He smiled when her fingertips brushed his nipples, so she did it again. With his eyes still closed, he captured her hand and pressed it to his lips.

And that was another thing. Her entire body had revved up for more, only he seemed to want to sleep. Of course, he was probably tired. She got that. After all, he had saved the world. He'd also gotten up to lock the house and retrieved his holster and guns, but then, they'd done it again, only they hadn't exactly made love. Oh, no. They'd made the most exquisitely slow love. It still had her purring. She'd found the perfect answer to her stress. *Gabe.*

Shelby stayed her quest, content to explore in other ways. Lying tucked into him as she was, his arm around her, his fingers under her arm, she noticed things. His profile. The sexy mess of hair she'd run her fingers through. His ridge of tiny hairs on his right ear. The shadow of a long day's scruff on his face. The way his fingers curled around her hand.

The minty taste of his tongue. His nose, a very straight and normal nose that flared every once in a while, as if it too was taking in her scent the same way she took in the smell of the great outdoors on his skin. His breath. Nuances that belonged to her and her alone.

"I love you, Shell," he murmured, his eyes still closed. "Stop staring at me. Go to sleep."

"I can't," she confessed, lifting up on one elbow to watch his handsome face. "I've just had the most mind-blowing experience of my life. How can you just go to sleep?"

"You want more?" He peered out of the corner of one eye at her, the hint of disbelief in his tone sparking her libido all over again. The darned thing seemed to have a mind of its own. And no off button.

"Yes, please," she whispered, a giggle lifting up from her heart. "I want your body. All of it. Every last inch. Again."

The man was cunning. In no time at all, she found herself facing the other direction, her back to his very impressive front, and his arm around her chest cupping her right breast.

"Then you shall have it," he growled into the nape of her neck.

Who knew sex could make that part of her anatomy so ticklish?

A rash of goose bumps shivered over her bare shoulders at the speed with which he'd manhandled her body. And this new position. Sweet.

That was all it took. She succumbed to the sweetest death, the death of her old self, her past life and all her childhood fantasies. This new dream was better and worth changing everything for. Living for. Maybe even dying for.

He buried himself inside her with one quick thrust.

Ahh. My very favorite Gabe part.

He woke to an empty bed. Not what he'd expected. *And a noise.*

The palest light of pre-dawn shimmered through the heavy curtains. Alarmed, he hurried into his cargo pants, sliding his holster over bare shoulders. The sight of him half-dressed and armed in the kitchen might scare Shelby, but then again, *it might not.*

No quiet breakfast-making kitchen sounds. No hint of bacon frying. A prickle of fear dumped acid into his gut. *Where is she?*

He opened the bedroom door to a dark hallway. A too-quiet house. The hair on the back of his neck lifted. He pulled both pistols, securing their power in his hands.

Might be over-reacting. Let's find out.

Three long strides took him to the front room at his left, the kitchen at his right. A shadow moved near the boarded up front room window. The same sound. A whimper. Gabe flipped the front room light on. Anger flooded his soul.

Fallon. The sonofabitch had Shelby pressed against his chest, one hand over her mouth, a snub-nosed revolver stuck in her neck.

Gabe raised pistols both on target, every fiber of his being begging to be let loose to destroy the man who dared touch Shelby. His inner sniper analyzed the odds of getting a clean shot off without hitting her. Not good with adrenaline hitting his body with a freight train load of flight or—fight, damn it!

"Let her go."

The poor thing's eyes were wide, her chest heaving. Both hands clutched Fallon's arms, her elbows jutting in front of her. At least she'd requisitioned Gabe's black TEAM polo for morning-wear. *Smart decision.* It hung to her knees, but the thought that it might be all she had on stalled his heart.

What else did Fallon do to her while I slept, damn it?

The bastard sneered, his lip cut and his nose bleeding. The fact he was dressed from head to toe in Army green added to the demented look. So did the Green Beret expertly angled over his bristly crew-cut. The black ink of Army-shit tattoos covered what his short-sleeved shirt didn't.

The man had to be stark raving, certifiably nuts to be dressed in spec ops gear, right down to his spit-polished black boots. He nailed Gabe with a cold, hard look over Shelby's shoulder. "Where is she?" he snarled.

"There's no one else here," Gabe countered quickly, hoping to God that Shelby kept her cool.

"I won't ask again," Fallon bellowed. "Where is she?"

"Who are you looking for? Do you mean—"

BLAM!

The round blasted Gabe backwards over the kitchen table and to the floor. He found himself blinking up at the ceiling, gasping for air that wouldn't come. Heat engulfed his right shoulder, radiating down his arm and outward to his fingertips. The coppery scent of blood—his blood—filled his nose.

Shit. I'm—shot?

Shelby screamed.

Damn. I've failed her. Too.

"Gabe. No! Please let me go to him and—"

"Shut up, bitch! On your knees. Watch and learn something smart for a change."

Gabe struggled to draw in one solid breath, but the sheer weight of the pain drilling him to the floor stole it back again. He clutched the hole in his shoulder. Bloody. Hot. Gut-wrenchingly painful. The kitchen filled with shadows and bouncing white stars. Panic choked him, but he shoved it back inside where it belonged.

Not now. Get up. Gotta get up.

Rolling to his knees, all he knew was that he needed to live long enough to finish the job. He lifted his head and forced his vision to clear. By then, Fallon had Shelby kneeling, her hair wound tight in one fist, and the revolver hard at the back of her head. He kept jerking her off balance, toying with her.

It pissed Gabe off, even as wrecked as he was.

She clutched at Fallon's wrists and forearms, struggling to keep her knees on the carpet. Her sweet face was paralyzed with fear, like a fawn in a wolf's jaws, already given up and prepared to die.

Gabe braced himself to rise. *It's not going down like that, Shell. I promise.*

"I'm only asking one more time, *hero*." Fallon jerked Shelby's head back, the barrel of his gun pointed downward at her skull. "I'll blow her away the second another line of shit comes out of your yap. Where's Stewart's wife? Where'd she go, gawddamn it?"

"Richmond," Gabe rasped, his eyes searching the floor for the pistol he'd dropped when he fell. He lifted to one knee, gripping the edge of the kitchen table with a bloody hand. "Let her go. She's got nothing to do with this. She can't hurt you."

Fallon growled and released Shelby with a mean shove. "Get on the couch!"

She scrambled on all fours to Gabe instead.

"Get the hell away from him!" Fallon roared, stabbing a finger at the couch. "I said sit!"

"You've hurt him," she cried defiantly. "I won't let you hurt him again."

Gabe groaned at her foolish insolence. *She thinks she has to save me?*

Fallon cocked his head in annoyed disbelief at the crazy woman in front of him. He aimed at her, his eyes wide and crazy. "I got news for you. You ain't no sniper and you ain't no soldier. All you are is bait. Now git your ass on the couch where you belong!"

No. Don't do it. Don't shoot her.

Once again, Shelby angled herself into the line of fire. "You're right. I'm no soldier, but he needs my help."

"Shell. Move," Gabe gasped, his strength fading, but needing to keep her alive. "Do what he says."

The damned woman never did know how to listen. She yanked a kitchen towel from the table and used it as a compress to slow the bleeding instead of doing what she was told.

"I don't give a shit if you're God." Fallon stomped into the kitchen to snare his victim again. He yanked her to her butt, dragging her backward by her hair, his eyes fixed on Gabe the whole time.

Shelby kicked and struggled, scratching at Fallon's hands in her hair. "Ow! Stop hurting me! You've already killed Mr. Stewart. Isn't that enough?"

Fallon's eyes bugged out in rage. "It ain't enough! I want it all."

He tossed her against the front door, rolling his shoulders as if a mighty weight sat there. He couldn't have looked more fierce—or more in pain. "You're gonna die, bitch. Your dumb-assed boyfriend, too. Then I'm gonna burn this shithole of Stewart's to the ground. Maybe then I'll start feeling better. Maybe not. Might need to kill every last one of his guys, too. Especially that piece of Mexican trash he's got working for him. Shit. What'd he do? Collect every worthless stray that came along?"

Izza? What could this bastard possibly have against Connor's wife?

Gabe knelt at the kitchen table, nearly on his feet. He needed to draw Fallon away from Shelby, so he egged him on, risking death. "What you got against Izza Maher?"

"He hires a lousy slut instead of a real man? He deserved to die!"

Shelby had landed on her butt in the corner by the door, the bookcase behind her. She extended a hand toward Fallon, and for a moment, Gabe thought she might be in the middle of working a miracle. A damned scary miracle.

He took advantage of the distraction and scanned the floor for either of his weapons.

She kept trying to help this sick bastard. Did she really think Fallon was worth saving? "You're sick, aren't you? You need help. You might have radiation poisoning. I can help."

The hard light in his eye softened. She lifted onto her knees, and—

No way in hell. Not this guy. Gabe spotted one of his pistols. He jerked it of the floor and on target. Muscle training took over.

BLAM!

The 9mm in his shaking hand roared with authority. Shadows danced at his peripheral. He wiped the burning sweat out of his eyes. *Damn. I'm not going to last.*

Fallon staggered backward.

Shelby ducked low and scurried into the hall.

Gabe crouched, cupped his bloody right hand with the other to steady it, and fired again.

Fallon backed into the sheet of plywood over Kelsey's front picture window.

Gabe climbed to his feet and advanced, firing a third time. *Die, you bastard. Die.*

Fallon refused to drop his weapon.

The kickback of each discharge pulverized Gabe's bleeding shoulder, but who cared? He was all out of human kindness. His pistol roared again.

Two final rounds pinned Fallon flat to the now bullet perforated plywood. He stood rigid, his knees locked in death and his damned weapon still in his clenched hand. The arrogant bastard sneered, as if he had anything to say about who would live or die. He lifted his lip, scornful to the bitter end.

Holy hell, Gabe ached to shoot him again. And again! But it took every ounce of strength he had left to hold that smoldering piece steady in his hand.

Fallon's jaw sagged. No ugly threats formed on his blood-slick lips now. The revolver slipped out of his limp fingers. The bastard fell, stiff as a plank to the floor.

About damned time.

Gabe looked down at the weapon in his palm, dazed, yet grateful. Funny that a friend this powerful should feel so warm and so deadly at the same time.

"Did he hurt you?" he asked, needing to know. "Touch you? Anything but—"

"No," Shelby answered quickly. "I tried to call for you when he grabbed me."

Must be what woke me. Gabe staggered, going down for the count. Adrenaline pounded in his ears, but he still had work to do. That was why he'd been born—to clean up the ugly messes that life revealed so that good women like Shelby didn't have to. *No matter what.*

He lurched on unsteady legs to where Fallon lay staring at the ceiling. Gabe dropped to one knee before he keeled over and peeled the man's revolver out of his fist, securing it in his own belt. With two bloody fingers, he closed Fallon's gaping eyes. *Good women don't need to see that, either.*

Shelby launched herself at him. "No, no, no! Gabe."

He stiff-armed her before he fell on his face. The war might be over, but one last duty remained. Man's work. He stiffened his spine and snapped his fingers, his palm extended. "I need... a sheet. Or something. Now, please."

Shelby scrambled into the hall. In a second, she was back. She shoved a clean folded bed sheet into his bloodied hands, but damn. Focusing on this one last thing took a lot of effort. The walls moved. He stumbled on his own feet. Time was running out.

"Bastard," he hissed at the dead man. "You don't come into good people's homes to kill 'em."

Clutching the sheet to his chest, he flipped it with one hand, but it only half-opened.

Shelby pulled the sheet from his fingers.

"No." He tried to pull it back. "I got... this."

"And I've got you," she said, unfurling the sheet over Fallon's body.

Gabe bowed his head, the wretchedness of death now concealed beneath a mantle of white. Like snow. With big, wide red splotches. *Good enough.*

"You're shot, Gabe." The anguish in her voice stabbed him.

His knees buckled, and down he went. His mission done. Kelsey. Shelby. D.C. Safe.

"Call... 911."

"They're on their way." She dropped to the floor, cradling him the same way Taylor Armstrong, his best bud, had done on another far off battlefield on another Godawful day.

"Call Mark, too." The dim kitchen light faded into shadows. His mind drifted. "Where's Zack?"

She eased him flat to his back, her tears falling like rain. "Zack took Kelsey to Richmond and Mark's home sleeping, remember? Hold still. I've got you now."

The shock of his predicament set in. *Of all the damned luck. Find the woman of my dreams. Die to save her. Lose her anyway. Doesn't seem fair.*

He had so much to tell this woman, so much of his heart he hadn't given her yet. He clutched her fingers, needing her to know one thing for sure. He gurgled, his throat and mouth filled with spit he couldn't seem to swallow. "I love you, Shell. Know that. Be sure."

"And I love you, Gabe. *You* know that."

"I... do." He sucked in a wretched pull of pain that in no way resembled breathing. Shadows filled the room. Ghosts.

"You're going to be okay," she cried.

No, I'm not. Not this time, Shell.

She knelt over him, and the damned ceiling spun round and round until he had to close his eyes before he fell off the—floor.

Her hands on his chest hurt so damned bad. He pushed her away, but Shelby wouldn't back off, and he didn't have the strength to make her. Then he knew. The bullet was still inside. Still hotter than hell, and his heart wouldn't stop pumping until every last drop of blood eked out of him through the hole in his chest.

Still, he had to ask. "Am I... dying?"

"No, no, no." The tears dripping off her chin denied her words. "I won't let you."

Silly girl. You can't control this. None of us can. I am too dying.

He pulled her down for one last kiss. "'S okay, Shell. Don't... cry. Love you, my... silly... beautiful girl."

She dipped her head into his face, her eyes swimming with heartache. "I love you, Gabe. Don't go. Don't leave me."

"Shh." He pressed his lips to hers, needing the touch of her mouth and the taste of her lips to fasten him to this reality. This earth.

Her fingers clutched the side of his head. The kiss she blessed his mouth with burned in a really good way. He inhaled the scent of her into his soul. One last time. Roses and vanilla. His favorite flavor and now his last memory.

With a ragged breath, his mind flew home to the One Star State. *Mom. Dad. I'm not coming home like I promised. I'm so damned sorry. Don't cry, Mom. Please, don't cry.*

Shelby lifted up out of his arms and morphed into—*a guy?*

Gabe squeezed his eyes tight, then opened them again, seeing things for sure. The guy was still there. But who? *Zack? No. Not Zack. Not Mark. Who then?*

He pressed harder on Gabe's wound than Shelby had. The heels of his palms dug in. He growled like a sonofabitch, "You're not dying, damn it. You hear me, junior agent? Not tonight."

Gabe blinked at the fierce scolding. He'd heard one just like it once or twice before. Kind of.

His world contracted. The hole in his chest became everything. Blackness welled up through the floor. It overwhelmed him, with tentacles that wrapped his body limb by limb until only blurry vision remained. Blurry vision he couldn't trust. *Who is this guy?*

Icy-cold shadows sat upon his chest, tapping impatiently to be off. He tried one more time to push the hard hand away, but he couldn't make it move. It seemed at war with the shadows. Sad blue eyes lasered through the blurry darkness.

No. It can't be. You're... dead.

Chapter Thirty-Five

Talk about the nick of time.

Shelby tried, but there was no resisting the fierce man who'd banged Kelsey's back door wide open in a rush, dropped his gear bag beside the kitchen table and commenced emergency first-aid on Gabe as if he knew exactly what to do. The guy simply knelt opposite Shelby and covered her blood-drenched hands with his. Together they compressed Gabe's bleeding chest wound.

Alex.

He'd glared at her with frosty eyes that took her breath as quickly as they'd taken stock of Gabe's shirt she wore, the state of his house and the dead man on his front room floor. Alex should've glowed. He radiated enough anger and hostility.

"Any air bubbles?"

"No, but I'm afraid he'll die if the paramedics don't hurry."

"Like hell he will." Alex brushed her hands out of the way. "Not one more goddamned time. Not now. Not ever again! Sonofabitchin' bastards. None of this should've happened."

Shelby sat back on her haunches and watched him work, her heart in her throat. Alex seemed to think he held the deciding vote, that Gabe couldn't die just because he'd said so.

"You're Alex."

He nodded with one short sharp glance, his hands cupped over the cloths she'd used to staunch Gabe's bleeding. "Where's my wife? Where's Kelsey? Is she safe?"

Shelby wiped her tears with the back of her bloody hand. "Yes. Zack took her to Richmond."

"Good. Damned good. Good man, Zack. Gabe, too. I only hire the best, and I'm not going to change." Alex pressed with all his might into Gabe's chest. Veins bulged up his neck and across his forehead. "Live, damn you. Don't you dare die on me," he hissed.

"Kelsey believes in you," Shelby offered, needing to connect with this intense man before the paramedics arrived. "She loves you."

He closed his eyes, his lower jaw jutted forward. "God, I've hurt her. Too much this time."

"You left the rose, didn't you?"

Alex nodded, the anguish in his voice raw. "Bastards killed me. Kept me under. Wouldn't let me leave so I showed them. I left. Had to. They kept finding me. I kept breaking out. Damn them all to hell."

He couldn't seem to speak without cursing, but Shelby didn't care. The man knew what he was doing. He'd stopped the blood flowing from Gabe's wound.

"She knew you'd never hurt her," Shelby assured him, placing her hands over his again. "She never doubted you, Mr. Stewart. Not once."

A siren shrilled in the distance. Help was on its way. She focused on Gabe. His breathing had shallowed, but remained steady. He'd grown pale, his handsome features sunken, and his lips gray. Shelby pressed her mouth to his ear and let her broken heart speak. "Please don't die on me, Gabe. Not yet. Please—"

"He's not going to die, damn it," Alex growled.

A heavy fist pounded at the front entry. Shelby hurried to let the first responders in. Cautiously, she unlatched the bullet-riddled door. Three men in paramedic uniforms stood on Kelsey's steps.

"Your badges, please." Trust was no longer a given. What had happened to Alex would *NOT* happen again, not on her watch. All three handed over their badges. *Good enough.* They were who they claimed to be.

She stepped aside and allowed access, pointing to Gabe. "Two GSW victims. One survivor. Take care of him first."

Alex came to stand with her, his bloodied hands fisted at his side while the medics dropped to the floor and worked frantically on Gabe. One inserted an IV line into his arm while another applied a pressure bandage to the hole in his chest. The third barked stats into the two-way radio on his collar, communicating with the hospital.

"Fallon?" Alex sneered at the sheet-draped body beneath the window.

"Yes. He was inside when I got up this morning. Said he wanted Kelsey, but Gabe intercepted him. Fallon shot him without remorse. Gabe returned fire, but Fallon wouldn't give up his gun. Gabe kept shooting until he did."

"Good," Alex spat. "Rat bastard deserved to die."

Shelby winced. The rage emanating off Alex was so strong, she couldn't picture Kelsey with him. Kelsey was everything he was not.

Alex stood alone. He seemed out of place, as if he wasn't sure if he should stay or leave. A growl rumbled deep in his chest, no doubt an internal curse that had more to do with his wife not being where he needed her to be. He'd come home for *her*, not the aftermath of a bloody shootout in his front room.

Shelby reached for his hand. "Can I ask where you've been all this time?"

He accepted just the tips of her fingers in his grasp. "In the service of the damned President of the United States. Like I had a sonofabitchin' choice."

"You were there last night, weren't you? You were at the World War II Memorial when Sam and Gabe diffused the dirty bomb. You know Mr. Becker."

Alex snorted. "Hell, yeah. Bastard killed me. Stop asking. I can't talk about it."

"Gabe saved the world. At least he saved D.C." She needed Alex to know what kind of a man his junior agent truly was.

"If that shirt you're wearing means what I think it does, you're a damned smart woman." He released her fingers. "Damn it to hell. I want my wife."

A good Marine does not waste time lying around in a hospital. Yes, Gabe had been shot. Yes, he was a little slow on the uptake and tired easily, but *so*? Leathernecks don't lie around waiting to heal. They keep on keeping on. Forward. Charging ahead. *All that crap.*

Gabe knew it now. Fallon never meant to kill him—at least not with that first shot. The bastard's bullet missed Gabe's lung upon entry, but shattered. One pesky fragment had ricocheted off his left clavicle and lodged against a rib while another pierced his lung. Not a big deal for a hardheaded Marine who had already survived the loss of his foot. One little bullet hole was damned near nothing.

The good doctor in the emergency room dug the bullet out, along with the other pieces, and sewed him up. Gabe spent the night flat on his back with Shelby close by while two units of blood dripped into him along with whatever was in that IV bag. By then, he'd been pumped full of antibiotics and pain meds. He was feeling a little worse for wear, but good enough.

Besides—Alex was alive! That news alone gave Gabe the energy he needed to get back on his feet. Shelby had whispered it to him the moment he woke up from surgery. Kelsey had been right all along. *Alex was alive!*

The local news coverage blaring across all channels filled in the details. While Gabe and Shelby were busy helping Sam Becker diffuse the bomb and save D.C., Vice President Winston went and got himself killed. That was the explosion they'd heard.

It seemed the VP was in a hurry to leave D.C. He'd ordered his helicopter to standby on the White House lawn, then showed up with three Secret Service agents and a stranger on his heels. The helicopter pilot's account of the events made for sensational news.

Winston had said he needed to be in the air within minutes. *"Make it so."*

Once the chopper lifted off, the VP got a little weird. He ordered the stranger to shoot one of the three Secret Service agents. When the stranger refused, the other two agents turned on him and fired.

The pilot seemed outright baffled at what went down on his watch and mostly behind his back. He'd tried to set Eagle Two back on the ground, but the VP bellowed about some bomb. Said he had to get out of D.C. before it went off. *Keep flying!*

While the VP ranted, the stranger returned fire with both renegade Secret Service agents, but not before one of them accidently shot the VP. Again, the frantic pilot attempted to set the chopper down despite the VP screaming at him not to land, but the craft had lost its hover. He had no choice. It crashed. Its rotors took out a good portion of the White House front lawn and the fence. The fuselage, recently refueled with jet fuel because the VP specifically demanded a full tank, burst into flames.

The pilot explained how he never showed up with less than a full tank in Eagle Two anyway. In his opinion, Vice President Winston must have gone berserk.

The stranger and the honest Secret Service agent pulled the VP and the pilot from the wreckage. Before they could return for the renegade agents, the craft exploded. The stranger, whom nobody seemed able to adequately describe except for his icy-blue eyes, dodged back into the flaming aircraft and retrieved the VP's briefcase.

The hero of the night ended up being the first D.C. police officer on the scene. The stranger slapped the VP's briefcase into the bewildered man's chest and told him to *"make sure the President gets this."*

Details were still sketchy, but the FBI announced they had linked a local terrorist organization called *Chaos Now* to the renegade Secret Service agents and possibly Vice President Winston. Police held the chopper pilot as a possible co-conspirator, although he protested he knew nothing. The stranger who'd assisted in rescuing the pilot and the VP? Nowhere to be found.

"I'm going," Gabe told Shell again. He'd already re-attached his prosthetic before breakfast arrived. *Time to move.* "Get these tubes out of me. My boss is alive and I'm going to find him, wherever he is."

"It's an IV line, not tubes," she replied, "and no. You're staying. Get back into bed."

"I'm going." Both bare feet were on the floor by then. True, only one could feel the cool linoleum. Again, so what? With two good legs or not, Marines don't end operations in a flimsy hospital gown with the guys sending rude get well cards and flowers. Or worse yet, paying a visit. No way. They hustled back to HQ and debriefed their CO. Gabe needed to move out of there. Fast.

Shelby had other plans. "Stop being difficult. You're staying."

He lifted his ass off the bed, despite the draft on his bare derrière. "And I said—"

"You're staying," Zack muttered at the open door. "Cover that rearview, Cartwright. Damn it. Ladies are in the room."

Gabe glanced over his shoulder, dropping back to the bed because there stood Kelsey, her eyebrows lifted in surprise. He waved her and Zack into his room while he tucked a sheet over his legs, ignoring the heat wave creeping up his neck. The last thing she needed to see was his ass, but did she already know that her husband was back in town? He gulped. She had to know. It was on all the news channels. But if she did, why was she there?

"Kelsey! You're back." Both ladies hugged each other as if they'd been separated for years instead of one long day and a night.

Zack ambled in, offering the seat by the window to Kelsey. He dropped a brown paper bag near the counter. "I brought you a change of clothes and your boots, kid."

Gabe tamped down his excitement, not sure how to break the news. Zack didn't seem to know, either. What'd they do? Avoid all the news channels all night long?

"What the hell have you and Kelsey been doing since Mark told you to get out of town?" Gabe had to know. He would've been glued to the news, waiting for the dirty bomb to blow. What could've been more important?

Zack crossed his arms over his chest and shot Kelsey one of his famous spiked eyebrows. "Don't ask me. Ask the boss."

She shrugged and lifted her brows too, only she looked guilty. "I wouldn't leave town, Gabe, and he couldn't make me, so, umm. We spent the night at my new vet's animal hospital. Because of Dr. Carin Davis, my boys are going to be okay. Whisper took a drink of water this morning and Smoke got to his feet."

"And I've got a kink in my back that runs all the way down to my boots," Zack growled, his hand to the back of his neck. "She slept in the kennel with Whisper and—"

"And you slept with Smoke?" Gabe asked, a big shitty smile cracking his face. What a cool picture, this big tough ex-Marine sleeping on the ground with a sick dog. All night.

No wonder they hadn't heard the news, but wow. Were they in for a surprise.

Gabe wanted to be on his feet when he told them. He tried again. "Give me a hand, Zack. Come on. Get this IV line out of my hand. I've got something to tell you."

All he got in answer was a shrug from two massive shoulders and the twinkle in Zack's brown eyes. "Don't look at me, bro. I've been where you are. You've been shot. I say you're staying."

"Like hell. He's going."

Oh God, no. Alex had just cleared the door. Damn. He looked ready to get back to work, dressed in his charcoal-gray business suit, crisp blue shirt, and black tie—and shocked as hell to see Kelsey.

She jumped to her feet, one hand to her mouth. "Alex?"

He froze. "Kelsey?"

Holy shit. Gabe didn't want to be there the day a woman kicked his boss's ass, but there he was, smack dab in the middle of what was no doubt going to be the Armageddon of all marital discords.

"Alex," she whispered. "You're... alive? You're here?"

The man took two long strides into the room, his arms outstretched before Kelsey threw herself into them.

Shelby sidled closer to Gabe, clutching his hands as the scene unfolded.

Kelsey had hold of Alex's neck, her cheek pressed to his, her eyes closed and tears flowing. "You're alive. I knew it. No one but Gabe and Zack believed me, but I knew it."

The saddest groan crept out of Alex. No words, just a fierce intensity as he held his wife for the first time in too many days. He'd closed his eyes. Sheer agony etched his clean-shaven face, but his fingers were clamped onto his wife like grappling hooks.

She leaned back enough to look up into his face. Her hands smoothed over his nose and cheeks, up to his forehead and down the side of his face again, never breaking contact. Raking through his hair. "Where have you been?"

He didn't answer, just kept holding her, the darkest shadow in his gaze.

The unthinkable happened. She cocked her arm and slapped his cheek with a hard right. "Tell me, Alex." Her voice pitched ragged. "Where have you been?"

He never let go of her left arm while she slapped him again. "Tell me! What was so important that you had to do this to *me*? To *us*!"

Gabe held his breath.

Poor Alex, his face reddened from the slaps, his eyes glistening.

Poor Kelsey, tears dripping over her cheeks, her brows spiked and—So. Damned. Angry.

"You let me bury you! Do you have any idea how that felt? God, Alex, I saw your dead body at the morgue. I shook all of your friends' hands and cried with them at *your* damned funeral. Roy and Murphy were there. Everyone was there. Every single one of your friends. *Our* friends. How could you do that to me? To them?"

He bit his bottom lip, as in he really bit it. A thin trickle of blood tracked down his chin, but she wasn't through. She launched herself at him, pummeling his chest. "Say something. Damn you! Say something!"

He took the hit, another wretched groan lifting out of him, until, at last, he snagged her flailing wrists and pulled her struggling body into his chest. He buried his face in the crook of her neck. Still no explanation. No defense. Just sorrow so thick that Gabe could taste it.

Her rant turned to sobs in the circle of his arms, her face buried in his dress shirt. "I'm so mad at you," she whined, her arms and hands moving under his suit jacket and over his back. "I knew you were alive. I knew you had to be doing something critical for national security or... or maybe the world... or something, damn you. I knew you'd never hurt me on purpose. I just knew it."

The man still hadn't offered a single word of self-defense, just held his wife as if he'd never let her go again, her feet lifted nearly off the floor. Great shudders shook his shoulders. Even with his eyes squeezed tight as they were, he could not hold back the tears that trickled down his face.

At last three very definite, very pain-filled words growled out of him. "I. Love. You." That was all. No excuses. Just a battle weary warrior's binding declaration to the sadly treated lady of his heart.

Kelsey sighed, and it seemed everyone in the room sighed with her. This was the hardest homecoming Gabe had ever witnessed.

"I missed you." She hiccupped, her hands smoothing up and down his back under his jacket, comforting him. Maybe even forgiving him. "God, my poor Alex. I've missed you so much."

Shelby sniffled, drawing Gabe's gaze from his boss. The woman was a mess, crying along with Kelsey. Gabe handed her a tissue from his bedside table, then took one for himself. Zack watched from the other side of the room, his arms folded across his chest, his eyes hooded.

"I never stopped loving you. Not even for a moment," Kelsey cried, still burrowing into her husband's broad chest, her head under his chin, and Gabe couldn't deny the energy of this powerful couple. Now. At what had to be the worst moment of all their time together, they were locked in a death grip as if they were the only two in the room. Only it was more like a life grip, more binding than death.

Shelby lowered to the side of his bed, so Gabe scooted over and made a place for her to sit. She laid her head on his shoulder, crying at the tender scene that was taking place in front of them. Like him, she had no words.

At last, Alex eased Kelsey away enough to tip her chin up to meet his eyes, his thumbs on her teary cheeks. "I'm so sorry."

She sniffed once, then lifted up on the tips of her toes. "No, Alex. I'm sorry," she said, caressing his cheek. "I shouldn't have hit you. I do trust you. I always have. I always will. And I know you. You would never hurt me. I was just so angry." She'd barely offered her lips when he crushed his mouth to hers, and she was off her feet and in his arms.

God, that kiss. He ravaged her mouth and she gave it right back to him, her arms around his neck as if she'd never let him go again.

Gabe had to look away, the tender scene too intimate. Shelby sobbed into his neck, and he had a hard time holding it together, too. His eyes kept tearing up. Damn. Could any two people love each other more than the couple locked together in unconditional love right there in his hospital room? The kind of love that could forgive the unforgiveable and do it with a simple sigh? The kind that seemed able to see beyond anger and still cling together in the middle of a damned ugly storm?

It all made sense now. The Stewart's tiny home. Their meticulously groomed yard. The tidy shed. The remodeling. It was a damned oyster with a hidden treasure. A pearl of immeasurable worth. The woman Alex loved.

The scorching, feral kiss ended with a lingering hug and straying hands that brought a smile to Gabe's lips. He knew the feeling, because he wanted to get his woman into bed, too. Under the covers. Bare-assed naked and ready to play. *Argh.* He forced his mind from the pleasant thought before his misbehaving body got any harder.

When Kelsey stood on her own two feet again, Alex ran a quick hand over his face, while Shelby offered the happy couple the box of tissues. She returned to Gabe's side where he could get his arm around her.

Kelsey blew her nose and wiped her eyes, still very much locked to the side of her man and still crying. Alex hadn't let her go, his right arm securely around her waist.

"Did you ever sneak into our bedroom, besides the night you brought the rose?" she asked.

He shook his head, his eyes misted. "No, but I wanted to. This is the first time I've held you since I hid you at Olsens' place."

"Oh," she murmured. "Then I really was dreaming all those other times when I thought you were there. Umm, do we know the Olsens?"

Another shake of his head. "You don't. I do. Craig is Murphy Finnegan's Army buddy. A damned good man."

"So it really was you who saved me? Not Sam Becker?"

Alex growled. "It was me, damn it. I saved you. Not him. Becker only told you that to throw you off track. He needed you to think I was dead until this whole mess was over and done. Damn him."

A small smile tweaked Gabe's lips. His boss was one possessive man where Kelsey was concerned.

"God, I love happy endings, Boss." Zack's sarcastic voice disturbed the reverent moment. "Don't be looking to me for no hug and kiss, though. I'd just as soon kick your ass. Where in hell have you been?"

Alex blew out a deep breath. "You're right, Zack. I've been in hell, which is why I'm here now. It's time I set things straight. I'm going back to work today, and I need my two best bodyguards on my six. You coming with, or do you plan to stand around the rest of the day and blow smoke up your ass?"

Gabe caught the attitude of a damned hard man, a man he could follow. He placed a quick kiss in Shelby's hair. "I'm going. You coming?"

She wiped her nose one last time. "I wouldn't miss this for the world."

Chapter Thirty-Six

The whole back-to-work moment couldn't have gone better if Alex had planned it. He made a commanding statement walking into what had once been his TEAM headquarters without so much as a warning. And alive.

Gabe adjusted the sling immobilizing his arm. He'd made it to his feet and intended to be all he could be. Pain meds worked wonders. He'd donned the clothes Zack had brought.

Shelby stayed at his side. There'd be no relaxing until this showdown was done.

Mark Houston looked up from what had previously been Mother's workstation where he stood with Maverick and Taylor. He did look more rested than he had the last time Gabe had seen him. But he was wary. Instantly defensive. His left brow lifted. His shoulders squared when he spotted Alex. He leveled an accusing stare at Gabe and Zack, and *ouch. Damn it. That hurt.*

Gabe offered a shrug in return, feeling like a traitor to his beleaguered boss.

Maverick gave him a silent nod. Taylor very nearly smiled, if one could call the twitch of the corners of his mouth a smile. Everyone else seemed frozen in place. *And that clever saying about a place being so quiet you could hear a pin drop? Times that by a couple million, why don't cha?*

Once Alex drew to a halt, the whole damned world stopped turning. Again.

Mark nodded at Kelsey first, then the man who used to own The TEAM. "Alex."

Not Boss? Ouch. Not off to a good start.

Alex returned the nod. "Mark. I hear you did a great job while I was gone."

"We did." Mark's gaze flittered back to Gabe. "Why are you not in the hospital where you're supposed to be, *Junior Agent*?"

Gabe cleared his throat. "Duty called, umm, Boss."

Mark's gaze narrowed, and remorse flooded Gabe. He'd just slapped Mark in the face, figuratively maybe, but just the same. Being here with Alex was all-out treasonous to the man who'd salvaged a dying team in the middle of damned tough times.

Alex tried again. "This is still the best team in town."

Mark's upper lip curled in a definite *'No shit, Sherlock'* sneer.

No one spoke. Hell. No one dared breathe.

"The President will be here in thirty minutes," Alex continued evenly.

Still Mark didn't speak, his eyes still locked on the ghost in their midst.

Alex ran a hand over his head, and Gabe wanted to referee or something. These two seemed locked in a stare-down that wasn't going anywhere, but Alex had made it clear before the elevator doors opened on level two. He'd do the talking.

Kelsey had taken position at Ember's counter. Zack still stood at military rest behind Alex, another open declaration in support of the treacherous renegade in their midst and a slap in Mark's face.

Alex looked around the circle of his personally handpicked agents—or at least they *were* his. Right now they worked for Mark, and they seemed to know it. None of them had so much as smiled at their former boss. They seemed to be waiting on a cue from their leader, and that person wasn't Alex. Not yet.

"Thanks for helping Kelsey these past couple of weeks," he offered.

"What? She forgive and forget already?"

Mark's sarcastic question drew Alex's ire. He raked his fingers over his head. Gabe cringed. *Here it comes.*

If Mark only knew what had transpired at the hospital between Alex and Kelsey, he wouldn't bait Alex as he had. The man had a flaming, nasty temper on a good day. It wouldn't take much to goad him. But Mark knew that.

Again, Alex faced the newly baptized-by-fire owner of the best covert surveillance team on the East Coast. "What do you want me to say?" he asked quietly. "I had no choice in this, Mark. Hell, I didn't even know I was deep undercover until I woke up the day after my sonofabitchin' funeral. By then, some joker was in my grave, my wife was devastated and all my protocols had kicked in."

"Your protocols?" Mark lifted his brow.

"My will—the legal document that turned this place over to you, David, and Harley." Alex looked around the group. "Where's—"

"Wisconsin. Safe," Mark said icily.

"Good. Good. I take it Libby and the girls are there, too?" Mark nodded.

"And all the other families?"

"Safe," Mark hissed.

"Harley's boys were born then. Are they doing okay? Damn, I'm sorry I missed that, but they—"

"Stop bullshitting me, you arrogant sonofabitch!" Mark bellowed. "Where the hell have you been?"

"Working."

Mark folded his arms across his chest and glared. Gabe had to give it to him, he wasn't making this easy, but The TEAM's reaction was just as interesting. All along, they'd argued Alex was alive, but now that he stood in front of them, they were hostile.

It wouldn't matter in the long run. Alex would only tolerate this standoff for so long. Any second now, he'd tell them to go to hell, march into his office with Kelsey and slam his door until he was ready to talk with them.

"I'd be pissed if I were you. It was a damned dirty trick they played on us."

Mark grunted. "You mean *you* played."

Everyone should've been paying better attention. Izza had just arrived with Connor. Apparently, they'd stopped to pick up breakfast on their way to work. She dropped an armful of brightly colored fast food bags on Ember's counter and headed straight to Alex. "You'd better have a damned good reason for what you did to Kelsey. And us."

He acknowledged her with a curt, "Izza."

Wrong move, Boss. Gabe took a full step away from Alex. Izza was mad. Damned mad.

"Hey. I'm talking to you. Did you knock me out?" She took a menacing step closer, her hands clenched into fists and sparks in her eyes. "When Taylor, me, and Steven tailed you? Huh? Did you knock me out and tie me up? Did you put a yellow sticky on my forehead with a stupid smiley face? Did you?"

He smirked. And that was all it took.

She cocked her arm back to deliver a solid punch, but Alex caught her wrist and easily spun her back to his chest. Izza had anticipated the countermove. She turned a full circle, kicked his feet out from under him and tackled him to the floor, business suit and all. Square into the middle of his chest, she let him have it, fists flying.

"You're an ass! You let us think you were dead, and we buried you, and... and..."

"Izza. Stop." He grunted under her assault, dodging her fists but not before one connected and she clipped his chin. "I didn't... ouch... do the smiley face, damn it."

"I thought you were dead! We all did, damn you! I saw you die. I thought I saw you..." she collapsed, crying unashamedly into his shirt. "God, Alex. You're Jamie's godfather. You gave me away at my wedding. You can't pull this kind of bullshit on people who love you. You just can't."

Mark and Connor gave them both a hand up off the floor, but Alex kept an arm around Izza while he rubbed his chin. "Sonofabitch, I've missed you guys."

When Mark clenched Alex's shoulder, Gabe relaxed.

Rory spoke up next. "I didn't have the heart to tell Tyler you'd died."

Ember wrapped her arms around both Alex and Izza. "And Harley named one of his baby boys after you. Did you know that? Alexander Marcus and George Patrick. The Mortimer twins.”

And the showdown was over.

Everyone swarmed Alex. Izza still bawled, and Gabe didn’t mind if he wiped his eyes, either. There was a lot of back thumping and handshaking, not the norm for guys and gals who could eliminate a target at one thousand-plus yards without batting an eye. Even Zack mellowed. He snagged a breakfast biscuit and doctored a cup of coffee from the new coffee maker at Mother’s desk.

“Where’d the FBI take you?” Connor wanted to know. “We know Becker shot you, but the round was some kind of paintball gizmo. The paramedics were phonies, too. What’d they do to you?”

“The Bureau’s got five lower levels I knew nothing about,” Alex explained, “including a complete dispensary. Physicians. Staff. The whole nine yards.”

“They shot you with a muscle relaxant and a mixture of cow’s blood,” David informed him. “Vecuronium bromide, to be precise. That’s what was on your clothes, Gabe.”

“No wonder I felt like shit,” Alex said. “Damned crap gave me hallucinations. Bastards kept me under five sonofabitchin’ days. Waited until everything was over before they had the balls to wake me up and tell me they’d destroyed my life.”

Gabe shuddered, knowing exactly how Alex must’ve reacted. The Bureau might not be as dumb as they seemed. They must have restrained him while they explained, probably from ten feet away. The man was lethal on a good day.

"We saw you at the morgue," Mark said somberly. "Sure looked dead to me."

The tougher-than-nails boss chewed his lip, a shadow shifting over his face. "Guess it really was me. That Vec crap turns a man into a corpse. Slows everything down to damned near hibernation. Must've made for a convincing viewing and funeral. Assholes."

That explained a lot. The Bureau had a lot of nerve to fake an American citizen's death, much less a man of Alex's notoriety like they did. Unbelievable.

"They totally screwed your civic rights," Gabe said.

Icy blues zeroed on him. "I remember you. In the car when I died. At my funeral. You were there, weren't you? You stood by Kelsey through the whole damned nightmare, didn't you?"

Gabe could only nod. *Hell, yeah, and I'd do it all again. That's... who I am.*

"God, I'm sorry, guys. I'm sorry for everything." Alex motioned Kelsey back to his side and released Izza to Connor's. "Sons of bitches put us all through hell."

Ember still had a tight grip on his other arm. She leaned into him and kissed his cheek. "But you're back now. You're home. That's what matters."

He blinked through watery eyes, nodded at her, but a hoarse "yeah" was all he could muster. He dipped his nose into Kelsey's hair and closed his eyes.

The elevator pinged and a dozen Secret Service agents flooded the office. Another contingent swarmed through the stairwell fire doors at the same time. Within seconds, there was standing room only in the work area.

Tension spiked higher when the elevator opened again and the President of the United States, Thomas Beauregard Adams, entered the office with yet more security. Every agent stood at attention, their backs straight and their eyes forward.

President Adams had run and won on an independent ticket that purported bi-partisanship above all else. Somehow, he'd gotten elected in a close contest with the traditional parties. He was the American Dream in the flesh. He walked straight to Mark with a nod to Alex.

The man was as big as Mark, broad chested, thick necked, and every bit a country boy turned politician. His brown hair was fastidiously trimmed. His nails manicured. He looked as if he'd rather spend his days outdoors instead of behind his desk in the Oval Office. Like Alex.

"This your team?" President Adams asked, both hands gripping Mark's.

"Yes, sir, Mr. President," Mark acknowledged stiffly.

"Mark. At ease, son. Please. Be at ease. I'm not here to make more work for you people—not after what I've just put you through." He straightened his tie, then changed his mind and took it off, handing it to the agent at his side. His suit jacket went as quickly. "As I'm sure you've heard by now, the Vice President was killed last night in a tragic helicopter crash. What you don't know is that he wasn't the target of *Chaos Now*. I was."

He paused as murmurs of surprise rippled through the group. "That's right. Winston was the wizard behind the curtain. At least, he thought he was. He funded the malcontent, Ron Fallon. In the process of their little revolution, I was designated to die tragically at their ground zero, along with thousands of others. From what I'm told,

Fallon built a dirty bomb with enough explosives to take out most of the Mall and a couple of Potomac bridges, too. The radiation alone would've wiped the District of Columbia. Sons of bitches, every last one of them."

Gabe nearly grinned at all the *sons of bitches, bastards, Goddamnits,* and *assholes* flying around the office. Alex was a prolific curser all by himself, and President Adams was too by the sound of it. Tough men the world over talked the same language.

Ahh. Home sweet home. Nothing ever sounded better.

President Adams did an about face to Gabe, his hand extended. "Special Agent Becker tells me you were responsible for stopping the bomb, that you did so at great personal risk, son."

Gabe swallowed hard. He accepted his President's hand, surprised Adams knew who he was. "Thank you, sir."

"No, young man. Thank you. I understand your girlfriend assisted, too. Is that right?" He winked at Shelby. Apparently, the President already knew everyone.

She shrugged, her pretty face a delightful rosy glow. "Oh, no. I mostly watched and, umm, yeah, I mostly just watched and prayed real hard."

He grinned. "Me, too, young lady. Me, too."

President Adams pulled Alex to stand beside him. "It was only through the heroism and sacrifice of this guy here that we have irrefutable proof of Winston's planned sabotage."

Alex looked steadily into space while the President clutched his shoulder.

"This guy here had the audacity to face Winston down, to convince him he was through playing Mr. Nice Guy. That he was sick to death of the status quo in the country, enough that he wanted out of his marriage and his business. Enough that he'd faked his own death to put an end to it. The whole shebang." President Adams snapped his fingers. "I only had two men I could trust with my life, Alex Stewart and Sam Becker, so you people blame me. All of you. It's my fault. I'm the one responsible for what you've been through. I tasked the FBI to procure your boss, and believe me, I gave him no choice once they did. He was under direct orders from me as his Commander in Chief, as well as a black ops non-disclosure. You all know how binding that is."

Gabe blew out a breath through pursed lips. *Damn. The President was behind this? Who'd have thought?*

President Adams turned slowly and looked each agent in the eye. "I needed a man I could trust without reservation— someone the Vice President would find believable as well. Winston had to think that Alex was fed up with governmental bureaucracy enough that he'd deserted his wife and joined a subversive underground terrorist cell. It actually worked very well. Once Alex was *eliminated*, so to speak, he was able to infiltrate Winston's inner circle while Sam Becker worked Fallon's. Can you believe my VP was arrogant enough to think a man like Alex would turn on his wife and country?"

He took a deep breath. "I thought Winston would be a good fit for the compromises this administration needed to make. These are tough times. We all need to work together. I chose wrong. As it turned out, the bastard also wanted your boss to work for him as an undercover assassin. Once I was out of the picture, Alex was supposed to eliminate Fallon and Sam Becker. Winston wanted an enforcer, a hired gun in his new regime. Someone without a conscience. Someone like him."

President Adams paused to shake his head. "God bless us all if he'd been successful."

He glanced toward his contingent. "By the way, I'd like you all to meet my newest Secret Service agent."

Becker stepped around the army of security, offering that annoying devil-may-care smirk. "G'morning, Mark. Winston thought it was his idea to recruit your boss, so we let him think whatever he wanted, didn't we, Alex?"

Alex grunted. "Bastard."

Gabe wasn't sure if he meant that term of endearment for Winston or Becker. It fit either. Murmurs of appreciation and wonder filled the room. The TEAM's hostility was gone. Alex was back—in more ways than one.

"By the way." Becker stepped closer to Alex. "You have something that belongs to me."

Alex passed whatever it was in a gripping handshake with the man who'd shot him. Gabe guessed maybe video or audio evidence. Maybe a USB drive. The look in Alex's eye, however, wasn't one of friendship. Becker was still the assassin who'd taken him down. Alex would most likely never forgive Becker for what Kelsey had gone through. Gabe couldn't. Didn't plan to even try. Sam Becker might be one of the good guys, but he would always be scum to Gabe.

Becker gripped Alex's hand tightly. "It's been a privilege working with you. I'd appreciate the chance to do it again. I hope you'll consider that."

Alex didn't return the compliment.

"Any more questions?" Becker asked.

"Just one," Mark said to Alex. "Was that you on the riverbank or not?"

Alex nodded, his lips pursed tight, his gaze drifting to his wife. "Me. We intercepted a phone call—some jerk luring Kelsey. Almost didn't make it in time, damn it."

"You lied about the boots. He never gave you his boots, did he?" Kelsey glared at Becker. "It was Alex all along. I knew it."

Gabe looked for Shelby, and damned if the girl wasn't already watching him. He winked, needing to connect with those pretty violet-blues. Just because. She came to his side, her hand gentle on his shoulder.

"You're the bastard who tied me up," Izza accused.

Becker's shoulder lifted in a half-shrug. "Yes. It was me. I meant it as a sign that we weren't hostiles."

"Those smiley faces smacked more of crazy," Steven muttered.

"I guess we all share a touch of crazy, don't we? I mean we do kill for a living."

"Only if we have to," Alex added.

That seemed to catch Becker short. "Believe me, if there had been another way—"

Alex pinned him with those icy-cold blue eyes, and Becker had the good sense to break the connection first.

"Why were you trying to get inside Kelsey's house?" Mark asked.

"I promised this guy I know that I'd find a way to let his wife know he was still alive. I wasn't supposed to get caught."

"But you were never actually inside, were you?" Zack asked.

"Hell, no," Becker replied. "I couldn't get close enough." A shadow of regret flickered over his face. "The collateral damage on this op was worse than any of us anticipated, but we had to protect our President. Our country. I am sorry for what I put all of you through, and especially you, ma'am." He turned to Kelsey. "But I would do it again if it meant saving my country."

"What I don't understand is why Whisper and Smoke didn't make a sound when you approached Stewart's backyard fence," Gabe said. "How'd you trick them?"

"Believe me, I almost didn't. It was pure luck that I was downwind. Never would've gotten close otherwise."

"Agent Houston," President Adams interrupted the questioning, taking firm hold of Mark's hand. "You and your team have been badly used. There is nothing I can say or do that will relieve the pain you must've felt. Not only did I steal your boss and let you think he'd been murdered, but I also stole your information technologist and let you think she'd quit."

Gabe turned at the sound of the elevator. Everyone else, too. *Great timing.* There stood a very sheepish-looking Mother. She waved a five-finger fluttery kind of a wave, her head ducked into her shoulders as if afraid to join her team. She mouthed *'sorry'* to Mark from her safe distance.

"*Et tu, Brute?*" he asked. His shoulders sagged as yet one more prodigal returned home with, hopefully, a good reason for what she'd done.

Slowly, she approached the man she'd betrayed the worst. "The President called me. He needed my help. What was I going to say?"

Mark extended his hand. One shoulder lifted as if he no longer cared. "That you're ready to come back and work for me again."

Her eyes brimmed. Her lips pinched. She rushed into him for a hug instead of a handshake, her silvery head pressed against his shirt. "I'm sorry I lied to you. Can you forgive me?"

"Yeah," he said with a big sigh, one arm around her and the other brushing something out of his own eye. "It's that kind of a day. You're re-hired. Get back to work."

President Adams interrupted. "The truth is, you guys are too damned good. You got close to unraveling my operation before I could stop you. I couldn't take the chance of your intercepting Fallon before we knew exactly what he was up to. We suspected a dirty bomb. Just couldn't verify when or where. And I couldn't let you decrypt that file on Eagle Two, Agent Tao. As it was, you nearly destroyed months of careful planning."

David grimaced and bowed his head. Gabe, too. Being caught hacking into FBI files wasn't something any of them wanted to admit to, especially not to the top guy.

Once again, President Adams glanced around the circle of agents. "Each of you has my sincerest regret for the way this had to be handled and my deepest condolences for the pain I put you through. But, you also have the gratitude of a nation that, even though they'll never know what actually happened last night, they'll honor your sacrifice by getting up tomorrow morning for another day in our nation's capital. They'll live the rest of their lives like nothing happened."

Gabe glanced at Alex, his eyes riveted to Mark's, as if asking for the way forward.

"It's also important you understand the vital role you played in protecting Kelsey Stewart," President Adams continued. "We had no idea Fallon would target her. I owe you a debt I can never repay. I dare say, Alex feels the same way."

"But why'd they target Kelsey?" Gabe had to ask.

"Simple. Fallon hated what Alex stood for," Becker explained. "The man was borderline psychotic. Winston might have believed our cover story, but Fallon always suspected Alex. He figured he could force him out in the open by going after all Alex held dear. The jackass almost did it."

At last, the President went around the group, shaking each agent's hand and taking the time to chat with everyone. He seemed to know a lot about them, from the names of Mark's daughters to the fact that Ember owned a cocker spaniel named Taffy.

Mother served everyone coffee, apologizing and explaining as she did.

President Adams ended at Mark, who happened to be chatting with Gabe at the time.

Mark had suffered more than most. He'd taken the reins of a tough but shattered business at the worst possible moment and made it work so well that it threatened a joint FBI/Secret Service operation. That said something for a ragtag team of patriots who felt they still had work to do. A nation to serve.

President Adams nodded toward Alex, who still stood at his side. "Don't be too hard on this guy, okay? If I'd a known he'd keep running out on me to check on his wife, I'd never have considered him for the assignment. Is he always this big of a pain in the ass?"

"He is, Mr. President," Mark agreed as he shook the President's proffered hand.

Alex rolled his eyes, but Gabe caught the exhaustion on his boss's smirky face. He'd been through the wringer, too.

Out of the blue, Kelsey cleared her throat. "Excuse me, Mr. President. May I say something?"

He winked. "I am eternally in your debt, ma'am. You go right ahead."

The room stilled.

Gabe snared Shelby's hand, hoping for more good news.

Alex pulled Kelsey close, peering down at her as if he'd really rather go home and just *please, be left alone.* "Yes, ma'am?" he asked, a tender twinkle in his eye.

She placed her palms in the middle of his chest and took a deep breath. "Alex, I want the world to know I always believed in you. I never gave up."

And damn it, Gabe wiped another tear off his cheek before someone noticed. Had to be the pain meds. What the hell kind of a jarhead cries like a baby?

Kelsey made it worse. She fingered Alex's tie and with the cutest shrug, looked him square in the eye and said, "Alex. Honey. We're pregnant."

And the crowd went wild.

Chapter Thirty-Seven

"Sit down. I'll take it off for you." Shell gave Gabe that determined, it's-my-way-or-the-highway spiked eyebrow.

They stood together in his bathroom, locked in yet another friendly confrontation. He'd been resting for days, on strict orders from Mark not to return to work for at least a month, one of the perks of working for The TEAM. After a hard op, agents were often assigned time off with pay, especially if wounded in the line of duty. Gabe's downtime happened to come with a sexy Certified Nursing Assistant, also paid for out of TEAM coffers.

Zack had retrieved his Land Rover from the Metro PD impound lot, none the worse for wear. He volunteered to dog sit Whisper and Smoke while Alex and Kelsey took off for somewhere in the Pacific to soak up the sun and each other. Even grumpy Harley had stopped by Gabe's with an apology for acting like an ass when times got tough. He'd brought Little Alex and Georgie, two of the cutest babies on the planet according to Shell.

Gabe shook his friends hand, gave Harley one of those chest bump, man hugs and called it good. Life was too short to hold grudges for no good reason. Gabe didn't intend to start now.

Poor Mark was still hard at work managing The TEAM while Alex was out of the country, but he'd changed. A lot. Not being lead dog probably helped his cheerier disposition, but Gabe knew better. Mark had been tested in one of the hottest fires imaginable and The TEAM had survived because of him. He'd come out a little scorched, but tempered like those extra sharp USMC knives a lot of men and women on The TEAM carried and carried proudly. Gabe knew it to his soul. If the day ever came that Alex stepped aside, Mark was already battle-hardened and capable. The TEAM would follow.

And then there was Shelby. She made herself at home in his new bachelor pad, then proceeded to fix meatloaf and real mashed potatoes instead of his customary instant spuds for dinner their first night together. Pretty clever. She knew the way to a man's heart. It worked.

She showed all the signs of hyper-vigilance, and startled easily, but those symptoms would fade over time. Or not. The guilt, relief, fear, and other mixed-up feelings were part and parcel of surviving any life-threatening trauma. What mattered most was to be that survivor in the first place.

Her close call with Ron Fallon had humbled her. She wanted to learn to shoot and had already signed up for a self-defense course taught by the local police. Better yet, she'd been accepted into the local school of nursing. The next time she passed herself off as Nurse Sullivan, she'd have the credentials to back her up.

Despite his injury, Gabe countered her current bossy order with his own get-out-of-my-way spiked brow. He hadn't needed help getting in the tub before. He wasn't going to start now. "I've got this," he'd said firmly.

But Shell wasn't most women. She'd accepted his removable limb as a matter of fact, but in the process, somehow, she'd also considered it hers to care for. "Come on. Let me help."

And that was where the rubber met the road.

He took hold of her shoulder to emphasize his point. "No. You need to back off."

Her eyes widened in surprise followed instantly by contrition. "I'm doing it again, huh?"

"Yes, ma'am. You are. I know you're here to help, but I'm capable. 'Sides, it's the hole in my chest that's recuperating. Not my foot."

They'd had this conversation before. Her relentless need to control had met a brick wall named Gabe, and he wasn't going to change. He lowered his butt to the tiled edge of the tub, removed his prosthetic and the sock that covered his residual limb, setting them aside.

She took a step back. "Okay then. I'll be outside if you need anything. Just call."

"You know I will." He eased his legs into the tiled tub, the one thing he'd demanded his builders include in his new home. It sported a handrail and bench, so a guy with one foot could sit while he showered. Again, it was no big deal. A man did what a man had to do.

He would've dropped his boxers, but she waited a minute too long at the door.

"There is one thing I do need," he whispered slyly as he turned the shower on and maneuvered to the center of the bench. Pulsating water streamed over his legs and foot. He'd intended to disrobe once she'd left, but plans change. They hadn't had any real time together since that last night at Kelsey's *and* Alex's home. It was time.

Of course, she came straightway to help.

Silly girl.

He pulled her onto his lap, right under the shower spray.

"Gabe. Stop. You'll get your bandage wet."

He snapped the glass shower door shut, being careful not to stress his shoulder. With her tipped back in his arms, he covered her protesting mouth with his.

Shell responded fiercely, turning on his lap to face him, the water streaming down her back. With her knees at his thighs, she returned kiss for kiss, and he forgot all about their power struggle.

"This is happening kinda fast," he mumbled in case she needed a way out.

He untangled his tongue and lips from hers, shaking his head to clear what little logic might be left. He meant to tell her there were bath sheets in the linen closet if she wanted to dry off and leave. He should've told her he had an extra bathrobe she could wear while her clothes dried in the dryer. He wanted to remind her he was flawed, that he'd made unforgivable mistakes in his life, but...

He didn't.

"Not fast enough." Her fingers skimmed efficiently over his chest and stomach. The glow in those violet depths drew him with every flutter of her lashes. His heart stuttered, skipped a beat, and revved into overdrive.

She traced a lazy line of pure electricity down his belly with her fingernails. "We can stop if you want."

"No." His answer came out much too fast. "It's just that—"

"It's just that you think too much." She kissed him less chastely, her tongue tenderly asking, her teeth tugging his lower lip. "You'll give yourself another anxiety attack, and what will I do then?"

As if in answer, she slid off his lap and stood. Shell unbuttoned her top. Until now, he hadn't noticed the yellow giraffes and pink monkeys on her navy-blue scrubs. Yes, the scrubs were part and parcel of her OCD-ness, but right then, Gabe didn't care.

Giraffes and monkeys slipped off her fingers to the shower floor. With a provocative wriggle, her bottoms joined the soggy ensemble next. She toed them to one side.

Her shoulder-length hair turned darker in the water, drizzled with streaks of blonde. The girl was color coordinated right down to her underwear. Okay, now he cared. When did navy-blue get so—hot?

"You do this for all your patients?"

"What do you think?" Her bra joined the monkeys and giraffes, her breasts set free.

"Not... thinking... too much... right now." He devoured her with his eyes. God, this woman had the loveliest breasts. Not grapefruit. More like peaches. Delectable. Sweet-as-honey peaches. With nipples.

"Remember. You started this." She grabbed the body wash with a devilish smile. Squeezing some into her hand, she began with her neck and shoulders, working the lather into a cascade of bubbles over her—everything. He groaned, his body overloaded with sensual stimulation in his usually lonely shower stall.

"Are you sure you don't need my help?" she asked with exaggerated innocence, her lips pinched together in a pout.

Shell topped her floorshow off by leaning backward to rinse. Water and suds sluiced over her curves and bumps, dripped off her hair, and that did it.

A man can only take so much. He lifted off the bench, balanced on one foot, ready to play.

"You'll slip," she warned, blinking the water out of her eyes.

"Believe me. I've already fallen." He kicked his boxers to the floor, pulling her back to the bench. "You're too beautiful to resist."

She stood quietly at his knees, her fingers on his shoulders as he looped a finger into each side of her panties and pulled them down. And off.

Apparently, nudity turned Shell into a completely different woman. Violet eyes had never looked so dark. She pushed him back to the wall and straddled him again, her lips pressed to his as mischief turned to passion. Water slipped between their over-heated bodies, adding to their steamy lust. Her groans of pleasure filled his ears and his heart.

"I love you, Gabe. Don't think. Just do."

He aimed to please. With one hand firmly attached to her backside, the other between her shoulder blades, he slipped into her body with one quick thrust. When she arched her head, he buried his face between her breasts, certain he could never get enough.

She laced her fingers through his hair, his hands pulling her closer and closer, steamy fireworks detonated again and again. Over. Around. Under.

She might have been a novice when they'd first fallen for each other, but Miss Shell was a natural. Better yet, she knew what she wanted. Him.

At last, they relaxed against each other, drenched under the gentle spray, both exhausted and breathing hard. But so damned satisfied.

"You're something else." His hands still clasped the bottom of his naked lady. "Do you know what I think?"

"Hmm."

"I'm thinking I'm glad I bought this place. We'll have plenty of room for a while." He meant to discuss the logistics of child rearing. How many? How long between births? You know, the other things they liked to argue about.

She stilled his lips with her fingertip. "Are you going to talk all day or are you going to kiss me?"

Gabe grinned. He could take a hint. Tipping her back in his arms, he ended the discussion the way it began.

Silly, beautiful girl.

THE END

Sneak Preview of MAVERICK

Book 9
In the Company of Snipers

Pretty girl.

She looked too young to be riding the brute beneath her, but up she went through the new grass rippling in waves across the steep mountainside. At least Maverick called it a mountain. Who knew? These people in Wyoming called everything a hill. Maybe that's all it was.

He'd heard her before he saw her, which only made him more curious. She called the heavyweight beneath her Star as she'd charged by, praising him as he dutifully grunted uphill and made it look easy. Already lathered with sweat, Star sounded more like a pig than a horse. That's why Maverick had bothered to look in the first place. A wild pig would've made a few tasty meals. A horse? Not so much.

The warm morning sun warmed his aching shoulders after the cool night sleeping on the—*hill*. His old guitar rested against the bag, ready to go. He'd just rolled his sleeping bag and stood to stretch the stiffness away before he got back to the work at hand. Walking.

The peaceful sight of a delicate woman on horseback, her denim-covered legs hugging the animal's massive body, soothed Maverick. It called to his soul of all things wild and free. Of no holds barred. Of hope. Of all the reasons he'd walked halfway across the continent in the first place.

For a moment, all was right with the world.

Life used to be different. He could've stayed employed and privileged in Virginia. Paid too much. Worked too little. His boss had certainly tried to talk him out of leaving.

"You'll always have a job here, son," Alex Stewart said at their final handshake.

Maverick respected Alex like few others, but the need to leave the past behind was a siren's call he could not ignore. Sick and tired, his heart ached as much as his life sucked. He'd returned the hard man's grip, sublet his apartment and didn't look back.

Two good pairs of work boots got him a long ways from the Potomac River of Northern Virginia. Would've helped if he'd known where he meant to end up when he started walking, but truth was—he didn't. Didn't think. Didn't much care. Just walked.

He learned the hard way. Most big rig truckers could be trusted. Not all. Kansas sucked in the dead of winter. The interstates meant Highway Patrol. The back roads meant common folks who looked out for each other. Not always, but most of the time.

Nebraska resembled hometown Ohio in a lot of ways. The standing fields of corn, for one. The football mania didn't hurt. Huskers Red blossomed everywhere. Like a plague. Almost as bad as their nemesis and their better, the Ohio State Buckeyes, *God bless 'em.*

Maverick didn't know much about horses, but it seemed this reddish-brown fellow racing uphill wasn't the usual breed for running. The big guy would've been better suited for a plow or wagon, harnessed up, maybe pulling beer. He made a magnificent but massive sight, perhaps because the rider was so small.

She rode bareback, her legs spread wide to accommodate the girth of the horse, her fingers buried in the black ruffles of his mane. They moved as one, her head tucked into his neck, her long black hair blended with his ebony mane in the wind. Damned magical is what it was.

What man wouldn't stop to watch? Peace instilled into Maverick's whole being at the sight of those two creatures in sync with each other and nature. It didn't take much to imagine Star as a unicorn with a lovely fairy on his back. Looked like she had wings. Looked like they were flying.

The world had need of sights like this. It almost filled an angry man's empty, battered cup to the brim. Almost.

He turned away. Truth was it didn't even come close to filling the hole in his soul. The horse had no horn sticking out of that big forehead. The girl had no wings on her back. Magic lay dead and buried on a grassy hillside in Arlington National Cemetery.

Time to pack up and move on. Maverick's path lay elsewhere, somewhere along the highway below, not in the morning light on the hill in the middle of nowhere.

Until the beast screamed.

Maverick jolted around just in time to catch sight of the horse reared up on his hind legs, front hooves flailing and the hill collapsing beneath him. Another blood-curdling scream rent the morning peace, and over the edge he slid, slashing the air frantically and taking his elfin rider down with him in a cloud of red dust.

And God, Maverick couldn't run fast enough to the edge of the rift, his heart thundering while rocks and earth settled below. A clean, half-moon cut of the hill he'd thought was solid rock had dropped into the ravine below. Billowing dust obscured the sight below, but not the screams of what had to be a broken, dying animal.

Fear clutched Maverick's gut. *Not again.*

As terrifying as it sounded, Star's squeal amongst the sounds of clattering stones and sliding dirt meant hope. The horse might not make it, but that girl could be alive.

Maverick doubted it. Life was an unfair gift, ripped from a man without warning, meaning or care. He stepped off the edge anyway, his boots scraping yard long steps while he half-stumbled, half-slid on his butt the rest of the way. Panic hurried him, panic that he'd arrive too late. That he couldn't help once he got there. That God had played another damned cruel joke.

He kept going, at last able to distinguish the toss of dark mane through the dust-laden air. A screaming, snorting demon had replaced the grunting pig. No sign of the girl though.

Shit damn it.

"Steady boy," Maverick soothed the big animal as he approached from above.

The way the horse had slid down the mountainside worked to his benefit. He'd lain into the slide instead of fighting it, and ended up lying into the hill, buried on his left side more than his right. It also prevented him from tumbling end over end. Nonetheless, Star's legs and belly and his left side were firmly encased. Only his head and neck cleared the dirt. He struggled, shaking the dirt off his back and head.

Damn. No sign of the girl. She had to be dead. This was no rescue. Only another sucking body recovery. Maverick's stomach pitched. He forced a swallow. *Not again.*

Still above the horse and looking for any signs of her, Maverick crouched and placed his hand on the horse's neck. Star tossed his head, bared his teeth and growled. That was a first, but then what animal wouldn't growl when confronted by the scumbag who just might have yanked the earth out from beneath him?

"Take it easy, big fella. Just here to help." He stretched a hand to that big nose with flared, wide nostrils, half-afraid the gnashing, grunting animal might bite it off.

Star didn't. The horse nickered, stretched his nose and bumped Maverick's flat palm like he wanted another touch. Good enough. Maverick slid the rest of the way to the horse's head, searching for signs of cuts or blood. "'S okay to be scared. That was a helluva scary ride, big guy."

As if in answer, Star bowed his head. A shudder raced over the hide on his back and up his neck. An unexpected communication passed from horse to man. Hope flickered to life. This horse was in better shape than Maverick expected. Scared maybe, but damned spunky. Both good signs. Maybe the rider fared as well.

He stepped away from Star and slid farther down the ravine, studying the ground for signs of a body. An arm. An exposed hand. Anything. She had to be there somewhere.

A noise caught his ear. Maverick cocked his head to listen better. Star still wheezed and snorted, but this other sound was more soprano. Feminine. He climbed above the horse, planted his boots and stilled again, needing to find a living, breathing woman instead of a broken body.

The murmur again and there she was, on her side, her head angled uphill and covered with just enough dirt and dust to hide her from view. He ran to her, so damned glad for small blessings. With careful hands, he brushed the dirt from her face, nose and mouth.

"You're going to be okay," he lied because that's what first responders were supposed to say to survivors. Tell 'em what they needed to hear. Make 'em believe. "Hold still. Let me get you our of here."

A groan and a whimper lifted up from her throat.

His hands turned into scoops and shovel, his heart a hopeful locomotive unleashed as he unearthed the rest of her. He'd made it in time. A half-buried horse and an unconscious woman was not a good combination, not this far from the road or the nearest town, but *she would live. She had to!*

She lifted her one free arm to block the sun while he worked wordlessly to unbury the rest of her. A bloody scrape marked her forehead over her left eye, but no other injuries were apparent. After he'd moved most of the dirt, he ran his fingers firmly over her shoulders and arms, working his way to her wrists, checking for breaks or cuts.

She seemed to be in one piece, but she hadn't opened her eyes yet, her breath coming in quick gasps for air.

"Tell me what hurts, ma'am." He tried to get her to speak, mentally diagnosing the possible injuries she might have sustained. She must've flown clear of the horse before he fell. Might have broken an arm or a leg. Bumped her head. Internal bleeding. *God, I hope not.*

She snapped upright so quickly he was instantly in her way. "Star!"

"Now hold on." He grabbed her forearms and leveled her back to the ground. A tiny slip of a woman like her didn't survive this kind of trauma without serious damage. Something had to be broken. He smoothed two firm hands down the sides of her ribcage to her waist and hips, feeling for breakage and not sure what to do if he found any.

She shoved his hands off. "Who the hell are you?"

"You're hurt. You can't just jump up and—"

The prettiest dark blues glared up at him. "The hell I can't."

Thank you for reading Gabe!

Be sure to check out the rest of the guys and gals of Irish Winters' series: *In the Company of Snipers*

Other Irish Winters' books:

King of Hearts, Deuces Wild Series, *#1*

Joker Joker, Deuces Wild Series, *#2*

Smoke, Hearts and Ashes Series, *#1*

Ash, Hearts and Ashes Series, *#2*

Coming soon!

Seth, In the Company of Snipers, *#17*

One-Eyed Jack, Deuces Wild Series, *#3*

YOU are the key to this book's success!

Please tell other readers why you liked Gabe and Shelby's story by leaving an honest review at the retail site where you purchased it. Recommend it to your friends. Lend it. Most of all, enjoy it!

The best way to keep up with my new releases, giveaways, and actionable intel is to sign up for my spam-free newsletter at IrishWinters.com.

About the Author

Irish Winters is an award winning, Amazon best-selling author who, when she isn't writing, dabbles in poetry, grandchildren, and rarely (as in extremely rarely) the kitchen. More prone to be outdoors than in, she grew up the quintessential tomboy on a dairy farm in rural Wisconsin, spent her teenage years in the Pacific Northwest, but calls the Wasatch Mountains of Northern Utah home. For now.

She believes in making every day count for something, and follows the wise admonition of her mother to, "Look out the window and see something!"

Connect with Irish!
On Facebook: https://www.facebook.com/author.irishwinters
On Twitter: https://twitter.com/irishwinters1
Or at www. IrishWinters.com